JAZZ FUNERAL

■

Also by Julie Smith

JAZZ FUNERAL

A SKIP LANGDON NOVEL

■

JULIE SMITH

FAWCETT COLUMBINE

NEW YORK

A Fawcett Columbine Book
Published by Ballantine Books

Grateful acknowledgment is made to the following for permission to reprint
song lyrics:

CPP/Belwin, Inc.: Excerpt from "Breakaway" by Sharon Sheeley and Jackie
DeShannon. Copyright © 1963 (Renewed 1992) EMI UNART Catalog Inc.
Used by permission of CPP/Belwin, Inc., P.O. Box 4340, Miami, FL 33014.
International Copyright Secured. Made in U.S.A. All Rights Reserved.

Strong Arm Music: Excerpt from "Mercedes Benz" by Janis Joplin. Copyright ©
1970 by Strong Arm Music. All rights reserved.

Library of Congress Cataloging-in-Publication Data
Smith, Julie, 1944–
Jazz funeral : a Skip Langdon novel / Julie Smith.—1st ed.
p. cm.
ISBN 0-449-90742-2
1. Langdon, Skip (Fictitious character)—Fiction.
2. Policewomen—Louisiana—New Orleans—Fiction.   I. Title.
PS3569.M537553J39   1993
813'.54—dc20   92–54997
CIP

Designed by Ann Gold
Manufactured in the United States of America
First Edition: May 1993
10 9 8 7 6 5 4 3 2 1

For six young artists I admire:
Brooke Smith, cook; Tom Petersen, humorist;
William Petersen, guitarist; Marigny Pecot, painter and potter;
Erinn Harris, writer; and Aliza P. Rood, actor.

ACKNOWLEDGMENTS

Heartfelt thanks to the endlessly patient and generous people who helped piece this thing together, offering everything from medical and musical advice to much-needed company for walks on the wild side: Betsy Petersen, Chris Wiltz, Jim Colbert, Kit and Billy Wohl, Becky Alexander, Terrell Corley, Liz Scott, Chris Smither, Ed Becker, Steve Holtz, Michael Goodwin, Greg Peterson, Jamie Howell, Chris Smith, Captain Linda Buczek and Officer Joe Costanza of the New Orleans Police Department; Judy Laborde and Paul Henkels of Covenant House; and the kids at Country Day, especially Marigny Pecot and the three musicians, William Petersen, Langley Garoutte and Justin Rubin.

JAZZ FUNERAL

■

1

The newcomer is told three things by the old New Orleans hand: don't walk on the lake side of the Quarter, don't drink the water, and always take a United cab.

He is sometimes surprised to find the lake side is nowhere near a lake, but quite near what the natives call the "projects," housing so poor and mean it would make a preacher think about mugging, just to even things up. Only one project is near the Quarter, the Iberville. Others are scattered throughout the city, as is crime, which is said to be so prevalent Uptown gentlemen have taken to presenting their ladies with handguns for their purses. The ladies, in turn, dare not step out of their cars at night and stroll up their own front walks without pistol cocked and at the ready.

The newcomer is puzzled. Is this because urban crime came late to Louisiana, with the crack plague that hit the rest of the country, and the natives haven't yet adjusted? Or is it really, as they say there, worth your life not to heed the warnings?

Now and then the city does lose a tourist, but Californians and such are nonetheless bemused by the syndrome of pistol as fashion accessory.

And by the other advice.

"Why not drink the water?" they will ask, and they will be told with a shrug: "This is a Third World country." On further questioning, one is told something about sewage and chemicals, but the Sewerage and Water Board says the city's water is some of the purest in the nation. The first answer is probably the one that counts.

It is a position with which it's difficult to argue. New Orleans, though technically a city, is more like a nation unto itself; though legally a piece of America, is Caribbean in its soul, as exotic an adventure as exists short of navigating the Amazon.

The question of the cab has never been solved.

Steve Steinman, in town for one of the country's better bashes, the New Orleans Jazz and Heritage Festival, was puzzling as usual over the bizarre customs of the City that Care Forgot. He was haranguing his hostess, Detective Skip Langdon of the New Orleans Police Department.

"So I asked three people on the street. You know what one of them said? You're not going to believe this. 'Because most of the drivers are white.' How do you stand the way people talk in this town?"

"I never heard that."

"Well, the next one said United's more reliable, and the next one said they're the best. I said, 'What makes them the best?' and he said he didn't know, he'd never taken a cab in his life, that was just what he'd always heard."

"Me too."

"That they're the best?"

"Well, not exactly. Just that that's what you're supposed to do: 'always take a United Cab.' It's like 'wear clean underwear in case you get in an accident.' You hear it so early on, you never question it."

"Some detective," he grumbled.

Skip liked this: the banter, the endless, meaningless, companionable nattering. She wasn't used to the luxury.

But it was a challenge, living in one room with a man. The

world seemed made of elbows and laundry.

When Steve Steinman wasn't there, those wretched times when he was at home in L.A.—most of the time—the studio was an echo chamber, a place for listening to Billie Holiday and Sarah Vaughan, a cell to while away the lonely hours, to contemplate the melancholy of a gloomy Sunday.

But it was getting more cheerful, Skip reminded herself. She had painted it cantaloupe. She'd bought a painting by Marcy Mandeville, the artist whose work she'd coveted since her college days; and she'd upgraded her Goodwill sofa bed to one from Expressions. Her landlord, Jimmy Dee Scoggins, had kicked in a new taupe carpet. The place was cozy. It was fine.

It was only lonely on nights when Steve called and the sound of his voice made her ache. Or nights when he didn't call and she ached for the sound of his voice. Or other nights when, for no reason, her suddenly girlish heart went Southern on her and gave birth to the blues.

Usually when he was in town he didn't stay here. Or technically he didn't. He stayed Uptown with Cookie Lamoreaux, in a house with more rooms than most hotels. This time she'd thought she could handle having him here. *And I could,* she thought now, *if I just had a living room.*

The place even smelled different. Not bad—she just needed to open the windows more often. She had to laugh at her own old maidishness, and then at her quaint phrasing.

"What are you laughing at?" said Steve. She'd picked an inopportune moment. He had just buttoned his shirt and was admiring himself in Skip's newly purchased full-length mirror. "Something wrong with the outfit?"

"Don't be silly. I was laughing at myself."

"Well, why don't you just change? I mean I know it's an informal party, but maybe some shorts or something . . ." He let his voice trail off.

She was lying on the sofa, wrapped only in a towel, having flopped down because there simply wasn't room for both of them to move about at once. And there was another reason.

5

"I don't know what to wear."

As if on cue, a singsongy voice floated up the stairs: "Margaret Langdon!"

"Dee-Dee. Hot dog."

She jumped up, smiling.

"You're going to the door like that?"

"I always do. He dresses me."

"I beg your pardon?"

"I don't mean he hooks my bra or anything. He styles me."

Steve gave her the kind of look Jimmy Dee gave her when she mentioned Steve. In a way, they were rivals for her, she was coming to accept that. But they weren't rivals in the usual way. Jimmy Dee was gay. He probably couldn't have admitted he was jealous of Steve, or wouldn't have figured it out. He never said so, seemed always surrounded by an admiring throng, but Skip knew how lonely he was. A lot of his friends had died, and he didn't have lovers anymore. Or not often, not much outside his fantasies. They were best friends, she and Dee-Dee, she and her older, gay, eccentric landlord. He played at straightening her out—she was the depressed one, according to him—and she drew comfort from it. But she knew he needed someone to love. As did she. And he lived only steps away—in the building's slave quarters.

So when Steve Steinman had entered her life, Dee-Dee had reacted with as much testosterone as if they were married. And Steve, sensing male possessiveness even when it wasn't supposed to be there, had reacted accordingly. The fact was, they hated each other, and both knew it would hurt her to admit it. So they contented themselves with snipes, which she simply put up with. She kept thinking it would work itself out.

She flung the door open and hurled herself at the somewhat smaller frame of her dapper landlord, nearly burning her neck on the joint in his mouth.

With one hand Dee-Dee removed the joint, and caught her waist with the other. "Ah. Just in time, I see. You need me, don't you?"

Without waiting for an answer, he handed Skip the joint and

strolled to her closet. Skip didn't want any, handed it to Steve, who toked enthusiastically.

Jimmy Dee was also going to Hamson Brocato's party, but he was still hanging about in an old pair of shorts and a faded purple T-shirt. His impeccable casualness made cool seem the invention of middle-aged gay lawyers rather than high school hooligans a third as old.

"It's casual," he said. "How about your linen thing?" He pulled out a dress he'd made her buy, a kind of jumper, or over bare skin, a sundress.

"A dress?" She wrinkled her face up.

"Well, I certainly don't care what you wear! Why not just pour your tiny body into that *gorgeous* blue uniform?" He was going into his swish act, which was funny, but always intimidated her when he did it around hair and clothes—made her as unaccountably subservient as bossy hairdressers did. She was six feet tall and statuesque. Well, Junoesque. *Goddesslike*, the normal Dee-Dee said. The swishy Dee-Dee called her tiny.

"Okay, okay, I just don't know if it's very flattering."

Steve said, "It isn't." Which wasn't like him at all.

"Oh, it'll do. Turn your backs." Normally she'd have dressed in the bathroom, but tonight she didn't want to leave the men alone together. She searched for a neutral topic. "Jimmy Dee, tell Steve about Ham."

Hamson Brocato, their host for the evening.

He cut quite a figure in New Orleans, which automatically made him an object of interest for Steve, who couldn't get enough Big Easy lore. And, along with something called the Second Line Square Foundation, he was currently Steve's employer. Dee-Dee'd known him all his life.

"Well, he's producer of the JazzFest," Dee-Dee said with a shrug.

"Oh, come on," said Skip.

Steve knew perfectly well what Hamson did and Dee-Dee knew he knew. Ham had hired Steve to make a promotional video for his pet project, arguably a very good cause—and for Steve, a very good opportunity.

"Well, hell." Jimmy Dee was contrite. He could tell Skip was pissed. "Okay, where to start?"

"Where'd he go to school?"

"St. Martin's. Why?"

"Just checking to see if you knew."

Skip knew it was his little joke—everybody in New Orleans knew where everyone else had gone to high school. And if they didn't, they asked—usually in the first ten minutes of knowing someone. "Start with the po' boys," she said.

"Always a fine idea. I'll have an oyster one. Dressed."

Steve said, "Make mine potato."

Skip sighed. "Okay, I'm dressed. How about a gin and tonic instead?" The pot wasn't providing much social lubrication.

The men turned back around. "The po'boy," said Jimmy Dee, "is undoubtedly—despite blackened redfish, Paul Prudhomme, Oysters Rockefeller, Galatoire's, *and* the beignet—the zenith of New Orleans cuisine. What I would order for my last meal if I were a convicted felon. Oyster, of course. Not merely the world's greatest sandwich, but possibly the world's greatest meal."

"Hear, hear!" Steve was definitely interested.

"This town's equivalent of the hero, but the very comparison is a travesty and an outrage."

"Yes, but what does it have to do with Hamson?"

"Be patient, my boy." It was like telling fire to be cold. "You've heard, perhaps, of George Brocato?"

"No."

"Well now, he *was* a poor boy. Or so the story goes. Hence the name."

Skip spoke between clenched teeth: "Dee-Dee, you're being tedious."

"Am I?" He seemed genuinely surprised. "I thought I was building dramatically."

"To?"

"Poor Boys Po' Boys, of course."

"Ooooh." Steve sighed, contentment personified. "They just

came to L.A. Oh, man! Fast food heaven. I don't know how they do it."

"Well, the high prices help."

"Worth every penny. Cheap at twice the price. It's like having Mother's in L.A. Or Mumfrey's. Are you trying to say Ham's the Poor Boys scion?"

"Exactly."

"So George is the dad, huh?"

"Right. You'll probably meet him tonight."

"Well, I wondered why Ham had so much money. Oh, man, maybe they'll serve po' boys tonight."

Skip thought she'd never seen Steve reduced to such a pure level of infantile pleasure.

■

It was the eve of the second weekend of the JazzFest, second biggest annual party in the world's most serious party town—a Wednesday, with the JazzFest to swing once again into full gear in another few hours. It would wail Thursday through Sunday, as it had the previous Friday through Sunday. When it was over, some 300,000 people would have had their ears massaged and palates tickled at eleven stages and sixty-four food booths.

In other towns, thought Skip, festivals lasted one weekend, and weekends started Friday evening at the earliest. But here they were, kicking this one off on Wednesday. Sometimes she was glad she hadn't stayed in San Francisco, to where she'd once fled. Back there, she thought with distaste, you had to be up and jogging at six. Here, that was considered a good time to go to bed.

The party they were going to was a benefit to which Steve had been invited because of the little job he was doing for Ham, the promotional video for Second Line Square. Second Line Square was Ham's dream, some said his obsession. Ham had a plan to keep the JazzFest going year-round—or something approaching that.

He wanted a permanent structure, down by the riverside, that would house an ongoing festival of New Orleans music and become, according to his dream, the city's leading tourist attraction. The Jazz and Heritage Foundation's own two projects, the

Heritage School of Music and WWOZ, the jazz radio station, would be housed there, with the Heritage School much expanded. Preservation Hall would move there too, if Ham had anything to say about it. Five or six important groups would play at once, every night, and there would be lectures, films, interviews with artists, every cultural experience that could be dreamed up to showcase the city's musical heritage. There'd be food and crafts booths too, but all carefully monitored, only the highest quality. It would be New Orleans' answer to the Grand Ole Opry.

The place would be self-supporting—which meant it would have to be huge, and therein lay part of the problem. People said the same things they always said about development—it would wreck the view, it would take up space that ought to be parkland, it would create parking problems, and it would cost too much. So Ham had failed to muster support from the Jazz and Heritage Foundation, which ran the festival. It was a bitter blow, but certain commercial interests needed hardly any convincing at all to pump money into it, and so he had started the Second Line Square Foundation, which was currently in the process of whomping up support.

Steve's video—to be shown to civic groups and potential backers, would be snippets of the JazzFest interspersed with interviews supporting Ham's position—the Tower Records folks, for instance, telling the home folks how many European tourists come in to buy tapes of their beloved New Orleans music, how they beg to know where they can go hear it. There'd be statistics, numbers, every kind of educational rah-rah, all softened by the stuff that soothes the savage breast.

Ham lived in Old Metairie, what passed for a suburb in New Orleans. Folks who moved there from Uptown were sometimes wept over, practically kissed good-bye, and packed off with a team of huskies. Yet, if you took the expressway, it was about a ten-minute drive from downtown.

Ham hadn't actually crossed the line into Jefferson Parish—he was in the five-street transition area "near the cemeteries," where you got both the suburban safety of Metairie and the social correctness of a New Orleans address.

As they tooled down Metairie Road, past the landmark cemeteries, Steve said, "Okay, tell me what to expect."

"Lots of food. Jambalaya, crawfish pie—"

"What else? Who'll be there?"

"Big names in music. And the crème de la crème, I'll bet. I
don't really know because it's the first time he's done this, but it's
predictable when you think about it. He's probably invited everybody in town who's got money, and he'll lure them here with
celebrities. All the musicians he can get—and that'll be plenty."

"Rub elbows with Ti-Belle Thiebaud and eat five pounds of
crawfish."

"Well, we know *she'll* come. Aaron Neville's not such a sure
thing."

"Aaron Neville! You're kidding."

"Hey, baby, have you forgotten where you are? Aaron Neville,
Alan Toussaint, Wynton Marsalis—it could all happen."

"Holy shit."

"There's even rumbling about Nick Anglime."

"Oh, sure."

"Well, its not all that farfetched. He's moved to New Orleans.
To Audubon Place."

"Sometimes I wonder about you, Detective. Do you ever check
out any of these rumors?"

"What rumors?"

He guffawed. "*What* rumors! I come to this town every four
months maybe, and I never get here that there's not some new
story about a different celebrity who's moved here."

"Well, Alison Gaillard's husband's cousin, who just moved to
town, lives next door to the Realtor who sold him the house." She
watched him double over. He'd have been on the car floor if not
for his seat belt.

"I don't get it," she said.

"If you only *knew* how many of those stories I've heard."

"Okay. Fifty bucks says Anglime shows."

"Hell, no. Dinner at Arnaud's."

"Done." It was a bet you couldn't really lose, or she might not
have made it. She was aware there was truth to what he was saying.

Those sorts of rumors did fly—sometimes you were even shown the building that some movie star had just bought from someone your boss's wife's sister knew *really* well. But somehow the star was never seen around town, and eventually you saw somebody else watering the flowers at the house and knew you'd once again fallen for urban folklore.

So far she hadn't heard of an Anglime sighting. And if there'd been one, the word would be out.

Even Skip, who had barely been born in his heyday, knew "the American Mick." She liked his stuff, along with Dylan's and the genuine Mick's. She thought she'd have done well in the sixties. The music was good and people swore all the time. It was a decade with rebel appeal, and she was nothing if not a rebel—sometimes to the despair of the New Orleans Police Department.

"Somehow," said Steve, "I didn't picture Ham in this setting."

It was a gracious neighborhood, dignified without being stuffy —too many kids for that sort of thing. The trees were grown, the ivy trained. The houses were several decades instead of several centuries old.

"Why not?"

He thought a minute. "Oh, hell, it's not Ham. It's Ti-Belle."

"I see what you mean. But she's a new addition. He originally moved here with his wife Mason."

"*Mason.* That's a weirder name than Ti-Belle."

"What do you expect? She's from a good family. I guess they were your basic young affluent couple with a yen to send their kids-to-be to Country Day, which is right in the neighborhood."

"This is hardly the country, but you're right—what should I expect?" He'd stared out at the suburban heaven they'd entered.

"What happened to Mason?"

Skip shrugged. "What usually happens, I guess. Realized she got married too young. She's been gone five years, and Ham just never moved. Then when Ti-Belle came on the scene, I guess— well, I don't know. I'm seeing your point more and more. She's like an exotic flower in a bed of busy Lizzie."

Steve spoke in a different tone, suddenly excited. "What's going on?"

They had just rounded the corner and come into view of Ham's house. It was obvious it was Ham's house because there was most assuredly a party in progress—but it appeared to be on the front lawn. "Must be damn crowded if they're spilling out on the sidewalk."

She parked half a block away, and as they came closer, she noticed the noise seemed odd, unlike party noise. It was a little too shrill, a little uncertain. No one was eating, and stranger still, no one was drinking. The clump of guests clustered on the yard seemed to get quieter as she and Steve approached, to follow their movements visually. It made Skip self-conscious. What did they want? She thought she saw people she knew in the crowd, but she couldn't be sure. No one spoke to her.

Steve said, "Did someone die?"

2

"Let's go around back."

Good smells wafted. Ham had hired a lot of caterers, in keeping with local custom—the idea was to get a dozen or so crews from different restaurants to set up little backyard booths, each serving one dish so people could sample and stroll.

A trailer parked in the driveway had put on vast caldrons of crawfish to boil. They'd be dished up in baskets and devoured at newspaper-covered tables. But the tables hadn't been set up.

The restaurant crews, who had portable cooking units, were trying to look busy, but mostly they looked simply forlorn. Some had set up and started cooking, some hadn't; none was serving. A confused-looking bartender was surrounded by bottles, but had no table on which to assemble a bar.

"At $250 a pop," fumed a red-faced man, "you'd think we'd at least get a drink."

Skip saw her brother, Conrad. Not her favorite person, but a truly great information source. "Hey, Conrad. You remember Steve?"

Conrad looked as if he cared for Steve slightly less than Jimmy

Dee did. "Hey, Steve." He didn't bother speaking to Skip.

"Where's Camille?" Skip liked her brother's new wife a lot better than she liked her brother.

"Around front, I guess. Trying to figure out what's going on. You seen Ham?"

She shook her head. "We just got here."

"Well, looks like you beat Ham and Ti-Belle." He looked disgusted.

The shrill uncertain buzz they'd noticed was developing a hysterical note. This was a party that wasn't fun. Bemused, Skip and Steve worked their way back around to the front.

"Ham I could see," said Skip. "He could have had to work late —it's his busiest time. But where's Ti-Belle?"

"Oh, 'bout two houses away, I'd say. Approaching at a dead run, having just parked a Thunderbird with a squeal of wheels."

Skip had heard the squeal, but had paid it no mind. Now she saw a very thin woman approaching, hair flying, long legs shining brown, sticking out from a white silk shorts suit. Over one shoulder she carried a lightweight flight bag. Golden-throated Ti-Belle Thiebaud, the fastest-rising star on the New Orleans music scene.

Steve said, "I'd know those legs anywhere."

She never performed in any garment that wasn't short, split, slit, or halfway missing. Some said the whole country would know those legs soon. They said she was going to be bigger than large, larger than huge.

Thiebaud was approaching at a dead trot, fast giving way to a gallop. She was wearing huge hoop earrings. She had giant black eyes and shining olive skin, flyaway blond hair that looked utterly smashing with her dark complexion. Her skin clung to her bones, hanging gently, as naturally as hide on a horse. She probably didn't even know what a Nautilus machine was—no doubt started the day with couscous and syrup and didn't set her fork down till she went to bed. Obviously she'd never worked out a day in her life and never needed to. Skip had seen her perform, but never up close. She thought she might have just laid eyes on the most gorgeous woman in Louisiana, if you didn't count her pal Cindy Lou Wootten.

15

"How'd Ham get *her*?" she blurted.

A black man waved at the singer, tried to slow her progress, pretend it was a party: "Hey, Ti-Belle."

Thiebaud paid him no mind, but cast a look at the crowd in general. Skip saw twin wrinkles at the sides of her nose—one day they'd be there permanently, if she worried a lot in the meantime.

"Hi, y'all." She was trying to smile, but it wasn't working. "Excuse me a minute." She let herself in and closed the door behind her.

Almost immediately, a scream that could have come from anyone—the hottest Cajun R&B singer in America or any terrified woman—ripped through the nervous buzz.

Skip's eyes locked with Steve's. "Stay here."

For a second everyone froze; and then the heroes in the crowd started for the door. It was locked. Thwarted, they looked around, confused.

Skip pushed her way past them, badge held high. "Police," she said. "Everybody stay back."

She rang the doorbell.

"Miss Thiebaud! Police!"

The door opened and she saw the look in Thiebaud's eyes. Gratitude. *Thank God you're here*, said the eyes. *You take over and be the grown-up.*

Skip walked in and closed the door behind her, turning the lock. There was a purple backpack on a chair in the foyer. "What is it?"

"Ham. Ham's dead." Thiebaud turned around and padded toward the kitchen. Halfway there she said, "I think. I think he's dead."

Ham Brocato was lying on the floor with a kitchen knife in his chest, buried almost to the hilt.

He wore jeans and a black T-shirt with something written on it, Skip couldn't tell what. He was very white, very pale, as if lividity were well along, as if his blood had already settled on the other side of him. The floor was black with dried blood. But even if he hadn't been so pale, even if the spilled blood hadn't been so dark, you could have told from his eyes that he was dead. They were open, cloudy, staring at nothing.

He had been cooking. Smoke filled the house, along with the smell of burned roux. The stove was still on, very low, under a heavy iron pot. Neat piles of chopped vegetables sat on the kitchen counter—onion, green pepper, scallions, tomatoes. There was a pile of shrimp too, lying on the white butcher paper it had come in. It stank. The vegetables looked withered. Two neatly washed wineglasses were upended in the dish drain. An open bottle of wine sat half empty on a kitchen counter.

Thiebaud looked at Skip anxiously. "I'm sorry," said Skip.

"He's dead?"

"Yes."

Thiebaud's face twisted and she threw herself against a wall. Something came out of her that could have been a sob, but was more like an anguished sound with no name, a sound loud and almost musical; unconsciously so, Skip thought.

"Are you all right?"

"Yes. I have to throw up is all."

"Listen, I'm going to have to ask you to go outside. This is a crime scene."

"I can't—" She put a hand to her mouth and started down the hall, made it only halfway.

Damn! Who knows what else she did before I got here?

"I'm really sorry, but I'm going to have to ask you to wait outside."

"This is my house!"

"Is there someone out there who can take care of you?"

"I have to brush my teeth!"

Skip put a hand firmly on the small of her back and guided her to the door. "Does Ham have family members here?"

"Oh, my God! George and Patty—they're invited. And Melody. Ham's little sister. Oh, no! That poor little girl!"

"Okay, we need to tell them. Anybody else?"

"I don't know." She seemed to be having trouble thinking.

"Ms. Thiebaud. Look at me."

17

Dully, the other woman faced her.

"Do you need a doctor?"

"Hell, no. I've already thrown up. Why? Do I seem out of it?"

"A little. My name's Skip Langdon, by the way."

"And you're a cop? What kind of cop?"

"I'm in Homicide."

"Oh. You mean someone called you? You knew?"

"No, of course I didn't know. I'm just a guest. But I need you to help me now. Can you?"

Her eyes went dull again. "I don't know."

"Can you tell me who else I need to talk to? Who else here was close to Ham?"

"Ariel—Ham's assistant."

"That's all?"

"All I can think of."

"Okay, here's what I need you to do. Go out in the crowd, find a man named Steve Steinman, and send him to me. And don't tell anyone what's in here. Leave that to me."

"Ham's video producer?" She looked baffled. "Is he a suspect?"

"We'll talk later." Skip had to give her a gentle shove to get her out the door.

The errand served a dual purpose. Skip needed Steve to call Homicide—she couldn't use the phone in the house, for fear of disturbing prints. And she wanted to keep Thiebaud away from the family members. The nearest and dearest were always the most likely killers—and if Ham hadn't died in a crime of passion, Skip didn't know what you'd call a knife in the chest while playing Cajun chef. Better to keep the suspects separated.

A quick tour of the house showed the only out-of-place object was the purple backpack. On a service porch were folding tables, boxes of glassware, tablecloths, plates—all the rented equipment you'd need for a big party.

Otherwise, everything was immaculate, perfectly ordered, every bed made, every surface dusted—as if the place had just been cleaned for a special occasion. The house was strangely impersonal, as if decorated from a catalogue; better than a Hilton, but

18

not much better. The living room was oddly like the bedroom—
generic. But not done up with wing chairs and Audubon prints,
which was de rigueur in New Orleans homes of a certain class.
More anywhere-USA generic. Nothing especially went with anything else, nor did anything clash.

It was the last place you'd expect people like Ham and Ti-Belle
to live. But the chatelaine was just up from the bayou country, Skip
thought, and hadn't yet gotten into decorating, had barely had
time to buy fabulous clothes.

The guests were banging on the front door, kicking at it,
ringing the bell. What to do with them?

The last thing she should do was let them disturb a crime
scene, but there were a hundred people outside and more arriving
all the time. One thing she might do was detain people for questioning, but most of them probably hadn't seen much. Ham had
been dead a long time—maybe since yesterday. Yet she didn't
have official word of that. She thought the best thing was to have
the family, close friends, and caterers stay, send everyone else
home.

She found a phone on a slightly battered nightstand next to a
king-size bed covered with an ordinary, quilted spread, cham-
pagne-colored, clearly bought from a department store, and not
recently. She was looking at it longingly when she heard Steve's
voice.

She let him in, explained the problem, and told him to tell her
sergeant, Sylvia Cappello, that she, Skip, wanted the case. "Just tell
her I've got it," she said, "and I'll talk to her soon." She watched
his eyes come alive with vicarious excitement—he had a layman's
yen to be a detective. "And tell her I need two more officers; plus
a marked car for crowd control." He envied her, she could feel it.
She understood, but she had her own envy—he didn't have to face
that crowd. It was increasingly nervous and ugly, threatening to
break in and ruin the only part of the scene that might not be totally
hopeless.

She stepped outside and held up her badge. "Ladies and gentlemen . . ." This was a crowd that was ready and waiting. She had
their attention at once. "We need your cooperation. I'm going to

19

have to ask you to step back a little bit for just a few minutes.''

But they surged forward instead. Skip would have given her Marcy Mandeville for some backup, but she didn't even hear sirens yet. Thiebaud was near the door, leaning against a handsome man in his early sixties who had his arm around her. He was graying, had a large head on a pair of large shoulders. Despite the informality of the occasion, he was wearing a suit. The singer was white, rigid. Without warning, her eyes rolled back and she started to fall. Her companion struggled to catch her.

Attention shifted to Ti-Belle, and then, almost simultaneously, a marked car squealed around the corner. Skip breathed a sigh of relief. She got Thiebaud seated on the ground, head forward on the flagstones. She came around. ''What is it?''

''You fainted.''

The man knelt.

''George!'' Thiebaud reached for him, he still squatting and trying to keep his balance, she trying to lean close enough to get some comfort, finally having to hop over on her butt. Giving up the balancing act, he sat down and held her.

Ham's father, Skip thought.

Feeling awkward, finally standing herself, Skip found herself looking into the terrified blue eyes of a woman whom she took to be Mrs. Brocato. She was much younger than her husband, if that was who the man was; barely older than Ham. A very beautiful woman, the classic creamy blonde, dressed expensively, and like her husband, a little overdressed—if there was such a thing in New Orleans.

''Mrs. Brocato? I'm Skip Langdon with the police department.''

''Oh.''

Thiebaud wailed, ''Oh, George! He's dead! I can't believe it.''

People always said they couldn't believe it. But it was out, and at least Thiebaud had held her tongue until now. Patty Brocato's face cracked, but the fear in her eyes didn't resolve itself, give way to shock or grief. Instead she looked more frightened still. A maverick sound fell out of her throat, and she drew in her breath. Finally she said, ''Melody?'' the word almost a whisper, as if she didn't dare speak it.

It was a question, but Skip wasn't sure what the answer was. She said, "Your daughter? Ham's sister?"

Patty Brocato nodded, eyes alert, fixed on Skip.

"She isn't here. Is she with you?"

She shook her head, hand at her mouth. "She's gone." It was a whisper. Her head kept shaking, shaking. Her son was dead, her daughter was "gone," and none of it was happening, said the head. Skip understood the impulse.

George Brocato struggled to his feet, pulled Thiebaud after him, kept an arm around her. "What happened?" he said.

"We'll talk. Can you wait a minute?" As if they had something better to do. Skip told the uniforms to get the names of everyone at the party and send them home. As fast as they'd go.

Then she told the Brocatos their son had been murdered. Thiebaud filled in the details. More officers arrived, and two coroners' assistants. "I have to leave you for a moment." She got another officer to sit with them while she went back inside to preserve the one piece of evidence she knew must exist yet was so fragile it could be destroyed with the flick of a finger.

She went into the ordinary bedroom with the ordinary bedspread. She'd noticed an answering machine near the phone, and she wanted to know what was on it. The messages were all for Ti-Belle—and there were lots of them, apparently a backlog of several days.

That wasn't good enough. She returned to a room that looked like a study, one to which she'd paid little attention when she toured the house a few minutes before. The walls were wood-paneled, the furniture utilitarian, masculine. There was a computer, fax machine, copier, CD player, and other machines, some she didn't recognize. She had no doubt every one of them was state of the art. The answering machine looked as if it would hold an entire library of messages. Carefully, keeping to the edge so as not to destroy any prints, she punched the button marked "messages." The tape rewound for so long she nearly decided not to listen, just to tell the crime lab to get the two machines.

But then she thought, Maybe just one or two, and ended up playing them all. She'd been right. There was important evidence

21

here. The tape might even help the investigation fix the time of death. Most of the callers had left the day and time. Most of the messages were of two types. There were frantic ones from various people—mostly from Ariel, Ham's assistant, asking where the hell he was. These had all been made today, indicating Ham simply hadn't been anywhere he was supposed to be all day. The other type of message, interspersed with the "where-are-you" ones, began the tape—on Tuesday night, apparently—and continued throughout Wednesday. These were from "Dad" and "Patty," desperately trying to find their daughter Melody.

Skip went into the kitchen, where she now found Paul Gott-schalk from the crime lab, and told him what she had.

Back outside, she found George holding both women's hands, the three standing almost in a circle, making a barrier with their backs against the other guests. Skip felt for them, wished she could take them someplace private to talk.

"This is an awful thing," she said. "I'm so sorry." She let a beat pass. "Ms. Thiebaud, could you leave us for a few minutes?"

"Ti-Belle," said the singer, and left, eyes glazed. It seemed a strange time to get friendly.

George spoke before Skip had a chance. "Detective. We have to tell you something. Our daughter's missing."

Patty broke in: "Could someone have kidnapped her? They killed Ham and they—could they have taken her?"

"Can either of you think of a reason why anyone would want to kill him?"

"No!"

"No."

"Or Melody?"

"Melody!" Patty screwed up her face to cry, apparently not having dealt with the idea her daughter could be dead.

George simply said "No" again, and patted his wife's hand.

"Was Melody here with Ham yesterday?"

Patty spoke again. "We kept calling and calling—Ham wasn't home. But Melody—"

George said, "Patty." Just the word. As obvious as kicking her. He was telling her to shut up.

"Mrs. Brocato, I take it you're Ham's stepmother?"

"Yes."

"And Melody is his half sister?"

"They couldn't have been closer if they were full blood. Even with the age difference."

George said, "Melody's only sixteen. Ham was thirty-four."

"Why do you think she was here when Ham was killed?"

"We don't," said George.

Patty said, "But if they kidnapped her—"

"Mrs. Brocato, why would she have been here?"

Her husband answered the question. "She goes to Country Day. It's such a short walk, she often comes over after school."

"Is Ham usually home?"

He shrugged, and Skip saw what he was trying to avoid saying —Ham wasn't.

"Does she have a key?"

He nodded. Skip remembered the purple backpack on the chair in the entrance hall.

"What happened yesterday? When did you last hear from her?"

Patty said, "When I dropped her off, she said she was going to a friend's house after school. I was supposed to pick her up about five-thirty. But she wasn't there." Patty had trouble saying the last few words, and for a moment she looked her age, looked like a woman who'd had children and suffered, not merely like a perfect shape on which to hang lovely clothes.

She put a hand over her mouth until she was back in control. "Blair—her friend—said Melody had left about half an hour before. Just left, without saying good-bye. Blair said she had no idea why. She was on the phone at the time—heard the door close, but that was it." Patty shrugged. This was obviously old material to her, a road she'd been down all too often in the last few hours. "I came here to look for her—it was so close—I was sure she'd be here. But no answer. Nothing."

"Did you call the police?"

"Of course." The Brocatos spoke together, angrily. George said, "You know how much they did."

23

Skip shrugged. At least there'd be a report.

"We spent all last night on the phone." He spoke like a man who wasn't used to being frustrated, who usually got what he wanted, and quick. He didn't handle it well when he didn't. His face reddened as he spoke, his voice rose. He was a child having a tantrum. "We called her boyfriend, we called a dozen of her other little friends, we called her teachers, we called Ham and Ti-Belle, and then we called Ham and Ti-Belle back. We called everybody in the whole fucking town, and then we called 'em again." Obviously it hadn't sunk in yet that his son was dead. It was easier to be angry at his daughter.

"Has she done this before?"

They were silent for a moment, a moment too long. "Not really," said George. "Once she stayed away for hours, but never the whole night."

Skip thought maybe she had, maybe Melody was a bit of a handful. George seemed comfortable with his anger, as if he was well-accustomed to it, as if Melody was possibly the only thing in his life he couldn't control and he was nearly driven bats by it.

So of course she'd know that, and use it.

"We thought she'd be here tonight," Patty said. "Are you sure she isn't here? Can you send someone to check again?"

"Of course." She called one of the uniformed officers and whispered to him, but she knew it was ridiculous to send him looking. If Melody were there, she'd have identified herself and come in to find out what was happening. Would have used her key and walked in, probably.

Skip said, "What was she wearing when she left for school?"

"White T-shirt," said Patty. "And jeans. Running shoes. White socks."

"Purse, backpack, anything like that?"

"Backpack—I think." She closed her eyes a moment. "Yes." She looked up. "I can see her going in, slinging it over her shoulder. Purple, bouncing against her hip." In spite of the tragedy, she smiled at the memory. She might be a shallow woman—certainly had the earmarks of one—but Skip thought she loved her daughter.

Skip glanced at George and thought he was seeing the same thing on his mental TV—his daughter, running to her class. He looked hugely sad, as if the shock were starting to wear off, the adrenaline crash beginning. His face was grayish. He was suddenly no longer handsome. Just old.

"Is her toothbrush missing?"

"No," said George. "We checked. She wasn't going anywhere —they got her. They must have got her, that's all."

"Who's got her, Mr. Brocato?"

"Whoever killed my son's got her. Who the hell do you think I mean?"

"Do you know who that is?"

"How would I know that? If I knew that, wouldn't I tell you?"

"I don't know what you'd do, Mr. Brocato." *But if you rant long enough, maybe you'll say something truthful. Then again, probably not.*

Patty said, "I don't think she ever in her life looked forward to anything the way she looked forward to this party. If she's not here, she's dead. She's a musician, you know." She looked at Skip with limpid blue eyes, proud-mother eyes. "She's a very fine singer. Professional quality."

Sure. I'll bet.

"Why did she have a key to this house?"

"Why, she and Ham were close. She's close to Ti-Belle too. Looks up to her, like an idol."

"But if she has a key, she must come here when they're not home."

Patty looked at her lap. "Oh. Why, yes."

George said, "There's no decent bus service from here to Uptown, you know. And Melody practices with her band after school. So she couldn't be in an ordinary car pool. Patty had to come get her every day. She waits here sometimes. Till Patty can come."

He spoke defensively, as if he thought Skip might accuse Patty of getting her nails done when she ought to be picking up her kid. Which was probably more or less the case, she thought.

"This was her second home," Patty said. Was it her imagination, Skip wondered, or was her speech getting slower, more

25

Southern? No, it wasn't quite that. More country-sounding. It had a slightly pious note in it too. "She loves Ham and Ti-Belle so much. And they feel just the same about her. They encouraged her to use their home as hers."

Skip said, "Do either of you have a key to the house?"

Both shook their heads; neither spoke.

"Is Ham's car here?"

George's head swiveled. "Yes, it's the silver Celica."

Skip told them she had no more questions. They seemed broken, these two, as if at the end of their ropes. But of course, their ordeal was only beginning.

Skip fought to keep herself from feeling their pain—from getting enmeshed in the giant emotions that were soon going to batter them like giant ocean waves, forcing them to the bottom, filling their mouths with sand, turning them over and over, around and around, flinging them wherever the ocean chose—the ocean of grief, the maelstrom of despair, the bottomless sea of feeling no one can fight off when someone close dies.

She went to find Ti-Belle again.

3

The singer was in her car, leaning against the back of the seat, drained. She reminded Skip of a gardenia turning brown at the edges. "Can I go back in?"

"After the lab people are done. Do you have a place you can go in the meantime?"

She nodded. "Do you mind if we do it fast?"

Skip smiled. "I'd be delighted." She climbed into the front seat. "Who had keys to the house besides you and Ham?"

"Melody."

"Anyone else? Your in-laws?"

She made a face. "No. Andy Fike. The house cleaner. I guess that's all." She shrugged. "Unless Mason still has one."

"Could I have Andy's address and phone number?"

"I'd have to go inside to get it."

"I can get it if you'll tell me where to look."

"My Rolodex—on one of the tables in the bedroom."

"Okay. Look, I'm sorry if it upsets you, but I need to ask where you've been."

"Chicago. On business." She was propped on one hand, leaning slightly, her head inclined, her hair falling over her shoulder as if she were posing for *Vogue*. She spoke casually. It was the pose that bothered Skip. Too studied; too perfect. As if she needed rigidity to hold her story together.

"Your plane was late?"

"I beg your pardon?"

"You were late for your own party."

"Oh." A smile, a little rueful laugh. "Ham's party. He's a big boy. He can—" She stopped in mid-sentence; horror replaced bravado as she realized what she was saying.

Skip said, "It just seems odd you'd cut it so close."

"The plane *was* late."

"Did you call Ham?" She hadn't, and of course she would have if she were telling the truth.

"Well, I did, but he didn't answer."

"What flight did you come in on?"

"I really haven't the least idea. How could I, anyway? I just came back from a three-day business trip to find . . ." Clearly she couldn't bring herself to use the words. ". . . this, and you expect me to remember my flight number?"

"Maybe you still have your ticket. How about if we look at that?"

Ti-Belle put a hand to her forehead. "Look, could we have this conversation later?"

"I'd really love to, maybe over some iced tea or something, but I've got a murder to investigate."

The singer winced at the word. Her eyes filled. "You don't have to be so sarcastic."

"Okay. Let me be straightforward. I'm a police officer and you shouldn't bully me or try to shine me on; it makes a real bad impression."

"I threw away my ticket." She seemed subdued.

"Can you tell me who you saw in Chicago?"

"Do I have to?"

"Why would you mind?"

The singer shrugged. "Okay. Mr. Jarvis Grablow. Mr. Grablow at Bluestime Recording."

"That's the only appointment you had in three days?"

"I can't remember these people's names."

"Don't you have your appointment book with you?"

"I—actually, my manager sent me a typed itinerary. I threw it away after the trip."

"Okay, look. Just give me your manager's name. I'll check with him."

She sighed and gave Skip a name and number.

"By the way, what's Ham's assistant's name?"

"Ariel. Ariel Burge. Kind of looks like her name." She seemed slightly cheered, happy to have Skip's attention on someone else.

"How's that?"

"I don't know. Flighty or something."

"Okay. I think that's it for now. By the way, did I mention I'm a big fan of yours?"

"Thanks." The reluctant witness actually managed a smile. Skip started to move off, but Ti-Belle yelled: "Oh, hey, I forgot something."

"Yes?"

"Could I go back in and get my flight bag?"

"I'll get it for you." Ti-Belle had tossed it in a living room chair, and as Skip carried it back to her, she couldn't help noticing it sported no airline tags.

There were still a few people left in the yard, standing in clumps—friends of Hamson's, the uniforms said, who declined to go home, waited instead "to see if they could do anything." Skip was horrified to see that Steve Steinman was one of them. She'd forgotten all about him. The place being New Orleans, and Ariel Burge being a great man's assistant, another had to be she—ready to fetch and carry till she dropped as dead as Ham.

There were also people still arriving, and there probably would be for hours. Officers tried to send them away, and sometimes succeeded. But not often. Great clumps of onlookers were gathering on the sidewalks. The neighbors, after hurried suppers, had begun to stroll outdoors in T-shirts and shorts.

Skip found the folks from the restaurants packing up. The bartender, one Michael Boudreaux, had turned up first, and had noticed nothing unusual—except, of course, that the host wasn't home. He'd called the caterer he worked for and been told to wait.

"But didn't it seem odd that no one was here? Like a member of the foundation?"

"What foundation?"

"The Second Line Square Foundation—the thing this was a benefit for."

Boudreaux shrugged. "All I heard was the host's little sister was s'posed to let us in. Tables inside, everything we needed— everything rented in advance. All we had to do"—he gestured— "me and all the others, was go in and get what we needed."

"But who was going to set up?"

"Me. That's why I came early. Well, technically my boss—she was hired to do that and supply me, but she had another job." He shrugged again. "I did the best I could—positioned everyone— I mean, the other caterers, and all that sort of thing, but—" He threw up his hands.

So Ham had enlisted Melody to help him. It made sense—Ariel probably worked for the Jazz and Heritage Foundation, and if he wanted to keep it clean, he wouldn't use her for personal business. Ti-Belle was out of town—or something. And he himself couldn't be spared during the festival. What better helper than Melody? She'd probably been thrilled to be delegated.

Now, which of the stragglers looked "flighty"? The one talking to Steve Steinman, she decided. Short and slightly plump, with the big-hair look, ill-considered atop such a small body. It was very pretty hair, chestnut-colored and wavy, but if she wanted people to take her seriously, she should probably stop gelling it out a foot on all sides. Yet she was probably anything but flighty. She'd have to be damn good at her job to keep it.

The question was, how to approach her with Steve Steinman there? She wanted to tell him to go home, not to wait for her, to apologize for forgetting him, but she couldn't in front of a witness. She'd have to be dismissive; she hated that.

"Pardon me," she said. "Are you Ariel Burge? Could you excuse us, Mr. Steinman?"

Apparently, he was amused. She hoped Burge hadn't caught

the wink he gave Skip. She showed her badge. "Skip Langdon. Could you—"

"Ham's *dead?*"

"What makes you think that?"

"I heard Ti-Belle yell it out to George. But I was trying to play hostess and got stuck in the back. I couldn't get close enough to talk to her. Did he have a heart attack or what? What happened to him?" She was wearing jeans and a T-shirt, had obviously come straight from work.

It was always a problem, trying to get information without giving any. Oh, well, the coroner's wagon would arrive momentarily anyhow.

"I'm sorry. He is dead."

Skip waited while Ariel fumbled with a tissue. "I knew it. It had to be something. He didn't come to work this morning. Just didn't come in at all. Only everyone was so busy, no one noticed till about noon. He was never where he was supposed to be— always late, half the time didn't remember. So that's what we thought. I mean, everywhere he was supposed to be, whoever was there thought he was just somewhere else—do you understand?"

She was gibbering a bit, but it almost made sense. "You mean if you were supposed to meet him at the office and he didn't show up, you just thought he was probably at the fairgrounds?"

She nodded. "And vice versa. I knew he was missing appointments—oh, yeah, and his father and stepmother were calling about every ten minutes, but things just get crazy at the last minute. I looked for him, of course. But that isn't unusual. He disappears and I cover for him, you know? Track him down and light a fire under him. He's like that." She didn't even notice she was using the present tense.

"Like what? Irresponsible?"

"No, just overworked. He gets involved in things. He forgets what time it is."

"And misses appointments."

"Well, not usually, but it's happened. He gets way behind schedule. He's—he was—kind of a dreamer, the kind of guy who gets interested in something and forgets everything else. He's not

31

really . . ." She seemed to think better of finishing the sentence.

"Not really what?"

"Well, you wouldn't call him a ball of fire. You have to keep after him or his whole schedule falls apart. Anyway, it was about lunchtime that I kind of caught on he hadn't been *anywhere* he was supposed to be that day."

"What did you do?"

"Well, I was so worried, I drove out to his house, but he wasn't home. I mean I guess he was . . . already dead."

Skip spoke quickly to stem that train of thought. "So the last time you saw him was when—quitting time yesterday?"

"There is no quitting time during the festival. We work around the clock if we have to. But this party—this Second Line Square thing—it's kind of his pet project. It's—it was—really, really important to him. He'd hired the caterers and everything—all out of his own pocket—but nothing would do but he had to make his own special gumbo for a couple of the performers. See, they'd been at his house when he'd made it before, and he promised them if they'd come and be nice to the rich people, he'd make it again." She spread her arms. "He had a deal—what could he do? So just when things were at their hottest, he went home in the middle of the day to make gumbo."

"And that was the last time you saw him? When he left?"

"No, he called and asked me to bring him some tasso. He'd forgotten it, and his special, personal recipe wouldn't work without it." She rolled her eyes. "So he said."

"You must have been snowed under too."

"And yet he wasn't really demanding. Every now and then something like that came up, that's all. He was a great guy, Office —uh, Detective."

"Skip."

"He was the best. Everyone who worked for him adored him. Just one of those easygoing, teddy-bear sweetie-pie pussycats, you know what I mean?"

"I knew him a little bit. He seemed like that to me." But she'd seen men like that get clobbered—not murdered, but good and beat up in domestic disputes she'd been out on. The wife would be furious, maybe still brandishing a poker or frying pan, and the teddy bear would be mouthing, "Now, honey, you put that thang down, baby doll," blood running down his face, but eyes like velvet, voice like taffy, all hell breaking loose and still gentle as a cocker spaniel. She never knew what these sweeties did to inspire so much wrath.

"Ariel," she said, "when did you bring the tasso?"

"About three."

"Was anyone else here?"

"No. I mean, not that I saw. Ham just met me at the door and took the package."

"What was he wearing at the time?"

"Wearing? I don't know. Jeans, I guess. And, um, a T-shirt. Black. I know! A Radiators T-shirt."

"How did he seem?"

"Seem? Anxious, I guess. Real worried. Like he always gets this time of year."

"Worried?"

"Yeah. Like he just knows he just can't get everything done. He gets like a permanent crease between his eyes."

"Okay, I guess that's it for now. May I call you if I have more questions?"

"Sure."

Skip was halfway back to the house, intending to get Andy Fike's address from Ti-Belle's Rolodex, when she heard a kind of collective gasp, followed instantly by an excited buzz. Wheeling, expecting the worst, she saw only a gray-haired man in jeans and tank top getting out of a double-parked car. The car was a Jaguar and the man had a certain seen-it-all look. Who was he? And then a name floated up from the crowd, repeated over and over: "Nick Anglime, Nick Anglime."

He stood uncertainly, as if afraid to go any farther, and it looked as if he had good reason. Already people were starting to approach—neighborhood kids, mostly, the bolder ones. But, setting his lips, he apparently made a decision, moved forward. Ignored the kids. And Skip noticed for the first time how tall he was. It was easy for him to ignore people—he simply stared out over their heads. She remembered the phrase, "A giant of his generation." Apparently it had meaning beyond his talent.

"Officer," he shouted. "Officer!" Obviously he meant one of the uniformed ones—Skip was wearing the linen shift Jimmy Dee had picked—but his voice was so imperious she nearly answered anyway. His tone was that of a man calling for a waiter. But intimidation gave way to amusement—and an idea. She was about to meet the American Mick. She hoped Steve Steinman was watching.

A uniformed policeman strode importantly in Anglime's direction, but Skip headed him off. "It's okay, officer. I'll talk to him." His face fell like a kid's. Skip almost laughed.

She pulled out her badge and approached Anglime, stood close to him and looked up, mentally measuring him. She was six feet, and he was about six inches taller; quite possibly the tallest man she'd ever seen except for Hulk Hogan, whom she'd once glimpsed in the Dallas airport.

"Skip Langdon," she said. "Can I help you?"

"What's happened? Is someone hurt?"

Behind him, Skip saw the coroner's wagon arriving—everyone would know soon. "I'm afraid so. The party's canceled," she said.

"But—what's *happened?*"

A kid grabbed at him. "Hey, Mr. Anglime. Do you really live in New Orleans?"

"Later, please," he said.

Emboldened, two more kids came close. "Hey, Nick. Hey, Nick, how ya doin'?"

He looked as if he'd like to swat them like so many gnats.

What, thought Skip, *am I doing here? Starfucking?* Disgusted with herself, she went back to tell Steve Steinman good night. He happily lent her his rental car, saying he thought he could get a ride with Ariel. Declining the bait—for some reason she hadn't yet figured out, she trusted Steve—she went back to work.

At the moment she couldn't really tell who was a neighbor and who wasn't—certainly couldn't see who lived where—so she decided to save the block canvassing for later. She went back in the house to check some things—yes, there was an unopened package of tasso in the refrigerator, and yes, Ham's T-shirt said "Radiators" on it, obviously a promotional item for a local band.

And Paul Gottschalk was through with the purple backpack. Eagerly, Skip opened it. It contained books, notebooks, pencils, pens, and money. Every book and notebook had the name "Melody Brocato" neatly printed on it.

▪

She went off to see Blair Rosenbaum, the kid Melody had visited the day before. As it turned out, she could have walked and probably should have—Blair lived about a block and a half away, in a neat brick house with an oak tree in front. It was almost fifties, it was so wholesome. Blair's mom would have been a pretty blonde—someone who worked on it a lot, but still handsome— if it hadn't been for the vertical worry lines between her eyes. Skip's request to see Blair etched them a little deeper. But it was granted, on the condition that Mom could sit in on the interview.

Blair was tall and lanky—maybe even anorexic. And yet she'd probably look elegant in most clothes—in anything but the jeans shorts and oversized T-shirt she wore. It was the skull on the front of the shirt that really made the outfit, but elegant it wasn't. Blair kept her brownish hair short, which emphasized her giraffeness, as did her almond-shaped eyes. She wasn't a typical teenager, this kid —or not what most people thought of as typical. She was clearly smarter than most—a lot smarter. Skip knew that before she opened her mouth, knew it by the eyes, by the way she held her head, by a thousand nonverbal signals.

And then there was her height. Skip had been "too tall"—her own description—as well. Now her height was an advantage, but at Blair's age it had been a distinct liability. For Blair it wouldn't be—no doubt she'd already found some of its advantages. Probably had a modeling contract and the self-confidence of a CEO.

Her mother seemed ordinary in comparison. Blair was so exotic, she looked out of place in the comfortable living room with its earth colors and brass lamps. It was a tasteful room hung with oil paintings—real paintings, not family portraits, not prints, not photographs—which already made it unusual for New Orleans. But Blair needed royal purple. Or Italian leather furniture against a black-walled room. Abstract paintings that took up entire walls. High drama.

Skip said, "I'm here about Melody Brocato."

The almond eyes, so knowing, flashed for a split second, cooled instantly. Blair nodded ever so slightly. "I thought so. Her parents have been calling all day."

"Can you tell me what happened between you?"

"Between us? You mean, when she left? Nothing. I was on the phone. I never saw her go." The girl shrugged. "Maybe she thought I was rude."

"For talking on the phone when you had a guest? Were you?"

She shrugged again, a little defensively. Good: chinks in the armor. "We do that all the time. When one person gets a phone call, the other just does her homework or watches the tube."

"Then why would she think you were rude?"

"She wouldn't."

"Why did she leave, Blair? What happened?"

"I don't know. Nothing happened."

"Okay. Did you have a fight earlier?"

"No."

"Can you think of any reason at all why Melody might have needed to leave suddenly?"

"No."

"Do you know Hamson Brocato? Melody's brother?"

"Sure."

"What's Melody's relationship with him?"

"They're close. Really close. He's a cool guy."

"Would Melody have gone to see him?"

"Why not? He's right in the neighborhood."

"Did you talk about him on Tuesday?"

"No. Why?"

"Did Melody fight with him recently?"

Blair shifted her weight, becoming interested. "Not that I know of. Why?"

"Have you heard from her since she left here?"

"Since yesterday? No."

"Have you got any ideas about where she might be?"

"Not unless she's with Ham and Ti-Belle."

Yes you do. If you're her friend, you do.

But Skip knew Blair wasn't going to tell. She had her story and she was sticking to it. Skip also knew how to shake her up. She said, "I think I should tell you something."

Silence. But Blair's mother tensed. The interview would probably end up putting money in some cosmetic surgeon's pocket.

"I think I should tell you this is not a simple case of a runaway teenager. This is a murder investigation."

Both Rosenbaums gasped. Fear leapt into Blair's eyes, her left hand went to her heart. "Melody—"

"Melody's brother Ham was killed yesterday."

"Omigod. Ham! Oh. Poor Melody." Blair's body rocked. "Does she know? Oh—you don't know that. Ham's dead and Melody's missing. Omigod!"

She was quick. She had put the two things together and realized they might be connected.

"What time did Melody leave here?"

"About five, I guess. Five-thirty, maybe. What time was he killed?"

"We don't know yet."

"Omigod! Ham! Melody'll just die."

"Okay, you said they were really close. Had they fought lately? Were they getting along?"

"They never fought. Ham was like—well, he was more like an uncle than a brother. You know, because of the age difference. He's not that much younger than Melody's mom, can you believe that?"

Skip smiled. Blair was poised, but she was still sixteen.

"Actually— *Actually* . . ." She made the word momentous, telegraphed that she was finally about to let Skip in on something. Something private, for those under twenty only. "Actually, he was more like a father than an uncle. Melody's dad's so old and everything—well, I don't know if that's it, he's just not—he's not—" She was losing resolve.

"Not really a very good father."

"Well, maybe not. He's not very . . ." She searched for the right word, gave up. "He's kind of distant."

"And Melody's mom?"

Blair's guard went up again. She executed another of her habitual shrugs. "She's okay, I guess. But Melody likes Ham and Ti-Belle better than her parents." She glanced at her mother, looking slightly guilty. "I mean, they're young and hip, and Ti-Belle's famous." The elder Rosenbaum rolled her eyes, but Blair missed it. She had put a fist to her mouth. "Omigod. I can't believe he's dead."

"What did you think of Ham?"

"Me? What did I think? I thought he was really cool. I mean, chubby, but, you know: cool. He knew a lot of sh—uh, stuff."

"What kind of stuff?"

"Oh, music. You know."

"What about drugs?"

"Drugs! No way." Her eyes didn't stray even slightly toward her mother. And her face was so scornful, Skip might have believed her even if they had.

"So who are Melody's other close friends?"

"I don't know. The boys in the band, I guess. The ones she sings with. Doug Leddy and Joel Boucree."

"Was one of them her boyfriend?"

"Not really." Blair sounded uncharacteristically vague.

"Did she have a boyfriend?"

"Yeah. But I don't know if they were too close anymore."

"Why is that?"

Blair shrugged.

"What's his name?"

"Flip, uh, Phillips." She shifted in her seat, obviously uncomfortable.

Seeing Blair was closing down again, Skip left her and went back to Ham's block. Things were quieter now. Most of the neighbors had tired of the show and gone home. And most of the guests had gathered all the gossip there was and gone out in the world to spread it.

Skip started at one end of the block on Ham's side of the street, worked her way to the other, and came back down the block on the other side. When she was done, she had learned three things:

No one had seen Ariel deliver the tasso at three o'clock Tuesday.

Mrs. Thiel Greenleaf had been cutting some flowers in her front yard shortly before five o'clock that day and had seen Melody arrive at Ham's just as Mrs. Greenleaf was going back in her house. (She hadn't seen Melody leave.)

And half the neighborhood knew Ham and Ti-Belle fought— long, loud, and often.

4

Melody had done what everyone does in the movies when something awful happens. She had hollered "No!" at the top of her lungs, as if she could make it stop, turn time back and erase disaster, regain her innocence, and start being grateful for the imperfect world she had known up to that instant to ward off this new, shattered one.

She was embarrassed about that, felt silly. Oddly, the memory of her hysteria was almost as painful as the other memory—the moment in which everything had come apart. After yelling, she had simply stared for a moment, trying to hang onto history, to the moment before it happened, and then she had split. Forgetting her backpack, forgetting her name, practically. She had just run out of there and kept running until her lungs hurt, and then she'd settled for walking fast. Aimlessly at first, while she tried to figure out what to do.

She wanted a shower, she wanted to wash this thing off her, but she couldn't go home. She was absolutely, utterly, completely, devastatingly alone in the world. That much she knew. Unless . . . could she call Madeleine Richard? No way! She almost laughed at the absurdity of it. Richard was always saying how she was Melody's friend, she was her advocate, but who paid Richard? Melody's mom. She was bought. And she was an adult. No way was Melody trusting any adult. Not after what had happened. She was alone. Completely alone. Absolutely alone. She hadn't known it was possible to feel so alone.

There wasn't even a kid she could trust. Well, maybe Joel. Yes! Maybe Joel. But she couldn't just turn up at his house. And she certainly couldn't go to Flip's. And she'd run away from Blair's. That left exactly nobody.

She walked down streets she didn't think her parents would think to go, but she knew she had to get out of sight pretty soon. They'd come looking. She had to decide what to do. She had a few bucks in her jeans pocket, enough to take a bus, but—where to? And then when she got there, what was she going to do for money?

As she walked, as her tears dried and her head cleared, she became aware of a curious, liberated optimism, almost a high. The down side was she'd lost everything and everybody in one tragic ten-minute interval. But there was an up side, if she could pull it off. She was beginning to see the rosy edges of it, to hear one of her favorite songs in a way she never had before. It was "Me and Bobby McGee," a song she'd heard a thousand times, sung a thousand times, cried over. The line that was getting to her was, "Freedom's just another word for nothing left to lose," a sentiment that always before had seemed unbearably sad. But reverse it and what did you have? "Nothing left to lose is just another word for freedom."

Freedom!

That was something you didn't get when you were sixteen. What you did get was school at eight A.M., and your mom telling you what to do, and no car because your dad said you were too young, and no career, no real career yet because your dad said you were too young, and curfews because your dad thought you were a baby and just generally that sort of thing—prison, more or less, because you were too young.

The only way to get around it was to run away, and Melody

had never thought of that before. Why should she? Okay, so her mom and dad weren't perfect, but she had had Ham and Ti-Belle. And Flip, and her friends, and most of all, her music.

Which was the key. The rest of it was gone, but what really counted anyway? The music. It was her life. It was what she loved most and what she wanted to spend her life doing, and she could go so much faster, she knew it . . . it was the only thing she could depend on. It was what was going to get her out of this hole.

If she were on her own, she could sing—did she dare say it? —professionally. She could bypass high school and college and sororities and other people's weddings and her own first divorce and all that crap.

She could be a professional singer tonight.

Ti-Belle had done it. She could do exactly what Ti-Belle had done—get on a bus for the French Quarter and join a street band.

The great Ti-Belle Thiebaud had actually done that. Caught the bus in New Iberia or St. Martinville, somewhere like that, and roared right on down to the Quarter.

Yes, but Ti-Belle has a great voice.

Well, hell, I do too.

I think.

But I don't know. I've never had a chance to try it out. All I've ever done is sung at parties for Country Day kids.

I can do it! I know I can do it!

The debate raged within her even as she sat quietly on the bus, but it didn't matter. Maybe she couldn't do it, but she sure as hell was going to try.

She'd finally gotten the idea of following the railroad tracks to Schwegmann's, knowing she wasn't about to see any of her friends' moms there. Mothers of Country Day kids didn't shop at Schwegmann's. Melody laughed, knowing she was through with that crap forever. She was an artist now, above the petty concerns of the bourgeoisie.

Once at Schwegmann's, all she had to do was wait at the bus stop on Airline Highway, and zap!, she was on her way to *la bohème.*

Gradually, the memory of what had just happened began to recede in her consciousness. Thoughts of the past gave way to thoughts of the future. True, self-doubt intruded, but it drifted in and out. A horrible thing had just happened. And yet, she thought, I'm okay. I think I'm okay.

Daydreaming, looking out the window, seeing nothing but her own internal movie, she was actually happy. She saw herself singing on a street corner in the Quarter, tourists surrounding her, throwing money in an open guitar case, murmuring to each other, "She's good," as if it were the last thing they expected. "She sounds like Janis Joplin." "She's fabulous. What do you think she's doing here?"

And their friends would say, "She's a runaway, probably. Poor thing, they probably beat her at home."

Or she'd fool them; they'd never think she was underage. Some of them would be from large recording companies and one or two would give her their cards and ask her to lunch and buy her champagne (not realizing she was only sixteen). They'd say they'd recognized her talent and give her advice on what to do—help her make a demo tape, that sort of thing—she wasn't sure exactly what was entailed—and then they'd fly her out to California and sign her up.

And next year she'd sing at the JazzFest. Or maybe the year after—not next year, she might be recognized. She saw herself on the stage—a big stage, not one of the little ones for local groups —and this time she was also surrounded by admirers, but hundreds, thousands of them, and they wouldn't be expressing surprise that she was good—they'd know her by her albums. And when she came out, she'd sing her favorite song, Janis's song, "Get It While You Can." That's the way she'd warm them up, it would be her trademark, because it was what she lived by. You had to get what you wanted, what you could get, you couldn't go waiting around, because you might not be here tomorrow.

Melody believed that. The song was about love, but she thought it a metaphor for life. It didn't seem sad or tragic to her that she would die young, she just knew she would. Well, she didn't really know it, she just thought it was likely. She couldn't say why. It just seemed that way. Janis had died young, and her life had been wonderful, she had escaped her provincial Texas roots and people had loved her, had stood and cheered for her; Janis had achieved love on a national scale. And she had done everything there was to do before she was twenty-seven. She had defied convention and gone her own way, and been her own woman. The fact that she died young seemed romantic, almost poetic.

I know! I'll write a song about it.

She couldn't believe she hadn't thought of that before. What a wonderful homage, what a perfect . . . but wait. She saw why it hadn't occurred to her. Because she hadn't been ready. And now she was. If ever she was going to be, she was now, when she saw how fragile life was, how you could lose everything—including, maybe, your mind—in about thirty seconds.

Ham had turned her on to Janis Joplin. *I lost him and he gave me Janis.* She marveled at the tragedy, the fearful symmetry of it. The minute Melody heard those throaty, hoarse, all-body tones coming up from the bottom of Janis's toes, full-out, full-tilt boogie, which was the way she always sang, ("CCrrrryy, baaaaaaaaby!" or "Ttttrrrrryyyyyyyyyyyyy just a little bit harder!") she had thought, *I didn't know a white woman could do that.* She knew Etta and Irma, Bessie Smith, Billie Holiday, all the great blues singers—Ham had given her a terrific music education—but she'd simply had no idea a white woman could produce a sound like that. Ti-Belle sang great, sure—Melody'd love to be as good as Ti-Belle—but the fullness of Janis, the total involvement, the *feeling* there—that was something else again. She felt almost reverent about it.

Okay. She would write the song, and then next year, after "Get It While You Can," she'd sing it. It would be a beautiful tribute, and she owed it to Janis, who inspired her personally as well as artistically.

Melody got a comfortable, warm feeling, thinking about it, about all the good things to come. It was like being in a cocoon, or sitting dry in front of a fire on a rainy day. She came out, she saw the crowd, and through the magic of the inner television, she saw herself onstage, belting her heart out. Joel was there—she had another identity now, but she could trust Joel and she'd taken him with her, straight to the top. He was the only one from her past life she *could* trust, but at least there was one. He was lead guitar. She had a huge band behind her. Huge. All black. And she was black too. Somehow in the fantasy, she'd turned black.

I wish, she thought. *Don't I wish.*

She tried to readjust the daydream, see herself in a more realistic way, but she couldn't. She didn't know what the new Melody would look like, the Melody who wasn't a girl, wasn't a wannabe, but the one who'd metamorphosed—who was an artist and a woman, respected as such by the world. Not her family (her late family, she meant), not the kids at Country Day, but the *whole world!* She had that potential now, to be that person.

But she had no cultural context for it. Her dad was a business-man, her mom—what?

Somebody who gets her nails done.

Neither had graduated from college, but that wasn't the point. The point was, they didn't take her seriously. They didn't know what she was, didn't understand her. She hadn't been named Melody because they hoped she'd have musical talent, but because her mom had thought it was cute. Ham had been the one who introduced her to music. If it hadn't been for Ham, she'd probably be on drugs. Because music was her escape. Her escape and her inspiration. A place she could go to get away, to be somebody else, not to have to live where she lived, with those odd people she was related to. She didn't understand them. Why would you spend your life selling sandwiches? Melody could see it if you really needed to, but her dad loved it. What kind of person would make that his whole life, ignore his family, ignore the daughter he had late in life, who should have been the apple of his eye? Actually, he said she was, but he never paid attention to her except to forbid something. That was the way she'd describe her father: forbidding.

Her mother was worse. She didn't care about anything except her damned appearance. Melody was never going to wear makeup, never going to color her hair, certainly never going to have mani-cured nails. You couldn't even play the piano with nails like that.

Why couldn't she have been born a Boucree, like Joel? It wasn't so impossible; New Orleans was full of families like the Boucrees —the Nevilles, the Marsalises, the Batistes, the Thomases, the Lasties, the Jordans—families where music was life. It was the family business and you went into it. They taught you to play the minute you were old enough to hold a drumstick, and you were performing at the JazzFest by the time you were seven. It had happened to Joel. She'd watched him play last year with the Boucrees and had nearly jumped up and down, shouting that she knew him and not only that, she played in a band with him. That she, Melody Brocato, was that close to greatness. Of course, the Boucrees were black and so were all the others. Why couldn't she have been black? Been born into one of those big, warm, loving families where your mom cooked up great pots of red beans and rice while she sang a version of "Amazing Grace" that had passersby stopped dead in their tracks on the sidewalk—on the banquette, Joel would say.

Now she saw herself as a little girl. The singer-to-be was gone, but she was still black. She was sitting around the dining room table with her three brothers and two sisters and her mom and dad and her two uncles and they were eating greens and chicken and black-eyed peas, all laughing, teasing each other, but gently, with deep affection. It was all good-humored, sweet-tempered, no mean jokes, no nasty stuff like white people got into. Melody was about five. She had light skin and medium-curly hair that hung in ringlets, one especially, that hung down over her right eye. She had a winning smile and people were always patting her, saying how cute she was, not correcting her every two seconds and finding fault. It was so vivid she could almost smell those peas. It felt so good to be loved like that. Her life would have been so damned easy if it had happened to her. Why did white people have to be so fucked up?

She got off the bus angry, stomped for half a block or so till she came back to the present. But finally it occurred to her that here she was—free at last! She should be celebrating.

Oh, sure. Celebrating. No friends and no family and I'm supposed to celebrate.

It went back and forth like that. Just when she'd be feeling good, she'd remember, and then she'd have to get herself back up again. Okay, that was just how it was going to be. She wasn't going to think about it. She was going to pretend it never happened, those people never existed. She was someone else now, a street

46

musician soon to be a star. All she had to do was get herself a gig.

She wandered on down toward Jackson Square, and right in front of the cathedral were two guys and a woman, maybe in their twenties, maybe a little bit younger, playing some not bad to pretty decent music. She listened for a while. They knew a lot of local stuff, some Cajun kinds of things, some country—Melody knew everything they did, and really didn't think they were too bad, but from the looks of things this was no way to make a fortune. They weren't really drawing a crowd. On the other hand, a singer could make all the difference. Her palms began to sweat as she tried to get up the nerve to do something. She wasn't sure what. So she just kept watching.

The guitar player was cute, and looked young. Maybe not much older than she was. He wore torn jeans and a black T-shirt, and he was blond. Flip, her ex-boyfriend whom she never wanted to see again, was dark. And of course Joel . . . but she couldn't get Joel. He was two years older and thought she was a baby, treated her like a little sister. Besides, they had a professional relationship. Or so he said whenever she kidded around, sort of flirting but not really because she didn't dare. She couldn't see why you couldn't be in love with somebody you worked with, but Joel was the boss. He was a pro, so she had to listen. Or anyway, it used to be that way. Today was a whole new ball game. From now on she could make up her own rules.

The guitar player had good shoulders, slender build, and a cute butt. His skin was tan, not peaches and cream, but it was as clear and delicate as a girl's. If he shaved more than once a week, she'd be surprised. And something else she liked a lot. He had beautiful hands. Long fingers, very clean. Nice square-cut nails. She watched his hands as he fingered the guitar, and found herself wanting to touch them, wanting them to touch her. She watched so intently it was almost like falling into a trance. It felt as if there was nothing else in the world but herself and those fingers, so why shouldn't she simply go get them? The need to do it was almost overpowering. Dr. Richard talked sometimes about impulse control—her mom and dad both had poor impulse control, and so, sometimes, did Melody. If she managed not to embarrass herself by grabbing this strange boy on a street corner, that would be a step in the right direction. She knew this thing that was happening to her, she'd felt it before—she just didn't know how to handle it. She knew perfectly well it was caused by the runaway truck called hormones, but that didn't make it any easier. Or any less delicious.

It occurred to her suddenly that she could do it with this boy. This strange boy with the perfect skin, the pretty planes in his face —if he wasn't involved with the female bass player, she could do it with him. She felt her face go hot. Her palms started sweating again.

I could do it tonight.

Tonight! This afternoon, half an hour ago, there had been nothing, and now there was this. The only reason she'd never done it with Flip was fear. She'd hardly ever let him touch her below the waist because it got her too hot. If they did that too much, she'd do it, she knew she would, and then someone would find out and her father would kill her. She might get pregnant, that was always a possibility, but it wasn't as bad as her father's wrath. Actually, she didn't know if he'd kill her. But he'd yell, and she couldn't stand the yelling.

God, what a baby! I don't believe what I've done. I've sacrificed my womanhood because I'm afraid of my daddy yelling.

She hadn't put it to herself quite that way before. She was ripe, she was ready, she felt as sexual as anybody else, she was pretty damn sure of that, and yet she was a virgin. All because she was intimidated by a geriatric parent. It shamed her to think of it.

Tonight could be the night. It would be a rite of passage. She'd become a woman in more ways than one.

The band stopped playing. What were they doing? Gathering up their money, it looked like. Going.

Suddenly, reality intruded in a big way. Now was the time to talk to them, before they got away. But what was the use? They were going to hate her. He was, especially. What had she been thinking of? Did she imagine she could get anybody she wanted, any strange boy on the street? Was she crazy—what on earth would he want with her? She was just a kid with a biggish nose and fuzzy-looking hair. Anyway, he was probably involved with the bass player, the redhead.

Okay, she had to do it. Had to or go home, and she had no home. She spoke to the woman because she felt shy and it was easier that way: "I really liked your music."

The woman had on a white tank top that made her look washed-out. Her hair was a peachy color, like Sissy Spacek's, and she wore no makeup. She looked friendly, though, and she had a nice smile. "Thanks."

"Are you leaving?"

The drummer, who was overweight and whom she'd hardly noticed, gave her a look that made her cringe. He'd noticed her. He had little pig eyes that looked hostile. "We think we've got enough to go eat. What's it look like, Chris?"

The blond had been counting the money. He said, "Eight bucks, give or take."

"Shit!"

"Okay. Let's crank up again."

The drummer said, "What do you want to hear, Jailbait?"

Realizing he meant her, Melody felt embarrassed. "My name's Mel—" She stopped just in time, head spinning at what she'd almost done. "Janis!" she said, shouting to cover her mistake.

"This one goes out to Janis," he said, and smiled, his eyes crinkling. He looked almost appealing. "What'll it be?"

"How about 'Breakaway'?"

"Not without Irma Thomas," he sneered.

"I can sing it," Melody said. She was surprised they even knew it.

He rolled his eyes. "Oh, great. An audition."

The woman said, "Oh, hell. Let's just do 'Jambalaya.' "

Melody thought the blond—Chris, his name was—winked at her. She looked him full in the eyes, tilted her head slightly. "I can sing that too."

He shrugged, lifted an eyebrow. He was interested, Melody thought with amazement. Not in the song, but in her. Her palms started up again. "Go to it," said Chris.

She turned around to face the audience. No one was there, really. Just a couple of strollers in the square, and a few more down Chartres Street. That made it easy. Melody took a deep breath and started belting: "Jambalaya, crawfish pie, filé gumbo . . ."

The familiar words bounced off the concrete louder than she'd expected, raised the energy in the street like a parade coming through. Melody felt the shock of it, saw the strollers in the square point and start to walk toward her. She'd only sung in controlled situations before, had no idea how she'd sound out here.

Someone behind her said, "Holy shit." One of the guys, she couldn't tell which one. And that was all she needed.

After that, it was fun. Her feet started to move and magic happened. The music flowed through her like a gift from another dimension. She was a musician, she was an artist, this was who she was. She knew now, just as she'd known it the first day she'd sung the same song, and danced in front of her mother's full-length mirror, just fooling around but feeling the magic. She'd been about eight.

Part of what was happening, the sudden party feel of it all, was the song. She realized it even as a crowd started to gather. People responded to songs they already knew. But, hell, it wasn't just that, she was singing well. Really well. They were loving her. They were tossing money.

Melody finished the song, and before the applause had stopped, before she had time to catch her breath, Chris started "Breakaway." The others joined in, but Melody got there first:

> "I made my reservations
> I'm leavin' town tomorrow
> I'll find somebody new and
> There'll be no more sorrow . . ."

They did that and then they did "La Ti Da," and some others. Chris just started a song, never asking if Melody knew it. And she always knew it. The crowd never got huge, but people came and went and dollars piled up in the kitty.

After about an hour and a half, they took a break. The ugly guy, the piggy one, was all over her, hugging her, kissing her, sweating on her. "You are something, kid!"

Melody shrugged graciously. "You guys just needed a singer."

"Let's go eat," said the redhead. "I'm Sue Ann, by the way. And this is Chris." She leaned on him for a moment, sending a message, Melody thought. But Sue Ann grabbed the fat one too, around the upper arm. "And this is Randy."

They went over to Decatur Street, walked down to get a pizza, Sue Ann asking questions a lot faster than Melody could think of answers.

"Where are you from?"

Where the hell was she from? "Abbeville," she said.

"Funny, you don't look like a Cajun." This from Chris.

"Um, only on my mom's side." She wished she'd thought to get a story together.

"How long have you been here?"

"In New Orleans? Gosh. Seems like forever. How 'bout y'all?"

"Oh. Awhile." They didn't like questions either.

Chris kept looking at her sideways, keeping his distance, seeming amused, as if she were a hamster someone had brought him to play with. It made her nervous, but on the other hand, it was attention from the person she wanted it from. She wanted to get closer, to close the distance between them, but she didn't know how. She felt tongue-tied every time he spoke to her, wouldn't have known what to say even if she'd met him as Melody Brocato.

Oh, God. What if they ask for a last name?

Robicheaux. That was safe. Everyone was named Robicheaux.

But they didn't ask. They asked how old she was, or the piggy one did. "Eighteen," she said, not missing a beat.

The guys slapped each other high fives. Melody flushed, thinking they were congratulating each other because she wasn't jailbait after all, nearly dying of embarrassment. But Randy explained, "They all say that. We got a standing bet."

Angry, she said, "Who is 'they,' please?"

"Every cute runaway comes to the Quarter."

Sue Ann said, "Don't let 'em bother you. They're just a couple of small-town guys in the big city."

"Well, listen to Miss Sophistication," said Randy. "Like you're not from Meridian, Mississippi."

"Shut up, big guy, or you're going to bed without." If that meant what Melody thought it meant, it was good news.

As if on cue, Chris said, "Hey, Janis, where you crashin'?"

"Uh . . . well, I . . ." She couldn't come up with a single idea.

Sue Ann said, "You don't have a place?"

Melody shook her head.

"Want to stay with us?"

She shrugged—coolly, she hoped. "Sure." As if she did this every day.

They finished off their pizza and had a quick conference about which songs they were going to do tomorrow, Melody being careful not to suggest any of Janis's songs, lest they make the connection. Everything they knew, Melody knew. Not for nothing had she worked her butt off the last two years, with Joel and Doug.

Chris was the best musician of the three, almost as good as Doug, though he couldn't touch Joel, and he looked at Melody with respect. Did respect her, she could feel it. Considered her a colleague. The worst day of her life had turned into the best.

Melody wanted to go back and make more money, but they said you weren't really allowed to play past eight, and they'd stopped at eight-fifteen. They'd only made twenty-two dollars, and most of it had gone for the pizza. But to Melody it was manna. She'd started out with seven bucks in her jeans and now she was a professional singer.

She looked at her watch. It wasn't even nine-thirty. What was next?

"Beatty's?" asked Randy.

"What's that?"

"The runaway bar," Chris said. "It's where you'd go tonight if you hadn't met us. You'd have hung around, watching it get later and later, and then this one bar on Decatur would have started hopping, and you'd have noticed everybody in there was about your age. And you'd have gone in and a lot of guys would have hit on you and finally someone would have offered you a place to crash tonight."

"A guy?"

He shrugged. "Anybody. People take care of each other in the Quarter."

She was fascinated. "Are we going there?"

"Hell, no. I can't take that scene."

"Just for a while," said Randy.

So they went.

The bar, which opened out to the street, was essentially a three-sided room. The furnishings were basic, if you were being kind, and Chris was right—no one there was over thirty, probably not over twenty-five. This early, it was pretty sparsely populated, which Chris said was good, he hated it when it was crowded. Randy and Chris played the video games across from the bar while Melody and Sue Ann got acquainted. Mostly, Melody asked questions and looked around. Some punk rockers were starting to arrive, pretty tough-looking customers, and she bet there'd be more as the night wore on. She wondered how she'd look all punked-out.

Chris came back, Randy tagging behind. "I can't take this scene." He gestured with his head. The place was starting to hop. A lot of people looked pretty unsteady already. They got a six-pack and some go-cups and went out to the Moonwalk, all four of them. Melody wasn't too happy about it, but didn't feel she had a choice, since she was depending on them for shelter. She had a pretty good idea about what was going to happen—Randy was going to make a play for her while Chris looked on in that amused way he had.

Sure enough, the fat one fell into step beside her, sat down next to her when they reached the Moonwalk. That part was right. But Chris wasn't paying even the slightest attention. He was talking to Sue Ann, not intimately, just joking around, but Melody might as well not have existed.

Randy was going on and on about something that had happened to him in high school, something to do with football, punctuating his story by touching her leg, her arm, anything he could get away with. She wanted to tell him to stop, but then he'd sulk, and she didn't want to piss him off right at the outset. And she was still trying to avoid contributing to Chris's amusement at her expense. Randy had sucked down his first beer on the short walk and was now into his second. He smelled beery and sweaty; revolting. He had his hand on her shoulder now, leaning close, not merely touching, but really latched on, like a barnacle or something. The hand was dirty. There were black lines under each fingernail, on the knuckles. She was going to have to say something or throw up. Involuntarily, though, she looked around at Chris, wanting his help but not daring to admit it to herself. She caught his eye and saw his expression change from bland to alert. Not amused.

He said, "Hey, Janis, want to go down to the river?"

She said, "Sure," swiveling slowly, as if she'd expected it, known it was due. Later, she realized she must have looked utterly desperate.

There were benches like bleachers, which you could climb down and sit on, dabble your feet in the Mississippi itself. "Come on," said Chris, and clambered ahead of her. At the bottom they stood clutching their beers, peering into the stillness of the water. "Pretty, isn't it?" he said.

But it was more than pretty. It was vast and calming, soothing in an unexpected way that was new to her. "It's like . . . a mom," she blurted, and thought what a dork she sounded, what a baby.

But Chris nodded. "Yes. It's like being rocked. Just listening to it, just being this close. It's an entity. It feels like a thing with a personality."

She stared at him. She didn't know who he was, where he came from, but she hadn't expected this. She had thought he was handsome, talented, transient, and no one she could take seriously—in other words, someone perfectly suited to be her first fuck, to be used and discarded. She wanted it that way because it wouldn't get messy. Now she thought she could fall in love with him.

"I grew up near the ocean. In South Carolina, where it's like velvet. People who come there, Yankees, hate to go in—they say it's like being in a dirty bathtub. Because it's so warm."

"And what's it like, really?"

"Like heaven." He smiled at her, a shy smile, she realized, and liked that. "Just like heaven."

She smiled back, but didn't know what to say, just held his gaze. He didn't speak either, and she felt uncomfortable. She slid her eyes back toward the river, took another sip of beer. She twisted her ring the way she did when she was nervous, the cameo ring that Nonna, her father's mother, had given her. It had been Nonna's, which made it an heirloom, her mother said, and so she wore it, but it was too small for her. She had to wear it on her pinky, where it looked much too big, but she kind of liked that, thinking that at Country Day it passed for eccentric.

Chris took her hand, made her stop twisting, calling attention to her nervousness, which embarrassed her. "I wanted to tell you," he said, "your singing was . . ."

She waited, knowing he was searching for a word that would flatter her but still not compromise him, a low-key word.

"Extraordinary," he said finally.

The guy was cute, but the phoniness of it pissed her off. She snorted. "Extraordinarily what?"

She was pleased with the sound of her voice—brittle, edgy, just this side of hostile. The woman who spoke in that voice would brook no nonsense.

But Chris only laughed. "Tough cookie," he said, and let the suspense build for a moment. *Extraordinarily amateurish*, he might have said, and a piece of her was sure he was going to. She was braced, ready for it, sure she could take it, anything would be better than stupid, lukewarm pleasantries.

"What are you, a prima donna? You were great. And you know it too, don't you?"

She stared at him, shocked. "You really thought so?"

He touched her cheek. "Yeah." He said it so softly, she almost missed it.

Her stomach felt fluttery, a sensation she associated with stage fright. Again she looked ahead and took a sip from the can. She thought of reclaiming her hand, the one he was holding, but she found, on consideration, that she didn't want to at all. Involuntarily, she squeezed his hand instead, and immediately regretted it, knowing it sent a signal she hadn't meant to send.

Not looking at her, staring at the West Bank like she was, he spoke again. "What's your real name?"

"I told you. You don't believe me?"

"You just don't look like a Janis."

"I don't? What do I look like?"

Boldly, she turned to face him again, and he stared at her for a long moment. "Olivia," he said. "No—something Shakespearean. Viola. Juliet. Better yet, Julianna. Something Mediterranean and complex—and soft as the night."

"Desdemona?"

"Too sophisticated. Something with depth, but innocence."

Her cheeks burned. She didn't like being seen as innocent. "Are you really named Chris? It's perfect for you."

"I know. That's why I picked it."

"Are Sue Ann and Randy their names?"

He shrugged. "Who knows? I don't know who they are. But I know you. Your family has money, but they don't really appreciate you. They treat you like a kid and don't recognize your talent, maybe they're violent; maybe not always, but finally—today; yesterday. Maybe it was one violent incident that did it. You couldn't handle it anymore. So you ran away."

Tears welled as he spoke and poured down her cheeks by the time he finished. She wasn't even embarrassed, just caught up in the incredible, wonderful, unprecedented sensation of being understood. "Did it happen to you?" Of course it had; how else could he know?

"It happened to you," he said.

A sob came out of her, unbidden, unexpected, like vomit. She turned her back to him, covered her mouth with her hands, desperately trying to stem this humiliating uprising of emotion, aware that her back must look as if she had St. Vitus's Dance. He left her alone for a moment, and then she felt him move closer, turn so that he could hold her whole body tight to his chest, his arms wrapped around her from behind, his face against her cheek. It was so gentle, so thoughtful a gesture, it felt so warm and intimate that the sobs began to die almost immediately.

She put her hands on his, which were now crossed on her chest. "I'm afraid they'll find me," she said, whispering, though she didn't know why.

"What?"

She spoke more loudly, turned her face to his, or as far toward his as she could, so that she was in profile, their cheeks touching again. "I'm afraid of them," she said.

His mouth was at her ear. "I know," he whispered.

It didn't occur to her to question how he knew, only to marvel that he did. She struggled out of the soft embrace, hating to do it, but needing to look at him some more, and turned around to face him. She took both his hands, surprised at her boldness but needing to touch him. "I just ran away today."

"Do you want to talk about it?"

She considered, finally shook her head. "No. A lot of things happened. I feel like I lost everything at once. I mean, my family and friends and . . ." She paused, suddenly shy. She had been about to say "my boyfriend," but thought better of it. She said instead, "I can't go back. I can never go back."

"Your folks live in New Orleans?"

She nodded.

He looked at her for a long while, assessing. "Wonder how you'd look as a blonde?"

She laughed, the sound coming out of her as unexpectedly as the sobs had. She saw suddenly how easy it was going to be. "That's it! All I have to do is look different."

"That's what they all do—the runaways." He stared at her. "But I like the way you look now." He was kissing her before she saw it coming, his lips on hers, his tongue probing, his hands reaching for her face, tenderly, gently. It wasn't like kissing Flip, or anyone at Country Day, or anyone in the world, maybe. It was like fire and honey at the same time. So sweet, so impossibly sweet, but so incendiary, sweeping, like a brushfire. Flip kissed like a baby; this was a whole new category. Or maybe one kiss was much like another, maybe she was different. She put a hand on Chris's neck, to pull him closer to her. His skin was impossibly hot.

In a while, she said, "I need a break," and pulled herself away, reached awkwardly for her beer, but only succeeded in knocking it off the bench.

Chris pulled her back. "Let's go to bed."

There they were, the magic words. Everything was working out so perfectly according to plan that Melody couldn't quite keep up. She felt dazed, out of focus. Chris put his arms around her, simply held her, not pushing anything, which gave her time to think. And she realized it had all been a fantasy, that she'd never expected to end up like this, with Chris—to get the thing she wanted. She was so used to being thwarted—to being a child instead of an adult, always at someone else's mercy—that she wasn't prepared to get her wish. Or maybe she just wasn't ready to do it. It was something you thought and thought about and it was a big, big deal.

Oh, hell, be a grown-up.

I don't know if I can. What if it scares me? His penis. What if it's . . . I don't know, not what I expect. And what if he gets weird? What if he's rough or something?

"I don't know," she said. "I'm kind of mixed up."

"You've had a hard day." He whispered it, massaging her shoulders. "Are you tired?"

"Umm-hmm."

"Come on. Nothing will happen. I'll just hold you."

"What?" Did things work like that?

"Really. It'll be okay."

The scruffy apartment apparently had two rooms and a kitchen, but Melody saw only the first, the living room. A door off the hall was closed. Chris glanced at it only briefly. "Guess Randy and Sue Ann got the bedroom."

"Are they a couple?" Randy certainly hadn't behaved like it.

Chris shrugged. "Sometimes. Give me a hand, will you?" Melody helped him unroll a foam mattress with a grayish sheet on it. He threw down a couple of dusty sofa pillows and found a sleeping bag to use for a blanket. "You want to take off your jeans or anything?"

She shook her head and untied her shoes, trying to look nonchalant. To her relief, he removed only his shoes as well.

When he got into bed, she pressed herself against him, fitting her contours to his, wanting to get as close as possible—to be embraced like a child. And he held her as tight as a teddy bear. She was inconceivably grateful.

▪

She let Sue Ann cut her hair the next day. It wasn't too precise, but who cared? It was a modified punk look, spiked up with gel; irregular was what the whole thing was about. They played a gig on Royal Street (which was closed to traffic in the afternoon) to get money for the rest of the makeover. Everybody chipped in, and they all went shopping together. They got her sunglasses, clothes from the flea market, different makeup and hair color. They didn't stop at blond, they got purple too, for the bangs. Chris did her himself. Then Sue Ann did her makeup—a very light base to cover Melody's tawny skin, red lipstick, and plenty of black stuff on her eyes. She put on a pair of striped pedal pushers and an off-the-shoulder blouse. Sue Ann added some zany earrings, dangling fruit baskets.

Chris said, "You could knock on your own mother's door and say you're the Avon lady."

It was true, but Melody wanted to cry. She had a new name and didn't even look like herself. She couldn't help it, it was weird. And not only that, she was ugly. Chris probably hated her now.

But after they all had muffalettas, he took her hand and led her up the river, to Woldenberg Park, and talked to her about his music. He played songs for her, only for her, and asked her about herself. She told about Joel and Doug, first names only, hoping that was okay, and nervously twisted her ring.

Chris said, "You look sad."

"I was going to a party tonight. At my brother's house."

He put an arm around her, drew her to him.

She said, "Do you hate the way I look?"

He said, "Babe, it's not the packaging. It's you."

They necked in the grass till it was time to find the others and start raking in the money.

And that night, when it was all over, when they had made

nearly forty dollars apiece, and drunk a couple of beers, and once again sat by the river, Melody made love with him. She didn't even think of it anymore as doing it. What she felt for Chris was like nothing so much as cotton candy—so light, so magical you could barely see it, so sweet it would melt in your mouth. He touched her everywhere, for a long time, and he let her see him slowly, so she wasn't too shocked. She hadn't said she was a virgin, but he seemed to know, and he was so gentle, so careful, she might have been a small animal with delicate bones.

She loved the way his body felt, she loved him, but she didn't love It. Sex. Her pussy hurt and that was almost all she felt there. Everywhere else felt wonderful.

"It'll be better," he told her, and she knew it would.

It was in the morning, when they did it again. She almost liked it for itself, not just for the feel of his skin, the twin bumps of his butt under her fingers, the smell of him.

She showered and was surprised to see blood, but there wasn't much, it was no big deal. She looked in the mirror and almost recognized herself without the makeup. She was sure the eyes were changed, were more knowing—Desdemona instead of Juliet eyes. But they were still blue, still Melody Brocato's eyes, so she put on the funny shades she had bought with the others—red with little three-dimensional hearts at the top. She wore the pedal pushers again, with a lavender T-shirt to match her hair.

When she stepped back in the living room, Chris grabbed her, as if he couldn't stop himself, and licked a drop of water from her neck that she'd missed. She'd never been happier in her life.

And then, as they stepped out into the sunlight, she and Chris, she was happier still. She'd had no idea life could be so sweet. They linked hands, heading for Café du Monde for coffee and beignets. Could anything in the world be more romantic?

Chris said, "Want a paper?"

"Sure."

He popped into a store, but she stayed outside, feeling the sun on her freshly fucked body. Feeling fine.

"Here." He handed her the paper. It was like having a knight to do her bidding, she thought, and absently unfolded it. The headline said, JAZZFEST PRODUCER STABBED TO DEATH.

She realized she must have screamed. She saw her brother's name below the main headline: HAMSON BROCATO MURDERED. She was suddenly, unaccountably hot, burning up, and sick in the pit of her stomach, and she felt herself falling.

A voice yelled, "Janis!" and before she went out, she wondered briefly who Janis was.

5

Joe Tarantino shook his head. He was a blunt-featured, pear-shaped, working-class kind of guy, dark and dandruffy. Today he needed a shave and, shaking his head like that, as if it were the end of the world, he looked inconsolable.

"Where in the hell is Carlson?" Joe looked easygoing, but he hated tardiness, hated wasting time, and hated waiting. Skip thought it was fair to assume he was also feeling fairly pressured by so public a murder as Ham's.

Carlson was an officer from missing persons. Joe had asked him to join them this morning—himself, Skip, and Sergeant Sylvia Cappello—to confer about Melody. Impatiently, he picked up his phone, and magically, Carlson appeared at the door. He was a youngish detective, with brown hair, a beginning paunch, and acne scars. Skip knew nothing about him, hoped he had half a brain. Because she thought Melody was the key to the case.

After handshakes and introductions, Joe said, "Let's get started." Skip knew he wanted every detail. He was the kind of lieutenant who liked to know how things were going, liked to participate, plan strategy. It might have driven her crazy if she hadn't truly enjoyed working with him. Cappello, her sergeant, was great, she was just fine, but she was a little on the brisk, close-mouthed side. Joe had a sweet, avuncular quality that made Skip love him and ascribe to him Buddha-like wisdom he probably didn't have. Steve had once accused her of hero worship where Joe was concerned, and she knew it was true. He was her mentor, the lieutenant who'd had her transferred to Homicide, who'd believed in her at a time when she hardly believed in herself. Thanks largely to a certain sergeant named Frank O'Rourke.

She ran down the events of the night before for the other three, and threw in reports from the coroner and the crime lab. Ham's death had been placed at about twenty-four hours before the body was found, give or take. And no prints had been found on the weapon or the open wine bottle. So there was no physical evidence.

Joe said, "You found him about seven?"

"Seven-thirty."

"And when did the girl leave the Rosenbaums'?"

"About five-thirty the day before."

"That'd be about the right time, wouldn't it?"

Skip nodded.

"Yeah," he said. "Yeah. We gotta find her. We gotta find her fast. Carlson, what do you think?"

He shrugged. "Either someone's got her or she's in the Quarter; they all end up in the Quarter."

"Well, how the hell do we find her?"

Carlson leaned back in his chair, undaunted by Joe's impatience. "Now that's a right int'restin' question. They do pretty well over at VCD—used to work there myself." He meant Vieux Carré District, the French Quarter station, where Skip had worked before coming to Homicide. "They leave flyers, that's one thing; and they got some good connections. Quarter people are funny—some of 'em'll only talk to people they know. I'd call over there if I was you —no sense banging your heads against the wall."

Joe nodded at Skip, who nodded back.

"There's a few little tricks, though. The kids are like cockroaches—sleep all day, come out at night. If they do come out in

63

daylight, they might go to Jackson Square—it's free entertainment. At night they go to bars, usually after midnight—way after. There's a few I can give you the names of. We closed down most of the bad ones a year or two ago—on North Rampart Street. But there's still a few where they can go to meet some friendly chicken hawks and kiddie pornographers."

Cappello winced.

Skip said, "Somehow I can't see Melody getting into—"

"Get desperate enough, they all do. See, these kids don't think of sex the same way you do. Lot of them have been abused, especially in homes where the mother's remarried or got lots of boyfriends. To them, it ain't exactly an expression of true love. More like a way to make a few bucks."

"What I meant was, I don't see how she could be that desperate—she's been gone less than thirty-six hours."

He ignored her. "First thing they learn's they can't get jobs—too young, no experience, no references, half the time no brains. Oh, sure, they might luck out—get to be a waitress or busboy. Whoopie-do. But most of 'em are gonna peddle their ass one way or another. Even if it's just dancin' at Bayou Babies. But don't get the idea that's any great deliverance from evil—you go in there and see some fifteen-year-old kid shakin' her booty six inches from some guy's Adam's apple, I guarantee you you'll want to throw somethin'. And that's nothin' to what goes on upstairs. I never been there—I know this plumber got called over there. Says they got mattresses all over the floor and cribs along the sides. The kids sleep naked all over the place, anywhere they fall down, I guess. No tellin' how loaded they have to be to get through that shit."

"Who goes up there?"

"Preferred customers, I guess. I don't know."

"So we should look at Bayou Babies."

"Hell, I knew this mother looked there six times in a week, all different times, never did find her daughter. Kid was dancin' there, though. They all change their appearance, and they hang together, help each other. Lie for each other. They form packs is what they do." He turned to Skip. "You know how many buildings in this city are unoccupied?"

She stared at him, didn't have a clue what he was getting at.

"Something like thirty percent. Kids see boarded-up houses. They go in and sleep. They call them squats. Then there's a bunch of cheap hotels—one that's kind of famous. Know who William Burroughs is? They say he used to score junk there."

Joe was getting impatient. "How about a list of their bars, hotels, known hangouts?"

"Hey, there's other stuff. There's facilities, you know. Covenant House. And a church where they hand out vouchers for mattresses. You can check all those places too. Other than that"—he turned his palms up—"all you can do is sit on balconies."

Joe and Skip spoke together: "Sit on balconies?"

"Well, it's not good police work, but it's what I tell the parents to do. You just watch the crowds up there where you can see them and they can't see you. 'Cause if you walk into one of the kids' bars —and I don't even mean the chicken-hawk scenes, I mean the ones with the punked-out wackos and the game machines—they ain't gonna roll out the red carpet."

When he had left, Joe said, "Okay, what's our strategy?"

"Find Melody," said Cappello. "She's all we've got, she's almost certainly the key, and she might be in danger."

"Skip?"

"Yeah." She bit her pencil. "Yeah. It's the danger part that's getting to me. Obviously, Carlson just assumed she ran away. But we don't know that. Maybe she caught the killer in the act and he killed her too. Or took her somewhere to think about it. Maybe he's crazy enough to ask the family for ransom."

"It worries me too," said Joe. "And of course there's that other nasty possibility."

"Little sis did him?" said Cappello. "What for?"

"How do I know? She thinks she's a singer, right? Maybe he wouldn't let her sing at the JazzFest. Skip, you need any help? For the routine stuff?"

She shook her head. "I've got it covered."

The routine stuff. Might as well get on it. She had good friends at VCD. She phoned her buddy Vic De Sandro, who said he'd start on it right away. She called the Brocatos and suggested they have flyers made up. And then she asked the computer for criminal records: Ti-Belle's, Ariel's, George's, Patty's. And Ham's, for good measure. Everyone was clean. Next, alibis. George had been at work, Patty at home alone, then at the Rosenbaums'—two blocks from Ham's—then back home. Ariel had been at work, and once, about three in the afternoon, at Ham's house. Patty and Ariel weren't exactly out of the question. And George probably wasn't either. It wasn't worth pursuing now, but she wondered if George could really account for every hour of his afternoon. Had he been alone in his private office at all that day? She wondered if there was any trouble between father and son—if she found any, that was soon enough to check.

At the moment, she wasn't interested in any of these three; she'd saved Ti-Belle for last because everything about her begged to be scrutinized—her sudden rise from obscurity after hooking up with one of the city's most influential music mavens, for instance; the continuing fights with Ham; and most of all, the way she'd been late to her own party.

Skip called Chicago first—Ti-Belle hadn't been to see Jarvis Grablow. Then she called a friend who worked at an airline. The friend wasn't supposed to, but he could pull up a list of passenger names for every flight out of New Orleans on a given day. Ti-Belle had said "a three-day trip," so the friend checked both Monday and Tuesday. Ti-Belle hadn't gone anywhere. Now, that was worth pursuing.

But first, an all-purpose investigative call that could save hours and hours of snail's pace bumbling—to Alison Gaillard, long-lost Kappa sister with whom Skip had recently reconnected. Alison was a true belle who knew everything there was to know about how to get people to look at you and then how to keep them looking —a mistress of the Southern arts. She was someone with whom Skip hadn't had the first thing in common when they'd been at Newcomb together (ever so briefly, before Skip flunked out). But for some reason, after Skip had gone off to Ole Miss, and then to San Francisco, and then had come back reinvented as a police officer, Alison had taken her on as a project. Skip didn't get it, she was just grateful, because Alison knew everything about everyone;

and what she didn't know, she could find out in five minutes.

"Skip Langdon calling Gossip Central."

"I've already pulled your file, officer. You'll be wanting Brocato lore, I suppose."

"Alison, you're amazing. If the city'd let me, I'd pay you handsomely."

"Oh, you will, Skippy, you'll definitely pay, quid pro quo. And we might as well start now. Who did it?"

Alison knew perfectly well Skip wasn't going to spew out details of this or any case, but as the world's greatest gossip, she had to try. "You haven't given me anything yet. Besides, you're likely to know more than I do."

"I only know where the bodies are buried. I don't know who buried them. Well, not always, anyhow. But I've known the Brocatos forever—or anyway, I know their next door neighbor, which is just as good. Do you know the whole story of George and Poor Boys?

"No, but I'd love to." Skip took off her right earring and settled in.

"Well, George is a true self-made man. The story goes that he was cooking in a restaurant when he got the idea for Poor Boys—and I mean short-order-type cooking, by the way, not exactly cordon bleu stuff. He got his two brothers to go in with him—hence the name—and they somehow managed to drum up enough investors to make it work. It took them five years to get the first one started, with George going to night school while the thing gestated; getting a business degree. Charming story of family solidarity, except for one thing."

"Let me guess. They've done nothing but fight ever since."

"Ain't it the way, as my mama's cook used to say. George was married to a woman named Dorothy—Ham's mom. Nice woman, stuck by him through thick and thin. But the sad part is, she never got to enjoy the thick. Died about the time he got the thing going. Well, that was about the time people started knowing him, and so after this, the story's a little more reliable. Apparently, he was crazy about Dorothy, although this pretty much came as a shock to everybody because he just seemed like your basic stone cold workaholic. When she died, he went into what I guess could only be called despair—unless you want to say it was a drunken stupor. Good thing his brothers were around to take care of the business —he didn't draw a sober breath until the day he woke up married to Patty."

"Wait a minute. He got drunk and married her?"

"Well, I don't think it was quite like that. He got drunk after Dorothy died and stayed that way about six months; somewhere in that period, he married Patty. She was a real stunner, I gather."

"Still is."

"But the question is, what did they have in common—I mean with the age difference and Patty's abiding interest in her own appearance and very little else? When he sobered up, which he quite soon did, George was said to be a little confused about the matter. Of course I was too young to know them then, but I'd say now it looks like Patty's the one who drinks too much—and I'm not alone in that assessment either.

"But if the marriage was shaky, nature came along and settled the matter, in the form of Melody, whom George adores by all accounts. Always has. So I guess the marriage turned out okay after all. It's still extant." She paused, thinking about it. "I don't know. George is pretty cold, so maybe he didn't much care what she was like—she was female, she was gorgeous, she was his kid's mother. That's enough for some guys."

"Most of them, it seems like."

"Yeah, the only problem is, we end up pissing them off by having personalities."

"And Patty's got to have one. I didn't get much sense of her, though."

"She seems like a hard bitch to me—pretty much somebody who saw a good thing and went after it. But what do I know? Lately, she's been going to a lot of weird doctors for Chinese herbs and stuff. Maybe she's sick or something."

"What's her background?"

"Skippy, with women like Patty, that's the sort of thing one doesn't ask. Let's put it this way, whatever it is, it's not Uptown. She's a self-made woman as much as George is a self-made man.

Only she made herself by latching onto George."

Skip's sense of democracy was slightly offended. "Well, it'd be the same thing if she did come from Uptown."

"No, because that's where she's living now. If she was a poor girl from Uptown and married a rich guy in another town, that might be analogous. But if you're from here and you stay here, you're already made, there's no self about it."

"That's one of the things I hate about the place."

"Now, Skippy, it has its up side."

Like the relationship she enjoyed with Alison. She'd grown up on State Street and knew she'd never get all this dirt if she hadn't put in her preschool years in the neighbor kids' sandboxes. Skip sighed. It was a hell of a trade-off. She said, "Do you happen to know if George is just a guy who drank too much in a crisis? Or is he in AA?" She was thinking of the wineglasses in Ham's kitchen.

"Let me think." She was quiet only a moment. "I'm sure I've seen him drink. Sure—at weddings, things like that. I saw him with a champagne flute that time Lala Bettencourt married Bony Henderson."

"Bony?"

"For Bonaparte. It only lasted six weeks, but not because George Brocato didn't toast the happy couple."

"Tell me about Ham."

"Well, he was about thirty-four, I guess. Quite a bit older than we are, but I used to see him around, didn't you? Before he got incredibly famous. I always thought he was kind of quiet and nerdy, but then he turned up with all these cool musician friends. Funny how much better a guy looks if he's got an entourage."

"Look at George Lucas. What about the ex-wife?"

"Oh, Mason. Went to Sacred Heart. Perfectly nice lawyer. I guess I haven't really heard much about her, probably because there's not much to hear. Now Ti-Belle's another matter. She just dropped from the sky, like Patty. How do these women do it? Now you see them, now you don't, or vice versa. I don't know a damn thing about Ti-Belle and neither does anybody else. Burns me up. It's bad for my reputation."

69

Ti-Belle.

She was just a little too mysterious to leave alone. When Skip was done with Alison, she dialed Ti-Belle but got no answer. That figured—she was probably at George and Patty's. To go there or not? Somehow, it didn't seem urgent enough to disturb the family. Instead, she drove out to Melody's school.

Country Day might not be in the country, but it looked as if it was. Both building and grounds bespoke money and taste, cultivated the look of an Eastern prep school. It was amazing, Skip thought, how relaxed you could get just walking around there—though maybe not if you were a teenager. Between hormones and insecurity, it would probably take more than a few trees to calm you down.

At Country Day you reached the main building, a stately columned affair, by means of a circular drive, and when you entered, you were in a paneled living room. Coming through the big double doors, Skip stood for a second, taking it in. Eventually she decided to walk toward the sign that said "Headmaster's Secretary."

Country Day prided itself on developing a high level of social skills in its students, and the members of the administration proved excellent exemplars to learn from. Despite the trappings, stuffiness apparently wasn't the style here. The very mention of Melody's name brought concerned murmurings and instant efficient activity.

Skip was given the headmaster's study for her interviews, and in five minutes was closeted with one Sharon Sougeron, Melody's faculty adviser. In the brief time she had to study her surroundings, she realized she could have entered blindfolded, asked herself the question, "How will this room look?" and described it perfectly. The Uptown decorator, whoever she was, had struck again. Two wing chairs faced a leather sofa; the tables were shiny dark wood, the lamps brass, the prints Audubon, the walls paneled. A room in the same impeccable taste as a basic black dress, and every bit as daring. Ah, but the magnolia's a nice touch, she thought, as a gust of lush scent wafted through the window.

Sougeron was thirty-fiveish and a little on the plump side, with dark curly hair, worn short, and white, delicate skin. Between the curls and the curves and the pearly skin, she was the very picture of Southern womanhood, dressed in a white silk blouse and navy skirt, accessorized with chunky jewelry.

She wore a wedding ring, and Skip had no doubt she was heterosexual, yet as soon as she opened her mouth, the word "butch" came instantly to mind. It was something in her voice and her manner that all the makeup and jewelry in the world couldn't hide. She taught English, the principal had said, but Skip would have guessed gym.

Her voice was brusque and dismissive, the voice of someone who had more important things to do, and Skip wondered if it was always that way, with her husband, for instance, in tender moments.

Sougeron, of course, was well-aware that Melody was missing —she'd talked to Patty and George no fewer than three times on Wednesday, the day before. Whatever she'd said, she seemed to be regretting it.

"How could I know, how was I supposed to know? I just figured Melody'd run away—typical unhappy teenager. I wasn't even very sympathetic."

"How could you know what, Ms. Sougeron? Are you saying you know something that's made you change your mind?"

"Well, something's happened to her, it's obvious. Her brother gets killed and she goes missing? It can't be coincidence."

"I expect you know Melody pretty well. Can you give me a sense of her? If I met her, whom would I meet?"

"Well, if you could get past the attitude, she might be a pretty nice kid. But nobody's ever been able to."

"She's a troublemaker, is she?"

"No." She thought about it. "No, I wouldn't say that. I guess boys are mostly troublemakers; girls are just twits." Skip wondered if Sougeron would define the term. She waited.

"Melody's like a black cloud most of the time—a sullen, sour little girl." Sougeron held her elbows and shivered deliberately, as if shaking Melody off. "And when she's not sullen, she's bitchy and disrespectful."

"How's that?"

71

The teacher shrugged. "It's nothing you can put your finger on. It's just her attitude. Oh, well, wait—there is something you can pin down. She cuts class and she lies."

"Lies? About what?"

She shrugged again, obviously hating to be put on the spot. "About everything."

"Everything?"

"Whether she did her homework. Where she was yesterday when she wasn't in class. Everything."

"Do you have any idea how she gets along with her parents?"

"Only a mother could love her, I'll tell you that."

"You don't know anything specific?"

"She's a behavior problem. What does that tell you?"

"I don't know. What does it tell you?"

"She's probably as much a problem for them as she is for me."

"How about her brother? Did she ever talk about him?"

Sougeron shook her head. "She didn't talk to me about anything. Spoke only when spoken to, and then with reluctance."

"Okay. She cuts class, she's got an attitude—how does she manage to stay in school here?"

"Well, believe it or not, she's usually a pretty good student—but if she doesn't like the subject, you can't get her to do beans. And she's a very good musician, most people think, but I'm no judge of all that. She can write, though. She's not a bad poet at all."

"A poet? She wrote poems?" Skip's heart started beating faster. If ever there was a window to the soul, surely it was a teenager's poetry.

"Songs, mostly."

"What about?"

"Oh, you know. Love and beauty. Sadness. As if a kid that age could have a clue."

"Sadness? Can you remember any specifics? Do you have any of her work?"

"No, I don't save their work, I give it back to them. And I don't really remember what she wrote about. She's got a way with words, that's all. But she's not so brilliant anything stuck in my mind." She stood. "Anything else?"

Skip looked up, surprised. For a moment she'd almost forgotten the other woman, her mind occupied with trying to form a picture of the sullen, defiant teenager Sougeron had described. She hadn't yet gotten to the meat of the interview. "A few things."

Sougeron remained standing.

"Does she use drugs?"

"I wouldn't be surprised."

"Well, does she hang out with kids who do?"

"Officer, this is a private school. Kids who use drugs are asked to leave."

In the unlikely event anyone finds out about it.

"Who does she hang with?"

"Her best friend's a girl named Blair Rosenbaum. And she's got a boyfriend named Flip Phillips."

"Anyone else?"

"Maybe the kids she plays music with. Joel Boucree's one of them, I don't know the other."

"Okay. Thanks for your help."

The school counselor was next, a sixtyish man who liked his gumbo and his fried catfish, judging by his shape. He was short, with a reddish neck, white moustache, and bushy white hair worn slightly long for New Orleans.

"Mr. Nicolai, I'm Skip Langdon."

"Matthew," he said with a broad smile, and Skip suddenly had the feeling he was very good at his job. He was somebody who could probably put the kids at ease and convince them he was on their side.

"I was hoping you could tell me a little about Melody Brocato."

"Where she is, you mean. Lord, I wish I knew."

"Any ideas?"

He spread his arms. "Not really. All her little buddies are present and accounted for. I've already asked them if they know, of course."

He recited the usual list—Blair, the two musicians, and Flip.

"I just talked to Melody's faculty adviser. I gather Melody's a difficult kid."

73

"Well, I guess it's all in the perspective."

Skip waited, sensed a favorite theory about to pop out.

"If Ms. Sougeron's trying to ram English down their throats, it's only natural some of 'em are going to choke. The ones who do are probably the ones she calls 'difficult.' That's the reason I quit the classroom—I hate trying to make 'em do something they don't want to do. I just like to talk to 'em—listen to 'em. That way I haven't got a program, and that means they can't sabotage my program if they don't happen to feel like conformin'. Whole different perspective. You see?"

"So you figure you see a different side of Melody than Ms. Sougeron did."

"Oh, indubitably." Skip had noticed the studied way he dropped his final g's; now she was starting to think it must really cramp his style not to be able to smoke a pipe while pontificating. "I see an extremely creative young woman there."

"Ms. Sougeron said she writes good poetry."

"She's famous for it. The teachers pass it around it's so good." He rocked back and forth, as if he did have a pipe. "What'd Ms. Sougeron say? That Melody's sullen? Uncooperative? Something like that?"

"Matter of fact, yes."

"Well, what you got here is an exceptionally bright young lady. Bright, but not that crazy about school. Her teacher says sullen, but I'd say restless comes closer to it. If somebody put a gun to my head and made me pick the most gifted student in the school, she'd be in the running. Might be the one. 'Course it's hard to know till twenty years later when they've done it or failed to do it, whatever it is, but I'd say Melody's got a fightin' chance to be the one that does it. Most people'd probably pick one of the boys —a jock with all A's, somethin' like that, but they haven't been around as long as I have. Kids like that either get tired of being perfect—in which case they become drunks—or they keep on doin' it. Turn into pediatricians who work for the homeless on weekends, that kind of thing."

Skip was fascinated in spite of herself. "What's wrong with that?"

"Why, nothin', of course, but they're still just bein' good little boys. Don't ever develop any real sense of self, who they are. And they don't really . . ." He paused here. ". . . *achieve*, if you will. In a grand sense. Pediatrician might help a lot of local kids, even save a lot of lives, but a kid like Melody'd be more likely to find the cure for cancer."

"She's that smart."

"Not smart. This idn't about smart. 'Course smart helps, smart's a big part of it, but face it, Detective, most all the kids here are smart. Country Day hasn't got any real dummies. But we got some real conformists, and Melody's not one of 'em. She's a romantic; a dreamer. No tellin' what's goin' on under all those curls when she's starin' out the window, cheatin' Ms. Sougeron out of one more perfect little English student. Twenty years from now Melody could be the graduate Ms. Sougeron invites to come back and talk to the new kids, inspire 'em to go on to greatness like she did."

"She's a very good singer, I hear."

He nodded. "Yep. That might be how she makes it. Voice idn't that much, but somethin' about her—she's got . . ." He thought a minute. "Passion. That's what it is. And man, can she sing the blues. Like she knows what she's talkin' about."

Skip thought about it. If she'd had a voice, she could have sung the blues in high school too—what teenager couldn't? "As I remember," she said, "being sixteen is no root beer float."

He leaned forward. "Look, the stuff that goes on in these kids' homes'd curl your hair—best families in town and all that, but probably no different from what you'd get at Fortier or Warren Easton. That's families. Imperfect." He wrinkled his nose so thoroughly that Skip sensed what he wanted to say and didn't dare.

She stared him right in the clever blue eye. "Fucked up."

"As young Joel Boucree would say, 'You got that right.' In fact—" He stopped in mid-sentence, interrupting himself. "No, wait. Let's talk about young Joel a minute. He's a perfect example of the kind of kid Melody's not. Near-perfect test scores. Extremely high IQ. Works like a demon. Scholarship student, in fact—one of only ten or twelve blacks in the whole school, I'm ashamed to say.

Joel Boucree works his little butt off; if we had to vote, faculty and students, on 'most likely to succeed,' Joel'd probably win hands down, even though he idn't much of a jock. But he hasn't got any need to spend the next twenty years provin' himself. People have been tellin' him all his life who he is, and he's real good at pleasin' adults so he probably likes what they say. All he's got to do is live up to it. Now Melody's not so good at pleasin' adults—she's probably got to make her mark, one way or another. You see what I mean?"

Skip wasn't sure she did, but if she said so, she'd never get away. She said instead, "Does Melody strike you as more unhappy than any other melancholy teenager?"

He shrugged. "Probably not. Just more frustrated than most. Something's bothering her, though. She probably ought to be in therapy."

"Why do you say that?"

He thought about it. "I guess she just seems like she needs someone on her side."

"I thought—" Skip stopped herself. That was the role she thought Ham had played. She rephrased: "Did she ever talk to you about her brother?"

"Yep. She's crazy about him."

"Do you know about any trouble between the two of them?"

Nicolai looked astonished, as if he'd just caught on to something important. "You think she murdered him."

"He's dead and she's missing. So far I don't think anything more than that."

"Well, she didn't kill her brother. She loves him more than anything on this earth."

"She told you that? I didn't realize the two of you were that close." She hadn't really thought that much about their relationship—it just didn't seem to her the sort of thing a kid would tell a counselor.

"I've been around a long time. Some things you just know."

Oh, great. How much of what you told me is true and how much is stuff you "just know"?

6

Clearly, Joel Boucree, Doug Leddy, and Flip Phillips were next on the agenda, but talking to kids was a delicate business. It usually required an adult witness and parental permission. Often, it was accomplished only after difficult negotiations. However, to her surprise, Skip found the principal almost unnaturally helpful. The Brocatos, apparently, had leaned on her.

The proposal was this—the principal herself, Mrs. Murray, would phone the kids' parents and lean, in turn, on them, and she'd get Matthew Nicolai to sit in. In return Skip would do the interviews after school. Murray would hold Flip, but Skip would interview the boys in the band off campus, at a nearby garage where they practiced every Thursday afternoon.

Skip leaped at it—it would save tons of time and tears, and other things were pressing anyway. School wouldn't be out for hours, so Skip headed toward an address on Burgundy, fairly near Esplanade, where she'd been told she'd find Andy Fike, Ham's housecleaner.

It took Fike a good ten minutes to get to the door. Skip would have given up, but a neighbor urged her to keep trying: "Andy sleep a lot, and he sleep hard, but he in there.'' The old lady cackled like it was the neighborhood joke.

When he finally pulled it all together, he shouted down from the balcony, ''What in hell can I do for you?'' He was leaning on the metal railing.

''Disheveled'' would have been far too mild a word for his appearance. His brown hair—which desperately needed shampoo —stood up all over his head. His clothing looked as if it had been slept in, possibly for several nights running. His skin was pale, his face almost emaciated. He was either very wasted or coming down from something ugly. Crack was Skip's guess.

She held up her badge and identified herself.

''What can I do for you, officer?''

''Let me in and I'll tell you.'' She wasn't crazy about going into this particular monster's den, but damned if she was going to stand on the street and shout.

''Well, aren't you the pushy one.''

''Don't whine, Andy. Do you have a courtyard? We can talk there.''

''Oh, butch, butch, butch.'' But he started downstairs, no doubt delighted not to have to rush around hiding his drugs. He opened a gate that led to an unkempt courtyard. ''I was having a beautiful dream too.''

''Andy, how long have you been loaded?''

''Why would that be your business?'' He led her to a round table, plopped down in one of two Kmart chairs pulled up to it. Skip remained standing.

''I thought maybe you hadn't heard about Ham, that's all.''

For the first time, his drug-induced bravado slipped. ''Ham?'' He spoke in a high-pitched quaver. ''Ham's my brother. What about Ham?''

''You haven't had the TV on the last couple of days?''

''I haven't done shit, lady, except lie around blasted. So arrest me, okay?'' He offered his wrists for cuffing.

''Did you see Ham on Tuesday?

''Yeah, I saw him. I cleaned his house, like a good little fairy. Like I do every Tuesday. And then I get paid and I buy myself some rock and that's all she wrote. Is there some law against that?''

He sounded so outraged—just Joe Citizen fighting the gestapo —that she had to wrestle an incipient laugh. But she figured he needed a quick sobering up. ''That and murder,'' she said.

She thought he lost color, but he had none to lose; it must have been an illusion. ''Ham's dead?''

She nodded, waiting.

''But I just saw him—he paid me ten bucks extra, the crazy fool.''

''What time did you leave him?''

''I don't know. Two, I guess. Three, maybe.''

''Did he have any visitors?''

''No, but he—'' Fike stopped himself.

''What?''

''Nothing.'' He looked down, wouldn't meet her eyes.

''He was expecting somebody? Was that it?''

''Ham didn't tell me everything.''

''Andy, pay attention. This is a murder investigation. You know as well as I do that if I went in your house right now I'd find plenty of good reasons to arrest you. And I don't even need that. I could take you down to Homicide right now and ask you the same questions over and over, keep you there till you got very uncomfortable. Already you don't feel too good, do you? You want to spend the rest of the day with me?''

''You bitch.''

''Don't mess with me, Andy, or I'm going to make your life a living hell.''

''Oh, go to it, officer. Make my life a living hell. Things have been way too great lately. I need some variety.''

Obviously, threats weren't working. She was going to be in this weedy old courtyard all day if she didn't get something out of the sorry heap in the plastic chair. She sat herself down in the other one.

''What happened to you, Andy? You weren't always this big a mess, were you?''

A faraway look came into his eyes, as if he could barely remember. ''I'm a musician,'' he said, whispering.

"Uh-huh, and you got depressed, didn't you? Your friends started dying on you."

"The plague, man. I can't handle it anymore."

"But Ham gave you a job, kept you in rock."

"He never knew. He wouldn't have let me in the house."

"But he was pretty nice to you, and he's dead."

"Oh, shit." It was beginning to sink in.

"So just tell me, who he was expecting?"

"Oh, hell. Ariel. Why should I protect the bitch? He didn't have any goddamn tasso for his gumbo." He shrugged. "I could have gone to get it, but I told him I was in a hurry. Shit! A hurry for what? This shit? The bitch killed him! Fuck!"

"Are you telling me Ariel killed him?"

"I thought that's what you were telling me."

"Let's start over. Did you leave before Ariel got there?"

He looked away for a long time before answering. "Yeah. Shit! I don't believe what I'm doing with my life."

"Can you think of any reason Ariel would have to kill him?"

"No. He was good to his employees. Nice as pie to me." He paused and stared into the distance. "He was a real good guy," he said after a while, still staring straight ahead, not looking at Skip and not, she thought, speaking to her.

She thanked him and left.

She went to Mama Rosa's, ordered a meatball sandwich to go, and phoned the Jazz Festival office. A polite young man said Ariel had gone to the fairgrounds.

"You mean the festival's happening?" She hadn't thought to wonder whether it had been canceled.

"Well, Ham would have killed us if we stopped now. The board voted unanimously to make it a memorial to him."

It was a graceful solution, Skip thought. She collected her sandwich—and when she got to the fairgrounds wished she'd waited. The food booths beckoned, and the lines were only medium-long. By Sunday there'd be nearly eighty thousand people here. It was a wonder anyone ever got a bite, but everyone seemed to. Some people, it was said, went for the food alone.

Skip found Ariel holding a clipboard and looking harried, her wild mane blowing about her face. She had on a white tank top, pink shorts, and lipstick that exactly matched the shorts. Skip wondered how women did that sort of thing. Did they go instantly from clothing counter to makeup counter or did they already have every color of lipstick there was? And how did they get their brains to focus on a thing like that? She might have been born here, but she was never going to understand the South.

Ariel said, "We're going crazy without Ham. I know I should be with his parents today, but there's no one else—"

"Ariel!" It was a man's voice as harried as Ariel's own.

"Coming!" she screeched. To Skip, she said, "I've got to go— some prima donna's probably got Perrier in his trailer instead of Evian water. Is it important?"

"Yes, and I'll be quick. As his assistant, you're in the best position to know if anyone had a motive to kill him. Did someone have a vendetta against him? Had he fought with anybody? Gotten any phone calls—" Ariel put up a hand to stop her.

"Absolutely not." Though she had been in the act of turning away, racing back to her duties, she stopped and gave Skip a big smile. It seemed as if her cheeks got a little pinker, but maybe it was just the rosy glow of her outfit. "Ham was one of those rare people who was loved by everyone who knew him. Everybody loved that man, and that's the God's truth."

"Why?"

"Why?" She looked thunderstruck. "Why did we all love him?"

Skip nodded.

"Because he was a wonderful person." She teared up a little. "I still can't believe this."

"Ariel. I know this is hard. I'm not trying to start an argument, believe me. I just want to know what he was like."

"Well, he was such a take-charge guy. But so sweet at the same time. I never heard him raise his voice to one person, and I never heard anyone raise their voice to Ham. How many producers could you say that about?"

"Not many." *Probably not any.*

"Do you know what a nerve-wracking job this is?"

"Ariel!" the voice had a tinge of anger now.

Ariel seemed not to notice. "His employees loved him, his family loved him, the musicians loved him, the public loved him —he knew everybody, and he made all our lives a little better." She was regaining her composure, sure of her ground here. "You know what? Even his ex-wife loved him."

"Do you know her? Mason Brocato?"

She shook her head slightly as if to wake herself, glanced at her watch and stepped away. "I've gotta go."

Skip looked at her own watch. One-thirty. Plenty of time to see Mason before school got out—but first she had a piece of key lime pie.

She had a moment of doubt, not at all sure Mason had ever used Ham's name, much less kept it. But there it was, under "Attorneys": Mason Brocato, on Gravier Street.

Mason was just back from lunch, as what lawyer wouldn't be at that time? She was hanging up a plum-colored suit coat. The matching skirt was a mini that revealed slightly pudgy legs, but otherwise Mason was sleek. Her extremely short haircut was carefully sculptured, a work of art that probably had to be recarved every two weeks. Her skin was olive, her eyes grayish.

"I've just come from George and Patty's," she said. "It's so horrible. And awful about Melody too. What's going on, officer?"

"Call me Skip."

"Is Melody a . . ." She couldn't bring herself to finish. "Is she a . . ."

"Is she a suspect?"

Mason smiled. They understood each other.

Skip said, "Should she be?"

"I beg your pardon?"

"Do you know of any reason she'd want to kill Ham?"

"She's just a kid."

"A kid could have reasons."

"You mean like incest or something? I hardly think that's likely." Her smile had a frozen quality.

Skip shrugged. "Or an argument. Did Melody have a temper?"

"No. Yes. I think sometimes she did, but it's been five years since I've seen her much. There's a lot of difference between eleven and sixteen." Mason rummaged in her bag—a black leather one, as sleek as the rest of her outfit—came up with cigarettes and stared at them apologetically. "I still do this. I hope you don't mind."

"Of course not." *What's another dry-cleaning bill?*

As Mason lit up, Skip segued into the delicate part of the interview. "I'm wondering what your relationship with Ham was."

She blew smoke. "Fine. Very good. What's not to like?"

Skip smiled. "I keep hearing everybody loved him."

"Maybe they did. I didn't—after a while."

"Oh, really?" *Why not?* seemed too rude, even to Skip's ears.

"He was a nice man. A very nice man. Just a little maddening to live with, that's all. There were times when I could have killed him— Is every marriage like that?"

Skip remembered the reports of Ham's and Ti-Belle's fights.

"While we're on the subject, could I ask what you were doing Tuesday afternoon?"

She started. "I was here." As if as an afterthought, she said, "Are you asking if I have an alibi?"

Skip smiled again, hoping she didn't seem so smarmy Mason would smash her teeth in. "I guess I am."

The gray eyes narrowed. "From when till when?"

"Oh, say noon till six or seven."

Mason checked her calendar. "I had lunch with Belinda Causey and got back here about two. I had a client at three—do you want his name?"

"Please."

"My God." She sat back in her chair. "You're really serious."

"Just routine, as they say on television."

"Okay. Gray Paulson. He left at four-thirty. Then my secretary, Elise, left about five-thirty. I stayed till six and then went home."

"Do you still have your house key, by any chance?"

"A house key?" And then the light dawned; or else she was a

good actress. "Oh, you mean to Ham's house. You know, I haven't the least idea." She shook her head. "I honestly can't remember giving it to him."

Skip nodded. "Okay. Thanks." She paused, sizing Mason up. She was tougher than Ariel and hadn't recently been in love with Ham. "If everyone loved Ham so much, why did someone kill him?"

"Why are you asking me?"

"Because I think you probably knew him better than anybody."

Mason was silent. "I probably did," she said finally. "I probably did."

"I mean, you said there were times when you wanted to kill him. Was he pushy? Was he aggressive and abrasive?" Ariel had called him a take-charge guy—Skip had never known such a person who didn't have enemies. "How did he push people's buttons?" This was a key question, she thought: Ham had been killed in anger.

Mason ground out her cigarette, slowly, thoughtfully, certainly not in pique. "He certainly wasn't aggressive or abrasive. Quite the opposite." She gave Skip a good hard stare out of eyes that were starting to have a nasty glint in them. "He was such a goddamn wimp, I could have bashed his head in."

"I don't understand."

She sighed. "You wouldn't unless you had to live with him. Listen, I can't imagine why anyone who didn't would want to kill him. Who could be bothered? How could he raise that much emotion in anybody? Always trying to please, never wanting to hurt anyone's feelings." Her hands contorted like claws. "Aaaargh!"

7

Skip got to Country Day just after school let out. If she hadn't had a watch, she'd still have known—carpooling moms clogged the street; kids swarmed like puppies and were just about as cute.

She tried to picture Melody here. The Brocatos had given Missing Persons a picture and description—black curly hair, blue eyes, medium height, slender build. In the picture—which they'd passed on to her—Melody's nose looked a little longer than teenage girls usually wanted, and she looked more skinny than slender—especially her face, which was almost pointy. She probably thought she wasn't pretty; it was a rare kid her age who thought she was. Melody wasn't, quite, though what she was missing had nothing to do with nose or figure. She had masses of gorgeous hair, and with a little detail work, was easily capable of being a knockout. What she didn't have was self-confidence. She looked scared. On the other hand, her vulnerability made her attractive in a way—made you want to protect her. But it might not have that effect on everyone. There would be people who'd see it as a window to opportunity. Skip shuddered, hating to think of Melody on her own.

Maybe on her own with a murderer.

What was she like in her natural habitat, wearing jeans and T-shirt? Did she ever smile? Did she smile too much, pretending?

Skip spotted Blair walking with a guy who wasn't tall enough for her. She got out of the car, waving.

Blair waved back, reminding Skip of a model in a commercial —there was something languid and liquid about the movement. She loped over with her friend, whose fashion statement ran to clean wrinkles. He was a handsome boy, olive-skinned, brown-eyed, who should have been wearing Top-Siders but had opted for Reeboks. He looked as if he belonged on a sailboat, or at least a squash court. He'd probably been born in a country club.

Blair said, "We were looking for you."

"You were?"

"Mrs. Murray asked Flip to wait for you."

Skip turned to the boy. "You're Flip?"

He stuck out his hand, a credit to his upbringing. "Basil Phillips. What can I do for you?" The kid got right down to business.

"I wonder if there's someplace we can talk." She left off the word "alone," but looked at Blair in a way she hoped was clear.

Blair said, "We both need to talk to you."

Skip came alert. "You've heard from Melody?"

"No. We just want to tell you something." She glanced around. "Mr. Nicolai's coming right out."

Flip said, "Blair, I'll do it. Look, officer . . ."

"Skip."

He flushed, hardly able to deal with it. "Skip. What happened was, Blair and I . . ." He was obviously too discreet to complete the sentence. "I decided to quit seeing Melody, and I made the mistake of phoning Blair while she was there."

Skip wanted it nailed down. "You and Blair became an item behind Melody's back—is that what you're saying?"

Blair looked down, but Flip held Skip's gaze. His granddad had probably been a Confederate general. "That's about it," he said.

"You dumped her, in other words."

He winced. "I was going to tell her Tuesday night."

Skip turned to Blair. "So what really happened at your house?"

"I guess she was starting to suspect something—that's all I can figure. Anyhow, when Flip called, I said I'd have to call back, but maybe I looked guilty or something. She figured it out—I don't know how. She just knew. She grabbed the phone and yelled at him and he said something to her—"

"I said I was sorry." He had his hands in his pockets and his cheeks were still pink. Being caught out of school apparently wasn't done among the Phillipses.

"And what did she say?"

"She didn't answer."

"She handed the phone back to me," said Blair, "but before I could figure out what to do, she was out of there. Disappeared for a minute and came back running."

Nicolai joined them silently.

"Disappeared where? Where were you at the time?"

"We were in the kitchen. I guess she went in my room."

"Why would she do that?"

Blair closed her eyes, held her hands in front of her face, willing her brain to work. Her eyes flew open. "Her pack! She went to get her pack."

"You saw her leave with it."

"Yes. I came out and called her name, and then she came running down the stairs. I saw it but didn't think about it till now."

"Did she have anything in the pack that she particularly needed?"

Blair looked bewildered, thought about it. "No, I don't think so." She thought some more. "What do you mean? Drugs or something? Melody doesn't do drugs."

"Oh, really?"

Flip said, "Just a little pot." He looked at Nicolai and flushed. The counselor stepped back a foot or two, pretended interest far across campus. "She likes it, though. She might do other stuff if she had access to it."

Skip nodded. She'd been like that herself. It wasn't that the high was so great, just that it replaced the pain. "I appreciate you two being so honest."

Blair said, "Listen, I'm really sorry if I caused any trouble. I couldn't talk about it before, I just couldn't believe it had really happened, that she'd run away, I mean. I thought she'd come back, especially when she found out about Ham."

Skip was pissed. "Didn't it occur to you she might have been kidnapped?"

"Well, yes. But my telling what happened wouldn't change that and wouldn't help find her."

Skip had to admire a fine mind at work. "You're right, I don't guess it would. Why did you decide to tell now?"

She copped a quick glance at her boyfriend. "Flip made me."

Flip said, "Was there something else you wanted to ask me?"

"Yeah. I wanted to know if she came to your house, and if you're harboring her."

"No. Neither."

"Do you know where she is or even have any guesses?"

"No. I'll tell you what's odd—she hates her mom, do you know that?" Once again he shot a guilty look at Nicolai, but the counselor was down on all fours, searching for something in the grass.

"No. Why?"

"They just don't get along, I guess. And she never sees her dad, so she kind of always idolized Ham and Ti-Belle. That's where she'd go."

She had, seeking succor in a fit of adolescent angst. "What's the odd part?"

"Well, even though she was really unhappy at home, she never mentioned running away. Sometimes she talked about going to live with Ham, wondering if he'd take her in. She never talked about just . . . leaving."

"Blair?"

"To me either."

"Well, thanks, kids." *Hope you'll be happy together.*

When they were gone, she told Nicolai she liked his style.

"The invisible man act? Don't be fooled. If you'd tried to get tough with those kids, you'd have known I was there."

■

You could hear the band from the street, but it wasn't too loud to be a nuisance. The music was muffled. The home attached to the garage belonged to people who worked and therefore never heard a thing, Nicolai told her. Another group at the school had used the garage and put in the soundproofing. Melody's gang had more or less inherited it.

Skip knocked, yelled, finally made herself heard. A black kid let her in, a kid with a smile that could have sold breakfast cereal. "We be the Spin-Offs. Who you be?"

"Also known as the Fuck-Offs," said the little twerp on drums.

"I be the long arm of the law." She showed her badge.

The black kid quit clowning. "You must be here about Melody."

"Uh-huh. Are you Joel or Doug?"

"Joel Boucree. Uh, hello, Mr. Nicolai." Skip had no idea how the counselor had managed to stay unseen till that point. Both boys suddenly dropped their terminally cool acts and remembered their manners. As introductions were performed, she took a shine to Joel. He was a friendly kid who looked at least as bright as a button. Maybe a solid gold button. He was light-skinned, on the thin side, conventionally handsome. But not too handsome (if there was such a thing). He was the kind of kid matchmakers would call "nice-looking." She remembered what Matthew Nicolai had said about him: most likely to be most likely to succeed.

The other kid, Doug Leddy, was a little white nerd. He had narrow shoulders, wore glasses and a sneer. The kind of sullen little twit that gives teenagers a bad name. The kind Sharon Sougeron had described.

Right after shaking hands, he sat back down, started pounding the drums again.

"Don't mind Doug," said Joel. "He thinks attitude's cool."

"Fuck off, Boucree." He didn't even give Nicolai a look.

Skip said, "You're pretty brave to say that in front of a police officer."

"You going to arrest me?"

"No. I'm going to kill you if you don't stop that noise."

He played an ear-bending coda first. Nicolai cocked an eyebrow: Should he should stop it? Skip shook her head.

"Very nice. Now, fellows. Is Melody here?"

"Here? Where? In Joel's guitar case?"

She spoke to Joel. "When did you see her last?"

"Monday. We practice Mondays and Thursdays. I might have seen her at school Tuesday, but that was it. I went to Ham's Tuesday night, but she wasn't there."

Doug said, "You went to Ham's? Melody didn't even invite me. Goddamn—bitch!" He picked up a drumstick, walloped his snare drum, and threw the stick at the wall.

Nicolai said, "Chill out, Dougie."

"Shit!"

Joel said, "His parents are getting divorced."

"I don't need you to fuckin' speak for me, party boy."

"Listen, Melody didn't invite me to that thing. Ham did."

"Oh, right, for a minute I forgot what a star you are." To Skip, he said, "Did you know our man Joel played onstage at the JazzFest when he was seven? He doesn't ever let us forget either."

Joel looked hurt.

"Do you get along this well with Melody? The three of you fight onstage?"

Doug lowered his eyes. "We get along."

She'd guessed right. He couldn't stand being called unprofessional. She said, "What's it like, playing with Melody?"

She'd hoped for Joel, but she got Doug. "She's as good at the keyboard as any guy."

"Pardon me while I puke."

He gave her a puzzled look, apparently having no idea what he'd said wrong. "Joel brought her in when Gary graduated—he was our keyboard player before. I didn't want to play with a girl. But she's okay, man. She's okay. Thinks she's Janis Joplin, though."

"What?"

"Oh, you know. That's her favorite singer, and not only that, she identifies with her. Thinks Janis was some sort of misunderstood artist instead of a drugged-out mediocre musician who was really nothin' but a bigmouth Texas redneck."

Joel said, "She was a great singer, though."

"Yeah, if you like screeching."

Joel grinned at Skip. "Doug's really the misunderstood artist—you can tell 'cause he puts down anybody who makes it. And some people who just have more talent than he does—like Melody."

"I said she was okay."

"Yeah, but you're always knocking her singing."

"She's not that good, man. I can't help it—she's nothin' special."

"She's the best *you'll* ever play with."

Skip was getting tired of the bickering. "Did she ever talk to you guys about her brother?"

"Yeah. Thought he walked on water."

"She didn't do it, man," said Doug. "I mean, Melody's got a temper, she's a perfectionist, she can be a pain in the ass, but no way she'd kill Jesus H-for-Hamson Christ."

Joel said, "Hey, what's police work like? What's it like being . . . out there?"

She couldn't tell if he was trying to distract her or what. "Why do you ask?"

"Well, I mean, it's kind of unusual. For a woman and all. I was just wondering why you went into it."

Skip laughed. "Cause I'm a big broad and I can beat people up."

"Come on. Really." He looked so serious, so quizzical, she was sorry she'd teased him.

"Really? Well, really, I thought I might be good at it. I used to live in San Francisco, and while I was there I caught a mugger—just on the street. I saw him get an old lady's purse and I got him." She shrugged. "I guess I got hooked."

"How do you go about—you know—working on something like this?"

"Finding Melody?"

"Yeah, finding Melody."

"Well, I'm kind of just asking her friends what they think." She could have said she was asking if they knew where Melody was, but some instinct made the sentence come out like it had.

Joel lit up. "That's what I'd do. That's exactly what I'd do. You think I'd be a good cop?"

"You might. But I hear you're a good musician."

"Annh." It was an unenthusiastic sound, a shrugging off. Probably people had told him all his life he was a good musician; hearing it was like getting a cheek pinched by a distant aunt.

"So what about it, guys? You know where she is?"

Doug said, "Hell, no." *And I wouldn't tell you if I did*, his manner said.

"Joel?"

"Not really." But he hesitated.

"You've got an idea, haven't you?"

"Well, I know what I'd do if I were her."

Doug said, "If you were her, and what, man? You killed your brother? You got kidnapped? Get real, man. You don't know where the hell she is."

Joel ignored him. "See, I've been thinking about it. Her boyfriend . . . like, dumped her, is what I think. For her best friend."

Doug said, "How the hell do you know that?"

"Well, they been together for two days. It's kind of a clue." He turned back to Skip. "So I think it got too much for her and she ran away. I mean, she couldn't take it. So she split."

"Good. That could be it." *Almost certainly was, except it probably didn't get too much for her before Ham bought it.*

"The only question is, where'd she go?"

"Well, she'd need money, right? So she'd go where she could make it."

Doug said, "She's probably peddling her skinny ass right now."

"Would you can it, please?" said Nicolai.

"Think about it," said Joel. "She's got a talent. She could use that. What can she do that she wouldn't have to get hired for, wouldn't have to prove who she is, wouldn't have to take any shit of any description? Excuse my French."

Doug said, "Holy shit! She's a street musician. She always used to talk about Ti-Belle doing that. That's what it is. But wait a minute —why hasn't she contacted us? She can't just sing with no band."

"Well, I bet she went to the Quarter and found one." Joel beamed, like the good student he was, fully expecting an A for this one.

And Skip would have given him one if she could—that or a kiss. What else would a runaway do?

Panhandle.

But Melody didn't have to. "The Quarter?" she said.

"Sure. That's where the bucks are."

And where you could get lost in the crowds, where there was a dim, tiny chance you wouldn't run into someone you knew. Where Carlson from Missing Persons said they all went. But still, New Orleans for all its size was such a small town. "You wouldn't just get out of here?" she said.

"I wouldn't," said Joel. "I'd be scared to. You gotta remember, she's only sixteen."

8

On the off chance Ti-Belle was home, Skip drove the four or five blocks to Ham's house and found her Thunderbird parked in the driveway.

The singer came to the door in a melon-colored, terry-cloth robe. She looked fabulous, and anyone else in the same color would have looked like candy corn.

"Oh, hello . . . uh . . ."

"Skip. Sorry to drop in on you. I was in the neighborhood."

Ti-Belle didn't seem unhappy to see her. "Come in. I was just changing."

"How are you doing?"

The singer led her into the living room. "This is the first time I've been alone. I've been at the Brocatos' all day."

"Are your relatives coming?"

Ti-Belle tried a smile, but it didn't quite work. "I think I'm going to have to gut this one out." Before Skip could be so rude as to ask why, Ti-Belle said, "Excuse me. I'll put on some clothes. Coffee? Tea?"

"Nothing, thanks."

"I'll just be a minute. Really."

If she'd been crazy enough to stab Ham, could she be crazy enough to come back with a weapon? It was the police way to think, but Skip couldn't talk herself into it. If she'd killed Ham, it had been in anger, not because she was nuts. And you'd have to be nuts to assault an officer the day after your boyfriend was found dead.

She said, "While you're dressing, could I have a look in Ham's office?"

The singer thought about it a second, finally shrugged. "Why not?"

Ham had been a careful record keeper. His income taxes were neatly filed, his canceled checks stored in his top desk drawer. He had a good income, partly from his festival salary, partly from earnings on his stock in Po' Boys, but it looked as if he was the very personification of "generous to a fault." He'd written checks to Ti-Belle amounting to nearly $25,000 since January. And at the bottom of each one was written the word "loan." It was only late April; if he'd lent her comparable amounts the year before and the year before that, Ti-Belle owed him plenty. And she wasn't the only one—he'd lent small amounts to Andy Fike and to lots of people whose names she didn't recognize.

There was one other interesting category of check—large donations to the Second Line Square Foundation. Once again, it was reasonable to assume this was his habit.

He had savings, but they were going fast. In the four months of this year, he'd paid out nearly three-quarters of the amount he'd made the year before. He either had to quit spending or come up with some more money to make it through the year.

Ti-Belle padded back in, barefoot, wearing baggy calf-length pants and a floppy T-shirt. "Finding anything?"

"Can I ask why Ham lent you so much money?"

She colored. "You think I make a fortune, don't you? Because you know my name and you've heard me sing, you automatically think I'm rich. Well, I'm not rich. I wasn't even middle class until about a year ago. If you're a musician—if you're in any of the arts —how do you think you get from zero to a hundred? From singing on the street to the Ray-Ban stage?''

She answered herself. ''You borrow money, that's how.''

''Was Ham pressuring you to repay it?''

''No. He was generous. I told you that.'' Skip was about to ask about the fights, but Ti-Belle stomped out. ''Jesus, I'm thirsty! Want some iced tea?''

Skip followed her to the kitchen, which had been cleaned up. She wondered if Ti-Belle had scrubbed the dried blood herself. The singer was still talking, more or less to herself. ''Nerves. I get thirsty when I'm stressed out. I'm supposed to sing tomorrow, and I don't know what the hell to do.''

''You mean sing at the JazzFest?''

She nodded. ''I don't see how I can not do it—but on the other hand, I don't know if I should. I mean, I want to do it—for Ham —the whole festival is a memorial to him, did you know that? I think I have to do it, don't you? But would it be crass?''

''It's a problem.'' A PR problem, it seemed. An interesting thing to have on your mind the day after your lover's death. Ti-Belle looked a little pale, but she wasn't exactly puffy from crying.

''What do you think? Should I or not?''

It was the question Skip was hoping to avoid, but what the hell —Ti-Belle might think she owed Skip for the right answer, and it was obvious she'd already made up her mind what that was. All she needed was someone else's stamp of approval.

''Well, frankly,'' said Skip, ''I think you'd be conspicuous by your absence. They've kind of got you in a box by making the festival a memorial—that way if you don't feel up to doing it, it looks as if you didn't really care.''

Ti-Belle looked modestly at the floor for a moment, possibly to hide tears (or their absence). ''I s'pose you're right. I've kind of been thinking along those lines myself.''

My turn, thought Skip, and plunged in: ''Ti-Belle, I know this is painful for you, but I'm wondering if you know of anyone who might have a reason to kill Ham. Had he had any arguments with anyone? Any ongoing disagreements? Enemies?''

''Well, no, this isn't painful. It sort of helps—I do better if I keep my mind working. And I've been trying to think about that myself. In fact, I've kind of come up with a suspect list."

"You have?" Skip couldn't quite conceal her astonishment.

Ti-Belle looked proud of herself, almost smug. She slung hair out of her eyes, poured tea and handed Skip a glass. "Well, just in my head. Let's go to the living room—this place gives me the creeps."

She talked as she walked. Skip liked the way she stomped around barefoot. Even liked her slightly too frank revelations. Except for the obvious knowledge that she was gorgeous, she had an ingenuous quality about her, a kind of country style that befitted a career Cajun. "I gotta get out of this house. Soon. After the funeral, I guess."

"When's that?"

"Oh, Monday. When they decided to go on with the JazzFest, George and Patty decided that's what they'd better do."

"It'll be a jazz funeral, I'll bet."

Ti-Belle lit up. "Well, I'll bet it will! That's the only appropriate thing. Well, of course it will."

They had returned to the living room and sat, Skip on the sofa, Ti-Belle in a ladderback rocking chair. "About your suspect list. I'm all ears."

"Ariel comes to mind first of all. She's a rejected lover, you know."

Skip made a note, hiding her eyes. "Ariel. Could I ask how you know that?"

"Well, Ham, of course, after I mentioned she was always making goo-goo eyes. I thought he was so innocent he just hadn't noticed. But he said he'd kind of, you know, done it with her once when they were both kind of drunk, and she never could forget. It embarrassed him, but he had to put up with it. He sure wasn't going to fire her just because he was embarrassed. Ham wasn't like that."

"How long has Ariel worked for him?"

"Oh, three years, I guess."

"Did that incident happen before or after you came on the scene?"

She threw back her head, hair falling prettily about, and laughed as if she was truly delighted. "See, I'm not dead. I can laugh a little bit. If it was after I met him, then I'd be the one with a motive, wouldn't I?"

"You sure would." Skip held her gaze, smiling just as broadly as Ti-Belle.

"Well, it was before. Of course. Whatever else you say about Ham, he was an honorable man."

"Everyone says so." Saint Ham. "Who else is on the list?"

"His dad and his uncles."

Skip was shocked. "Acting in concert?"

"Oh, God, I hope not. But I s'pose anything's possible."

"Why would his dad and his uncles want to kill him?"

"Business disagreements. They were always arguing about what to do with the damned sandwich places."

"And what was the basis of the argument?"

She leaned forward, defiant. "Frankly, I never asked. I just never was that interested."

"How did you know about the arguments?"

"Oh, Ham'd be in his study talking on the phone, and then he'd come out all red in the face and huffing and puffing. And he'd say, 'Dad's crazy.' Or 'Uncle Joseph doesn't have an ounce of business sense.' Or something like that, which meant he was sick and damn tired of talking about it and don't get him started. Which I wouldn't have dreamed of."

Skip said, "Is that all your suspects?"

"Well, I can't decide about Patty." She paused and gave it some thought. "Yeah, I guess she's one. Just 'cause they hated each other. Patty and Ham."

"Why?"

"Jealousy, looked like to me. Just plain old jealousy, pure and simple. Patty married his dad pretty soon after his mom died. He was a dweeby teenager who was probably always trying to get attention, and cramping Patty's style."

"I take it you don't much like Patty either."

"Well, I don't mind her. It's just that she's so . . ." She searched for the word.

"What?"

"Worthless, I guess. Once I said she had pretty nails and asked her how she kept 'em so nice. She held 'em out, all ten of 'em for me to see, like some kind of window display, and said, 'Honey, I don't do shit.' With this big Southern Belle smile. Like she was real proud of it. I mean, if you're a parasite, do you really have to brag about it?" She was getting looser and looser as she warmed to her subject. "No wonder Ham couldn't stand her. That poor boy needed a mother, and his dad married a Barbie doll." For a moment her eyes filled with tears, presumably at the plight of the motherless, dweeby Ham. "That gumbo he was making—you know when he learned to make it? Then. When he was a kid. Patty didn't cook, and his dad wouldn't hire a housekeeper, so poor little Ham taught himself to make gumbo. It was his mom's recipe, except for the tasso. He was so proud of thinking of that." She cupped her face in her hands and brushed hard with the fingers. Skip couldn't tell if the tears were real. It occurred to her that, in Ti-Belle's estimation, just about everybody Ham knew had a motive for killing him.

"You haven't mentioned Melody," she said. "Is she on the list too."

"Melody?" She sounded thunderstruck. "Never! Little Melody? She adored Ham. And he adored her."

"She was on the scene."

"I know, and I'm worried. Maybe they got her too." Her chin trembled.

Skip said, "I hear she adores you too."

Ti-Belle looked puzzled. She nodded. "We're close. We're real, real close. But she hasn't called. Why hasn't she called if she's all right?"

"We're looking for her. Just as hard as we can."

Ti-Belle smiled dreamily, free-associating the way people do when they're trying to get their minds off something. "She's such a sweetheart. Reminds me so much of me at her age. Wantin' a ticket out. Wantin' it real bad."

"Ticket out? You mean . . . suicide?"

"Oh, never. Not in a million years. Do I look to you like that kind of person?"

"I thought you meant Melody."

"She's just like me. That's what I'm saying. Look, Melody's life's not a pretty picture. Whose is at that age? Honey, that's what the blues is about. Being sixteen and wantin' *out*." Right then she had such a bruised, bluesy air about her, so world-weary, so knowing, that she should have been sitting around in her underwear, chain-smoking and playing cards between tricks.

"What's so terrible about Melody's life?"

"Her parents don't give a shit about her."

"I keep hearing she's the apple of George's eye."

"La-di-da."

"I beg your pardon?"

"Look, you could be his favorite person in the world and you still wouldn't notice. If he hugged you, you'd probably catch a chill. And Patty's into makeup and hypochondria. Melody needs something." She leaned back, her point made. "And that's the blues. It's being in a town way too small for you, and itching. Just itching. Crying yourself to sleep but never losing hope 'cause you got your music."

The words were like something she might have said onstage to introduce a song, but the pain in her face told Skip how heartfelt they were. She was enthralled. And wondered if this was the blues too—perhaps a true artist didn't have to sing, just to tell her story. "And what was that town for you?"

"St. Martinville. I grew up with Cajun music, and it was the only thing in my life that made it worthwhile. We were dirt-poor and I was miserable—maybe my life was no worse than any other kid's, maybe I was just more sensitive. My little brother didn't seem to take it so hard. Maybe that's what makes you sing—you just take things too damn hard. Anyhow, I wanted out of there the worst kind of way. I got a scholarship to LSU and that was it. In the summer I'd come down here and sing in the Quarter, make enough money to go back to school a little while longer. Finally quit school—it did what it was s'posed to do. Got me out of there and over the hump."

"You could make enough, just on the street?"

"Oh, yeah. On a good day you might rake in two or three hundred dollars. But I waitressed some too."

"Did you talk about it with Melody?"

"Sure. That and everything else." Unexpectedly, she lost her animation, sat rigid, as if remembering something, and burst out: "Oh God, oh God, oh God, don't let anything happen to that kid!"

"Do you have any idea where she'd go if she ran away? Any special friends or relatives she might try to reach?"

Ti-Belle shook her head.

"Listen, on another subject—I hate to bring this up, but I have to ask you about your relationship with Ham."

She smiled, an ironic smile, bittersweet. "You mean, did I have reason to kill him? Oooooh, yes. And I loved him to pieces. We fought all the time. Absolutely all the time. Honestly, I don't think it was ever going to get better either. I think I might have ended up leaving him."

"What did you fight about?"

"Ham couldn't . . . he wouldn't . . . I don't know, he just couldn't take any kind of change at all. He was so passive, it was like living with a giant oak tree instead of a man. Just somethin' growin' in the middle of the road, stopping traffic. You realize this is the house he lived in with his wife?" She was angry now, her voice rising, her eyebrows working. "His wife! I've got no idea why I agreed to move in here. I guess I just loved him so much it never occurred to me there could be problems. But then after we'd been together awhile, we needed a place that was ours, not his. And certainly not hers. Well, he wouldn't even talk about it. He said this was where he lived. I mean! He'd rather keep it than me.

"He wouldn't let me buy new furniture. Now I don't mean he wouldn't give me the money; I might have cash-flow problems, but I do have charge accounts. I mean I'd buy something new, have it delivered, and he'd get anxious. He said it was mine, not his, and that made him feel pushed. Pressed. Smothered. Something like that, I never could quite get it. So I'd say, fine, let's go pick out something together, or even, you go out and get something. You see what this stuff is?" She indicated the contents of the room.

"Just any old thing. But if he picked out something he liked, then he'd have to decide what he liked, which he knew he couldn't do. He was just too damn neurotic. So I had to put up with this shit. I couldn't pick out something, and he wouldn't go with me to get something, and he wouldn't do it himself. You see why I wanted to kill him sometimes?" Her voice had risen almost to a scream.

She was quiet for a moment, and Skip thought the silence felt good. Ti-Belle could get up quite a head of energy when she was angry. No wonder the neighbors had heard the battles.

When the singer spoke again, it was in the quiet voice of remembered grief. "And now I'd give anything to have him back again."

"I know." *I know the right thing to say, anyway.*

"I've thought about what happened. It seems like he was talking to somebody and they got mad enough to really do it, doesn't it? Well, I could have done that, except that . . ." She shrugged. "It's just not the sort of thing you kill someone over. He was the most frustrating man in the world, but it was nothing personal. If you killed somebody, wouldn't you have to have a damn good reason?"

No. Blind rage is plenty good enough. Particularly if there's alcohol or drugs involved. But if Ti-Belle didn't know that, maybe she was putting up a smoke screen. Skip thought she'd poke around a little, see if she hit any sensitive spots.

"Did you fight at all about getting married? Did one of you want to and the other one didn't?"

The ravishing Ti-Belle spoiled her image by snorting. "He was still married to Mason!"

"What?"

"Yeah. Five years later. And that's over. Way over. Ham was just too damn wimpy to get a divorce. That would require positive action, and Hamson Brocato never took positive action, oh no." She was off again. Anger may have felt better to her than grief.

But this Mason thing was food for thought. "Did Ham have a will?"

"I don't know. Why? Probably not, why would he?"

Right, why would he? A man who couldn't even be bothered

to get a divorce wasn't going to make a will. It was funny, Mason had used the same word Ti-Belle had—wimpy. But Mason was no wimp. Why hadn't she taken care of the divorce?

Ti-Belle's thoughts were still on marriage. "Look, I'm not the kind of woman who just wants to get married. It just isn't my thing, maybe never will be. I've got a career going. I thought Ham was going with me, maybe as my manager. I used to think we'd work as a team, but I was starting to think it just wouldn't happen. Couldn't. Probably shouldn't."

"Why not?"

"Well, it turned out his main talent was schmoozing." She spoke with the sadder-but-wiser air of someone who's learned the hard way.

Skip thought she'd learned everything she was going to from Ti-Belle. It was time to play the bad cop. "Ti-Belle, I checked all flights out of here for a week. And I checked with Mr. Jarvis Grablow in Chicago. You didn't go anywhere."

The beautiful face registered disbelief and then panic. It was probably about to be replaced by anger, and if Ti-Belle was as volatile as she seemed she might attack. Skip got ready. But the human volcano had burned itself out. She fell back in her chair, defeated. "Oh, shit!"

Skip breathed a sigh of relief. "Where were you?"

"Oh, fuck!"

"You didn't really think you were going to get away with it, did you? With a shaky alibi like that?"

"Get away with what? I didn't kill Ham, for Christ's sake. I was with a man, okay? Ham got to me. He wore me down. I needed some . . ." She sniffled a bit ". . . some self-esteem from some-where. He wasn't around, he was putting everything into the JazzFest, I was frustrated, I felt like our relationship was coming apart. . . ."

"You don't have to make excuses to me."

She made a face that was like a funny little half smile. "I guess I was really talking to Ham. Do you have any idea how awful I feel? I was in bed with somebody else while he was getting killed!" Loud voice again. Mad at herself—or a good actor. "I might have saved him, do you realize that? If I'd have only been here."

She raced out of the room, Skip following. But she was only getting a tissue. She came back dabbing and patting at her face. "Actually, I feel better. I really do. I couldn't talk to anybody else about this, might as well be a stranger."

Skip smiled, momentarily the good cop. She said, "Who was the guy?"

"The guy? I have to tell you that?"

"Either that or get a lawyer fast."

"Shit!" She thought it over. "Okay—it was Johnny Murphy. My drummer."

9

As she shut the door behind the damn cop, Ti-Belle threw her Kleenex at it. But that wasn't good enough, so she went back in the living room and threw each of the sofa cushions across the room.

"Shit!

"Fuck!

"Shitfire!

"Motherfucker!"

They didn't make any noise, so she picked up a little ceramic box—ugly thing Ham wouldn't let her deep-six—and threw it against the wall. "Goddamn, motherfucker!"

To her disappointment, it only hit the wall and fell to the carpet. There was a good thwack, but no satisfying shatter.

"Goddamn, goddamn, goddamn!" She hated the cop, she hated herself, and she couldn't believe the goddamn motherfucking stupid mess she was in. About the only person whose ass she didn't currently despise was Johnny Murphy.

She went into her bedroom, thinking as always how much she hated the colorless, boring, unbelievably ordinary cover on the bed. God, it was going to be good to pick her own things. Was she crazy to have lived with a man who wouldn't even let her get a goddamn new bedspread?

But there'd been good things. There certainly had. And lots of them.

She dialed Johnny Murphy for the fiftieth time that day, but goddamn! No answer again. She spoke to the robot: "Johnny, it's Ti-Belle. I need you real, real bad. Please call me the minute you hear this, I don't care how stoned you are or who you got with you. This is an emergency, you hear me?"

What to do now? Oh, shit, what? The tears started coming again, just as they had before the cop came. Being alone was bad. Sitting on the bed, she looked in the mirror and hated what she saw. A crying, pathetic waif. Definitely not a dynamic, take-charge kind of woman, the kind who could have gotten from where she'd started to where she was now, on the brink of really making it big. If she didn't take charge right now, what was left of her life was going to fly apart like a bomb hit it. She found a pair of socks, put them on, got down and crawled, looking for her running shoes. Then she remembered Andy Fike had been there cleaning up—they'd be in the closet.

She got in her car and started driving. She was halfway across the causeway to Covington when it occurred to her to wonder where the hell she was going.

To find Johnny.

But Johnny doesn't live in this direction.

There was no turning back in the middle of the lake. Where in the hell was she going to look for Johnny anyway? She already knew he wasn't home, where the hell would he be? Practicing? More likely getting ripped with people she'd hate.

She was driving like a sleepwalker. She turned off the AC and rolled down the window, hoping the breeze would keep her alert. Why had she gotten on the causeway? Instinct, she thought. She probably just needed to keep moving for a while, and she needed to be outside. She'd walk when she got to the other side. Go to the banks of the Bogue Falaya and be with the world in a way that she couldn't in New Orleans.

The wind on her face was familiar, the whole situation was.

No wonder I'm doing this. I always run from the bad stuff.

It would get hot like this when she was a kid, the wind would be hot, and yet refreshing. Moving through it would make her feel alive. Being on her bike. She would get on her bike and pedal so fast her calves hurt, her calves nearly killed her, her chest felt raw, but that was okay, she was getting away.

"M'ay Ellen?" (Not "Mary." Her dad could never get the r in when he was drinking.) "M'ay Ellen, bring me a Bud."

The words echoed in her head as if they hadn't been uttered nearly twenty years ago. Twenty years ago she'd heard them, or nearly that long, a lifetime ago, and she hadn't thought of them since.

They hadn't had air-conditioning, and all the windows were open. Outside someone was cutting his lawn. The drone was pleasant, borne on the afternoon breeze with the sweet scent of the mown grass. Another drone came from the living room, this one not nearly so pleasant, in fact ugly, to Ti-Belle, depressing. It was the baseball game on television.

She didn't know why it depressed her. Because it reminded her of darkened rooms on a beautiful day, she supposed. Because her father was glued to it, not available to play, to take her out, even to get groceries for the family. Because it was the most important thing in the world to him, and she sometimes thought she was the least. Because it dominated the household, with its horrid drone and everyone's schedule planned around it. And because it was so utterly his territory.

She wanted to go lie down on her bed and let the tears run out of her eyes while she clutched her green and purple stuffed rabbit, her last year's Easter bunny, holding it up tight to her face so no one could hear her sob. The ball game took her that way. But she couldn't do that, even though she didn't have to babysit today because Jimmy was over at a friend's house. She had to figure out how to make macaroni and cheese. She had told her mother she could do it, and she was smart, she knew she could.

Then her dad called for that Bud. He's forgotten, she thought. She could go in there and remind him that Mama had one of her headaches and couldn't be disturbed. But then he'd get mad. She didn't know why he got mad about things like that, but he did, and she'd be the one he yelled at.

He'd say, "Shit! Goddamn headache! Goddamn! Again?" She'd try to leave at this point, but he'd say, "Don't turn your back when I'm talking to you!" And he might throw something. He might do that whether she stood respectfully or whether she tried to get out of the way, there was no way to tell.

The best thing was to bring him the beer herself. She went to the refrigerator. "M'ay Ellen? M'ay Ellen!" Oh, no. There weren't any more. But there had to be some beer—her father always drank beer when he watched the ball game. It had to be here.

There it was on the table. She remembered now. He'd gone out that morning and gotten it. She pried a can loose from the pack. Warm. He'd be mad about that. He liked his beer good and cold, he was always talking about it. What to do? Ice! She could put ice in it, like tea.

"M'ay Ellen, what's taking so goddamn long?"

"I'll just be a minute."

She pulled a chair up to the refrigerator, stood on it, and opened the freezer door. But the ice tray stuck. It was frozen in there. She had to get down and get a knife to pry it loose. Her dad was yelling again. . . .

The tray came loose so suddenly she fell backward, toppling the chair, hitting the floor. The knife nicked her arm and it started to bleed. She heard her dad's footsteps, heavy, threatening, like a bear coming to get her.

"What in the hell do you think you're doing?" (Except he really said "What in the hail," which she knew was incorrect from watching TV.)

"Just gettin' you a beer." She was in trouble; big trouble.

"Look at you! You're bleedin'. What the hail do you mean you were gettin' me a beer? You were up in that freezer, weren't you? What were you doin' up there?"

"Daddy, the beer was warm. I was just tryin' to get you ice."

"Ice! Ice! You don't put ice in beer! What the hail were you doin'?"

"I was—" She started to pick herself up.

"Don't lie to me." His voice rose, his hand went back behind his shoulder, cocked to hit. "Don't lie to me!"

"Daddy, I was just—"

"You were just. Don't tell me just."

Feet hit the floor and heavy steps came fast down the hall, her mother's, urgent. She looked awful in an old nylon nightgown in the middle of the day, no makeup, hair every which way.

"M'ay Ellen, what the hail is goin' on here?"

He turned toward her and smacked her hard. Ti-Belle was out the door, fast, the screen slamming behind her. If he caught her, she was dead, but she didn't think he would. They'd played this scene before, and she'd gotten away. She'd come back crying, sure he'd kill her, and afraid her mama was already dead, overcome with guilt because she'd left her alone with him, but her mama'd gotten away too, the distraction gave her time. She told Ti-Belle she'd done the right thing, to do it again if she ever had to.

"But Mama," she sobbed, "when he wakes up, he's gon' kill me."

"No, he won't, honey. He won't remember a thing." She pushed Ti-Belle's hair back behind her ears, just playing with it, nervous. "He'll be sobered up and sorry as he can be."

"What's that mean, Mama?"

"It means the devil won't be there anymore. You know when he gets like that? That idn't really Daddy, honey. The devil gets in him and makes him act like that."

She got away this time too. Grabbed her bike, hopped on and started pedaling, her dad chasing her down the street, a great big barefoot guy in his shorts, yelling like a crazy man. But a neighbor came out, an older man, and said, "Hey, Bobby, you go back in there where you belong."

And he had, but by then her mama had probably gone back to the bedroom and locked the door, so she was safe. Ti-Belle was pedaling down the road with the wind in her face, going to a place she knew—a place with a big creek where you could see tadpoles and dragonflies and lots of water bugs. There were trees there, one of them with steps nailed up it by some kids a little older than she was. She could climb up there and sit if she wanted to, just Ti-Belle and the tree, until her heart stopped beating so hard and her face wasn't red anymore. She sang when she was up in the tree, songs she knew and new songs she made up. She didn't have to be mad, or sad, or anything when she was singing.

Ti-Belle felt her face now. Was it red? It always had been when she ran for the treehouse.

But how did I know that? There was never a mirror.

It just felt that way, she decided. But it didn't now. She was cool as cucumber ice cream. But she had to take stock. She focused: Ham was dead and so was that part of her life. Fine. Good.

It sounds cold, but I can live with it.

Anyway, he isn't the first.

There had been another time when this had happened.

Jesus Christ. Proctor! Things were bad enough with Proctor here before this, but what now?

The shit was going to hit the fan in a way Ti-Belle couldn't imagine in her wildest flights of ballad-writing.

Oh, Jesus, oh, Mama!

Why hadn't she thought of it before? Proctor was going to destroy her.

She parked the car and got out, enjoying the breeze, distracted, thinking for a moment it might be a benevolent universe after all. It was April in Louisiana, how bad could things be?

No worse. No way.

She had to smile at herself. It was her optimistic nature that had gotten her through so far, but had things ever been anywhere close to this bad?

Yes. They had.

But now she had something to lose—a lot, on several fronts. Money. Love. Fame. Everything she'd always worked for and wanted and thought she'd never get. And Proctor was the one who was going to mess things up.

She walked by the river, taking in the rich smells, feeling the air soft on her skin, like silk, a fabric she'd grown to love lately. Until two days ago her whole life had been silky. Now it was starting to tear apart, to turn rough and ugly. What the hell was she going to do about it?

She was out of her mind with fear and anger. And grief, which surprised her. She was genuinely sorry Ham was dead.

■

Relatives came and friends went and George swam through it all. Actually, he was walking and talking, he knew that perfectly well, but he thought of it as swimming. Because the air resisted, as if it was water, and because of the way he experienced things as having a liquid quality, as if seen through water; water that wasn't quite calm, that rippled and blurred things, threw them all out of focus. He was walking fine, he was talking fine, but nothing seemed solid.

This is probably shock, he thought, and also thought it wasn't bad, he rather liked it. He couldn't remember this from the time before, when Dorothy died. All he could remember was searing pain. White-hot, razor-sharp. Maybe it wouldn't come this time.

Life was so peculiar. If anyone had asked if he loved his wife —if he cared for overweight, homely Dorothy—he'd have said he did, as a pro forma thing. She was the mother of his son, he was a Christian, he must love her. You were supposed to love your wife. He'd never have given it a second thought if she hadn't badgered him all the time. Did he love her, did he really love her?

Yes, yes, yes, goddammit, Dorothy. Will you just get off my back, I got work to do. We're poor, haven't you noticed? What kind of husband can't do better than this? Would I work so hard if I didn't love you? Now leave me alone, goddammit!

That was really the only way the word "love" had come up. He guessed Dorothy was a pretty good wife. She was there, what else was she supposed to be? She said maybe he loved her, but he didn't cherish her, like he said he would in the marriage ceremony. She wanted to be cherished. And Patty said the same goddamn thing, or something like it.

Well, hell, he must have cherished Dorothy, she just didn't realize it. The minute she was gone, it was like a fucking two-ton weight fell on his chest and crushed it. Crushed him. Crippled him. He missed her like a baby misses its mother. It had never once occurred to him that one day she wouldn't be there. Hell, Ham was only sixteen or seventeen, he couldn't really remember. Dorothy had been thirty-eight. Nobody dies at thirty-eight. And Ham had died at thirty-four! Was he ever going to learn?

But the thing was, it was the same both times. The love part, the cherish part, the part that was supposed to be all rainbows and little chirping bluebirds, that part you didn't notice much. It was just there, it was just life, it didn't really give you pleasure the way your work did, the way your own family did, your brothers and all. That kind of stuff. But wait—something had once. Melody . . . oh, Jesus, a stab of pain, grief, something bad. Melody, when she'd been a baby, a toddler. That was as close as he'd gotten to "cherish," he supposed. He used to see her walking on those chubby legs—running, she never walked—and he'd turn to bread pudding, all soft and sweet and squishy. He'd start feeling happy and he'd break out smiling. Just looking at her. That was the only way he could describe it. Just looking at her made him feel happy.

He went to the bar and got himself a scotch.

Nothing else had ever felt that way—not Dorothy, not Ham, certainly not Patty. Dorothy was the first girl he'd slept with. Well, not really the first, but the first Catholic one. And because she was Catholic and came from a real nice family that lived down the street, dressed modest, acted kind of quiet and all that, he knew she meant it. When she made love to him, she really meant it. And that meant a lot to him. That you could make love and both people would really feel different—not like when he knew the girl was just doing it because he wanted her to, or because it was what she did (pretty much screwed everybody)—that was a new idea. That had to be what they meant by love, and he knew damn well it was what *she* meant, and she was kind of cute and plump, certainly not fat at the time. And she was pregnant. So he married her. Why not? It was what you were supposed to do. And he'd never regretted it. Not once. As he'd told her all the time, whenever she asked. He could honestly say he'd never regretted it. But he still didn't understand why she didn't make him smile, like Melody had, yet it hurt so damn much, goddamn nearly killed him when she died.

Now Ham. Ham was another thing entirely. He knew it then, he knew it now, but you didn't say it if you were a man—he didn't want Ham. He just flat-out hadn't thought about what

112

having a kid would be like, and what it *was* like was a fucking lot of work. He resented that. He had to cook in filthy shitholes to take care of another human being who hadn't asked his permission to butt in. Then when he saw a way out, it was a goddamn lot harder because there was always a kid tugging at him, wanting stuff, needing stuff. And there was a lot of boring activity you had to do or everybody'd think you were a shit—like go to parents' night and Little League games.

Ham always needed something. Like a parasite. How the hell were you supposed to relate to that? To a little boy? Now, a little girl was different—girls were supposed to be pink and helpless and need you. They made it easy—they knew how to charm you and wrap you around their little fingers; for the first few years anyway. He couldn't remember much about Melody after about age five or six, maybe the time she started school. That was probably it. School. She got involved and didn't notice her old dad so much any more.

Ham as a young man was a problem. He never seemed to know what he wanted, what he could do. He certainly wasn't interested in Poor Boys. That would have been the obvious solution—some kind of sinecure George could arrange—but Ham said business bored the pants off him and refused to get his MBA. Didn't like a damn thing but listening to music, as far as George could see. And goddamn if he hadn't made it work for him. He had turned himself from a nobody—a worthless, good-for-nothing—into somebody. He was somebody in this town. George was proud of him, heard people talking about him all over town, could barely believe it was really his son they meant. Didn't see how he'd done it, if truth be told.

That was all well and good, but by then he had hot ideas about how to run the goddamn business, which George had been stupid enough to give him a part of so he wouldn't starve to death, and which all of a sudden didn't bore his pants off. Now he knew fucking everything.

George thought about watching Ham onstage at the JazzFest, everyone applauding, his son the man of the hour. It was fine. It felt fine. He was glad Ham had turned out all right after all. But

Ham still didn't make him smile, just to look at him. He'd never thought about that before. Why not?

It was because Ham was Ham, that was why. He'd see him up there and then he'd remember stuff—how the kid was always grabbing at his pants when he was in a hurry. Or whatever stupid fucking thing he'd said that morning about the way he thought the business should go. Or how silly he looked in a straw hat and those kind of Caribbean shirts he had made for him. Ham was a grown-up, not a cute little baby—and there was a lot of water under the bridge. It was hard to forget that kind of shit.

What distressed him, truly made him sad, maybe even sadder than Ham's death, was the realization that he'd never had that pleasure, that delighted feeling love was supposed to bring. It was like being cheated—so much pain now, so little pleasure then. He'd had thirty-four years to enjoy being a father, yet he hadn't. And he knew it couldn't be because he didn't love his son; he wouldn't feel so miserable now if there hadn't been *some* feeling. Life was so strange, so unfair.

He sat in a chair by himself, with his drink, and some relatives came over to pay their respects. It was hard to concentrate, hard to think what to say, not to let his mind wander back to whatever deep place it had just visited. And suddenly he realized how tired he was. All day guests, people, friends, relatives, acquaintances, people Patty knew, people he didn't care about. He wanted to be done with them.

Where was Patty? Maybe she'd get rid of them.

Over there, pouring someone a drink.

He got up and walked over, approaching from the rear, putting an arm around her, leaning close to whisper in her ear, catching her perfume. And to his utter amazement, he felt himself getting hard. This was Patty, his wife of seventeen years. But it was like being with a stranger; or being young again. He couldn't figure out what the hell it was like. It was just unexpected.

Instead of whispering what he meant to, he said, "I can't take it any longer. I feel like I'm coming apart."

She turned quickly, touched his cheek. "Oh, George."

He held her. "I think I have to go upstairs."

"Do you need help?"

He had known she would say that, though why a grown man would need help getting up the stairs in his own house, he couldn't imagine. But he nodded. "Come with me."

He put his face against her head—her shoulder was too far down—and let her lead him, gracefully fending off the well-meaning and intrusive.

When they were in the bedroom, she started to loosen his tie, but he took her hands away, enfolded her, kissed her with more passion than he had in eight or nine years.

"George!"

"I want you, Patty."

"You brought me upstairs to make love?"

"Yes."

"Now?"

"Feel." He put her hand on his erection.

She stared at him, unbelieving. "I could almost believe you're glad Ham's dead."

He said, "Aren't you?" And they stared at each other a long moment.

For answer, she kissed him again, grinding into him like a teenager. George felt strangely exhilarated. He couldn't remember when he'd been so turned on by Patty, when he'd had so much fun making love to her; the thought of the house full of mourners only excited him more.

As he picked her up and laid her on the bed, the answer to Why?—the question he hadn't consciously asked himself—came anyway: "So I won't have to think about Melody."

He squeezed Patty's breast, entwined a hand in her hair and yanked—too hard, probably—anything to enhance sensation, to turn his brain off.

▪

I must be dreaming.

Patty tried to remember when he'd made love to her at his own instigation. She couldn't. It was always her idea, and it was always desultory. Yet, feeling his fingers in her hair, feeling him pull it that way she kind of liked, she felt only annoyance.

How can I do this with a houseful of people?

It's what you want, isn't it?

I guess so. But why don't I feel anything?

She moaned as he stroked her breast. He said her name. He was wrecking her dress.

She started to unbutton his shirt. He stopped her and took off her dress, as she'd known he would.

I know him so well.

The thought almost made her cry, weep with longing for what she'd missed all these years. She wanted so much to enjoy this, and she wanted to please him.

But she was thinking of Melody, and her fear was consuming her. She couldn't seem to focus like George, and she envied him. She couldn't stop thinking. Try as she might, she couldn't turn off her brain.

Why am I doing this?

You know why. Because he wants to.

She'd just read *Women Who Love Too Much,* and had seen herself so clearly it scared her. She'd thrown the book out. But little lessons from it came back to her now and made her hate herself, despair for her marriage.

"What's wrong? Patty, what is it?"

She hadn't even realized she was crying.

"Oh, George, I love you so much." She wrapped her legs around him, buried her face in his neck.

When it was over, she said, "What are we going to do?"

She was sorry she'd said it, knew it had spilled out only because she was frantic. She thought he would say "About what?" and she would have to make something up, so as not to add to his load, not remind him when he needed to forget.

But he said instead, "Fuck the police."

"What?"

"We can find her, Patty. We're her parents. We'll look for her ourselves."

"We will?" She couldn't believe what she was hearing, George Brocato saying "we," including her as if she were his wife.

10

Skip stopped at Old Metairie Village to call Ariel. "I need to talk to a drummer named Johnny Murphy. Any idea where I can find him?"

She'd meant to ask for his address and phone number, but Ariel interrupted. "Johnny? He's around here somewhere." She yelled, forgetting to cover the receiver. "Hank! Have you seen Johnny Murphy?" Pause. "What?"

She came back to Skip. "He's drinking a lot today. He tends to do that. Hank said he left a while ago. You could try him at home or maybe Cosimo's."

"What's he look like?"

"Tall dude. Ponytail. Seems a lot older than he ought to."

As it happened, a man like that was hanging on for dear life at Cosimo's. His ponytail could have belonged to the old gray mare, but it wasn't only that that made him look old. Johnny had a lot of miles on him. He was handsome, or he would be if he'd get about forty-eight hours sleep, but he had "Bad News" written all over him. In bold type. Skip would have thought Ti-Belle's taste tended to the better-heeled, better-

117

groomed, and better able to give her a boost up.

She showed her badge and started to explain, but Johnny Murphy wasn't ready yet. "Hey, you really a cop?"

"Uh-huh. As I was saying, I'm investigating—"

"I just can't believe a little gal like you is really a cop."

Skip was six feet tall barefoot, and she was wearing two-inch heels. "Very funny, Mr. Murphy. Now suppose you tell me where you were Tuesday."

"Tuesday? Was Ham killed Tuesday? I hardly knew the man— why you asking me?"

"Why're you getting drunk like this? Feeling bad because of ol' Ham?"

"Lady, pay attention. I told you I hardly knew him. He did a lot for the city and all that shit, producing the festival and working on Second Line Square and all. But other than that, I don't give a rat's ass."

"Fine. So you wouldn't mind telling me what you were doing Tuesday. Also Monday and Wednesday."

"Now how the hell am I s'posed to remember somethin' like that?"

"Why don't you check your calendar?"

"Huh?" Drunken dopiness gave way to shrewdness. "Okay. Good idea. Why don't I check my calendar?"

He grabbed a leather bag he'd set on the bar, the kind of men's purse a man like him would never have carried if he hadn't been a musician, and extracted a battered pocket calendar. "Let's see now. Monday. Nothin'. Ti-Belle was out of town, so we couldn't practice. I'm her drummer, you know that, probably. Shit, you're a cop, you probably know everything about me. Monday night— nothin'. Tuesday I had a doctor's appointment. Asshole told me to stop drinking. Wednesday, Ham's party. No, I'm just kiddin'— fact, I was right here with Norm, wasn't I, buddy?"

The bartender smiled at hearing his name, but obviously hadn't heard anything else.

"You satisfied?"

"How long was Ti-Belle out of town?"

"Monday through Wednesday—all three. Right before the

JazzFest too. But hell, we're pros. We been through it all. We can play in our sleep. We didn't need to practice. Hell."

Skip wasn't sure if he was bragging, simply stating a fact, or trying hard to convince himself.

"You didn't see Ti-Belle on any of those days?"

He belched loudly, too far gone to bother apologizing. "Hell, no. Didn't do a damn thing worth mentioning. Oh, wait—yesterday I played tennis with Tommy Houlihan."

"Ti-Belle says she spent those three days with you."

"She what?" He guffawed. "Did I hear you right? Ti-Belle Thiebaud said that?" He was having the best old laugh in the world till suddenly the penny dropped. "Wait a minute! Ham was killed Tuesday, right?"

Skip nodded.

"And Ti-Belle says I was with her? Holy shit! You know what that means?"

Skip shook her head, smiling. Johnny Murphy was a pretty funny drunk. "What does it mean?"

"Means the bitch did it." He clapped her on the shoulder. "Hey, Sherlock, case solved. Ol' Ti-Belle just tried to use me as an alibi. Means she did it, right?"

"You're pretty quick to accuse her. Any reason she'd want to do her boyfriend in? You ever hear her threaten to?"

"Hell, no, she never threatened. I'm not accusin' her, I'm just lookin' at the evidence."

"All the same, you're not a bit shy about it. I might have thought you'd have a little more employee loyalty. Isn't she a good boss, or what?"

"Oh, I'm just having a little fun with you. Ti-Belle Thiebaud'd never do a thing that dumb—it might interfere with her goddamn motherfuckin' career, and we'd just hate that, now wouldn't we? Nothin' in this world is so fuckin' almighty precious as Ms. Thiebaud's brilliant career, and you can be damn sure she ain't gonna forget it long enough to stab her boyfriend. Her boyfriend who's about the most important dude in the state of Louisiana in the music bi'ness."

"So you weren't with her Tuesday. Is that what you're saying?"

"Yeah, that's what I'm sayin'. Can I buy you a drink? I'm so shocked and surprised by all this nonsense, I almost forgot my manners." For the first time, he was looking at her, narrowing his eyes a little, registering her femaleness.

For all his bombast and pseudocountry accent—she noticed it came and went—she liked the guy. She sensed he had done lifelong battle with a streak of sadness in himself, and hadn't won the war yet. People like that tried so hard to stave it off they were usually fun. She felt like bantering a little with him. "Now tell me something, Johnny—if I were a male cop, you wouldn't offer me a drink, would you?"

"Why I sure would. Would've a long time ago. I was just so distracted by your petite loveliness, I lost my head."

She emitted the obligatory chuckle. "I'd never guess you were Irish."

"Russian on my mother's side."

She could see it, she guessed. High cheekbones and deep-set, smoldering eyes. She said, "Johnny, you wouldn't kid me, would you? You really weren't with Ti-Belle?"

"Let me tell me something." To her amazement he sounded almost sober. There was an angry note in his voice that hadn't been there before. "I've known Ms. Ti-Belle Thiebaud a long damn time. A long damn time. I've been cleanin' up messes for her almost as long as she's been singin'. And I am not fuckin' doin' it anymore." He stuck a forefinger in her face, almost touching her nose. "You got that?"

"I think I got it, pardner. Raincheck on the drink, okay?" As she left, Skip clapped him on the shoulder. She couldn't explain it, but she felt drawn to him, wanted to help him in some odd way she couldn't define.

Out of the dark, out of the air-conditioning, in the sunlight and the late spring humidity, she felt depressed and wondered why. There was something about Johnny that seemed hopeless, she thought. Perhaps he was simply what he looked like—a man well on the way to killing himself with booze—and that was what had gotten to her.

She needed some gossip of the sort Alison probably didn't know, and Ariel seemed a likely source. What, she wondered, were the chances of Ariel's having a free moment? She called the festival office, fully expecting to be referred to the fairgrounds. But Ariel herself answered, sounding out of breath.

"Oh, Skip. I was just going home. I feel like I'm gon' die."

"Going home?"

"Well, going by the Brocatos'. It's the only chance I've had all day."

"Could you give me a few minutes? I'm in the neighborhood."

"Sure. I'll just pass out for a while. Wake me up when you get here."

The JazzFest office was painted a kind of grayish-lilac with rose trim—a muddy color, not entirely successful. But the reception area, converted from what had once been the Old Reliable Bar, was a cheerful peach. A young black woman who looked good in it told her Ariel was upstairs.

A ratty old carpet covered the stairs, contrasting in that wonderful New Orleans way with a handsome curving banister. Upstairs was the usual maze of offices. Ariel wasn't in hers but in Ham's, which was large, comfortable, and hung with JazzFest posters. She wasn't resting either, but talking on the phone. It was twenty minutes before she got off.

She grabbed a linen jacket. "Quick. Let's get out of here."

They went to the courtyard of the Maison Dupuy and drank Cokes as the fountain splashed. "It's soothin' here," Ariel said. "Ham and I used to use it as an escape." She smiled, leaning forward. "A working escape, of course. Briefcases everywhere, ink stains on our fingers, papers flyin' in the wind—still, it beat the office every now and then." She paused, struggling for control, and when she spoke again, her voice came out a squeak. "I still can't believe he's dead. I just can't believe it."

"Ariel, listen. You want to help me find the murderer?"

"Of course. I'm sorry about this." She dabbed at her eyes with her napkin, which was already damp from the Coke. "Being such a baby, I mean."

"Don't be silly. This whole town loved Ham, and it's going to take us all a while to get back to normal. I wanted to talk to you because I figure you know more than anyone else about the inner workings of the JazzFest."

"Well . . ." She seemed to be assessing that. "I might. I guess with Ham gone, I probably do."

"What would you think about being a little indiscreet?"

"Indiscreet?"

"I have some kind of unofficial questions for you. What the press calls deep background." She spread her arms, showing how expansive she was, what good buddies she and Ariel were. "Oh, heck. Let's call it what it is."

"Gossip?" For the first time since Skip had met her, her eyes twinkled; she smiled a real smile.

"Uh-huh."

"Well, for *Ham.*"

And they laughed together, just two fun gals having a real fun time together.

"I was wondering about Ti-Belle."

"Yes?" Ariel licked her lips, poised for action. She looked slightly predatory. Skip had chosen well.

"Well, I was wondering about her relationship with Ham. Did they get along well?"

Ariel looked disappointed. "Ham didn't really talk about that."

"But you probably saw them together a lot. I thought maybe you came to your own conclusions."

"Actually, they seemed perfectly happy. But I did overhear Ti-Belle telling someone else about a fight they'd had. It surprised me, to tell you the truth. Maybe that's why—" She stopped, raising her hand to her mouth. "I shouldn't have said that."

"It's okay. This is all confidential. And let's face it, Ariel— Ham's dead. Trying to protect him at this point is an exercise in futility."

She looked down at the table. "I guess so."

"They fought and maybe that's why . . ."

"Okay. You'll probably find out anyhow. Everyone's buzzing about it."

"Yes?"

"The word is, Ti-Belle's seeing Nick Anglime."

"Ah."

"I haven't personally seen them or anything—I've just heard it."

Skip took it in, raised an eyebrow, said nothing.

Ariel looked pleased with herself.

"You must hear a lot of things."

"It's one of the things I like about the job."

"I must introduce you to my friend Alison Gaillard."

"Who?"

"Someone you'd like. Tell me—was there any buzz about Ham?"

"You mean seeing somebody?"

Skip slouched back in her chair, the very picture of "nonthreatening." "Um-hmm."

"Not that I can recall."

"Ariel, you're blushing."

Her hands went to her face. "Oh, shit, I always do that. Well, hell. I was wondering if I should tell you. Ham and I got together once, a long time ago."

" 'Got together'? You mean you dated?"

"No. We just kind of fell into bed one night when we were working late."

"Just once? That was the whole story?"

"Yeah." Her voice said it might have been for Ham but it wasn't for her. "I guess he wasn't very interested. Or maybe he didn't want to get involved with an employee. So, hell. I went back to my natural color. That'll show him." She smiled, letting Skip know she was perfectly aware it wouldn't show him anything.

"I beg your pardon?"

"Sorry, I guess I left something out. I was a blonde at the time, and Ham told me a weird thing. He was drinking—we both were —we went for a late drink and ended up having too many. I guess it was his idea of foreplay—what he said."

"What was it?"

"He said he could only have sex with blondes, brunettes just didn't do it for him. I guess I didn't pay too much attention that night, but later, when he—you know—never followed up, I got mad about it. I thought, 'Right, Mr. Big-Shot Producer, you can get all the blondes you want, so why mess with mere brunettes?' Pissed me off."

"So you grew your hair out to show you didn't care?"

She touched her cheeks. "Oh, hell, I'm blushing again. I guess so. Only it didn't feel like that. I just got less interested in being a blonde. I mean, the remark really turned me off. Like we have to make ourselves into whatever they want, and they just reject us anyway. I was sick and damn tired of it."

"Was this before he was seeing Ti-Belle?"

She thought a minute. "I don't think so. But they weren't living together then—I do have *some* standards." She giggled. "Hell, I think I'll get my hair frosted."

"So after all that, he did move in with Ti-Belle."

Ariel nodded.

"And then what? Any more blondes in his life?"

"Not that I know of, and, honey, I made it my business to keep tabs. I mean, who's in a better position to know who calls? And what he's got on his calendar."

"That's why I thought we should have this little talk."

"Well, as far as I can see, he stuck close to the bitch."

"You don't like Ti-Belle?"

"I don't like her cheating on Ham. He was too fine a person for that kind of shit."

Skip suppressed a smile, knowing Ariel would have found cheating on Ham's part perfectly acceptable—with the right person, of course.

"Basically," said Ariel, "I think he was monogamous. Family man. The kind—you know—the kind you could really love." A sob, half checked, came out of her throat with a noise like "Whmmmmf." And tears poured, too many and too fast for her damp Coke napkin. Skip had to dig in her purse for a tissue.

11

Suzuki-roshi wrote: "In the zazen posture, your mind and body have great power to accept things as they are, whether agreeable or disagreeable."

This was Nick Anglime's goal, though Suzuki had a few things to say about goals as well. Which he would ignore for the moment. Today, Nick wanted to accept death, spend the day making peace with it. Death was here in his life, and not for the first time. He and his friends had done the usual things, things involving chemicals and strangers and fast-moving vehicles. Death happened.

Janis and Jimi, Jim Morrison, Keith Moon, Mama Cass, Richard Manuel, John Lennon—they'd died so fast, so soon after he'd come to love them. And there had been others, closer still, including Feather Willis, a woman who'd died in his bed. He'd had to call his manager, and his manager had sent some men to roll her up in a rug and cart her away—back to her own apartment, of course, not to be dumped by a roadway or anything so revolting, but Nick had been shaken. Had written a song about it, "Knock Me Over with a Feather," that had made him a million dollars, give or take. Yet he hadn't done it to make money off of Feather's death, he had done it because he had to; that was the song that had to be written then. If he had exploited her memory, as Rachel, his second wife, had insisted, then so be it—death was part of life, and that made it part of art.

All those other times, he hadn't known how to think about it, and he didn't know now. He knew how to miss the person, that didn't take figuring out, but he didn't have a philosophy to cover the subject. He wanted to, though.

For seven years, he had been pursuing spiritual studies. He would follow one path and then another—he wanted to sample them all, indeed believed in them all, couldn't see a reason for pinning himself down.

He was in a Zen phase now—his third; he kept coming back to it because sometimes when he meditated, he felt different, physically and spiritually. It made his mind different, his body different, the world different. The deeper he went, the simpler things got. That was one reason he did it. He was bemused that everything written on the subject seemed wildly complicated.

"We die and we do not die," wrote Suzuki-roshi. "This is the right understanding."

It bothered him how these people talked about "right"—right practice, right posture, right understanding, right livelihood. Half the stuff they wrote made it seem as if life and truth held a million options, but excuse him if this right business seemed a little on the dogmatic side.

He came out of his reverie, realized he'd lost the thread. This was the sort of thing his mind was doing today, detouring obses- sively—veering off, often toward Ti-Belle, the Crazy Cajun, as he'd come to call her ever since he found out she bleached her pubes. He'd fallen out of bed laughing at the time, and thinking about it now, he gave a loud hoot. It was his favorite thing about her. He'd known women with boob jobs and women with butt lifts and women who'd had every single one of their armpit hairs removed by electrolysis—even one who'd given up a rib or two to make her waist smaller. But he'd never in his life known a nut case who had black roots on her pussy. There was something just plain endearing about being so thorough—or maybe he was so nuts about her, he'd lost it.

That could be it, and he knew it. He was thinking about her mouth, her voice, her crazy Cajun stories, her legs, the way she'd pretend to know something she really didn't. He was thinking about her home alone, in that horrible suburban house, and wishing she was with him. And yet not wishing it. He needed space; he hadn't moved to New Orleans to be with a woman.

He had a spiritual anchor—Caroline Meyer was with him for a few months, Meyer-roshi, his friends called her, though she wasn't a roshi and claimed she wasn't even his teacher, just a more experienced student. Caroline said Nick was becoming obsessed with Ti-Belle (though that was more in her old friend role than in her roshi role). It was true, he was. It seemed to him that if you were trying to free yourself from desire, which he supposed he was, a woman, the very symbol of desire in Western culture, was the last thing you needed. (Caroline said that showed what an extremely inexperienced student he was—the idea, to her, was to observe what you did, be alert to it, but that didn't mean don't do it.) His discomfort was his own; Caroline declined to give it sanction.

He couldn't count the number of women he'd had—and had children with—and was currently still supporting, some in this very house, from time to time. Sabrina was here now with their daughter Mia; Gillian had left only a week ago. Eric and Scott were here too, the twins from his marriage to Rachel. And then he'd once had a little thing with Caroline.

He'd been through stages where women hid under his bed and in his closet, bribed people to get near him, tore at his clothes, wrote him tomes rather than letters, and poems and songs galore. Slept with his friends, hoping they'd get to meet him. Followed him from city to city and brought him gifts that creeped him out —nice things, stupid things, ugly things, it didn't matter, they were bribes. Bribes to get near him, to spend time with him, to get him to notice them, approve them, make them real to themselves.

He'd had women and he *had* women. The last thing he needed

was a woman. He wanted to live a quiet life, a spiritual and contemplative life, a life more or less alone, which he could do in this vast palace of a house, even with all his house guests and staff members. But he couldn't even read about death without thinking about Ti-Belle. He couldn't stand to be without her, couldn't wait till she came back.

"Volleyball?"

It was Proctor, sticking his head in. He was always organizing.

"I don't think so."

"Come on, you think too much."

"No, really. I think I'm depressed."

"Endorphins, baby! Endorphins." Proctor was dancing up and down in his shorts and T-shirt, trying to dribble the volleyball, ready for action.

"Y'all have fun." He looked back down at his book. He was irritated. Except for the kids, just about no one treated him like that. Proctor could get away with it because they'd been room-mates at Auburn. But just barely. Most people—except for Ti-Belle and all the exes—pretty much treated him like royalty, and he'd gotten used to it. He and Caroline were working on it. He wanted humility—it was something he knew he needed—but it was just so damn nice to have everybody hopping when he said rabbit.

So Caroline thought Proctor was good for him—because he wasn't even slightly intimidated by Nick's fame. On the other hand, Proctor was probably going to have to go soon. Because Ti-Belle hated him. *Hated* him. It was unreasonable the way she raved on about him. And it looked to Nick as if the feeling was mutual. He'd seen Proctor looking at her a curious way—not admiringly, which she wasn't used to, but with his eyes narrowed a bit, like he was planning an attack. Or maybe trying to stave one off, Nick wasn't sure which. These two weren't going to work out under the same roof. And if he had anything to say about it, Ti-Belle was coming here.

Yes!

He closed his book with a bang, realizing he was going to ask her soon, couldn't help it, was driven to it. He needed her and he wanted her and he was going to have her.

He could see Proctor and the twins through the open window
—it was nice today, too nice for the AC, so the maid had simply
flung the windows open. It reminded him of summers back in
Alabama, and so did the scene in the yard—adults and kids playing
together, shouting, having fun, as if death hadn't entered their
lives. His life.

He breathed down into his belly and held the breath. Then he
let it out, slowly, slowly, and sat there for a moment, contented,
even thinking of joining the game. But he wouldn't for a minute.
He'd sit here and savor his library, the most beautiful room he'd
ever seen outside of Florence or Rome. There was dark wainscot-
ing, then books to the ceiling. A fireplace. And naturally, leather
furniture. He'd chosen a deep burgundy to match the Oriental rug.
A tapestry hung on one wall, a three-hundred-year-old French
painting over the fireplace. (Rachel had chosen it on one of her
visits; he could never remember the artist and didn't care anyway,
but he liked the fact that it was old.) The room was the one he'd
always dreamed of having when he was a little boy growing up on
a quiet street in Birmingham. Rich. Not rich like Hollywood rich.
Rich like Old World patinas and craftsmanship. Rich like somebody'd put a lot of thought and care into it, and then his son had
come along and done it all over again; and Nick was the third
generation to leave his mark. Of course that wasn't the case—it
was something that had taken a decorator and Rachel three
months, but who cared?

Proctor had said, "You're the William Randolph Hearst of New
Orleans."

Which had made Nick laugh.

It was right on the mark. He'd picked New Orleans for his
castle because it was relatively cheap, it was isolated from the
glitter spots, it was Southern without being a backwater, and he
had good memories of it. From spending time here as a young
man, before he'd made it.

And because it had a music scene. Not a big heavy rock scene,
just a nice local scene he could observe and enjoy and not participate in. He was sick of that shit—performing, putting out. But he
still loved the music, loved to be around it. He'd been thinking of

getting involved with Ham's project, Second Line Square. He could throw benefits here at the castle.

The thing didn't look like a castle—it looked like a gracious huge home—but he wanted to do with it what Hearst had done at San Simeon. He wanted to get the finest of everything and surround himself with it. And then hole up to pursue his path.

The doorbell rang. James would get it, or Luellen. It was probably somebody for one of the kids. Or Caroline or Sabrina. Or maybe Nanette, the acupuncturist.

Luellen came in. "Mr. Nick? A young lady to see you."

"What young lady?"

"A young lady policeman."

"Oh." He couldn't think what to do. Did he have to see her? Should he have a lawyer present? But wait—it didn't have to be about Ham. Maybe it had to do with parking; or break-ins in the neighborhood.

He got up. Almost without thinking about it, he walked to the door, propelled by curiosity as much as anything else. "Yes?" And then, "Oh."

"Oh?"

It was someone he knew—the big mama who'd spoken to him at Ham's that night. He hadn't realized she was a cop. Or had she said she was? He'd forgotten? He wondered if she could sing —a woman with a build like that ought to sing Gospel or something. "I know you from Ham's."

"Yes. Skip Langdon." That was all she said. What did she want? Why was she just standing there?

"Well. What can I do for you?"

"I have a few questions. Not many, really . . . I wonder if you have a minute?"

She looked wistfully behind him, into the marble-floored foyer. She wanted a house tour. Well, okay. He knew how to get a woman on his side. She was a fan, probably.

"About ten," he said. "Would that be enough?"

"I'm sure it would." She smiled, happy now.

He let her in, led her into the library. Her mouth all but fell open. In a minute she'd say, "Have you really read all these books?"

But she went straight for his first editions. "*The Sound and the Fury. The Hamlet.*" Her fingers kept moving. "Everything but *Pylon.* Somehow I never connected . . . well, I mean . . ." She flushed.

"You think if you can sing, you're too dumb to read Faulkner? Ms. Langdon, I'm an ol' boy from Alabama; I had to read this stuff in high school, some of it. You know that song of mine about the boy named Joe? That's about Joe Christmas. From *Light in August?* You know it?"

She nodded, raised an eyebrow.

"Sit down," he said. "Can I offer you anything?"

"No, thanks." She was still staring at the room, but she had a confident air about her. Something told him she wasn't going to turn into a pliable little Gumby.

"How can I help you?"

"I'm here about Ham Brocato's death. I was wondering . . . did you know him well?"

"No. I'd have liked to, but I've more or less just moved here. In fact, I don't quite understand why you're here."

"Don't you, Mr. Anglime?" She had gorgeous green eyes and they didn't waver; but she wasn't giving him a chance to blink first. They were very amused eyes at the moment. Did she think he couldn't see that? She was starting to piss him off.

"No."

She shrugged. "Well, we're just talking to a few key people closely connected to the case—"

"Wait a minute. What connects me to the case?"

"We found your name in his appointment book. So I thought I'd ask when you last saw him."

His name in Ham's appointment book? He'd been to Ham's house once before the party, two months ago. That's where he'd met Ti-Belle—could the cop possibly mean that?

"I don't understand."

"Yes, it was an entry for next week—'call Anglime.' I thought maybe you were close friends."

" 'Call Anglime.' That's what you came out here for? Because he was thinking of calling me?"

She nodded.

"How could I know why he planned to call me?"

"I just thought you might." He thought she was smiling flirtatiously, inviting him to play a little game with her.

"Well, if I had to make a guess, I'd say it was to ask for a contribution to the Second Line Square Foundation."

She just couldn't smile enough. "Probably it was," she said. "Just as a matter of routine, do you remember what you were doing Tuesday afternoon?"

"Why Tuesday?"

"That's when Ham was killed."

"You're asking me what I was doing when Ham was killed? Officer, you're out of line. I hardly knew the man."

"I don't think it's out of line. You're a well-known friend of the family."

"Well, it is."

She stood. "I'm sorry, I guess I was wrong."

"You're sorry! Barge in here invading my privacy—I swear to God I'm going to report you."

"Listen, I'm sorry you're upset. New Orleans is a very small town and we're all upset. Ham leaves a big hole."

"I can't believe you're treating me like a suspect."

"Mr. Anglime, I'm sorry you took it the wrong way. You're not a suspect at all. I just thought I'd ask while I was here."

"Well, why did you want to know?"

She shrugged. "I don't. Really. I'm very sorry to have bothered you."

She started out the door, but he followed. What did she know? Was it better to say something?

"Listen, I have nothing to hide. I just don't appreciate you bargin' in and askin' these questions, that's all."

"I understand. I apologize." She was pleasant as could be, chest sticking out in her white blouse. This close, he realized how tall she was. Was she standing like that on purpose? He thought she was, but not for reasons of enticement. Because the pose gave her confidence—legs planted firmly, chest high; this wasn't a woman who'd be easily intimidated.

"I was home meditating."

She nodded. "I see." She let a few seconds pass. "Vipassana?"

He smiled. "No, that one's too rough for me. Zazen."

"Zazen? I thought that only took about twenty minutes."

"Twenty, thirty, or until your incense stick goes out. But you do it over and over again."

"Until you get it right?"

"Well, I don't think there's a wrong way. You just follow your breathing."

She was on the front porch now, doing a long good-bye. "You mean your mind never wanders?"

Was she psychic or something?

"Mine does," she said. "Thanks for your time." As she clicked off the porch, he thought, *She's not a cop; she's something else.*

"Wait a minute—can I see your badge?"

"Sure." She reached into her purse. She was a cop. One who knew zazen from Vipassana and all of Faulkner's titles. And she might or might not be psychic, but she sure as hell wasn't dumb. She was the first woman he'd ever met who made him nervous.

He sat down and thought about that; meditated on it. No, she wasn't. In his teens, they'd all made him nervous. If he had to be out in the real world, they probably still would. But here in the ivory tower it was different. Better. They all wanted to please him.

And he'd worked hard for it.

But still. The way she stood, that defiant don't-fuck-with-me way—it was intriguing. This was a woman who really didn't give a shit whether he noticed her or not.

It was not only intriguing, it was scary.

▪

Steve was lying on Skip's brand new, light-gray-and-white-striped sofa, a long-neck Dixie balanced on his bare chest. He wore a pair of khaki shorts and nothing else. The AC was off, the windows open, and the ceiling fan spun lazily. It was just twilight, but he had turned on one or two lamps, so that the whole room, with its cantaloupe walls, glowed invitingly. Coming in, key still in the door, Skip felt a great surge rise up from her chest and, to her horror, fall out of her eyes. She shut the door and turned around quickly, jerking off her suit jacket, so Steve wouldn't see the tears.

"Hard day catching felons?"

She kept taking off clothes, the sudden rush of tears gone, but the rush of soft feeling remaining—love, gratitude, whatever it was. Perhaps, she thought, it was simple aesthetic pleasure.

She was down to bra and panties now. She walked over and plopped down beside him, bending over for a big beery kiss. He could hold her with only one arm, the other being occupied with the beer. He circled her waist and let his fingers brush her back like feathers, coming to rest down around the dimples. She said, "What'd you do all day?" She didn't think she'd ever felt so completely at peace.

"My job," he said. "It turns out just because Ham's dead doesn't mean Second Line Square is. I've got a contract with the foundation, and they said go ahead and fulfill it." He sat up so that they were nearly eye to eye.

"Who did?"

"The board of directors."

"So you've been out at the fairgrounds."

"Yep. Saw Taj Mahal and Marcia Ball. And some local bands."

"Good stuff?"

"Uh-huh. Hungry?"

"Exhausted, mostly. But we could have gumbo. I made some and froze it."

"But did you thaw it?"

"Well, no, but—"

"Let's go out."

She was about to protest that she was too tired, but how often did Steve Steinman come to town? You gotta get it while you can, she thought. "Okay. But low-key."

"The Gumbo Shop."

"Done. A shower first, though."

"I think I might drink me a beer and listen to some tunes."

She slipped into the shower as he was putting on an Alan

Toussaint tape. She was loving the sense of easy domesticity.

He'd picked up all his clothes and things. And all hers.

That's why it seems so nice in there—because he's made it nice.

She hadn't expected that.

Jesus, he wants to go out, we'll go out. He wants my right arm, he can have that too.

The crowded feeling was starting to wane. This contented feeling was probably dangerous as hell. Couldn't last—had to turn ugly. Or just disappear along with Steve.

All the more reason to go with it.

Laissez les bon temps roulez.

It was a phrase for tourists, or so she'd thought till it popped into her head.

Well, hell, I'm a tourist in this country.

Being in love was a new thing for her. She didn't know what she expected, but it certainly wasn't this softness, this unaccustomed sweetness, as if life was a pillow, a pillow trimmed with meringue lace that you could eat at will, and it would miraculously form itself again, always as delicate and intricate as it had been before.

She put on off-white shorts and last year's JazzFest T-shirt, a black one dotted with musical instruments.

Emerging, she saw that Steve had likewise covered his chest, and had slipped on sandals. His T-shirt was from Disneyland.

"I forgot to tell you. Jimmy Dee called."

She grinned evilly. "Should we ask him to join us?"

"How about if we muddle along by ourselves?"

But as they walked to the Gumbo Shop, he said, "Jimmy Dee said he needed to talk to you."

"He did?" That was unlike Dee-Dee. To call instead of dropping by.

"He sounded a little upset." That was very unlike him. To show weakness in front of Steve; in front of her, for that matter. But maybe it was nothing. Maybe she'd forgotten the rent.

"I'll call him when we get back."

Steve patted her backside. "Did the little woman have a good day?"

Skip sighed. It was a gentler lead-in than usual, and he'd waited longer—a lot longer—but there was no getting around it: he remained fascinated with her work. Would pump her avidly for details. Though now that she thought of it, not so avidly as he used to. Usually it made her tired to talk about it after doing it all day, but on the rare occasions when he kept his distance, she quite enjoyed it—when she didn't feel like she had to perform and maintain discretion at the same time. And tonight she had something to say.

"A hellish day," she said. "Except for the last part. I keep worrying about Melody. What do you think of a nineties' kid who's got a thing for Janis Joplin?"

Steve shrugged. "She's got good taste."

"But Janis died."

"So did John Lennon—it happens to everybody, haven't you heard?"

"I don't know. I've just got a weird feeling she's got a self-destructive streak."

But Steve wanted the good stuff. "About that last part you mentioned. Was that by any chance the part where you had a little talk with Nick Anglime?"

"Now how'd you know that?"

"Well, who wouldn't if they could? Besides, I saw the way you just happened to manage to speak to him last night."

"That was for your benefit."

They got to the restaurant.

"They do a nice gumbo."

"Good. I'll have that and the shrimp étoufée."

"Just the gumbo for me." When they'd ordered, she said, "First I ran around all day listening to people's lies."

"*Everybody* lied to you?"

"Well, let's put it this way—they told their own versions of things."

"So how can you tell when they're lying? Do your palms itch or what?"

"I've got a better system."

"Check out their stories? Even I could do that."

"Okay, then. I get this weird feeling right behind my left ear. You want to hear about Nick Anglime?"

"I'm on the edge of my seat."

"Well, he lives in a baronial manor."

"What would you expect? It's on Audubon Place."

"The place isn't Southern at all. It's stone, for one thing. And inside, it's like a museum. All beveled glass and dark wood and Oriental rugs and Tang dynasty porcelain."

"How do you know the porcelain's provenance?"

She gave him a grin. "I made that part up. But it sure as hell didn't come from Pier 1. Even the walls were works of art; little designs painted on. Stuff on stuff. And colors so rich and deep you could sink in if you touched."

He nodded.

"And hung with sconces and mirrors and very dark art. European, I'm pretty sure, but I didn't recognize any of the artists. And the ceilings were three-dimensional."

"I beg your pardon?"

"I don't know—carved or something. Vaulted. Like ceilings in Italian palaces. Oh, and some were painted too—maybe frescoed for all I know. And the floors were marble—those that weren't parquet. I didn't go in the kitchen, but I guarantee you there's no linoleum in there. Probably Spanish tiles."

"Excuse me. The witness is speculating."

"It's like he has so much money, he has to invent things to do with it. Travel all over the world to find things to buy."

"Well, how'd it look?"

"What do you mean?"

"Gaudy or nice?"

"Aren't we snotty tonight."

"Well?"

She shrugged. "Both, I guess. It's fabulous. It's a sultan's palace."

"It's got some *harim*, I bet."

"I don't know. He might be an ascetic in some ways."

"I beg your pardon? The guy's living in a stately pleasure dome."

"Well, that's it—it's stately. More sedate than anything else. He's got kids living there too. Don't ask. You've been to Buddhist centers, haven't you? They're always beautiful. Very well thought out, but formal. Churches too."

Steve shook his head. "I don't know. I just don't see anything ascetic about spending all that money."

"I only said 'in some ways'—I guess I meant about the women. He just doesn't seem wildly sexual. And anyway, he's a spiritual seeker."

"That doesn't preclude sex, but I'm too fascinated to argue the point. Keep going."

"Claims he sits zazen." Something was bothering her. She paused, but it didn't come clear. "I can't tell you why, but I don't get the impression he's a wildly committed Zennie."

"Why not?"

"I'm not sure. The weird ear feeling, I guess."

Steve slurped gumbo. "He seemed like a dilettante?"

"A little. I don't know. He seemed tired. Burned out, I guess, but not from drugs. At least not recently. Just . . ." She spread her arms helplessly. ". . . tired of life, maybe. I can't explain it. I thought he was going to be mesmerizing, but he hardly has any personality at all."

"Oh, come on."

"Well, not that you can get at."

"Hold it here. Baby, this is Nick *Anglime* we're talking about. That's the closest we've got to Elvis himself in terms of star power. Are you telling me that you, Detective Margaret Langdon, are so sophisticated you just weren't impressed one little bit?"

"Impressed!" She started to giggle. "Omigod. *Impressed!*" She laughed till tears ran down her face and had to be wiped by the more alert Steve. Other diners stared, and the waitress brought a glass of water. Steve merely waited.

"Impressed!" she said, when the power of speech returned.

"Skip. You're more tired than I thought. You want to go home?"

She still couldn't stop laughing. But finally the thing spent itself, and she drank her water. "Was I impressed?" she said. "I nearly wet my pants. Like you said, this is Nick *Anglime* we're talking about. He doesn't *have* to have a personality. Listen, I stammered, I fished for words, I couldn't meet his eyes. Are you kidding? *Impressed!* I'll tell you about impressed. It was all I could do not to roll around on the floor and beg to kiss his ring or something."

"Well, I'm glad he wasn't mesmerizing or anything."

"Okay, okay. Maybe he was just a tiny bit mesmerizing. I mean, aside from the fact that he's an extremely good-looking dude, there's something else. It's that he's withdrawn. By not giving you the slightest notion who he is, he makes you want to know. The more withdrawn he seems, the more fascinating it is in a weird kind of way."

"You're sick."

"Well, think about it. He's the nearest thing to God in the pop culture pantheon. So you go in all ready to sit at the feet of greatness, and you don't get greatness."

"And that just makes you want it all the more. I guess I can see it." He was staring down at the bill, probably figuring the tip.

Shyly, she stroked his first two fingers. "You want dessert? Bread pudding?"

"Are you kidding? I just ate the equivalent of three meals. Anyway, we'd have to go to the Palace Café for that. You're way too tired."

"No, I'm not. I want to walk through the Quarter."

"What for?"

"I want to look at street bands."

"Look at? Doesn't one usually listen to them?"

"I want to check out runaway teenage singers."

"Melody!"

She tried not to look smug. "Sure. Where would you go if you were sixteen and knew a tune or two?"

He looked at her with respect. "That's brilliant."

"My weird ear thought of it."

He looked jazzed. "Let's do it. But no bread pudding. Beignets."

They walked to Royal, and over to Jackson Square on the way to Café du Monde, but didn't see a sign of a teenage singer. Over their beignets, Steve said, "I'm going to go to Cookie's tonight—give you a little time to recover."

"What?" She'd heard it, but she didn't want to believe it.

"I thought I'd go to—"

"I meant . . . why?"

He touched her hair. "Look at you. You're beyond bushed."

He's seen me with a concussion. Could I look worse than that? I must be a hag.

Desperate to register a protest, yet not knowing what to do, she said nothing. It had been such a perfect evening, how could this be happening? He was the one who needed time alone, that was obvious. It was a first in their relationship—he always wanted to be with her, never slept at Cookie's even when he was officially staying there. It was a first, and it was probably the beginning of the end. He'd had enough of her already, couldn't take her in large doses, and the irony was, she was falling more deeply in love every second.

But of course she knew that it wasn't irony at all—or at least not irony in microcosm. It was the greater irony of the tolerance difference between the sexes. She'd heard about it, read about it, endured endless complaining about it from women friends.

But I never thought it could happen to me. I was so cautious. I let him take the lead in everything. I didn't dare let myself feel anything until I was sure about how he felt. I did everything right, dammit!

Alone at home, feeling like a deflated balloon, she called Jimmy Dee.

"And where," he said, arriving joint in hand, "is that terrifying bear of a man. You did call me for protection?"

"I thought you wanted me, Dee-Dee darlin'."

"Well, listen to Little Miss Double Entendre. You didn't used to have such a filthy mind."

She accepted a hit of his joint, something she seldom did lately. "I'm just trying to keep a stiff upper lip."

"Uh-oh. The bear growled?"

"He went to another cave." She handed back the joint, catching Jimmy Dee's look and considering the tone she'd set with her earlier remark. "Oh, hold it, I didn't mean—"

He puckered his lips, clowning. "Tell it to Dr. Freud, tiny one."

"I didn't mean another woman. He's not like that."

"Listen, you don't have to convince me. He's not my boyfriend. If that isn't it, what's wrong?"

"He wanted to be alone. I think he's getting tired of me."

Dee-Dee grabbed one of her feet. "Oh, who could be tired of a great big gorgeous thing like you?"

"Why'd he go away, then?"

He started massaging the foot. "Darling, do you speak English? He said he needed time alone—why make it complicated?"

"That wasn't exactly what he said. He said he wanted to give me time alone."

"How thoughtful. For a bear."

"Well?"

"Well, what?"

"What do you think?"

He shrugged. "You do look kind of peaked. Shouldn't you be hopping into bed—with the big case and all?"

"Do both feet, Dee-Dee. That reminds me—I never saw you last night."

"Oh, but I saw you. I got there about the time you were cozying up to Nick Anglime. You had bigger fish to fry than ol' Jimmy Dee."

"Never." She gave him a pat. "What'd you call me about, anyhow?"

"Well, I wanted to tell you a couple of things."

She lifted an eyebrow.

"Including something I shouldn't."

"Ummm. Let's get married."

"Listen, I got bad news today."

Her foot, flexing happily in his grasp, went dead still. She could feel her hands get cold. Jimmy Dee was HIV negative and celibate lately—too depressed to get it up, as he put it—but he was still getting tested every six months after several decades of doing whatever he damned well pleased. And then doing it again. (Or so he told it—she personally thought he'd be dead if he'd

141

really led the life he described, probably of fatigue.)

Seeing her expression, he said, "Oh, my dear, it's not me."

"Jesus, Jimmy Dee! Don't do that to me!" She smashed a pillow in his face.

"You sweet thing, your true feelings are coming out. Leave the bear for me."

"Oh, Dee-Dee, you ass." She said it because she loved him and he was half her size and gay; in a way, it was tragic they could never be a couple, and now and then it got to her—particularly at times when she was already inclined to feel sorry for herself. "What's wrong?" she said.

"My sister's . . ." A gurgle came out of his throat. He struggled for control.

She had had cancer several months ago, had had her spleen removed. Skip said, "The cancer's back."

He nodded. He had gone to Minneapolis to be with her for the surgery. He was her only adult relative, he'd said at the time, but more than that Skip couldn't get out of him.

"I can't do this," he said.

"It's okay, Dee-Dee. You don't have to say anything." She tried to catch him, to give him a hug, but he stood up, avoiding her.

"There's more." It came out a croak.

Skip moved back on the sofa, giving him room, and patted the place beside her. He sat down and swallowed, staring out the window, not looking at her. He swallowed again, finally said, "I don't think I can talk about it." His voice was thin and high.

"Later, Dee-Dee. Another time." He let her pat his knee. Touching seemed okay, just not closeness; she could understand it. He reminded her of children—of herself as a child—batting away at well-meaning adults dispensing comfort.

"Drink?" she said. "Cognac? It's supposed to revive you."

He nodded, smiling a little, still unable to speak.

She brought him the cognac and poured a little for herself. She knew he was depressed—any gay man in New Orleans who wasn't had to be kidding himself—and she knew he smoked so much pot to keep reality at bay. Hell, she was depressed herself. She took a healthy sip, savoring the richness, rolling the brandy on her tongue, losing herself in the pleasure of it.

In a few minutes Dee-Dee said, "The epicurean cop at home."

"Beginning to go slightly cross-eyed."

"I'm going to tell you something you never heard, okay?"

"I've just gone deaf."

"My firm represents a giant conglomerate that shall remain nameless, but which would very much like to own Poor Boys; they've been trying hard to buy out the Brocatos. However, the outcome is still very much in doubt."

"And therein, I gather, hangs a tale."

"One simple sentence, my dainty darling; one sentence tells the tale: some members of the board want to sell and some don't."

"Ah." She sat up straight, alert as a hunter. "And who might they be—these fractious board members?"

"Brocato family members. Every one of them."

"Ham was one?"

He nodded.

"Which side was he on?"

"Sorry—that's as much as I know."

She wondered why he had told her this—it was unethical, she supposed, violated some code or other. It was probably because he wanted to give her something, felt close to her tonight.

But he said, "Use it well, Thumbelina. This isn't meant to be a precedent-setter. I feel sentimental about Ham is all."

12

■ ■

Melody woke up on the sidewalk, Chris bending over her. "What's wrong? What is it?" he said, and she remembered. And would have passed out again if she could have.

"I don't know. I just got sick."

"Come on." He helped her up, and she could walk perfectly well, but she pretended; leaned on him all the way back to the apartment.

"I want to lie down."

"Maybe it's hypoglycemia."

She nodded. But when he brought her some toast, she found she couldn't eat. "I have to sleep," she said, and rolled over.

When she awoke again, she was alone. She didn't know if it had been half an hour or several hours, but she had slept soundly, had fallen asleep immediately. Lying there, on the smelly sleeping bag in the dingy apartment, she felt like puking her guts out. That was the phrase that came to her, and surely the muscle action couldn't have been that different, but it was sobs, not vomit, that were issuing from her belly; from her pelvis; perhaps from her toes. From the bottom of her being, each one as wrenching as a fit

144

of vomiting, but none so purging. And that was what she wanted. With each sob, she tried to cast out the knowledge that Ham was dead, free herself of this despair, this hopelessness. But it remained like an anchor in her soul, dragging her back, taking her again and again to the depths.

She screamed, she rolled around on the filthy bed, she tried to think what to do. No plan presented itself, but one thing became obvious: she couldn't bear to see Chris. Or the other two, Sue Ann and Randy. How was she going to pretend that nothing was wrong? Her *brother* was dead.

She said it to herself: *My brother is dead.*

But the words had no meaning at all, she couldn't begin to comprehend them, understood only the dolor that had invaded her body and captured her spirit. Understood only that she wanted to die if she had to hurt like this.

She got up to go to the bathroom and was surprised that she could still walk, her motor skills were intact, though she occasionally bounced off walls, but that was due to shock and lack of focus, she thought. She hadn't thought she'd have the strength to make it, had thought she might have to crawl. But strength she did have, she wasn't actually sick, just out of it.

On the way back she strayed into the kitchen and opened the refrigerator, not out of hunger and certainly not out of curiosity, but because that's where her automatic pilot happened to take her. There was some ketchup and mayonnaise, some bottled salad dressing, a box of days-old doughnuts. With no enthusiasm, she opened the box and closed it again, not even registering what kind of doughnuts were in it. And then she happened to notice a can of beer.

Barely realizing what she was doing, she popped the top and took a swallow. She took it back in the living room and over to a table where she could sit and look down at the street. She swallowed and stared, swallowed and stared, paying no attention to either action, simply letting her mind roam free, and it worked much better than she could have imagined. If anyone had asked her what she was thinking about, she couldn't have answered. Her mind, though not still—she was aware of movement—was al-

145

most literally blank. "Almost" because she knew it really wasn't, every now and then came into focus to catch the tail end of some thought, almost like seeing it with peripheral vision. But for the most part she didn't notice her thoughts, had found some inner space to go to, where she could cover her pain with gray clouds. When she finished the beer, she felt better.

She thought, *The thing to do is stay loaded.*

She could do that. She had money and she was tall enough to reach the bar. And she had the sense to know that no matter how ugly she looked to herself, for some outlandish reason there would be men who'd be interested, who'd offer her things. Drinks. Pot.

She could get by.

She went back into the kitchen and got a rock-hard doughnut, knowing she couldn't afford to fall off any bar stools. If someone took her to a hospital, or some juvenile facility, or jail, her parents would find her and she was dead. So she had to remember to eat. It was the only thing she did have to remember except a key . . . but there wasn't one.

Who cared? She probably wouldn't be coming back here anyway. She had no idea where she'd sleep that night. Maybe outside. By the river. In an alley. She'd be too wasted to notice.

She found her sunglasses and, slipping them on, stepped into the glare, biting into the doughnut, feeling it give beneath her teeth, crunching it but not tasting. She threw it out. She could get a Lucky Dog. She'd lived in New Orleans all her life and never had one. The thought almost cheered her up.

She ate the hot dog, went into an Irish bar and got a beer. But not soon enough. The dog had hit her stomach with a thump that dislodged feelings, stirred up thoughts—about what it meant that Ham was dead, what that would do to her life. She drank quickly. She couldn't think about that.

A man sitting two stools down from her, a short guy with muscles and a tan, played an Irish song on the jukebox. The sadness of it penetrated every cell of Melody's body, locked her into a grim spasm of desperation so strong, so severe that if she didn't tense all her muscles, keep them tight, not give a millimeter, she'd fly apart,

146

faint again, maybe melt, she didn't know; she just knew she had to stay tight to keep it together.

The man said, "You cold?"

She shook her head.

"You looked cold. Holding your elbows, curling up almost."

She knew she was making a spectacle of herself.

She tried to uncurl but couldn't. "The song is so sad."

"That it is," he said. "That it is." As if that was the only fact he knew in the universe. Melody wished he would talk to her—about anything, it didn't matter much. It might be distracting.

She wanted to talk to someone about Ham, to somehow rid herself of this horrible burden she was carrying, but she reminded herself anew that she had no friends, no boyfriend, no family. She was alone. Except for Chris, of course, and she couldn't talk to him. A thing like a roach, all crawly and ugly, lodged in her throat when she thought of it. Wasn't there anybody?

Madeleine Richard!

But no, not Madeleine Richard. She'd already been through that. Richard would turn her in.

She got another beer. Was there someone in the Quarter? Surely there was someone. How could a musician not know someone in the Quarter? A musician and a sister of Ham Brocato's. Ham! Of course. She did know someone—someone Ham and Ti-Belle knew. Someone she probably couldn't trust, but who couldn't be bothered turning her in either. Somebody she'd always liked, who was as much an outlaw as she was.

He lived way on the other side of the Quarter, near North Rampart, dangerously close to Treme. Ham had told her never to walk there alone, but Ham hadn't known that one day soon she was going to be completely alone, no one to walk with, no one even to lecture her, as he had.

■

He didn't answer his bell. But where would he be? Nowhere.

She knew he had to be home—he didn't go anywhere else anymore, except to Ham's once a week. It was very sad, Ham had said—the wreck of a fine musician. Ti-Belle had laughed: "Another of Ham's strays."

She looked through the courtyard gate—yes! There he was, in a ridiculously brief blue bathing suit, eyes closed, stretched out in the sun, skin like milk, and a squeeze bottle of sunscreen right beside him. Why was he bothering? she wondered. He was always going to look like *pompano en papillote*.

"Andy! Andy, it's me! Melody."

He didn't budge.

"Andy Fike! Wake up!"

A kid about her age, black, but somehow nothing like Joel, came ambling down the street. "Wha's wrong, baby—your boyfriend throw you out?"

"No. I just, uh—dropped by."

The kid moved closer.

She noticed that two more black guys, also their age give or take, were about to join them. Should she be worried? "What do you want?" she said.

"I don't want nothin'. Just thought you might need some help."

She had on the sunglasses, but she glared anyway. It made her feel powerful. She planted her feet about a foot apart and faced him. "Thanks, anyway. I'm fine." She kept glaring. The other two were getting closer.

"Hey, DeJuan," one of them shouted, "what you got down there?"

He gave Melody one last, assessing stare. "Dyke," he shouted. "Just some ol' dyke."

He trotted off to his friends. Melody knew it was crazy, but her feelings were hurt.

Where does he get off calling me a dyke? He didn't interview me on my sexual preferences. Why would he say a thing like that?

Andy Fike rolled over and blinked. "Who's that? Wha's happenin'?"

"Andy, let me in, godammit! It's Melody." Her legs were beginning to shake. DeJuan and his friends were long gone and probably hadn't meant any harm in the first place, but tell that to her body. Sweat was breaking out around her hairline, in her palms.

"Melody? Melody fucking Brocato?"

"Oh, shit, I shouldn't have come here." She turned and started to run, feeling as if she'd like to run all the way to the river and jump in; she'd had enough.

"What'd I say? Hey, Melody, come back. Melody, dammit, come back if it's you!"

For some reason, she turned around and looked at him. A jockstrap, or something white, was showing underneath the bathing suit. His hair stood up in a million unintentional spikes—not punk, just pathetic—going every which way. He was as pale and skinny as a straw.

He said, "Melody?" again, as if she was about as likely to come calling as the governor.

"You were expecting Liza Minelli, maybe?" One of his favorites, Liza.

"You're a blonde!"

And somehow he sounded so comical, so outraged, that she burst out laughing, fear and anger momentarily vanquished.

"You like the look?"

"That's your voice. I know that's your voice. Take the glasses off."

She complied.

"Jesus Christ! Say something."

Instead, she sang to him, a line or two from Janis:

> "Oh, Lord, won't you buy me a Mercedes-Benz—
> My friends all have Porsches, I must make amends."

"Holy Christ! That's the most amazing transformation I've ever seen in my life."

Melody giggled, unexpectedly pleased with herself. "Really? You really didn't recognize me?"

"I still don't. Come closer."

She walked toward him. He scrutinized her face. "Well, I guess so. I guess I can see it a little bit. But, honey, you could fool your own mother with that getup."

"You wouldn't rat on me, would you, Andy?"

He didn't answer for a moment, apparently thinking it over. "Come in a minute. I think we've got to talk."

She went in the gate. "I came to see you, Andy. You're the only person in the world I trust." That was a lie, but maybe it would keep his trap shut.

"You smell like a brewery."

She grinned, all sophistication and nonchalance. "You got another beer?"

He sighed. "All right. Wait here."

"No! Forget it."

Instantly seeing through her, he said, "I'm not going to call your parents. Come on—watch me through the door."

For some reason, he didn't want her inside—but that was okay because she had a feeling it would depress her. When he had gotten them each a beer, he said, "I'm sorry about your brother."

She looked down at the cheap table at which they were sitting, nodding. She couldn't manage to say anything.

"You know the whole city's looking for you."

She nodded again, feeling accused.

"Well? Tell Papa. Why'd you run away?"

Oh, God, I should have known! Why didn't I think of this?

It honestly hadn't occurred to her that he'd ask this.

It was the beer. I shouldn't have come here half drunk.

She was now sober enough to realize it had been a stupid idea, an alcoholic whim she should have left alone. And yet . . . she still wanted to talk to someone. She said, "I don't want to talk about it."

"Honey, you're being silly. You want everyone to think you did it?" He spoke in the shrill, overexcited voice of the truly irritating know-it-all queen. She wanted to pop him one, but suddenly it occurred to her that she could say what she was thinking—things could hardly get worse.

150

"Oh, don't be such a queen."

To her surprise, he laughed, preening a little; apparently pleased. "Well, did you do it?"

"I come here for help and this is what I get? Of course I didn't do it. I must have been crazy." She got up and started to leave.

"Mel, wait a minute. You're in trouble, kid."

"What are you going to do about it?"

"I'm going to light up a doobie. You woman enough for that?"

She sat back down. The beer wasn't really doing it right now. "That's the best offer I've had all day."

He pulled a joint out of his shoe, which he'd taken off to sunbathe.

Melody didn't have much in mind about what to do with her life, had started to think of it as fragments, laced together with beer and pot when she could get it. She wasn't even interested in singing right now. She was so depressed it even occurred to her to go home—but the consequences of that seemed far too much to bear.

I could get raped sleeping outside, she told herself.

But she couldn't imagine being raped. And she could imagine facing her parents today. Tomorrow. Any time, this wasn't about time. She could never face them again.

But I have no place else to go!

Back to Chris's? Somehow, that sounded almost as bad. She couldn't be in love, feeling the way she did, knowing what she knew, being who she was. She didn't even think she could sing, and they wouldn't let her stay there if she didn't sing and she didn't . . . put out? The phrase had popped into her mind, but surely it didn't apply. Chris wasn't like that.

The one person in the world she really wanted to see was Ti-Belle. But she didn't want to talk to Ti-Belle. No way she was going to talk to anyone about what had happened, and that's what they'd want to know about.

She wanted to see Ti-Belle's set tomorrow, that was what she wanted. Was she crazy to go?

She was way too stoned to know. She looked at Andy. Should she go home? Should she ask him if she should go home? Talk about it with him?

He was as stoned as she was, and it gave him a consummately silly expression.

"Mel," he said, "what's a girl with bruises around her belly button?"

She shook her head, at a loss for words, not believing he was trying to tell her a joke right now.

"A blonde with a blond boyfriend." He brushed her thigh with his fingers. "You can appreciate that, right?" He fingered her hair and, feeling how heavy it was with spray and gel, pulled his hand back in disgust. "Icccch."

"Andy, I've got to go. You're not gonna rat on me, are you?"

"Wait a minute. You never did say why you wanted to see me. You need a place to stay?"

"No thanks. I've got a blond boyfriend."

Oh, shit! Why did I say that?

"Oh-la-la."

"I'm just kidding. I've got to leave town, I guess. I just wanted . . . to say good-bye to somebody."

"Come here, honey. Give me a hug."

Ichhh.

"I'm going to miss my bus."

She ran all the way to the river side of Bourbon Street, where there were places she knew she could get served. But suddenly she was unaccountably tired. She needed to sleep again. Where to go?

By the river. Where she could feel the sun, where the river itself would be a warm and comforting presence, like the lap of a giant mother. She was so sleepy she could barely walk. But she did, somehow, more or less in a daze, until she got to the levee, where she curled up on the grass just behind the Café du Monde, looking, she hoped, not at all like a drunken, runaway murder suspect, just an afternoon stroller having a little nap.

She could hear the drone of bees, she thought, though maybe it was machinery somewhere, and occasionally whistles blew on the river, whistles on the paddleboats. The sun felt delicious, gold and lovely on her skin. The air hung heavy, river air. She felt like a baby, snug in a crib.

She awoke slowly, not too much later, she thought, but she didn't have a watch and didn't care anyway. She wasn't scheduled to bow to the queen today.

She was aware that something had awakened her, of a vague feeling of uneasiness starting to give way to dread. Filled with panic, she opened her eyes, tightened her body. A man was sitting close to her, too close to blame it on coincidence. He was a grown man, not a boy, a white man in his thirties, perhaps, or maybe his forties—all men that old simply looked alien. This one wore khakis and a madras button-down shirt, not filthy but limp, as if they'd been worn a few times. He had a beard and glasses, slightly greasy hair. He was fat and probably tall too, and staring at her. She gasped; her whole body twitched. She sat up, ready to defend herself.

"You could have gotten hurt," he said, "lying out here like that."

She was afraid of him, didn't know what to say. She started to slide away on her butt.

"I had to run off a group of black guys talking about what they'd like to do to you. Young lady, this is New Orleans—you can't just go sleeping in public."

Melody was sober or at least beginning to be—sober enough to have a dull, thudding headache. Whereas before, she had thought she would look like a happy tourist who lay down after an enormous lunch and happened to doze off, now she thought she must have looked like a junkie, probably a junkie prostitute, some sort of street flotsam who'd be treated as such, preyed on by criminals, rousted by cops—or worse, arrested. She must look that way to this man.

"Thank you," she said, and started to get up, looking around to see if they were alone.

He stood also. "I told 'em I was your father. After I sat down, you were okay, but don't you do that again. You're not going to be so lucky next time."

It sounded like a threat. She tried to smile. There were people around but she still wasn't sure how to extract herself. "Thanks," she said. "I'll be careful."

He held out his hand to shake, but she thought, *What if I step closer and he takes my hand and grabs me? And then tells people he's my father?*

She had to shake, there wasn't any choice. She started to step forward, but at the last minute changed her mind. Turned and ran. But before she ran, reluctant entirely to abandon the manners she'd had drummed into her every day of her life, she said, " 'Bye."

She ran down the Moonwalk, past it, and at first it was fun. There was a banjoist there, a white man playing "Ol' Man River," but he started talking as she ran past:

"You know, folks, when you go to Disneyland, you expect to see Mickey Mouse—come to New Orleans, you get to see me."

It was funny, though she knew it wouldn't have been in any other circumstance. But running by like that, just getting a glimpse, it had a life-in-the-city feel to it. She was of the city herself, of its sidewalks and pavement. She had winged feet, like Mercury, would probably lift off, she was going so fast.

She ran through Woldenberg Park almost to the aquarium, across the streetcar tracks, down Bienville Street and to the corner of North Peters. She had a choice now—she could go to Canal or double back. But toward Canal the street was nearly deserted. She doubled back, still flying, but flying slower now, past the aquarium parking lot . . .

Why wasn't there a goddess with winged feet? There was Diana of the Hunt, surely she had to run fast . . .

I am Diana!

But if I'm a goddess, why do I feel like throwing up?

She slowed down, looked behind her. No sign of the man. And she did throw up, in the gutter.

She looked behind her again, and, pretty sure she wasn't being followed, ducked into Tower Records to catch her breath. Her throat hurt from vomiting and she wondered if she stank. She examined her clothing. It seemed okay, but her breath must be something else. She went out to Walgreen's and got some mints.

She was aware, once again, of the need to eat; not hunger, just an empty feeling that told her she'd better do it if she intended to drink some more. She knew a cheap place, and there was just time to get there before it closed. She got some red beans and rice, thinking soft and squishy food would be easy to get down, but it wasn't. She had no appetite at all, and she kept thinking of Ham, which made her throat close. She could only get down a bite or two.

She really needed to eat. She kept telling this to herself. Two lines came to her that rhymed: *I lost my brother today. I miss my brother the worst kind of way.*

And she knew what she had to do. She would write a song. *Blues for a Brother.* It would be her tribute to Ham. But even as she thought that, she knew that wasn't the main thing. She had to have a way to grapple with this agony, to get it out of her, to be done with it. It wouldn't work, she knew that; she'd written plenty of songs about lesser pains in her young unhappy life, and the emotions hadn't gone away.

There wasn't any choice. Once the fit was upon her there was no stopping. It gnawed at her, chewed at her, wound her up and spun her around, wouldn't let go until it was done, until it had spent its fury and left her sweaty and breathing hard.

She needed paper—her napkin? No, she needed lots. Back to Walgreen's, where she bought a thick notebook and a couple of Bics, the black ones she preferred. She never used pencils, they made ugly gray marks.

Now what?

Kaldi's. There was plenty of light there and she could get coffee. Her head ached from the beer and tears—mostly the tears, she was pretty sure. Kaldi's meant crossing to the back end of the Quarter, walking nearly to Esplanade, and she was impatient: Phrases were coming, little bits of melody. The first two lines, the ones she got in the restaurant, were hopeless. This was going to be the best song she'd ever written, a classic, like "Jambalaya." Irma Thomas herself would sing it; so would Charmaine Neville, and Marcia Ball—everybody would. It was going to be that good, Melody could feel it; her mind was humming, it was boiling inside her.

But she had to put it aside for the walk, had to remember to be on the lookout, ready to duck if she ran into anyone she knew.

The coffeehouse had carrot cake, and to her surprise it looked good to her. She got some, and a cappuccino. Sweet things would go down, it turned out. She ate every crumb of the cake and felt better; it didn't seem right, but she felt almost okay. As long as she didn't think about anything.

She sat there a long time, she didn't really know how long. Maybe an hour, maybe three. She drank two cappuccinos and quite a bit of mineral water. The song started to take shape. Well, sort of. The first ideas she'd had now seemed sophomoric, but she was getting more; they were coming thick and fast. Better ones; more complex imagery. She wrote a couple of versions, three or four verses, then new ones. Her mind wouldn't stop.

But suddenly her body gave out. This had happened before, when she practiced with Joel and Doug. She'd be going along great when all of a sudden everything turned to jelly—arms, shoulders, legs—and she felt like throwing up. Once she actually had thrown up, causing both guys to worry that she was pregnant. Right now she felt awful. Her mouth was full of acid coffee taste and her stomach hurt. She went outside to get some air.

Okay. Better. She wasn't going to throw up, but what she needed was a shower. Should she go back to the band's place? They wouldn't be there, for one thing—it was too early. For another, she didn't want to. Didn't know why she didn't, just didn't. She started to feel panicky. Where the hell was she going to sleep tonight? Not outside. Not after what had happened with the weird guy who told her to be careful.

I'll think of something.

She started walking, trying not to think, especially about that. She walked toward Jackson Square, toward the cathedral, then turned away. She wanted to see Chris, just eyeball him. If she found the band, they'd want to know why she'd fainted and why she'd run away and shit like that. Even having someone ask how she felt now, was she okay, would be an intrusion she couldn't handle.

She didn't need anybody, she didn't want anybody. Realizing it, she smiled, threw up her arms in triumph. This felt pretty good.

A hell of a lot better than the loneliness of yesterday. As her tiredness seeped away, the cramped, spent feeling she got after hours of focusing was replaced with the satisfaction of having done good work. She felt almost exhilarated.

She stopped to listen to a saxophone player, a black man, middle-aged, kind of round and chubby-cheeked. He was good, and it made her sad that he had to play on the street. Would there be a job for him in her band? Probably not, she probably wouldn't have horns. She thought of Ham and his dream, Second Line Square, and that made her sad too. But still, it was a good thought. She'd carry on his work, maybe form her own foundation; she'd put that side of him in the song.

The man came to the end of his song. "Baby, you want to get stoned?"

Melody nodded, still under the spell of the music.

"Come on. We'll go to my place."

"I thought you meant here. Maybe by the river."

"No, no, I'm stayin' with a friend. Got some weed back at the place."

Melody nodded and fell into step.

Am I crazy? she wondered.

But the thrill of adventure—and perhaps, just perhaps, the edge of depression—outweighed what she knew to be good sense.

"Herbie," the musician said. He offered to shake. "What's yo' name?"

"Janis."

She couldn't think of anything for a while, finally said, "I liked your number."

He shrugged. "Been doin' it all my life. Don't pay nothin'. I just do it."

She pondered what he was saying, but couldn't make sense of it. They walked in silence, and when they got to the friend's place, Melody thought it must be a very close friend indeed. It was one room with nothing in it but a double mattress, a couple of night tables, and a chair. The sheets on the mattress looked pretty grimy.

Herbie sat down on it and rolled a joint. Gingerly, Melody took the chair. Finally she got up the nerve to ask, "Did you mean you play music because you have to? Because there's something in you that has to?"

"Huh?"

"I mean, you said, 'I just do it,' even though it doesn't pay. I was wondering what you meant."

"I'm wonderin' what *you* mean." He offered her a fat joint.

"I don't know." She laughed. "I don't know what I mean."

She did know, but she couldn't make herself understood. She felt small and inadequate. Decidedly unhip. Herbie was a man who probably used music as language, rather than words, and had little need to talk about the fact.

"Hey, baby, you okay?" he said.

She nodded, found she couldn't speak anyway. The grimy sheets were starting to look sort of poetic, like they could be the inspiration for a line in a song.

Somebody'd beaten her to "Empty Bed Blues." Something less obvious anyway, something about grinding poverty and barely scraping along.

"Why don't you come over here and sit by me?"

Melody heard steps on the stairs outside. Herbie's friend? Would the two of them gang-rape her? Or was it a woman, a jealous woman who'd stab her lover and his . . . holy shit, his what? *Guest?*

Get real, Melody.

"Janis? Come here, babe." He patted the mattress beside him.

Melody's heart pounded like John Henry's hammer. *I have to get out of here.*

"What's wrong? What's wrong, Janis? Everything's all right, baby. Ol' Herbie ain' gon' let nothin' happen to you."

Why was he asking her what was wrong? And why was he taking that smarmy tone? It wouldn't fool a two-year-old.

She got up and bolted. Opened the door, slammed it behind her, and flew three flights down to the bottom, passing a young black man in a baseball cap, nearly knocking him off his pins. He called after her, "Hey, motherfucker!"

But not a word out of Herbie. She ran all the way back to

Bourbon Street, where she could blend into the crowd, and even then kept looking around her. She bought a praline, and then another, and walked endlessly, around and around this block and that, up and down, neck constantly swiveling for Herbie and his band of rapists in baseball caps.

When she started to come down from the pot, she began to realize what an ass she'd been—going to a strange man's apartment, fleeing, all of it. There wasn't a piece of it she could make sense of, and she felt a fool. The independent, exhilarated feeling had drained off, and what she wanted now was a pair of arms around her. She thought briefly of her mother.

Ha! Fat chance.

She wanted to cry. To cry into someone's shoulder and have her hair stroked and no questions asked. She went back to the band's apartment, as she'd known she would all along.

It was dark when she got there, and she thought that was good. If they were asleep, Chris would let her in and she could just slip into bed beside him and hang onto him and that would be that.

She knocked a long time before he answered. "Who the hell is it?"

"Melo—Janis!"

The door opened so fast a cool breeze brushed her cheek. He was naked. "You split on me."

"I had to. I'm sorry, I—"

"Listen, I'm with someone else."

She stared, not taking it in. She'd only been gone twelve hours, thirteen, fourteen at the most. "Someone else?"

He shrugged. She kept staring, trying to process the information.

Finally she said, whispering, barely able to make the sounds, "Could I sleep on the couch?"

He stepped aside and padded back to the mattress on the bed. Vaguely, Melody was aware of another face shining somewhere in the bedding. But she caught only a glimpse; she was fascinated by the sight of Chris's naked backside, smooth and nearly white in the dark.

I've never seen that before, she thought, and almost keeled over from

159

the pain of it, her first sight of a lover's butt, yet she couldn't enjoy it because her brother was dead and she had no family or friends. And the lover was headed toward someone else. The enormity of it, the way it all piled in like that, put her on overload. She miscalculated and fell on her way to the couch. Now she had humiliation to add to the pile. She felt the sobs beginning to rise as she picked herself up and stumbled toward the bathroom, making a racket, bumping into things, unable to cork the deep, ugly sounds from her throat, the sounds of a baby with croup struggling for breath. Yet even so, she heard Randy and Sue Ann fucking in the bedroom.

That's it. I'm going to die, she thought, as she turned on the hot water. That was the last thought she had. She tore off her clothes, stood in the shower, sobbing her guts up, standing there till her fingers wrinkled, and then made herself a bed of wet towels and curled up in the tub. Her mind was a perfect blank, aware only of the water and the rhythmic sounds of her grief.

13

It was late and everyone had gone when the phone rang. George had fallen asleep fully dressed, on top of the covers, and Patty was applying acupressure to her face. She had learned a system guaranteed to keep her skin youthful to her dying day, and it might be helping, but it wasn't the answer. The signs were starting—ten more years and she'd have to have her face done; she was resigned to it. Still, she made tiny circles at a dozen pressure points every night.

People had called all day, of course, but the phone had stopped ringing sometime ago. Surely only one person would call this late. George sat up in bed: "Melody!" But he was groggy with drink and grief, and it was Patty who got to the phone first.

"Patty? Andy Fike."

"Who?"

"We've met. We've met several times. Don't you remember me?"

Patty was furious. The caller was drunk or otherwise loaded, and had a hell of a nerve. This was a house of mourning. But something, she didn't know what, told her not to hang up. "I'm

161

afraid I don't," she said, unable to keep the frost from her voice.

"I'm Ham and Ti-Belle's housecleaner."

A dim memory emerged, of someone pale and lanky, a little unhealthy-looking. "I see."

"Shit, I don't know why I'm doing this. A kid needs its mother, that's why. She's too damn young to be on the streets."

"Melody? You're calling about Melody?"

"Look. I read the papers and all." His voice was lower and suddenly he sounded sober. "I just wanted you to know she's all right."

"Is she with you?" Patty could hear the urgency in her voice. She hadn't meant to telegraph her terror.

"No. God, no, she's not with me. But she came over today. I saw her."

"What did she want? Why did she come to you?"

"She's a friend of mine." He was suddenly defensive.

"Do you know where she is?" Patty was practically yelling.

"Hell, no, I don't know where she is. Jesus, try to do some people a favor—" He hung up.

She simply stood there, holding the phone in her hand, staring at it, and felt George's arms go around her, supporting her. It was an unaccustomed gesture.

He said, "You look like you're about to fall."

"She's okay."

"Come on. Let's sit down and talk about it." Gently, he led her to the bed. He was so solicitous, so different from his usual self. Dignified in his grief, Patty thought. Suddenly she felt the loss of this George, the one who was present now, yet normally absent from their daily life. Having him now, like this, made her realize once again how much she was missing, and any happiness she might have felt at the news of Melody was dispelled. Nor was the irony of it lost on her.

I'm crazy, she thought. *This is why I'm not happy. Because I'm crazy. I can't be happy. I don't know how.*

And yet she knew that was wrong too, that no woman could be happy with the everyday George, the one she lived with. She told the story of the phone call.

George was excited. "Where does he live? If she went to visit him, that gives us a starting point."

"Well, here, I guess—I don't see how he could have cleaned for Ham if he didn't."

"Let's call Ti-Belle and ask her." He started to dial, but Patty stopped him.

"George, wait. If Melody's in New Orleans, we can communicate with her."

"What do you mean?"

"Let's call the *Times-Picayune* and make a plea. Beg her to come home."

He stared at her as if she had just grown horns. *He thinks I'm stupid*, she thought, and maybe he did, usually. Maybe that explained his dumbfounded expression.

"That has some merit," he said finally. "That really has some merit."

Patty fairly preened.

"They'll talk to us and they'll run it—they've been pestering us all day. This way, we control the situation."

He called the paper. Without consulting Patty, he issued the statement:

"Melody's mother and I want to say something to our daughter. We love you, Melody. We miss you. Please come home to us. We need you."

Just those few simple words. Patty listened with pride as he evaded the inevitable questions: Was Melody's disappearance connected with Ham's death? Was there fear that she'd been kidnapped? Had she gotten along well with her brother?

Everything short of, "Why'd she kill him?"

"George," she said when he had hung up, "we have to call that detective. Langdon—the one at Ham's party."

"About Andy, you mean? No."

"No?" Patty didn't get it. "But maybe he's the one. Maybe he kidnapped her."

"We're not leaving it to the damn cops." He started to put on his shoes. "Call Ti-Belle, will you? Get his address."

Not sure what he was planning, Patty didn't protest, didn't

dare confront him. She dialed Ti-Belle. "No answer."

He grabbed a phone book. "Here it is. Andy Fike—shit. Burgundy Street."

It wasn't a terrible neighborhood, but it wasn't the sort they'd normally visit. George looked at his watch. "I'll be back in—" He stopped. "No. Come with me."

Patty couldn't believe what she was hearing. "Come with you?"

"To drive. I don't want to try parking there."

"What are we going to do?" But it didn't matter, as long as they were doing it together. She had already pulled on jeans. She zipped up and looked for a T-shirt.

They went downstairs and she watched George go into his study, take something from a desk drawer and pocket it.

"What's that?"

"A gun," he said casually.

"A gun? For what?"

"A gun, Patty. Did you think I said nun?" The old George. "You have one—why shouldn't I?"

"I just didn't know you did."

"There's a lot of things you don't know about me."

He could say that again, and he probably would. He said it often. He seemed to like it that way.

They didn't speak on the way to the Quarter. When they had pulled up in front of Andy Fike's building, George said, "Drive around the block until I come out. If she's in there, I'll have her in ten minutes. If I'm not out in fifteen, call Langdon."

George was a big strong man who could do anything, so far as Patty could see. If anyone could pull this off, he could. But if Fike had kidnapped Melody, he wasn't your everyday business problem. Patty had a frisson. She said, "George. I love you."

He gave her a half smile and a chin chuck.

"This guy might have killed Ham." She didn't know why she said it, she knew he had thought of it. It sounded like nagging, and she wished she could take it back.

He was out of the car now, his back toward her. He made an

impatient gesture at shoulder level. Quick, dirty, and eloquent: "Leave me alone."

That was George. Mr. Leave-Me-Alone. But right now she felt oddly bonded with him; they were in this together, rescuing their daughter. She drove.

He was on the sidewalk the second time around, alone. He pushed her out of the driver's seat, obviously having a need to control something, to assert himself with a piece of heavy machinery. He accelerated way too fast for the neighborhood.

"God, what a dump!" he said.

"She wasn't there?"

"Not now, and God help her if she ever was."

"Why'd the guy call us?"

He shrugged. "He's an addict. Maybe he was trying to get money. Did he ask you for any?"

"No. George, maybe she was never there. Maybe Fike's like one of those people who confess to crimes to make themselves feel important."

"Shut up!" His face was a study in dark fury, and suddenly Patty understood how much he had wanted Melody to be there, realized how out of character it had been for her gray-haired, dignified husband to storm a Quarter apartment with a gun. He was hurting. Beguiled by the action, she'd forgotten that. Overcome with a need to help, to make him feel better, she rubbed his leg. That was all she dared do.

Finally she said, "Are you hungry?"

He didn't answer at first. After twenty blocks or so, miles it seemed like, he said, "Yeah."

"Yeah?" She'd forgotten what she asked.

"I'm starved."

"Me too." Neither of them had eaten during the day.

When they reached home, they went in and fixed themselves sandwiches, ham for him, roast beef for her, with potato salad on the side. There was plenty of everything today. It was a house of mourning.

Sitting with her husband, munching in the middle of the night,

Patty forgot Ham, forgot even Melody. For a while she felt euphoric, knowing they were together, that in some way he was enjoying her company.

"Patty, I'm going to find her." He looked so impossibly sad. "If Fike didn't lie, she's here. We're her parents, we can find her."

He had said "we" again. Patty tried not to show emotion, to let him know how much that meant to her. She nodded solemnly. "Yes. If we can't, nobody can."

He seemed to perk up at that, to want so much to believe her that he actually did. He gave her another half smile, and she would have given her trademark blond hair to see a real smile, would have turned backflips while baking an apple pie, if he'd been into that sort of thing. But he wasn't, and, despite this afternoon's encounter, sex didn't tempt him either. Silence was what he seemed to want from her. Tonight she gave it willingly, thinking of it as "silent support."

Tomorrow, together, they would find their child.

■

"Ti-Belle, honey, you're gettin' yourself in a tizzy."

She wasn't in a tizzy, she was in a fury. And with Nick, of all people. *Nick, who I'd have killed to be with* — oops, don't say that, Ti-Belle.

Well, it's true. I'd have killed to be with him before I was. This is the fucking man of my dreams. How can he be such a shit? "Tizzy? That's all you can say?"

"Baby, calm down. Try to tell me slowly what you're so upset about."

"I can't, goddammit! I can't *speak* without sputtering!"

"Honey, can I get you a drink or anything?"

He was so damn solicitous she could puke. This was the way he was — she was learning that about him. He wouldn't confront, he just got nicer and nicer — and farther away from the subject.

"Did it ever occur to you I might be a suspect in my lover's murder?"

"Well, honey, I don't suspect you. How could I?"

"That is the point, Nick Anglime — don't you see that?" Her voice had taken on a quality that was belligerent and whiny at the same time. It was probably the very definition of shrewish, she thought, but she could no more stop herself than turn black. The pressure had built and something had to blow. "Wait a minute, dammit."

She went in the bathroom and splashed her face and counted to ten. She still felt just as nutty and furious as she had before, so she did it again. And then she did it a third time.

When she came out, she said, "Yes. You can get me a drink."

He was on the floor of the library, in the lotus position. He unwound his long, muscular legs. "Gin and tonic?"

She nodded, went to the open window and breathed in jasmine. She was still furious, but she thought if she sipped the drink, she might be able to speak without sputtering.

"Okay," she said when he handed it to her. She composed herself, remaining near the window. She thought the tableau probably looked romantic, and didn't want to move. She was wearing a retro-style dress, white with old-fashioned "princess lines" and a halter top, short flared skirt. Marilyn Monroe style. She hadn't exactly dressed for pleading for her life, but as long as she was reduced to that, the dress was probably a plus.

"Okay, look. We were together when Ham was getting killed. Therefore, I couldn't have done it. So a cop asks where you were when Ham was killed, and you don't even alibi me."

"Sweet cakes, I didn't get the feelin' she was interested in you —I kind of got the idea she thought I might have been the guilty party."

" 'Oh, Ti-Belle, you selfish bitch. Ti-Belle, you must think the world revolves around you.' Do you have to be so goddamn judgmental, Nick Anglime?"

"Honey, could we start over? I don't remember calling you a bitch."

"You said all I ever do is think about myself. Well, I'll tell you something—I protected you. I said I was with someone else."

"Baby, I don't mean to nitpick, but doesn't that leave me without an alibi?"

"You! You live here with an entourage of ten people. You don't need me." She'd flown off the handle when she heard

Langdon had seen Nick. She'd given her Johnny Murphy's name to hide the affair, but now it was obvious the cops knew anyway. So if they knew she'd lied about Johnny, and Nick didn't alibi her, where did that leave her?

"Sweetheart, I'm real sorry I made you mad. What can I do for you right now?"

"Placate, placate, placate. All you know how to do is placate."

"You haven't known me long enough to know what I know how to do." For the first time his voice held anger, a sulky anger, the kind that simmered and bubbled. Ti-Belle's heart speeded up; she realized she was frightened. The last thing she wanted was to turn him against her.

But she had to get her point across. "Look, Nick. I just don't see why you didn't tell her I was with you. What could be simpler?"

"Well, I didn't know what you'd told her, for one thing."

"You could have at least set it up, just in case. 'I was with a friend,' something like that. Now, if you have to say it was me, it'll sound like you made it up."

"I didn't think of that, okay? The woman made me nervous."

"Made *you* nervous? You, Nick Anglime? Are you crazy? That cop was slobbering like a teenager—you could have told her you were with *her* and she'd have believed you."

"Look, how am I supposed to alibi you when I can't? Am I supposed to perjure myself for you? Is that the next step?" Now he was the furious one. But why? Ti-Belle couldn't figure it out. She was the one with the beef.

"Nick, what are you getting so upset about? One minute you're a perfect little lamb and the next you're acting like a crazy man."

"You want me to lie for you—is that it? Is that what you're mad about—that I didn't lie?"

"What are you talking about?"

"I'm talking about the fact that you left for an hour and a half in the middle of what was supposed to be a daring weekday rendezvous—which was your idea in the first place. Frankly, I'm starting to wonder if I was set up."

"Set up! How dare you!"

"Well, what the hell else am I supposed to think?"

He was deserting her. She felt her chest start to heave. "You don't trust me."

"Why don't you just tell me, then—where the hell did you go Wednesday?"

"I went to get a dress to wear to Ham's damn party—isn't that what I told you I did?"

"Yes, ma'am, you did tell me that. But then when you didn't come back with any packages, I got to thinkin' maybe you had another lover on the side."

"Shit!" Ti-Belle pulled a book out of the nearest bookshelf and threw it at him, the first book that came to hand—she didn't care if it was a first edition *Moby Dick*.

It caught him in the chest and he clutched it to his body like a baby. "Don't *ever* throw my things! Don't *do* that ever again!"

"I'm *sorry*."

Like hell I am.

"This was the dress I bought, okay? I didn't think you'd be interested in my damn dress. I didn't want you to think I'm one of those women who just shops, shops, shops all the time. So I left it in the car, is that okay?"

"It just seems pretty weird that you'd leave in the middle of things like that."

"Damn you! I take three days off, turn my life upside down to be with you, and I just have this one thing to do from my real life—"

"Okay. Okay, Ti-Belle." He was backing away.

She wondered if she was coming on too strong. But probably not, she thought. The men she attracted weren't afraid of a strong woman. She liked that about them—about Nick. Her anger was losing steam. "Okay what?" she said.

"Okay, I'm sorry. I'm really sorry. I did the wrong thing and I'm sorry."

She felt the muscles in her chest start to loosen. Her anger was ebbing as swiftly as it had gathered. She smiled at him, happy they were making up. "Really?"

"Really."

"I'm sorry I got mad."

"You've been under pressure."

She nodded, felt a flash of misery at the mention of Ham, and quickly turned her mind off. That's what she'd been doing when the subject of Ham came up; the way she'd taught herself to get through.

Nick came over and put his hands on her waist, set off so well by the white dress. But it was a tentative gesture. She felt the indecision, perhaps the fear, in his fingertips. He said, "What can I do for you, baby?"

Come out of your damn shell.

She wasn't about to say it aloud. She loved this man; loved him much more than she'd loved Ham, miles more than she'd loved anyone she'd met in her young life, and she desperately wanted to be with him. But he was so different from her. Ti-Belle wanted to be out every night in every joint in New Orleans with every musician for miles around; and all Nick wanted to do was stay home and read and meditate. Was it age? she wondered. Nick really was getting on—maybe he just didn't have the energy she had. But a person didn't have to surrender to that. She'd seen other people in their forties who were young and fun; surely that was the healthy way to be.

He'd probably picked her because she made him feel young. Because she was young, and youth was contagious. She could make it contagious anyway. She could be good for him. She was determined to. She was going to keep him just as young as he wanted her to, even if he only wanted it subconsciously. She knew that was why he wanted her—what else could it be?—and the way to keep him was to accept that and be who she was and help him be all he could be.

"Sing with me," she said.

"Do what?"

"Do wha'?" she mimicked, and laughed delightedly. He was so cute when he was like this. "You sound like some funny old cartoon character."

"You want to sing? Now?" He sounded baffled.

"Sure? Don't you ever sing for pleasure? It helps me get out of the dumps."

"You're not mad at me anymore?" He was smiling. He looked ten years younger. Ti-Belle made a silent vow to remember the effect it had when she got mad.

"Well, I won't be mad if you'll tell that big ol' cop the truth."

An odd expression flicked over his face—confusion, perhaps? Ti-Belle couldn't be sure. He replaced it with a smile, a weak one, but recognizable. "Come on. Let's sing."

They went into the music room and Ti-Belle sat at the Bosendorfer. While he tuned his guitar, she played a couple of his old songs to get him in the mood. Even before he was finished, before the instrument was ready, he couldn't help it, he started singing along.

They did his songs and one or two of hers, some old stuff—Beatles and Rolling Stones—and a little Neville Brothers. Ti-Belle had actually had an agenda when she suggested the little singalong, but she had so much fun, she forgot she'd been plotting and planning. The whole thing just seemed natural.

"We're great together!" She was beside herself.

He gave her another of his almost-smiles. "Not bad, hon."

"Oh, come on, Nick, tell me you aren't having the time of your life."

"It's fun. I'm not sayin' it's not exactly fun."

Ti-Belle felt disappointed, rejected. "But what?"

"I'm just so glad I don't have to do it for a livin', I could spit."

"You don't miss it? Not even a little bit?"

"Honey, I don't miss performin' and I don't miss havin' my teeth drilled without novocaine."

"Why don't I believe that?" Because she didn't want to, she knew that perfectly well. Ti-Belle had a really great idea to boost her prestige in the music business—she wanted to sing with Nick professionally. And now that they'd sung together just for fun, she wanted it for more reasons than simple greed—she'd never felt more in love in her life, more exhilarated than when they were doing it. And if she'd felt that way, how could he have felt any different? He couldn't have—nothing else made sense. The whole thing was to get him in touch with his feelings, guide him along, pull him out of this depression he was in—she saw his quietness that way, as depression—and lead him back to living rather than just observing, to having fun again.

Nick said, "Sweetheart? You with me?" She realized she must have phased out. She had been thinking about her first performance experiences, on the streets, and later in coffeehouses, and of how much her music had meant to her, how it had saved her life when she thought about it, where she'd be now (in jail, probably) if it hadn't been there for her.

Then she had thought of Melody, of how very much Melody reminded her of herself, except probably not as talented. But still she wished the same for Melody—to get by, get through, with the music to help her.

For the ninety-ninth time she wondered where the hell Melody was. How could a kid that young just disappear? And why didn't she call? She didn't want to think about possible answers.

She said to Nick: "I'm sorry. I was just thinking about Ham's little sister."

He smiled. "Your protégée."

"My missing protégée."

He put his arms around her. His sweetness made her think of Ham, and she felt panicky, as if she were about to lose it, before she could get her mind back on Melody again. Even so, her voice sounded whiny and she had to sniff as she said, "You just don't know, Nick. You don't have any idea."

14

George had lived with this damn family for nearly sixty years, but he couldn't believe what he was hearing.

"Who are you assholes?" he roared.

"Who are you calling asshole?" his brother Joe roared back.

"His son's dead and not even buried yet—can't you give him a break?" He knew Patty meant well, that she was defending him, but he couldn't help it, he found her voice unbelievably irritating, almost wanted to cross over to his brother's side so as not to be associated with her.

He hollered, "Patty, for Christ's sake, shut up!"

Joe and Philip, Rod's kid, started yelling at once. Joe said, "You're going to ruin it for us, George. Thirty years we put into this business, and we can cash in, we can retire in style, and you gotta stand in the way."

"Bullshit! Bullshit!" screamed Philip. "Don't put it on Uncle George. It's you and Dad against the rest of us."

George's brother Rod shouted, "I swear to God you're disinherited."

"Disinfuckingherited! You can't disinherit me. I'm a shareholder in the fucking company. What you think, you can just throw me out? You crazy old man!''

George winced. Had the board meetings always been this way? Or did this one seem so brutal because he was rubbed raw? Usually he would have been furious because they hadn't cancelled out of respect for him—as if they'd understand the concept. But not today—today he hurt too much, and not just because of Melody and Ham. Because of them too. His brothers, his sisters-in-law, his nieces and nephews—the damn hypocrites who had come to his house yesterday to offer condolences and today were trying to sell him down the river.

He couldn't summon an ounce of fury—only sadness and bewilderment, a sense of everything caving in on him. He really didn't feel like fighting. For all he cared, they could take the damn company and— He stopped himself. That was what they wanted. That was why they'd refused to cancel the meeting. They wanted to hit him when he was down.

I can't let them get away with it.

The words formed somewhere in the back of his mind, like an echo, a vague reminder of something he'd forgotten. But he had to start caring, had to muster some of the old fire. Had to get through this.

I'll need Patty's help.

The thought surprised him. Usually he considered Patty a necessary hindrance. He needed her to serve on the board and to vote the way he told her to, but this was his show and he didn't need her horning in.

Well, that was before. Today, he did need her. He squeezed her thigh under the table. Startled, she looked at him. He gave her a little nod. It meant: "Help me," but would she know that after he'd just told her to shut up?

A couple of the younger ones were now putting in their two-cents worth, the ones who were mad about Philip's saying it was Joe and Rod against everyone else, because it wasn't. It would be a lot simpler if it were—it was split more or less down the middle, and Ham's death could make the difference. Only Hilary wasn't here today, and Hilary sometimes went one way, sometimes the other, depending on whether or not she was mad at her dad. Christ, he sometimes thought that was what the whole thing was about—getting back at each other. Maybe hurting each other just for the hell of it. He'd thought that about Ham.

A truly amazing thought ran through George's brain: *Do I sound like they do?*

Patty was talking. "Ladies and gentlemen, I honestly don't think we're going to accomplish a goddamn thing this morning."

Her voice was icy; haughty. George wasn't sure he'd ever heard her sound like that. "I do not like any of your attitudes, and I am absolutely appalled at your lack of respect for our bereavement. I move we table the motion until the next meeting."

The room was dead silent. George stared at his wife as if at a stranger. Where was the shrew with the nasty, desperate wail? He hadn't known she had this in her—this strength, this ability. It unnerved him.

Somehow, it was done and they were out of the conference room, George feeling almost as if he were underwater. He had thought to work today, for an hour or so at least, but now he saw that that was impossible. He just wanted to get out of here; he wanted to look for Melody. But the receptionist hailed him as he and Patty walked by.

A woman was waiting for them. He didn't recognize her at first, though obviously she thought he would.

"Hi," she said, and smiled with her head tilted a little, tomboy-style. "I'm Skip Langdon. We talked at your son's house."

Patty caught on first. "Oh, yes. Detective Langdon."

He took her into his office—it was small for three people, but he certainly wasn't going to conduct a police interview in the reception room.

She said, "It sounded like quite a meeting you were having in there."

George simply sat in stony silence. How dare she!

"Listen, I'm sorry to be rude, but I could hear every word. And I'm afraid I have to ask you some fairly personal questions."

He raised an eyebrow, a gesture that always intimidated Ham and Patty, and sometimes some of the nephews.

175

"I understand you and Ham had some business differences."

"Where in hell did you hear that?"

She shrugged. "I don't think that matters. I just need to hear the story from you and not somebody else."

"You heard right. Ham and I had our differences."

"I understand it was a pretty important difference."

"Could I ask how this could possibly matter to you?"

"I'm trying to find out if he had any enemies, Mr. Brocato."

"Now wait a minute—"

But she held up a hand. "Not you, of course. But things got pretty volatile in there."

"You honestly think one of his own relatives could have murdered him? Over a few sandwich stands?"

She might as well have rolled her eyes for all her expression left to the imagination. "I just need to know his part in the business."

Patty nudged him, mouthed something. Why the hell didn't she leave him alone?

He said, "All right, Detective Langdon, I'm gon' tell you everything. Why? Because I have nothing to hide. Poor Boys is considering selling out to a large conglomerate for a very tidy sum of money. S'pose to give 'em an answer on Monday, but turns out we still can't agree. Can't even agree to go ahead and take a vote." He sighed and resumed. "Many board members believe this is the best way to go and that we can still retain our power in the company if we make the right deal. Others believe that greater profits are to be made by pouring a little more money into our own small company and beginning to diversify. Ham was on one side. Patty and I are on the other."

"I see. Is Melody a shareholder as well?"

"Well now, that's a stupid question and you know it. We're not about to let a sixteen-year-old vote, now are we?"

His rudeness had the desired effect. Her cheeks reddened and her voice got a little louder. "Someone would have to vote her shares. Would that be you or Ham?"

"What the hell are you—"

Now she was spreading her arms, all coolness again. "Mr.

Brocato, I take it a lot of money is at stake. They were two important players in a very big game."

"I vote Melody's shares, dammit. Tell me something—why aren't you out finding my daughter?"

"I'd like to be, but I'm talking to you right now." She enunciated very carefully, stopping just short of contemptuousness. And then her voice turned sweet as pie again. "However, I did find something out that you might want to know."

George could feel himself sitting up straighter.

"Yes. Her boyfriend had dumped her."

"That sorry Phillips boy. I warned her about that little wrinkled-clothes so-and-so."

Patty said, "Flip? But he worshiped her."

"Anyway, that's why she left Blair's."

"Well, that explains it all." Patty always did jump to conclusions. "She did run away, then."

"Oh, Patty, come on. Her brother's dead!"

The detective broke in. "If y'all don't mind, I really need to fill in a few details about Ham's life. The other night I felt as if—well, it wasn't the best time to talk."

Patty said, "We appreciate that, Detective." Why couldn't she keep her damn mouth shut?

"What do you need filled in, Ms. Langdon?" She'd given them a present—the news about Melody—and now she expected something back. Didn't it embarrass her to be so transparent?

"I was wondering if Ham had any enemies."

"Enemies! Ham? Why, Ham was the best liked young man in Orleans Parish."

"He got along okay with his ex-wife?"

"So far as I know."

"And Ti-Belle?"

George merely nodded, not about to dignify that with an answer.

"Melody?"

"He loved that girl more than anything. They got along like wildfire, because of the age difference, I think—by the time she

177

came along, Ham was too old for sibling rivalry. She was more like his niece than anything else.''

"Can you think of any reason why Melody would want to run away?''

"Well, sure,'' said Patty. "The boyfriend.''

"Anything else?''

"Detective, we've been over and over this ground.''

"I don't remember that.''

"In our own minds. With each other. Wouldn't you in our position?''

She settled back a little in her chair and looked George in the eye. She smiled, friendly as a fox. "I guess I would. I wonder if you could tell me who Ham's lawyer was.''

"Jimmy Calhoun, I think. Why do you need to know that?''

"Sometimes it's helpful in these cases.'' She was cagey, George thought. Not someone you'd want working against you.

Patty said, "George, I think we should tell her about Andy Fike.''

He shrugged. Why not?

Patty did.

And in the end George was glad. Because the smart-ass detective did a slow burn all during the telling of it. "Did you call the police at all?''

"No.''

"Are you crazy? Do you want your daughter found or not?''

"We investigated on our own.''

She put a hand over her face, shook her head, and more or less moaned.

She'd pretty much lost it. George liked that.

▪

After a brief and utterly unfruitful visit to Andy Fike, in which Fike acted as if he were the severely wronged party and even pretended he couldn't remember what Melody was wearing, Skip sat down disgustedly at her desk. She would have liked to spend about half an hour running or riding a bicycle instead, to let off a little steam, but there was far too much to do.

Ham's financial problems worried her. He needed cash, pure and simple—she already knew that. And that would certainly explain why he was so eager to sell the family business. A man who needed cash might have been pretty active in campaigning among the board members to get his way; which in turn might have made someone wildly opposed want to get rid of him.

Skip sighed. It was possible, but it didn't seem likely. She dialed Jimmy Calhoun: Ham hadn't left a will.

"So what does that mean?" asked Skip. "Who inherits?"

"Well, he never got around to getting divorced," Calhoun said. "At least he didn't do it through our firm. And, hell, we were at St. Martin's together—he'd have come to me. Matter of fact, we had lunch a few weeks ago and I nagged him about it. He said I was worse than Ti-Belle."

"He did?" That didn't square with what Ti-Belle had told her about the relationship.

"Well, no, actually. But I did nag—thought he might want to marry that little Cajun before she got away. But I don't know—he just looked kind of unhappy when I brought it up."

"So does Mason inherit?"

"Absolutely. If there aren't kids, the wife gets the loot."

When she got off the phone, she started to feel the first pangs of lunch lust. She thought of the tuna fish sandwich she'd brought, and decided it was going to be seriously inadequate. How to beef it up? Potato chips were too salty, a piece of fruit too wimpy. Now, an order of fries—that was more like it. And after lunch, she had a plan. A plan involving Ti-Belle. The phone rang.

"Lunch?"

"Cindy Lou Wootten. Where you been, girl?"

"Working my butt off, same as you. But listen, I got to eat, you got to eat—and you've got a case to fill me in on."

This beat the hell out of a lonely tuna sandwich. "I've got a little chore out at the fairgrounds—how about we eat at the JazzFest?"

"If you can get us in free, I'll be there in ten."

"I think I can wait."

Cindy Lou Wootten was one of Skip's favorite people. She

could talk about suspects—indeed whole cases—in a way no one else could. She would analyze and postulate long after anyone else —even Steve—would have been bored silly, and she was nearly always right. And the best part was, it was perfectly ethical to talk about cases with her (which it wasn't with Steve) because Cindy Lou was a psychologist who frequently worked with the police department. A forensic psychologist, schooled in the dark corners of the criminal mind.

But mostly, Skip thought, she was street-smart. She was a black woman from Detroit who claimed to have learned everything she knew about crime before she ever got to high school, and Skip half believed her.

She also happened to be the most beautiful woman Skip had ever seen; but better still, she had a way about her, a kind of confidence and poise that Skip thought she might develop if she lived to be seventy-five. Nobody messed with Cindy Lou, not even Skip's nemesis, the contentious Sergeant Frank O'Rourke. O'Rourke had once tried, and come a cropper. And playing out that tiny drama, Cindy Lou had earned Skip's undying admiration.

There was only one thing about the brilliant, beautiful Cindy Lou—she fell for all the wrong guys and was perfectly cheerful about it. If it had been anyone else, Skip would have suggested therapy. But she seemed more or less to enjoy the melodrama in her own life. Skip didn't get it; she was just glad she had Steve Steinman—she wanted no part of the dorks Cindy Lou brought around.

As usual, the sight of her friend made Skip feel dowdy and cowlike. Just a hair bigger than petite—and quite tiny of waist and hips—Cindy Lou arrived in chamois-colored linen walking shorts with matching jacket and immaculate white linen tank top. Skip was wearing black cotton slacks with a pink T-shirt—functional, that was about it. *Oh, well,* she thought, *it wouldn't matter if I had the good outfit. Everybody'd still look at her.*

"After lunch I thought I'd go terrorize a witness—probably bring her back for questioning. Care to join me?"

"Always a pleasure."

"Let's take my car."

"You're not going to terrorize my favorite Cajun singer, are you?"

"Afraid so. Why—is she also your favorite suspect?"

"It's nearly always the wife or girlfriend—you know that. But hell, I don't know anything about this mess. Fill me in."

Skip told her on the ride over. As they stood in line for soft-shell crab po' boys, she got ready for opinions—Cindy Lou always had plenty.

But she wasn't her usual bantering self. She was very solemn, very focused. "You've got to find Melody. That kid's in a heap of shit."

"Tell me about it." Skip was slightly abrupt, angry to be told once more what she already knew. It was hot and her hair felt damp.

Cindy Lou said, "You think she did it?"

"What's the motive? Everybody says she and Ham were so damn close and loving."

"So what does that tell you?"

"Too close maybe. He tries something with her, she goes nuts and stabs him."

"Uh-uh, I don't think so. A sixteen-year-old kid is nearly grown. If he was a sicko, he'd have done it earlier."

"Maybe he did and she got tired of it."

"The wineglasses bother me."

"Oh, give me a break. Anybody'd who'd screw their little sister wouldn't draw the line at giving her alcohol."

"They might. People are funny, you know? But I don't know —the glasses just have an adult feel to them. Like two people were talking and one of them said the wrong thing."

"Betrayal."

"Yeah."

"Couldn't that work for Melody too? Like maybe he said he was going to marry Ti-Belle and she got jealous? Or she wanted her band to play at the JazzFest and he said no? Something like that?"

Cindy Lou shrugged. "Let's face it, there are only four choices —either she did it, she didn't do it but she's afraid she'll be accused of it, or she saw something; and she ran away."

"Well, if we believe Andy Fike, she wasn't kidnapped. What's the fourth choice?"

"A variation. She was seen seeing something and she's being pursued. In which case, she could have been caught by now. Any way you slice it, she's in a heap of shit."

Skip felt panic rising inside her. Yet she was helpless to do anything other than what she'd been ordered to do.

"Who do you like best?" Cindy Lou said.

"Ti-Belle, I guess. Just because she's lying. But I can't see a motive for her either. If she wanted to be with Nick, why not just leave Ham?"

"You know the answer to that—the classic crime of passion. They're having a friendly talk over a civilized glass of wine and he says, 'okay, get out of here, you Cajun slut. I never loved you anyhow—you dye your hair and give a lousy blow job.' "

Skip laughed. " 'And not only that, but you can't sing.' That's when she used the knife—forget the blow job."

"Now you got it. That's the sort of stuff people kill over." Cindy Lou took a big bite out of her sandwich. "You know, we haven't got a damn thing like this in Detroit."

"Must be why you're here. Certainly can't be the weather."

"You know why I'm here, honey. 'Cause the average law-abiding southerner has a criminal streak two yards wider than any mob boss Detroit ever spawned.

"Listen. There's something I think I need to tell you. The fact that the kid left on her own volition—and I guess we really think she did—doesn't bode too well for her state of mind. We know for a fact her boyfriend dumped her for her best friend—there's two big losses. Next she either kills her brother or sees him killed —big loss number three (even if she killed him), and number four if someone she trusts did. Then there's the fear—either of the law or the murderer—which is also going to contribute to depression. And there's the fact that she's currently homeless and probably penniless. She probably feels like she doesn't have a friend in the world."

"What are you telling me, Cindy Lou?"

"I'm afraid she might be suicidal."

An imaginary clock ticked louder every second. "I never even thought of that."

"And by the way, I hope you're not overlooking Andy Fike. Maybe he never saw Melody at all—just started that stuff to hide the fact he killed her and buried her in his courtyard."

Melody was becoming a flesh-and-blood kid to Skip—it was as if she'd known her and was missing her. She was starting to feel panicky every time she thought of the girl on the streets alone. "Cindy Lou, stop! She's only sixteen."

"Well, you know how people are. No damn good."

"God, you're professional."

"Honey, the more psychology I study, the less convinced I get that I'm ever going to understand the human animal."

Skip was ready for a change of subject. She made her voice playful. "Well, that reminds me. Who're you dating this week?"

Cindy Lou took the last bite of her sandwich. "Whoa, that was good! Well, this week is right, babe. I just broke up with a guy who couldn't decide between me and this cute blond librarian. Male."

Skip shivered. "Sounds dicey."

"Oh, no problem. He wouldn't sleep with either of us. He was into spiritual relationships."

"You meditated together?"

"Breathed. He was into breathing. Don't knock it if you haven't tried it."

"I do it a lot, actually. Sweet potato pone?"

Cindy Lou nodded, and they edged into the pone line. "This is different. You play music and trance out."

"No drugs?"

"I'm telling you, girl—you get high. You get weird. I mean it."

"I don't mean to be rude, but do you really need to get any weirder?"

Cindy Lou ignored that. "So anyway, now I'm going out with this musician."

"Married?"

"Uh-uh."

"Coked-up?"

"AA all the way."

"Poor, then."

"Well, let's put it this way. He's doing pretty damn well for the amount of experience he's had. I think he's got a future."

"Uh-oh. I think I just got it. He's young, right?"

"And gorgeous."

"Okay, how young?"

"Twenty-six." Cindy Lou was thirty-four.

"That's not such a huge age difference."

"Yeah, but he lives with his mama."

"Well, gosh, Cindy Lou, big deal. You can always go to your place." The truth was, he sounded a lot better than many of Cindy Lou's bright ideas—especially if he was in AA. To be twenty-six and already done with addiction was a feat.

"Yeah, we could. But then his mama has to·look after the kid."

"He's a single father?"

"Yeah. Cutest little boy—you should see him."

"Okay, twenty-six, a single father, poor—"

"Well, look, none of that's really the problem. The thing is, I met him through his mama."

"Oh. She's a friend of yours."

"Well, not exactly. You know that program I'm in at Tulane? She's my adviser."

It was always that way. Cindy Lou collected men the way a kid picked up shells at the beach—utterly effortlessly. And all of them seriously flawed. Skip would have thought she simply wasn't discriminating if she hadn't seen the ones Cindy Lou dumped—the ones the average psychologist might have called "suitable."

"Well, I would too," Cindy Lou had said when Skip remarked upon it. "I just don't like suitable men."

15

■ ■

Melody had walked right by a friend of her mother's with no problem at all. So when she saw Chuckie Parsons, a kid from school who had a crush on her, she deliberately caught his eye and smiled seductively around the Sno Ball she was working on. He actually looked around to see who she was smiling at. Of course, she wouldn't have dared do it without the red shades, even with the makeup and hair and all, but even that might have been okay. Her eyes looked like something off of Cleopatra's barge.

She would see people she knew at Ti-Belle's set, she was sure of that, but she felt pretty confident. Meanwhile, she was waiting in the gospel tent, her perennial favorite.

Most of the groups were black and many came from high schools, schools Melody had never heard of. Some of the singing was incredibly good. All of it was fun. But the thing that fascinated Melody, the amazing thing that had struck her the first time Ham had taken her here when she was eight or nine, was the way some of these kids were really adults. The stars, that is.

What would happen was that the star—it could be a girl or a boy—would step forward and perhaps speak first, say a few words for Jesus, sounding like a preacher, getting to do something completely adult, unlike anything in Melody's experience any white kid ever got to do. Maybe the kid wouldn't speak, maybe she'd just sing. Then she'd get the whole choir going, she'd be leading her own choir. She'd get the audience to join in, and here would be this crowd of people from all over the country, adults in every kind of job—blue collar, white collar, anything you could name—this incredibly disparate audience ranging from good churchgoing people, folks from the Seventh Ward, to sophisticated music-lovers who'd made the trek from California or New York—and a seventeen-year-old kid would have the audience in the palm of her hand. She'd have been taught everything she needed to know, the poise, the leadership, the musicianship, and she'd be an adult and a star.

Melody watched the New Orleans Spiritualettes, the Christianaires, and the Second Morning Star Mass Choir, then took off for Ti-Belle's gig.

Ti-Belle looked fabulous. She had on a yellow dress with black polka dots, kind of a sheath thing, with a square neck—very retro, very Ti-Belle. Her long, gorgeous hair was platinum, stunning against her olive skin; it was parted on the side and usually fell over her eye, which meant she had to shake it back pretty often, and that was always dramatic. She was positively elegant in her raw skinniness. Melody was rhapsodic, just looking at her.

Then Ti-Belle began to talk about Ham.

Melody blinked tears. She should have realized this was coming. Ti-Belle was talking about their time together, how much he'd meant to her and to her career, her music, how easygoing he was, how patient, how everyone depended on him because he never got mad, he never got upset. Melody was struggling like hell not to cry. She truly couldn't afford to ruin her makeup. She couldn't cry—after all, Ti-Belle wasn't crying. And why not? she wondered. What had she done to keep herself together?

Melody knew. She knew exactly what Ti-Belle had done. She had seen her do the same thing countless times—she'd stood in front of the mirror and practiced and practiced until she was perfect. Ti-Belle did not ad lib. No way was she going to get onstage without having it down pat, without knowing she could stay in one piece while saying it. Melody didn't even know how many hours it might have taken; it could have taken all night, and Ti-Belle wouldn't have flinched. She was a perfectionist.

She said now that her set was for Ham, that this first song in particular was dedicated to Ham, that it was what she had to do now. Then she sang a verse, a cappella, of "St. James Infirmary," belting as if this was a talent contest and the winner got to be Madonna. She had changed the words slightly:

> Let him go, let him go,
> God bless him,
> Wherever he may be.
> I may search this wide world over;
> I'll not find a man like him.

Then the band came in and she sang the whole song. If there was a dry eye when she was done, it would have to have been the miserable orb of a person so insensitive he might as well be dead, Melody thought. She herself was openly bawling, having given up the fight to save her makeup. She didn't dare take off her glasses, so they were thoroughly steamed up by the time the song was over. There being no choice now, Melody removed and dried them quickly, keeping her head down. But she was sure she needn't have bothered. All eyes were on the utterly riveting Ti-Belle, who now broke the elegiac mood with a song of her own, one of Ham's favorites, she said, called "Afternoon Delight."

It was rollicking and bawdy and the folks loved it. From there on the performance soared into the stratosphere. Melody, so overcome only a few minutes before, was transported to a new level of ecstasy, a musical ecstasy, a pure, vibrating, physical pleasure that was like a drug high, only better. Or an orgasm. She hadn't had one yet, but surely it couldn't be better than this. She threw her hands high above her head, swung her hips, moved her feet, and boogied like she'd been born to it. And she had, she had, she was born for this—she knew, even in her trance, her zoned-out no-holds-barred ecstatic transport, that that was the title of a song she'd write

187

soon, after she finished Ham's song. It would be about music and what it meant to her, but not the creative process, just the physical, primitive sensation, the thing the cave people must have felt the first time one of them beat on a hollow tree and invented the drum.

She forgot all about Ham, all about everything except the music and the sun and the luxuriant pliancy of her own lithe body. She was singing, dancing, screaming, hands waving in the air, in seventh heaven, when all of a sudden she felt something.

Eyes.

She knew what eyes felt like. She could tell when a boy was looking at her in class and when someone in the next car was staring in the window. Someone was looking at her now.

Quickly her own eyes swept the crowd, and she saw who saw her. Someone who was moving toward her. Her nemesis. The last person she wanted to see, or expected to see. A person who shouldn't be here if there were any logic left in the world. But there hadn't been for four days now, and she couldn't worry about it. She had to go.

Bodies pressed close to her, thick as a Mardi Gras crowd, everybody boogying but staying in their own space. It worked fine so long as no one disturbed the equilibrium. Melody was messing it up bad; plowing through like some human bumper car—" 'Scuse me; sorry"—but still getting dirty looks.

The way it worked at the JazzFest, there were a couple of tents —one for gospel, one for contemporary jazz—and other than that, open-air stages, lots of them, of greater and lesser importance. The more important ones drew the bigger crowds, of course, and the crowds could expand as much as they needed. They thinned on the edges and eventually melted into the greater, strolling JazzFest crowd.

Ti-Belle was at the Ray-Ban stage, the biggest and most important; before he died, Ham had made sure she was far the most important act on at her time. The crowd she'd drawn was enormous, probably the biggest of her life. Melody felt as if she were moving through Jell-O, in slow motion. Then she was at the end of the crowd. She started to run. And hit somebody head on, fortunately a large man, possibly a biker, someone who was only stunned, not hurt. But he was angry. She might have got away, but she heard him pointing her out to her tracker.

Where to go? If she got into another crowd, she might be able to disappear, or she might get trapped. The tracker had binoculars; Melody had seen them, thought that was odd, and then had seen the figure start to move. She had to disappear altogether, become invisible even to the possessor of high-power magnification.

She knew how she'd been spotted, and it had taken a clever person to do it. She had painted her nails scarlet, made her hands look like someone else's, except for one tiny thing — her trademark cameo ring. Everyone knew about the damn ring, and yet it was such a tiny detail, who would spot it? Someone watching her dance, throwing her hands up in the air, the only parts of her body that stood out of the crowd, that could possibly be identified. Why hadn't she thought of that? In a fury, she jerked the ring off and tossed it into the crowd. "Finders keepers," she hollered, and all might have been well if the finder hadn't been a girl of nine or ten.

"Mees, mees," she screamed, and with a sinking heart Melody realized that she was foreign, Jamaican perhaps, or African, that she didn't speak English, and that, childlike, wanting desperately to do the right thing, she wouldn't rest till she returned the ring. She was small, and fast too — she'd catch Melody and slow her down, keep her there being polite until the tracker could get to her.

Melody turned around and shouted over her shoulder, "Keep it! It's for you. Keep it, keep it!"

The tracker was gaining. The girl stopped for a second and pointed, possibly telling the story to her mother or sister. Someone else, someone with more English, shouted, "Mees, mees! Your ring — I have your ring."

Melody tried again. "Keep it. It's yours — wear it in good health." She had learned the phrase from television.

More people were chasing her now — a crowd of black people, shouting, most of them children. What irony, Melody thought, everyone Uptown was afraid of getting robbed by black people, and here was a whole fifth grade class and all their chaperones trying to chase her down to return her property.

She was getting close to Congo Square now, the part of the Jazz

and Heritage Festival dedicated to the African part of that heritage.
The original had evolved from a slave market to a voodoo site and
black culture center. This one had rethought the market idea and
given it a more palatable twist. There were T-shirts for sale here,
as everywhere at any festival, and some cassettes, and that was
about the end of ordinary merchandise. The rest was all dashikis
and djellabas and rattles and jewelry and curious musical instruments. It was a great place to shop; Melody could spend hours
there. But right now it was about the last place she wanted to be.
If her pursuers were African, someone here might speak their
language and try to help them out, and the shopkeepers would all
have seen a running white girl. She was doomed.

Desperately, grasping at anything, she picked up a scarf, something to make her look different. She grabbed it as she sped by,
shoplifted as the owner's back was turned. But a customer saw and
pointed.

"Hey!" the merchant shouted. "Hey, you thief!"

Shit. It was hopeless. She was nearly numb with depression and
she was breathing so hard her lungs were probably going to burst.
And then she'd be dead. She hoped it wouldn't be a painful death.
After all this, surely she deserved simply to slip away. She turned
a corner.

"God damn you! Watch out, bitch!"

She had run right into a man who hadn't had time to move.
"What you want?" he yelled, outraged. He was a big man, and for
some reason he had grabbed her wrist. She couldn't move.

She'd probably have given up right then, except that due to the
circumstances, she was jammed right up against him and he'd
asked a question. She thought later that the smell of patchouli
incense that someone was burning had been a contributing factor.
That and adrenaline.

What you want?

There was nothing for it but to give an honest answer.

"Hide me," she said, and she looked into his eyes, wishing she
weren't wearing the shades. "Please, please, hide me." And because
his chest felt strong and good against hers, and she could smell his
sweat, it occurred to her to reach for his crotch with her free

hand, to brush it lightly and to whisper, "I'll give you a blow job."

The shouts were getting closer. Without a word or change of expression, the man raised the piece of India print fabric that covered his table of wares and pushed her under it. Just like that. One moment desperation, the next a dark, enclosed space all her own.

Melody crouched and concentrated on the pain in her chest, sure she could be heard breathing at fifty paces. She wished there were a way to lie down.

The first group of pursuers had closed in. "Blond bitch run through here? Red shorts?"

No answer. Probably her benefactor had merely shrugged.

"Hey, man—she stole somethin'. Come on—you seen her?"

More silence. Melody imagined him shaking his head.

There was a rustling as the shopkeeper hurried by, he and whatever entourage he'd gathered.

Melody's chest sounded as if it were inhabited by frogs; every breath was a croak.

The second wave came. A lilting, lovely voice.

"You see a young lady? She lose her ring." The little girl was probably holding up the ring, all innocence, brown eyes wide and gentle.

"What did she look like?" the man said.

"Oh, she have two-color hair, white and purple." Mass giggles. There must be a dozen children out there.

The man laughed too. "White and purple? Now how I'm gon' forget somethin' like that?" There was a pause. "She went by a minute ago. That way."

Okay, that was it. Except for the tracker. Her nemesis was still out there, and she couldn't warn this man, couldn't tell him not to pick up the cloth at the wrong time or she was screwed.

He did. He picked it up now. "Is that all, sweet pea?"

Melody closed her eyes and shook her head, desperate. "Ten minutes. Please, okay? Just ten minutes more."

"Sure. Sure, baby. Stay just as long as you like."

She closed her eyes again. Her breath was coming more evenly now, her pulse slowing down, and she realized how hot she was.

Her makeup had probably melted, but that was the least of her problems. The tracker could have heard her talking to the man, could easily stick around till he lifted the cloth again, and there she would be, staring dead-on into the eyes of the enemy.

She squeezed her closed eyes tighter, banishing mental pictures, bits of her old life, and tried to think what to do next.

Okay, if the tracker was there, what?

Run. Get out of there fast.

And if not? She had a potential ally here, and her benefactor seemed a nice man, but there was a problem—she'd made a deal with him and he was bound to insist on payment. Maybe violently.

Melody wondered how that would be. Could she just sort of close her eyes and think of something else? Wasn't that what nineteenth century ladies did? She could, she supposed, if she'd made a slightly more basic offer.

"Hide me and I'll fuck you?" What would have been wrong with that? She could have gotten through that, probably. Why had she gotten fancy?

The truth was, Melody had only a very dim idea what a blow job was, and wasn't at all sure she could actually perform one; knew she couldn't without coaching. This guy probably thought she was a pro. What would he do when he found out he'd been had?

Anyway, how strong was her stomach? This guy was a stranger, and a pretty big one at that. His dick was probably in proportion, and she knew she had to put it in her mouth (though she hadn't a clue what the next step was). Could she do that? Quickly, she put her hand over her mouth to stop the noise coming out of her throat. Just thinking about it, her gag reflex had kicked in. She had to get out of here.

She lay still and thought. Finally she got up the nerve to roll out from her hiding place, to stand facing her benefactor, smiling, knowing she was about to pull a double-cross and wishing it didn't have to be that way. Her eyes darted, looking for the tracker. No one she knew was in sight. She smiled at the man; seductively, she hoped. She even moved closer to him, touched his chest with her breasts and moved back, teasing him a little.

"Ready to collect?" She wished her voice was breathy.

He smiled. He was really very handsome. "Mmmmm-hmmmm, baby." All lazy and nice, like he did it all the time, bought sexual favors from fleeing criminals.

Fleeing minors, she thought, aware that a grown man shouldn't have made such a deal with her. She had no reason to feel guilty —the man was a child molester.

She turned and looked over her shoulder, still smiling, still seductive. "Catch me."

He looked surprised, but not yet daunted. Apparently, he still thought it was a game.

Melody ran, dodging men, women, and children, ran in earnest and as if she were desperate. "Help!" she screamed. "Somebody please help! Police! Rape!"

She sneaked one more look and saw the man staring after her, frozen, terrified to move an inch.

16

Nick was watching the swarm around Ti-Belle, hanging back on the sidelines, thinking that this was perhaps the first time in his adult life that such a thing had happened—that he was not the center of attention. He was currently being as decidedly ignored as the tall chap with the video camera in the other corner. He was enjoying both the anonymity and Ti-Belle's success. As a matter of fact, he realized he was grinning like an idiot, and kept trying to remind himself to stop in case the fellow with the camera decided to notice him.

Ti-Belle had been truly brilliant. He was so proud of her he would have busted buttons if he had any. It was a pleasure to be associated with such a woman.

"What'd you think?" said Proctor.

"Oh, man," said Nick. "Oh, man, oh, man." And then was conscious of having become speechless. However, with Proctor, who'd seen him throw up the first time he got drunk, it hardly mattered.

Proctor seemed uncomfortable, a little pissed that Ti-Belle was getting so much attention. He had a thing about her, and Nick just couldn't see it. Ti-Belle, of all the women he'd known, was the most accomplished, the least likely to want him for his money.

I've never been with a singer before, he thought with surprise. Why not? he wondered. Had he been too egotistical? Too reluctant to share the limelight?

I didn't know what I was missing.

This felt good.

Somebody was pushing her way through the crowd, ruffling feathers, more or less making a scene. It was a tall woman, hefty, someone he'd seen before, trailed by another woman, a black one who could have been a movie star.

He remembered. "Hey, there's the cop."

Proctor said, "The black one?"

"The big one."

"The fat one?"

"That one." She'd made it all the way to Ti-Belle.

She held up her badge: "Police. I'm going to have to ask you all to leave."

Ti-Belle looked as if someone had hit her. Red spots had appeared on both her cheeks. "You can't do that!"

"Do you want to talk in front of everyone?"

"Talk! What do you want to talk about now?"

It was getting ugly and there was still an audience. Nick stepped forward. "Would everyone leave, please?"

Ti-Belle was shocked. "Nick!"

He wished he could signal her that it was okay, that he was still on her side. Proctor started to herd people out.

Ti-Belle turned her fury on the cop. "What the hell are you doing here? Whatever it is, couldn't it wait half an hour?"

"I'd like you to remember that I'm a police officer and I ask you to treat me with respect." She sounded like somebody's mom. Somebody's mom who's just discovered the grades aren't up to par, or the car's wrecked. Nick kind of admired her style, but at the same time he wasn't immune from it. Despite his best efforts to remain calm, his neck prickled slightly. He moved closer to Ti-Belle and slipped an arm around her waist. Held her tight so she'd know she was okay.

"Hello, officer."

Now that he was there, Ti-Belle was losing it. A sound came out of her as if she had asthma, and then she turned to him, put her arms around his shoulders and hung on like a two-year-old, shaking with the effort of holding herself together.

He bent his head and whispered for a while, but he wasn't at all sure she heard. Her body had taken over; what was happening with her was happening somewhere he couldn't reach. He turned his head and caught the cop's eye.

"You're here about Ham?" he said.

"I'm here to talk to Miss Thiebaud," she said primly, in that way cops have, that smug, arrogant way that made him want to belt them.

"She was with me that day," he said. "We were together the whole time."

Ti-Belle, tight against him, kissed his neck to let him know she'd heard and she was grateful. He was glad he'd done it; it would be good for both of them.

"Well, it's about time somebody broke down and admitted it," the cop said.

Ti-Belle let go of him, turned around, astonished. "You knew all the time?"

"I knew you two were seeing each other. Tell me—were you together all day Tuesday?"

"Yes," they said together.

"There was no time at all when you were apart?"

Ti-Belle shook her head. Nick held her tight around the waist. "No," he said.

It went on like that for a while, light fencing, the cop trying to pick a hole here, a thread there, and then she asked him to leave.

Ti-Belle nodded, letting him know she'd be okay, and he knew she would be. She was strong. True, she'd been under a lot of pressure—various kinds of pressure—and she'd nearly cracked, but with his support she was fine. The minute he'd spoken, he had felt her spine straighten, felt her drawing strength from him.

He left. Proctor, who'd been banished, was waiting for him. "She okay?"

"She's going to be fine. You think we can walk around awhile?"

Proctor sighed. "We can give it a shot."

Nick didn't perform anymore, he was practically a recluse, he did everything he could to discourage any sort of public following, and yet whenever he went out, he still got mobbed. Anywhere. He couldn't go to the cleaners without autographing his ticket.

"Come on, these people are cool. Let's go get a Sno Ball."

They walked in silence for a while, tense, expecting to be approached. Finally Proctor said, "What'd the cop want?"

"Hell if I know. Had some kind of bug up her butt about Ti-Belle's alibi. Picked a hell of a time to come, didn't she?"

Proctor shrugged. "I don't know. It worked."

That struck Nick funny. He threw back his head and laughed like he hadn't in a long time. "Well, you're right about that. It did work, I guess. Now the whole world's gonna know 'bout me and Ms. Ti-Belle."

Proctor let a beat pass. Finally he said, "Her show was good, I thought."

Nick couldn't tell if he was changing the subject or not. "Yeah, she was hot," he said, going along with it. Then he said what he wanted to say: "I'm crazy 'bout that little Cajun."

His friend didn't answer.

Nick wanted to know why, but didn't know how to ask. He said, "She's a great girl, isn't she?"

"Seems to be," said Proctor, and he shrugged again, as if getting rid of something. His voice sounded vague.

Nick said, "I think I'm gon' get married again."

"Oh, Lord, Anglime, what does it take? You got a houseful of ex-wives, and fifty-seven varieties of gurus, and not one shrink, I just noticed. Don't you think you ought to get one? When in the hell are you gonna learn your lesson?"

Nick grinned. He'd said it. He'd surprised even himself, hadn't really known until he'd spoken it, and now that he had, he liked it. "I'm not kiddin'. She's the one."

They were in the Sno Ball line now, but these lines were always the slowest. Proctor said, "I'm not going to say how many times I've heard that one."

"Well, it was always true. You know anybody else who's so friendly with all his exes?"

"Nick, baby, this is costing you. It costs money to get married, in case you've forgotten. I mean, I know you're feeling all romantic and everything, but get real—we both know the expensive part's at the other end. And anyway, you can have anything you want—I mean anyone you want doing anything you want any time you want. Why go through all that crap?"

"I like bein' married. That way you've got a deal. See, if you don't get married, they just get pregnant and make you support them and the kids and you never have any say about it and it still costs you but you don't have anyone to watch movies with."

"Chocolate Sno Ball," said Proctor to the vendor, and when he got it, he said, "You know, it's all I can do not to smash this thing on top of your pointy head?"

That struck Nick as funny. He laughed like a loon and thought how good it was to be in love. He hardly ever laughed.

"Hey, I mean it, Anglime. You're the craziest dude I ever met."

Nick now had his own coconut concoction. "Let's go hear some zydeco."

They headed toward the fais do-do stage. Proctor said, "You sure about Ti-Belle?"

"Surer'n shootin'." He laughed again. "And I've done a lot of that in my time." He was having the time of his life; it wasn't every day he made puns.

"She just doesn't seem like that kind of girl—the midnight-movie type."

"What do you mean? Ti-Belle loves movies."

"I'll bet she'd rather act in them than watch them."

Nick considered. "Well, she is ambitious. But hey, bro', that's fine with me—somebody in the family's got to be. Sure ain't me, now is it?"

He was having so much fun, and Proctor's mood was so serious. Dark, almost. "I worry," he muttered. "I just worry, that's all."

"Okay, spit it out. What are you so worried about?"

"She wants a career, Nick. She wants it worse than air. She's good, but she needs something and she knows it." Proctor punched him in the chest with his index finger. "You, Nick. You know what I think she really wants? She wants to get you working again—with her. She needs you to perform with her."

"So you heard us singin' last night."

"How was I going to miss it?"

"Wasn't bad, was it?"

Proctor raised an eyebrow, forebore to answer.

"Well, it wasn't now, was it?"

"How was it going to be bad? You're good, she's good—and you've got chemistry. Of course it wasn't bad."

"Know what? I kind of like the idea."

"You *what?*"

"I mean it. I do."

"Is this Nick Anglime speaking? The same Nick Anglime who swore five years ago he'd never work again even if ordered to at gunpoint? Remember what you said? 'They can kill me, I don't care. I'm not doin' it one more time.' "

"I was tired at the time."

"Man, you are somethin'."

"Well, that little gal's somethin'. I want her and I'm gon' do whatever it takes."

"What about your spiritual life? How're you going to spend the rest of your life meditating and studying?"

"Well, I am. I'll just do it between gigs and makin' love to my wife. You don't get this, do you, buddy?"

"That's what I've been trying to tell you."

"The spiritual stuff is about being afraid I'll live my whole life and miss out on what's really important. Do you get that much?"

"Most people would kill for your life, but so far as a normal human being can get it, I get it."

"Ti-Belle's what's important. It's that simple." He looked

straight ahead, certainly not at his friend to say what he had to say, and spread his arms. "Love, baby. Love's it. The whole ball of wax."

"Nick, you've been in love before."

Nick had used Proctor to think the situation through, and he didn't like the turn the conversation was taking. Proctor's voice was starting to take on a carping note.

"Lighten up, would you? Let's go find some young ladies to dance with."

They'd arrived at the fais do-do stage, where two ancient black men who looked and sounded as if they came from a bayou where English wasn't spoken played the harmonica and the washboard. Their voices were pure and sweet, and they were as good as seventy-five percent of the artists at the festival. Nick figured they probably had a combined income of $15,000 a year, and wondered how he could help them.

All around the stage couples twirled gracefully to the charming old tunes. Cajun dancing had become popular, but you had to go out in public to learn it. It had never occurred to Nick to do that.

He realized now that he could have hired a dance instructor to come to his house—hell, maybe he could have gotten Ti-Belle to teach him, she was a Cajun, wasn't she? But then where could you go dancing if you were Nick Anglime? You couldn't just hop over to the Maple Leaf like you lived in the neighborhood. This was the first time he'd been to a public place where it was happening. It was a deliciously anachronistic sight—everyone, men and women alike, in shorts and baseball caps, Reeboks on their feet, going through a set of motions from another era, a softer, sweeter time when "fais do-do" was more than a quaint old phrase. It was from "faire dormir," Ti-Belle had told him—you brought the babies to the party and let them sleep while you danced.

He wanted to do it—and Nick Anglime was a person who got what he wanted. There was a girl on the sidelines in black shorts and a black T-shirt with tiny, multicolored musical instruments on it. She was a little fat with too much makeup, hair a little too high and sprayed too stiff—the kind of girl Uptown New Orleanians called a "charmer" (pronounced "chawama" in imitation of the blue-collar whites they called yats). But she was tapping her foot and looking like she was just dying to dance. She was way too young to know who he was.

He tapped her on the shoulder. "Do you know how to do this?"

She turned to look at him, eyes bland and a little blissed out —he loved the way women here were relaxed, didn't get bent out of shape when a stranger approached. Suddenly she gasped, and he half expected her eyes to roll back in her head; but she turned red instead of white and yelled, "Christie! Omigod! Christie!"

A dancing yat couple, the woman in white shorts and dainty white sandals, the man, spare tire barely covered and then only sometimes by a T-shirt that kept riding up, stared at her, startled. The woman yelled, "Audrey! What is it?" Then saw Nick. Her jaw dropped.

The sight of a dropping jaw was something Nick had seen enough to last him several lifetimes. In fact, he sometimes thought he had open-mouth karma. Maybe he'd been a dentist once.

It wasn't a pretty sight. It was a truly ugly sight.

"Holy shit!" said Christie's dancing partner, and Christie squealed, "Nick *Anglime!*"

Nick was pissed. He said, "Audrey, why the hell did you do that? Did I do something you didn't like?"

But Proctor was pulling at his elbow. "Nick, we got to get out of here."

He was right, oh so right; and they were just a bit too late. He should never have stopped to tell Audrey off. She grabbed his sleeve as he turned to go. And other people, having heard Christie's squeal, turned toward him.

Audrey said, "I'm sorry. Hey, listen, I'm really sorry. Were you going to ask me to dance? Did I blow that? Just tell me—did I blow it?"

He couldn't deny who he was. That would make him look churlish. The best thing, he'd learned by experience, was to be polite, Britishly polite, polite to a fault, but keep moving. "Audrey," he said, "I think you're a delightful girl and it's been lovely meeting you."

He put out his hand to shake. She took it in two wet, sticky paws and said, "You called me Audrey."

"Only because it's your name," he said, and extricated his hand. Proctor was clearing a path.

He heard his own name, louder than the music, being carried on the afternoon breeze, traveling like news of war: "Nick Anglime, Nick Anglime, Nick Anglime . . ."

People magazine had once called him the most famous American, had compared his celebrity to that of Elvis. Elvis had probably never been out without a brace of bodyguards in his life.

And people called him self-destructive.

Nick had chosen not to live his life that way, had become a near-recluse instead.

People pressed at him now, closed in, asking for autographs. Some of them, having no paper available, wanted him to sign their hands or wrists. "I'm sorry," he'd say with a disarming grin, "I don't sign body parts," but he did sign some people's programs. He and Proctor threaded their way.

It was going okay, maybe a little slow, but they were making progress, until he felt a hand close on the flapping sleeve of his Hawaiian shirt and start to tear it.

"Oh, shit!" He'd been here before. Things could turn nasty.

Proctor's hand closed on the other hand. It was a woman's. "You let go of me," she yelled, in that unbelievably irritating accent the yats had.

"Okay," said Proctor, holding on. "Okay. It's going to be all right. You just let go of my friend's shirt and everybody'll be happy."

Instead she used the distraction to press closer to Nick, press her sweaty body next to his. She put her head down and before he could budge, bit him. Bit him on the neck.

"Goddamn!"

Nick's first impulse was to turn around swinging, but he couldn't, the woman had his sleeve and Proctor had her arm. Failing that, he sent his elbow behind him, hard. He couldn't help it, it was pure reflex. She still had her teeth in his neck.

"Ow!" She pulled away, releasing his neck, releasing his

sleeve, but with her right fist she began to beat him, raining blows on his shoulder and the back of his head. He tried to duck, tried to get away, and Proctor tried to block the woman, but the crowd surged. The smell of Dixie beer was beginning to escape from people's pores. Nick was aware of the same sick panic he'd once felt when a rock audience had rushed the stage.

Because they all wanted a piece of him. That was what the whole autograph thing was about, the whole thing of getting him to talk to them for a minute—they wanted a piece of him metaphorically, and how much imagination did it take to extend the metaphor? Early in his career he'd had dreams of being hung up on a stick like a scarecrow, and pecked to death by tiny birds, thousands of them, that landed all over him.

"Police! Step back, everybody. Leave the man alone." It was a woman's voice, a familiar voice, the voice of the big cop who'd just humiliated his woman. A few minutes ago he'd hated her, now her voice was a nightingale's.

"Everybody, be cool. Everything's okay, just give the man some air, that's all. Hey, Mr. Anglime. How's it going?"

She walked over and put her arm through his, cool as you please, a good-looking babe in business clothes, could have been a publicist or something except for the badge she was waving with her free hand.

"Police. Let us through, please."

The woman who'd bitten him had wound up to hit the cop, but she'd quickly seen she wasn't big enough to win in a fight with that one, and stepped back. Nick wondered if she'd sue for the elbow whack he'd given her. People sued him for breathing, and had for years.

When the biter gave up, the fight went out of the crowd. The sudden meanness that can come from too much beer had passed, and the more accustomed mellowness had slipped back home. Couples who'd stopped dancing to join the fray were starting again to twirl and two-step.

Nick said, "First time I've ever been rescued by a woman."

The cop grinned. "It'll cost you one autograph."

He couldn't help it, he liked her. She was a nervy damn broad.

Proctor said, "You okay, Nick?"

"Except for a bitten neck. The skin isn't broken, is it?"

The cop looked, standing close yet remaining professional. He liked having her that close. He wasn't used to big women—and she was definitely big, not just tall. There was something about it he liked—something vaguely maternal. He'd never go out with a woman that overweight, but still, there was something.

"Looks okay," the cop said.

"Shit," said Nick. "This is the last time. I'm never doing this again."

"Never doing what?" asked the cop.

He wasn't sure. Never going back to the JazzFest? Never going out in public? He was tired of feeling like a prisoner. How the hell was he supposed to live?

17

"**O**fficer! Officer Langford!"

Skip looked around to see a very distressed young man waving frantically. He looked worried and upset in that exaggerated way only those under twenty can look—it usually means they've missed a question on an exam or something equally earthshaking, but it made her want to hug them and play Mom.

She waved and walked over. "It's Langdon," she said, "but thanks for remembering my face."

"Oh. I, uh . . ." He seemed not to know what to say.

"You're Flip Phillips, aren't you?"

He nodded. "Melody's ex."

It was all she could do not to laugh. High school kids and their "exes" were so wonderfully dramatic about their three- or four-week relationships.

"I saw Melody," he said.

"Here? Today?"

"A few minutes ago. See, I knew she'd come today to see Ti-Belle sing. So I cut school to come find her." He looked extremely pleased with himself. Skip was willing to bet he'd never cut school in his life and wouldn't have done it today if he hadn't convinced himself it was for the greater good of the human race. This one was no Ferris Bueller, but he seemed pretty smug about bringing off such wildly criminal behavior. Skip was happy for him; he seemed a young man who had far too many rules in his life, most of them of his own making. Wrinkles seemed his only vice. Even now, in the most casual of settings, he wore a button-down shirt—wrinkled but correct to the point of stiffness.

He put his hands in his pockets and looked down at his shoes. "I've been feeling really bad about what I did."

"Dumping Melody?"

He winced. "I wouldn't exactly call it that."

Skip was rapidly changing her assessment of him—beginning to think he had a great career ahead as a white-collar criminal. He was enjoying his first foray into the forbidden, and proving to have great capacities for denial. She wondered if he'd think of a way to describe cutting school without exactly calling it that.

"I wanted to talk to her and tell her I was sorry. I guess. I don't know—I just wanted to see her. To be sure she was okay."

Skip nodded.

"Well, I didn't see her at Ti-Belle's set. There were a million people there, and anyway, I was looking for the wrong Melody. She's completely different now. See, later I was just standing around, looking over the crowd, still trying to find her, and I saw these knees—"

"I beg your pardon?"

He was blushing slightly; becomingly. "There was this girl I saw with gorgeous legs—they reminded me of Melody's—so I was, you know, checking her out. And she had Melody's scar. Melody has a little crescent-shaped scar on her right knee. So I think, Melody's legs, Melody's scar, holy shit! And I look up and the girl does a double-take and starts running."

"It was Melody?"

"Well, yeah, it had to be. But I know her really well. Better than anybody else, I bet, and I didn't even recognize her."

"Did you chase her?"

"Of course." He shrugged. "But she's not that tall and I guess it wasn't hard to get lost in the crowd."

"Okay. What does she look like now?"

"New Age. She's got short blond hair that's purple in front. And different makeup or something. I don't know—maybe she had plastic surgery."

"You're absolutely sure this was Melody?"

"It was Melody's scar. I know that scar."

"Shit."

"What?"

"Oh, nothing. Nothing to do with you." And everything to do with Andy Fike. She sighed. "Okay. Let's go find her."

"What?"

"Let's walk around till we find her."

"Okay. Sure." He seemed delighted to be told what to do. This was a kid who was most comfortable taking orders. In a way, she could see how he and Melody had been attracted to each other— she was the outlaw, he the good citizen; halves of a whole.

They started to walk, eyes peeled and scanning. Something was bothering Skip. Why was the kid blowing the whistle on Melody? Was the whole thing an elaborate hoax?

She made him wait while she put in a call to Andy Fike, who was home as usual, and slightly slurred of speech.

"Andy, how'd Melody look yesterday?"

"Pretty good, for a chick that's been through what she has."

"Damn you, Andy. Start describing."

"Okay, okay, five feet three, skinny, blond, blue eyes."

"Anything else about her hair?"

"Short, purple in front, ugliest thing I ever saw."

"I could kill you, you know that?"

"Hey, you never asked what she looked like—I figured you knew."

Sure.

But at least Flip wasn't lying about that part. She caught up with him again. They walked for nearly half an hour, Skip turning over different strategies in her head and coming up with no clever, devious way to confront the kid.

Oh, hell, she finally decided. *Go for the direct approach.*

"Hey, Flip," she said, "why'd you decide to tell me about this? A lot of kids would have helped their friend get away."

He was walking beside her, so she couldn't see his full face. But his neck turned a good deep red. "Yeah, I know. There's nothing worse than a snitch." He paused, apparently finding it hard to talk about. This was a kid who worked so hard to do the right thing, he probably went nuts when a dilemma came along. "I really really thought about it. I've got to say I still don't know if it's right or not. I'm pretty sure she wouldn't want me turning her in—stands to reason, doesn't it? But I thought of what she told me her shrink said once—I mean, she was really mad about it, but I know Melody and I think it was true. She said Melody's her own worst enemy a lot of times. So I thought about all this, and when all's said and done, she needs to get found. It's the only way out. Anyway, she got real mad at me when Dr. Richard said that and I kind of agreed with her. I mean, not about everything, but a lot of stuff."

He was babbling on and Skip was barely hearing him. She had heard only one word. If Skip had been mad at Andy Fike, that was nothing to the way she was currently feeling about George and Patty. Why in the living hell hadn't they told her?

"Her shrink?" she said when Flip paused for breath, aware too late that she'd shrieked the query.

Flip stared as if she'd gone crazy. "Yeah," he said quietly. "Her shrink. Like a head doctor?"

"Why didn't anyone tell me about this?" She knew it was an unreasonable thing to ask, but at this point she couldn't keep her mouth shut. A teacher had said Melody should be in therapy— why hadn't she thought to ask if she was? Why hadn't anyone thought to tell her? Surely if Melody was in touch with anybody, it was her therapist.

"I'm sorry," Flip said. "I didn't know it was important."

"Flip, listen, I'm the one who's sorry. I shouldn't have yelled —it's not your fault."

"Well, it is partly, I guess."

"Come on, forget it. Just tell me who it is."

"Dr. Richard," he said, almost instantly cheered up. "Madeleine Richard." He pronounced it Ri-SHARD.

"Thanks. Are you tired of looking around?" They'd now made several complete tours of the fairgrounds, and the crowds were getting thicker by the minute.

He said, "I have a feeling she split after she saw me."

"Okay. Can you get home okay?"

He looked insulted. "Sure."

"You'll call if you hear from Melody?"

"Yeah. Yeah, I guess I've got to." He was Atlas bearing the weight of the world; the kid was going to have wrinkles in more than his clothes before he was thirty. "Listen, I want to say something else about Melody. I was right about her coming to see Ti-Belle, wasn't I?"

"You sure were."

"She'll come again on Sunday. When the Boucrees sing."

"Oh, yes. Joel's her buddy."

"She just worships him is all." Skip thought she caught a hint of jealousy in his voice.

She went back to headquarters to check messages and do some catching up. There was a message, all right—a note from Frank O'Rourke, her least favorite sergeant. It was terse, arrogant, and utterly typical: "Report to me at once."

Why the fuck should I? came to mind, but it was almost instantly replaced by a nagging horror, a deep-seated dread.

She grabbed up the note and went to Joe Tarantino's office. He was talking on the phone, but motioned her in anyway. For five minutes she cooled her heels, mentally composing her letter of resignation if Joe told her what she thought he was going to tell her. He hung up the phone and said, "You're as white as that paper you're holding."

She said, "Am I permanently assigned to O'Rourke?"

He sat back in his chair, lips together. "Damn, Skip. Cappello got hurt."

"Oh, shit." She didn't normally swear in the presence of superiors, but this was the "oh, shit" found in every black box of every crashed plane—the universal lament of pilots about to get a second set of wings.

"A suspect pushed her down a flight of stairs." He paused. "Hurt her back real bad—looks like it's going to be about six months."

"Oh, shit," she said again. It had happened so fast; it could happen to anyone—worse could.

"I know how you feel about O'Rourke. Listen, I wouldn't have done this if I had a choice."

She nodded. "Thanks, Lieutenant. I know you wouldn't." She knew he'd already said too much. He'd more or less apologized for assigning her to O'Rourke, even though that was his privilege. He wasn't going to say any more, and he certainly wasn't going to back down.

She went to find her tormentor.

"Langdon. Where the hell have you been?" He got up and led her to an interview room, bellowing as they walked.

"At the fairgrounds. Seeing Ti-Belle Thiebaud."

"What for, may I ask?"

"Trying to find out where she was at the time of the murder."

"And did you?"

"I got her alibi. That's all."

"Did it check out?"

"I just got back. Haven't checked it yet."

"Check it."

She thought she'd scream. But he wasn't nearly done and she knew it.

"Run down the case for me, Langdon. What have you done, what are your plans?"

Feeling like a child in the principal's office, she did, ending with her afternoon with Flip.

"The kid's out there, goddammit."

"Why goddammit? We know she's not dead, and we know what she looks like."

"Why the fuck don't we have her?"

"I think there's a good chance she'll contact this Richard. I'm going over there now."

210

"Langdon. Have you checked Thiebaud's police record?"

An unbelievably condescending question. "Of course."

"How about the other suspects?"

"Who are the suspects?"

"You tell me, Langdon—you're the officer on the damn case."

She took a breath, trying to control her anger. "The parents, the uncles, the cousins, the assistant, the girlfriend, and Melody."

"Forget the uncles and cousins. This is a crime of passion, Langdon. Who *probably* did it? Just speaking statistically?"

"The girlfriend, but—"

"So who're you going to work on, Langdon?"

This was ridiculous. She'd just told him she'd *been* working on Ti-Belle. "Look," she said. "She's got an alibi and no motive."

"You don't know whether she had a damn motive, do you? Maybe Ham said he was porking the assistant, and the Cajun stabbed him. And you haven't checked the alibi, you just told me that."

"Actually, I've checked it with the guy she said she was with. I was just going to do a little more work on it."

"What work?"

"Ask the servants."

"Who's the guy?"

"Nick Anglime."

"Nick Anglime." O'Rourke rocked back in his chair. His face took on such a look of smug contempt she wanted to break his nose. "You believed him, of course, because you're star-struck like some kid Melody's age."

It felt as if the temperature had gone up ten degrees. Skip's neck and face were scorching. Sweat was popping out at her hairline. She clenched the edge of her chair, to give her anger a place to go. And still wanted to fly at his face. She swallowed, trying to think, and wondered if her eyes were bugging out from the effort of control. Finally, she thought of Cindy Lou. What, she wondered, would Cindy Lou do in a situation like this?

When the answer came, it was so right she almost smiled. Her fingers relaxed. Cindy Lou wouldn't answer his insulting questions, would decline once and for all the bait he kept cramming down her throat. She wouldn't sit here submissively, like some kid getting chewed out at school. She'd call him on his own bad behavior. Suddenly, Skip was calm as a Buddhist monk.

She said, "Oh, Frank, don't be such a bully," got up and left.

He shouted, "Young lady, you come back in here!"

She tried not to laugh out loud. She wanted to look—sure he'd turned a gorgeous shade of watermelon—but she wasn't turning full-face around. Instead she gave him only a glance over her shoulder. "That's it for today, Frank." She kept walking.

He followed, bellowing, "Goddammit, Langdon, I'm your sergeant."

Now they were in the middle of the cavernous squad room. People were staring. Skip still felt cool as a gin and tonic. She stopped and turned around. "Fine. What would you like me to do?"

"Follow up on Thiebaud, goddammit."

She nodded. "Of course." And glided back to her desk. Actually, you didn't really glide when you were six feet tall and didn't tell your weight, but she felt she came close.

Certainly she would follow up on Thiebaud. Just as she would if Frank were moldering in the grave. She was a professional. She'd follow up on other things as well. She simply wouldn't mention them to Frank.

First, she went to do what she'd intended all along, declining to be stopped by the fact that she'd now been ignominiously ordered to do so. She went to Nick's to poke around.

The housekeeper answered her knock. "Is Mr. Anglime here?"

The woman disappeared, came back and said he wasn't. All as Skip had suspected.

"Okay. I wanted to talk to you anyway." She produced her badge, explained her mission, and asked who had been at the house on Tuesday.

The housekeeper, of course, said she couldn't answer a question like that—that would be up to Mr. Anglime. But fortunately, along came a kid of about nine or ten who didn't stand on ceremony. "Hey, are you the lady cop? What do you want to know?" And once again the housekeeper went in search of Mr. Anglime.

He showed up shirtless, buckling his belt, hair uncombed. Skip was willing to bet he'd been having a little nap with the lovely Ti-Belle. "What the hell is this?"

"I wanted to see if there was anyone here who remembered seeing Ms. Thiebaud on Tuesday."

"You think you can invade my house, disturb my guests, distress the staff—"

"Mr. Anglime, this is a murder case. If you'll let me know who was here Tuesday, I'll gladly see them on their own turf."

"What the hell do you think you're doing?"

"I'm trying to see if anyone can back up her story—and yours."

"Mine? What are you talking about? Lady, I'm Nick Anglime. Who the hell do you think you are, questioning what I say?"

With those words, Skip's stage-struck state shattered like a skim of ice. Suddenly she felt much more composed, for the first time in command with this man. She shrugged; even smiled. "It's my job."

Something in her manner must have communicated itself—or else he simply realized he'd acted like a jerk. "I'm sorry. Of course it is—I don't know what I was thinking of."

He let her in and said to the housekeeper, "Jessie, take care of Officer, uh . . ."

"Skip."

He looked at her, puzzled.

"It's Langdon; but call me Skip, please." They'd been through this; he wouldn't remember the next time either.

"Oh, yes." He turned back to Jessie. "Help her any way you can."

Jessie looked as if she'd rather eat toad stew. "This way, please." She led the way to the kitchen, where there was a beautiful long pine table, as nice as most people's dining room tables, and asked her to sit. A man was in the kitchen making iced tea—the same man who'd been with Anglime at the JazzFest.

"Hello," he said, but didn't introduce himself, just went on with his project as if she and Jessie weren't there.

"How may I help you?" Jessie asked, the prim words spoken

in a soft black accent, as warm and sociable as she'd been aloof before.

When Skip repeated her mission, the housekeeper started reeling off names. There'd been a possible total of eleven people in the house Tuesday, including herself, aside from Anglime and Thiebaud.

They were Jessie Swan, housekeeper; James Fayard, another housecleaner and handyman; Sabrina Kostelnik, ex-girlfriend; Mia Anglime, her daughter and Nick's; Eric and Scott Anglime, Nick's sons with a Rachel Anglime; Caroline Meyer (aka Meyer-Roshi), Zen consultant; Nanette Underwood, acupuncturist, herbalist, and masseuse; Ricky Roberts, cook; April Thomas, clerical worker; and Proctor Gaither, old friend.

When Jessie Swan got to Gaither, the man making tea waved to acknowledge that was he.

Of these, houseguests included Kostelnik, the three children, Meyer, Underwood, and Gaither. Of the other four, none lived in and only Swan was full-time. Yes, she, Jessie, had been there Tuesday and, sure enough, so had Ms. Thiebaud. "All day?" asked Skip, thinking it didn't matter what she said—she was in her boss's house and likely to lie anyway. She'd interview the others on their own turf.

"All day and all day the day before and all day the day after," said Swan.

That should have been that, but Proctor Gaither spoke up. "Except for when she went shopping."

"Well, I didn't know about that." Swan was slightly huffy.

"Sure. Tuesday afternoon? Around three or four, I think."

"Well, I don' know," repeated Swan.

Skip said, "When did she return?"

But Gaither shrugged. "I don't know. I just saw her leave, and then she was around for dinner."

So Ti-Belle wasn't getting off the hook quite so easily.

"Tell me something, Mr. Gaither."

"Proctor."

"Proctor. Doesn't it get awkward with Ms. Kostelnik and Ms. Thiebaud around at the same time?"

"Awkward?" He seemed genuinely to be considering the idea. "No, I don't think you'd call it awkward."

"You wouldn't?" She held her breath, not sure he'd answer.

But he was surprisingly forthcoming, even glib. "Sabrina and Nick are very good friends—so long as they don't spend too much time with each other. She's having a hard time, he wants to do right by his kids, so he lets her stay here, and the two of them bend over backward staying out of each other's hair. He wants her to learn a useful trade, so she can get by on her own. Nanette's teaching her Oriental medicine."

"You don't have to go to a special school for that?"

He touched his chest. "You're asking moi? I'm just an ol' boy from Alabama."

"Just out for the JazzFest?"

He nodded. A shadow crossed his white-bread, good-ol'-boy face. "Getting divorced. Took some time off."

"This is some household."

"Never a dull moment. Nick's a child of the sixties; look what he's built here—an updated, upgraded, upscale commune, complete with resident guru—two if you count Nanette." He shook his head. "No, she's more like—don't take this wrong, okay?—she's more like a connection. Nothing illegal; nobody'd be so un-nineties as that—but she's got what makes us feel good, even if it's liver compresses nowadays."

"Do they work?"

"Are you kidding? I don't even know what they're supposed to do. Nothing wrong with the massages, though."

Skip half turned back to Jessie Swan, who was still sitting primly, patiently. "Is she around? I'd like to talk to her."

Swan shook her head. "No'm. She and Sabrina went out some place with the roshi. Took the kids."

"Ricky Roberts?"

"Day off."

"Popeye's, here we come," said Proctor. "By the way, he cooks only nonfat vegetarian, and he can do macrobiotic if you really want it."

Skip made a face; couldn't help it, it just happened.

215

"Don't knock it—it's some of the best food you ever had. The man's an artist."

"Well, I'll need the artist's phone number," she said to Swan. "Also April Thomas's—she comes one day a week, I presume."

Swan nodded, and went to look up numbers.

"What's the roshi like?" she asked Proctor.

"Quiet. The one-hand-clapping type."

She raised an eyebrow.

"I wasn't being sarcastic—I just meant she's quiet. She's certainly not a freeloader, if that's what you're thinking. Nick's known her only about five years less than he's known me—and he's known me a millenium. But she's not really a roshi and doesn't claim to be—we just call her that because she's—you know—holier than we are. She used to manage a club in the Village, where Nick had some of his first gigs. Then she got into Zen, studied to be a monk, and married another one. They split up, and got into some kind of tangle about money that she ended up being embarrassed about in the Zen community. She and Nick ran into each other again at Tassajara, she told him the whole story, and he asked her to come here and be his teacher until she decides what to do next. She designed the zendo and everything."

Skip sighed. In matters of meditation, she could use a teacher. Swan came back, gave her the numbers she needed, and then Skip left, thinking Proctor Gaither had been a shade more talkative than was natural.

18

$\blacksquare$ $\blacksquare$

Patty stood in front of the little shotgun on Calhoun near Fontain-
bleau Drive, thinking it must not have been painted in fifteen years,
you'd think no one lived there. The lawn hadn't been mowed
either. Her brothers usually kept up the lawn, but perhaps the
house was so shabby they couldn't do it any more, couldn't find
the heart even to do a few simple things. They couldn't afford to
have the house painted, couldn't do it themselves—being too tired
on weekends, too involved with their own families, maybe too
depressed. And no one in the family would accept money from
her, not that much anyway.

But they'd take a few little things, and today she'd brought
clothes that she no longer wanted, some food that mourners had
brought, an extra ham, a turkey, cakes, things she and George
couldn't eat. Before she left, she would give them money too, and
they'd spend it on medicine, doctors, the usual things. They never
had extras and they never seemed to want any. Not that they were
so satisfied with their lives; they just didn't connect the notion of
themselves and luxury. Even tiny luxuries—she knew one of them
would wear the denim dress she'd brought, and one might take the

simple silk, but the evening dress would probably be cut up and made into costumes for children's recitals.

She was depressed, just standing here, being here, and she hadn't even gone in yet. A sense of futility hung over the Fournot house, always had, because of the illness. There were six of them, Patty and three sisters and two brothers—her mother had had them all before she knew she had it, or knew she could pass it on to them.

Her mother had been forty-two when she went blind for a couple of weeks and miraculously regained her sight. She had had a religious conversion before the other symptoms came on—the thing the doctors called "clumsy limb," the slurred speech that made her think she'd had a stroke, and the facial pain. Whoever heard of facial pain? When her mother would say her face hurt, neither Patty nor the others would know what to say; they thought she must have gotten drunk and fallen down.

After an endless series of tests and misdiagnoses, one of the dozens of doctors she went to finally realized she had chronic progressive multiple sclerosis. A woman in her church had MS; she was relieved, knowing it was something you could live with. But there were two different kinds, the doctor explained: the kind the other woman had, which tended to relapse and remit; and the kind she, Lorraine, had, which would only get relentlessly worse, and which "ran in families." Frannie, the second oldest sister, had come down with it eight years ago, at the age of thirty-two. The worse it got, the more her husband drank; he'd left her, finally.

Desiree took care of her and Lorraine. She lived here, in this small house, with her husband and two children and the two sick women.

No one came out to meet Patty. She went up the steps and knocked, lugging the clothes and a hamper. Ten-year-old Ashley, home from school, let her in, looking at her sleek hair, her tight Joan Vass pants and matching swingy little top, with the awed eyes of a child who's never been shopping anyplace fancier than J.C. Penney. "Hi, Aunt Patty."

"Hello, sweetness." Patty bent to kiss her, trailing the gift castoffs, nearly upending the hamper.

"Watch out!" It was her brother, Martin, catching things, taking them from her, but sounding angry.

"I've got more stuff in the car," she said, and went to get the turkey and some lasagna, trailed by Ashley. No one else followed.

The two of them muscled the stuff into the kitchen, where Desiree was chopping onions and crying.

"Des, for heaven's sake. Let me do it."

It was like old times. While she was still in high school, Patty had saved enough money for contacts, which meant she could chop onions without crying. When she'd lived in this house, it had always been her chore.

Gladly, her sister handed over the knife and stared at Patty, a vision in the chic little cream-colored outfit, whimsical lemon flats on her feet, white-blond hair falling to her shoulders.

Ashley came and caught the sheet of hair in her hands: "Aunt Patty, your hair's so pretty."

"Yours too, sweetness," said Patty absently. Ashley's was thin, mouse-colored, and badly in need of shampoo. Patty looked up at her sister, caught her staring. "What is it, Des?"

"You do that so well. Like a professional."

Patty was embarrassed. She probably hadn't chopped an onion since she married George. "How's Mama?"

"The same."

"And Frannie?"

"Lively this week for some reason. They know you're coming —I've brushed their hair." And she clomped off to the last room, the one where they lived, in the two hospital beds Patty had bought for them. "Mama! Frannie! Patty's here."

"Well, where is she?"

"I'm coming, Mama."

She finished the onions, washed her hands, and went in, feeling a little lift at the prospect of seeing her mother. But she didn't look well, looked even less well than usual, smaller somehow.

Just about all she could do now was chew and swallow—and click the remote control for her television. She could talk, but she sounded as if she were drunk. Her limbs were limp, soggy logs. And Frannie was nearly as bad.

They were both diapered, didn't even know when they excreted. Their limbs were rolled in sheets and cushions. They had to sleep on egg-crate mattresses to prevent bedsores. They were prisoners, but at least they could speak, they could eat. Patty thought how much worse it would be if they couldn't communicate.

Frannie's hair was almost completely gray now; she was younger than Patty and looked nearly as old as Mama. The television blathered, as always in this room. The blinds—not even miniblinds, ancient venetian blinds, were closed. Patty had never seen them open. She couldn't imagine what it would be like to live in one room, a dark one, and had begged Des to open the blinds every day, but Des said the patients wouldn't permit it, they wanted nothing except to watch television, and who was to deny them their one pleasure? As if Patty meant them ill.

Martin had come to fix something, but now he brought chairs for Patty and himself and Des, so they could visit in the sickroom. It was stuffy and hot and it smelled of urine.

"We heard about Ham on the TV, Patty." Her mother's voice was barely a quaver. "We were worried sick about you."

"I'm sorry, Mama. I phoned and told Des to tell you not to worry."

"Couldn't help worryin'."

"Well, I know. That's why I came. I wish I could have come yesterday, but I was so busy with George . . ."

"That's how it always is."

"Yes." Patty couldn't tell whether her mother meant to let her off the hook, merely meant that was how it was with husbands and family deaths, or meant that Patty always put her and Frannie second. "I brought you some cakes and things."

"Don't have much appetite lately."

But Frannie said, "Chocolate?"

"Lemon. With white icing."

"Oh." There was a silence, and finally her mother said, "I'm sorry about Ham, Patty."

"Thank you, Mama."

"Who killed him. Melody?"

"Mama! Why would you say a thing like that?" Did her mother think she'd done that bad a job of raising Melody? That she'd raised a killer?

"Well, it just seems natural, don't it? Melody bein' missin' and all."

"Kidnapped," said Martin. "That poor child's . . . Ashley, you go play now. Don't listen to this."

"I just can't believe this is happenin' in my own family," said Patty's mother. "I want to cry my eyes out every time I think about it."

Desiree nodded. "It's been real hard on all of us."

"Well, I'm sorry, I . . ." Patty realized she didn't know what to say. How did she apologize for her stepson's murder?

Martin gave her a narrow-eyed look that said, "How can you look that good and rich and act that dumb?" Or so it seemed to Patty. She was the oldest; he was the second youngest. She'd left when she married, and missed a lot of his growing up; they hardly knew each other, and she hardly knew Des and Frannie either, she'd been gone so long. The others barely remembered her, she thought. They treated her like an outsider, and yet she tried— didn't she try? Not that they noticed. She would offer again, but first she must ask the question she'd come to pose.

Ashley hadn't heeded her uncle; she was hanging in the doorway, taking it all in, looking at Patty as if she were a movie star. "Is Melody okay?" she said, and Patty thought she saw the beginnings of tears in her eyes.

But Desiree, her mother, spoke before Patty could, "Yes, precious, Melody's just fine. You go out and play now."

It struck Patty as odd that they weren't more worried about Melody, about their niece and grandchild, who was only sixteen and missing, possibly kidnapped as far as they knew. She had called Des and spoken to her only briefly, and no one had called her back. No one in the huge Fournot family, full of siblings and in-laws and their issue, had called or come over after her stepson had been murdered and her daughter gone missing.

The thought flickered and died. She was barely aware she'd thought it before she got busy explaining the actual situation to herself.

They're intimidated. They don't dare come visit me Uptown, and they don't want to call because George spooks them—they wouldn't know what to say if he answered the phone. They can't worry about Melody, because she seems like a fairy princess to them. They'd be worried if they thought she was human, but they just can't grasp the idea that anything could happen to her.

Then again . . . maybe they know something I don't.

She asked her question. "I was wondering—has Melody called here? Or turned up, maybe?"

Her mother snorted. "Turned up? Why, she wouldn't know the way."

Patty felt her face go red. It was true she'd only brought Melody over on Christmas and her mother's birthday, though Melody adored Ashley, seemed to like the other children as well, to be happy to have cousins. But George thought it depressed her to come, and Patty thought he was right. George didn't come at all anymore. In the days when he had, he hadn't spoken for hours after except in monosyllables. Patty found herself stripping and jumping in the shower, or else going swimming after a visit. She never thought about it, just did it.

She and George slaved to keep Melody in the best school, in beautiful Country Day, with its arches and deep green walls upstairs, its five working artists on the faculty. They gave her a magnificent house with her own room and bath, and all the clothes she had time to shop for. They'd given her music lessons. Her life was perfect, privileged; as parents, they believed in that, preparing her for life—at Country Day, they even talked about that, preparation for life. They made the kids eat lunch with different kids every six weeks, kids they didn't even know, so they'd learn how to handle themselves in different situations.

But this was sad, it was dirty and crowded and scary, because illness was always scary, and that of your relatives, those close to you, much more so. Patty didn't want her exposed to it any more than George did. She hadn't brought Melody here much; and yet, she *had* brought her here. She wasn't some kind of snob who didn't want her daughter to know her own relatives. It hurt her that her mother thought so.

"Melody loves to come here," she said. "She loves you, Mama."

Patty didn't know if that was true, but she knew it was true that *she* did, did love her Mama and didn't understand where things had gone wrong between them. Understanding that was what she meant as soon as she said it, she felt herself tearing up, hoped they wouldn't notice.

Her mother's eyes got a faraway look. "I doubt that girl loves anything, really. I don't think she knows how to love."

"If Ashley's listening, you'll hurt her feelings. She's crazy about that child, and you know it." Patty's voice was rising, but she felt guilty, somehow; it wasn't pure. She didn't feel like a protective mother animal, didn't know why her mother's comment made her so mad. She pretty much agreed with her. Melody did like small things—Ashley, and animals, and babies, but she hated her own parents, certainly Patty. Once Patty had thought the girl had a bond with George, but after she reached puberty and started hating the whole adult structure of the universe, she turned against George as well.

"She's not a bad child," said her mother. "I don't really think she's bad."

She's just a selfish little bitch.

"She just needs some guidance."

"Well, how're y'all feeling, Mama and Frannie?" she said, making her tone light, canarylike, taking charge, changing the subject.

"I feel fine," said Frannie. "I b'lieve I'm gon' be the first person with this thing to get better."

Her mother said: "Nobody gets better with this thing." She cackled like it was funny.

Patty put a hand on the blanket, feeling mushy flesh; useless flesh. But even so, her mother's leg felt smaller than it had, she thought. All of a sudden she knew Lorraine wasn't going to live much longer—the doctors had been predicting her death for years. Des always said she was too mean to die, and her mama liked that, had taken it on as her special slogan and had lived ten years longer than anyone thought she would, declaring her meanness nearly every day, if anyone would listen. But she was going to go soon.

"I mean it, Mama," Patty said. "How are you?"

"Well, I get the spasms a lot."

Patty cocked her head like a parakeet.

"Most times I can't feel a thing in my legs—haven't for years, but when the spasms come, it hurts me so bad I holler; Des has to bring warm towels in to make it stop. You know how you can scratch an old dog's chest and his hind foot'll jump around? Tha's what the spasms are like—jus' like a dog's hind leg. We're runnin' out of towels too—ours are so threadbare you can almost see through 'em."

"Oh, Mama! I'll get you some towels. You know you don't have to want for anything if you'll just tell me what you need. I want to get you a house so bad! You suffer so much, you and Frannie. Wouldn't you like to have a bigger place, something with some nice big windows and ceiling fans?"

Her mother made a sound that was somewhere between a cough and a snort, something like "harrumph," but more explosive. "You couldn't buy us anything like that."

"Well, George could. You know he could, and he'd be glad to. He wants to, Mama. You know that."

"I know y'all are talking through your hats," said Frannie. "You're not gon' do anything of the kind. You've been sayin' you would for years and you're not gon' do it."

"But Mama always says she won't move!"

"I'm not takin' any of your ill-gotten gains, Miss Patty Big Shot. I know why you married George Brocato, and it sure wasn't for love. You can just forget it if you think I'm touching one floorboard of any house that man buys for me."

The room went out of focus. Patty felt her head tilt, spinning, out of her control. She always offered the house, they always refused. But this was new.

"Mama!" said Martin.

Des said quickly, "She's overtired." Hustling Patty out, tiptoeing, she whispered, "The medicine does her this way. Sometimes, anymore, she just isn't herself."

Patty's throat had closed. Patty and George had supported the Fournots from the beginning of their marriage; George had insisted. A hammer thudded in the back of Patty's head. The tears wanted to come out, but she couldn't let them, couldn't drive home if she got started.

■

George had been on a similar errand, had looked for Melody at the homes of his brothers and nieces and nephews, even the ones who'd been so nasty earlier that day. Nasty was a way of life with the Brocatos; you lived with it.

He'd never noticed it that much before. But today, with the weight of his son's death heavy on him, he couldn't stand it, felt as if walls were closing on him. His brother Phil and Phil's wife, Nan, didn't even ask him in, just kept him standing at the door, Phil saying, "Hell, no, she's not here, why the hell would she come here?"

Nan had said, "Be nice to your brother," and Phil said, "Why should I be nice to him?"

"Because he's your brother."

"Hell, you're my wife, I'm not going to start being nice to you —why should I be nice to him?"

Phil thought he was funny, and usually George would have forced a smile, might have been genuinely amused; he really couldn't remember the man he'd been two days before, when he'd had his children, when he hadn't felt so lacerated and naked.

"Bicker, bicker, bicker," he said. "Nobody in the whole damn family even knows how to be nice!"

His brother had said, "You and Patty do it too—come on, admit it, George, you wouldn't be a Brocato if you didn't."

And before he thought, he didn't even know what he was saying, George retorted, "We don't care enough to bother."

Phil said nastily, "Well, why not, George?"

He had no idea what his brother meant by that. He walked away, furious, huffing, but as he got in his car, the words echoed.

Well, why not, George?

Phil had said them so accusingly.

Why not what? Why didn't he and Patty care? Patty cared. She was like a leech. Why didn't George care? Care enough to bother bickering with his wife?

He shook his head, clearing it, wondering if he was short of air —he was sitting in the car, letting it warm up, even though it was eighty-two outside.

It wasn't about bickering. But his brother had asked a question that had been nibbling at the edge of his consciousness lately: Why didn't he care?

Patty's who there is to love—why not love her?

That was the question, wasn't it? With Ham gone, with Melody gone, *missing*—she was only missing—with the underbrush cleared out, so to speak, he was feeling closer to Patty, needing her almost.

This morning he'd almost forgotten what he didn't like about her. He thought about it. There was nothing wrong with Patty. She was pretty. She was a good mother. She must be a good wife, she did everything wives were supposed to. She wasn't Dorothy, of course . . .

How could you miss a woman who'd been dead for seventeen years?

He wasn't exactly sure how a shrink would put it, but he thought he knew the answer, sort of—*if you had half a brain, you wouldn't. You'd get over it.*

Like a man.

He was humiliated. Was he really in love with a dead woman? But he thought it couldn't be—he hadn't been that crazy about her when she was alive.

He put the car in drive and drove away far too fast.

Well, if I didn't love Dorothy because she got pregnant and I got stuck with her, and then I never loved Patty because she wasn't Dorothy, what the hell's wrong with me?

He'd never had a thought like that in his life.

It's the damn assholes! The Brocato assholes.

Looking at them, listening to them, turned his stomach—there must be other ways to live.

Phil lived near Audubon Park, and to George's surprise, he found himself going there, heading for the zoo. He had a weird feeling Melody would be there—an overpowering feeling. He was as sure as he was of her name that she was there now, that he'd find her in the next few minutes. Where else would she be? It was her favorite place.

Yet, once inside, wandering among the moms and kids, the sudden elation left him. It wasn't such a brilliant deduction he'd made. It was the final fuck-up of a man whose whole life was a fuck-up. Not his whole life. Not his business life. Just this sleep-walking—or whatever it was—involving Dorothy and Melody and Patty.

And Ham. Maybe Ham most of all.

What the fuck's wrong with me?

I hate myself.

The zoo wasn't Melody's favorite place. Melody was a young woman. He didn't know the young woman. The zoo had been the child's favorite. He didn't know when she had gotten away from him.

Or when Ham had.

19

George found Patty at home staring out the window, apparently as depressed by her efforts as he was by his. He felt a tenderness for her, an odd identification. "Baby, I know what you're going through."

She looked at him in surprise. He had put his hand on her shoulder. She almost jumped.

"Listen, I know a guy. A private detective."

"You mean the one Johnny Dupre got to spy on his wife?"

"How'd you know about that?"

"The man's pond scum. I don't want him anywhere near our daughter."

He took her hands and tried not to notice the surprise in her eyes. He felt the energy running from her body to his; it was strangely exhilarating. "Patty, I thought we agreed we were going to work together to find her."

"I thought we did too."

"Did you think I'd go back on that?"

"But I thought you just said—"

228

He interrupted her. "Trust me. Would you trust me, please? I'm just going to ask the guy for advice."

He dropped her hands and strode to the phone, not waiting for an answer. He said it was an emergency and waited for the guy to call back. Patty went upstairs to wash her face.

When she came back, he said, "Let's go to the Quarter."

"But she's been there. She told Andy Fike she was leaving town."

"She'll be there." He spoke more grimly than he meant to, teeth clenched, jaw muscles working.

"You're so damned arrogant."

Could that be Patty speaking? She never spoke to him like that. It was as if Ham's death had changed her, changed him, changed them all forever.

He could have tried to mollify her, but he didn't, he was too impatient. He said, "She'll be there, Patty. Come on. They all end up there. That's what the guy told me. There's a whole scene down there."

"Scene?"

He thought he could see fear in her eyes, hear it in her voice. The guy, the detective, had told him things he didn't want to hear, didn't want Patty to know about. He hustled her out the door. "A runaway scene," he said, trying to keep his voice neutral. "He said to try a place called Covenant House—a shelter for homeless kids."

Patty looked puzzled. "Melody's not homeless."

"Come on, dammit, Patty. Listen, it's a nice place, the guy said. They call it the Hilton for the Homeless."

"Where is it?"

"North Rampart."

She said nothing, merely opened the car door and sank down, looking out the window.

He might as well have said they were going to the Desire Project; no mother wanted to think of her kid on North Rampart, the street that divided the French Quarter from Tremé. Right now it was one of the roughest neighborhoods in New Orleans. Still, the

Cov was a nice place, the man had said; if Melody were there, she'd be fine.

It looked okay, he thought. He could see hope in Patty's eyes as she took in the neat brick building, the large, carpeted, pleasant reception room—well, technically not a reception room, perhaps. The sign called it a Crisis Center.

"We're looking for someone," he told the young woman at the desk. "We don't even know if she's here."

"A kid?"

"Yes, a kid. I thought that's what you have here."

A young black woman came into the room, carrying a baby and holding a toddler's hand. She looked about nineteen.

The receptionist was looking at Patty and George as if they'd just arrived from Mars. "Are you her parents?" She sounded unbelieving, even accusing.

"Yes."

"I'm sorry. We offer sanctuary. We can't really tell you if someone's here."

"She's sixteen, for God's sake."

"We can keep underage kids for seventy-two hours before we're required to notify their parents."

"Bullshit!"

Patty said, "George!" and he realized he'd bellowed. The receptionist was nearly the color of a frying pan, one of the blackest people George had ever seen, yet he had the sense she'd turned pale. She stood and backed away, her eyes jumpy, like a rabbit's.

"Ms. Ohlmeyer," she said. "Could you come talk to these people?"

In a nearby glass-fronted office, an older woman, perhaps fifty, looked over the rims of her glasses. She was black also, and dressed in a black dress, one that looked comfortable to George, suitable for moving fast if she had to. It had a white band down the front, with buttons on it. The woman was overweight and, though her face looked serious, even stern at first, she had a maternal quality that George picked up immediately, that he associated with overweight women, and liked; that made him feel comfortable. She wore no jewelry except a wedding band and a pair of gold hoop earrings. She looked bored, but she came out of her office and stood politely. "Yes?"

"We're looking for our daughter."

"Come in." Her voice was rich as meunière sauce.

Like the receptionist, she rather pointedly didn't ask their daughter's name.

"We don't get many parents," she said. "You took Johanda by surprise. A lot of our kids aren't really runaways—some of them are, sure, but a lot of them are what we call 'push-outs.' " She shrugged. "Their parents don't want them."

"Don't want them?" George could see Patty struggling with the concept. "Why wouldn't their parents want them?"

"They can't afford them. Say the mother gets a new boyfriend and her daughter's sixteen—well, she's a threat two different ways. Sexually and economically. The boyfriend's a meal ticket— the mom doesn't want to lose it."

"But that's terrible."

"Or some of the parents are crack addicts."

"Not white people!" Patty blurted, and George could have kicked her.

But Ohlmeyer smiled. "You'd be surprised."

George struggled for control. "Look, Ms. Ohlmeyer. We didn't push our daughter out—she ran away."

Ohlmeyer's face took on a wary, purposefully cheerful, but slightly phony, look, the look people get when they're about to tell you bad news. "You know, kids usually don't run to something; they don't call them runaways for nothing. They leave because they can't handle conditions at home. Our kids are here for four reasons: neglect, emotional abuse, sexual abuse, or other physical abuse. Ninety percent of our kids have been abused."

She leaned back in her chair, letting them take it in.

Patty said, "You don't understand. This isn't anything like that."

If he didn't shut her up, she'd probably say, "*Melody goes to Country Day. She takes music lessons.*" He realized that he was on the verge of saying it himself.

231

Ohlmeyer said, "She must have had a reason for running away."

"Look, this isn't your average runaway case—"

Patty interrupted him. "Do we look like most of the parents you get in here?"

"We don't get that many parents. But look, I think I can reassure you on one thing—we do offer the kids sanctuary, but if a kid isn't being abused, home is where she belongs. We encourage all our kids who can to go home."

"But you won't tell us if our daughter's here?"

Ohlmeyer stared at them, assessing. "I've got a funny feeling. Look, I'm about to go out on a limb—are you the Brocatos by any chance?"

George saw Patty's eyes close with relief.

"Yes," he said, and Patty said, "She's here."

"Well, no, she's not here. I just recognized you from the papers. You have all my sympathy, Mr. and Mrs. Brocato." She clucked like a hen. "Mmmmm mmm, you surely do. You're right, this isn't your average runaway situation. I've been thinking about Melody a lot; we all have—that poor child."

Patty looked as if she might cry. George said, "We won't take up any more of your time."

But Ohlmeyer said, "You're serious about trying to find her?"

"We're her parents!"

Ohlmeyer shrugged. "We've got kids in here who came home one day and found their parents had moved. But look, Melody's out there somewhere—" She stopped. "Pray God." She looked seriously at both the Brocatos.

George said, "We know she is. She's been seen."

"Well, probably what she'll do is what they all do—she'll try to meet other kids. That's how they get along here. They help each other; live off each other. They get jobs as waitresses or, uh, dancers. Your best shot at finding her is to go where the kids go." She started writing things down. "Go to Decatur Street—here's the names of some bars they like. Go to Jackson Square. If you think she's dancing, Bourbon Street."

"Dancing?" said Patty.

232

It was preposterous. Melody dancing on Bourbon Street?

Ohlmeyer shrugged. "Go sit on a balcony. Watch the crowds go by—you might get lucky."

"That's your best advice? Go sit on a balcony?"

"At least there they can't see you. If you go in the bars, you'll stick out."

After the initial shock, George had rethought the dancing idea. Melody was too young to get a legal job, and probably not desperate enough—he fervently hoped—to turn tricks or deal drugs. Dancing might seem an adventure to her. "Which clubs hire underage dancers?" he said.

Ohlmeyer looked almost pleased. "Bayou Babies gets most of them," she said. "The one with the ugly sign."

■

They all had ugly signs. Bayou Babies, in fact, looked less offensive than most.

It was only afternoon, but a near-naked young woman gyrated on a stage clearly visible from the door. Or visible until a man blocked the doorway, a man who'd been wearing the same wilted clothes for a while and had splashed cologne over stale sweat. He stood so close George felt himself start to gag.

"I'll have to ask you to—"

"We're coming in!" George snapped, handing him a folded bill to get him out of nostril range.

The dancing girl wasn't Melody, and his first thought was to leave, never mind the two-drink minimum, until he saw the girl on the bar. She was lying there on her side, her feet got up in some kind of mermaid's tail, but the rest of her stark naked except for the two-by-two-inch G-string they all wore. She rested her head on her right hand and had her left arm folded over her breasts, so that the effect wasn't erotic, merely shocking. Shocking because she was a teenager with a pageboy, a kid about Melody's age, looking as if she was lying by a swimming pool. Shocking because her face was a baby's face, the face of a child whose worst problem ought to be algebra. She wasn't even wearing makeup.

He was staring at her, trying not to gasp, not to change expres-

233

sion, when he heard Patty say, "Oh my God."

He turned toward her—toward the center of the club—and saw what she saw: a short-haired girl with walnut-sized breasts, brand new, just sprouting, barely budded little things. She was standing on a chair, pulled up to a table, pumping her pelvis. The girl was thin, like Melody, wearing only the ubiquitous G-string and a pair of knee-length boots. Her crotch was about six inches from the face of the man sitting at the table.

"Don't look," he said to Patty, he didn't know why.

A waitress led them to a table and brought them a pair of five-dollar Cokes. George stared at a landscape dotted with "table dancers" like the girl with the walnut breasts. In the center was a carpet-covered stage, inhabited by three more naked beauties, performing on their backs—doing somersaults, leg lifts, getting into contortions that looked like weird yoga postures. They probably were yoga movements, it dawned on him—these clubs didn't have choreographers; the girls probably had to use whatever they knew.

But these girls were background—the table dancers were what hurt. High school kids shaking their booties in men's faces. It made him want to throw up.

Patty reached for his hand. "Do you see Melody?"

"No." It came out like a squawk. A girl came and whispered to Patty, who answered. The girl drew up a chair.

"She asked me if I wanted to buy a table dance for twenty dollars to embarrass you," Patty said. "I said we'd give her twenty bucks to talk to us."

George nodded. "Do you know a girl named Melody?" he asked, knowing how futile it was.

She shook her head. "My name's Tulip." She spoke in a high, baby voice.

"How old is that girl?" He pointed to the one lying on the counter.

"Twenty-two. Me too."

What was there to say? *Where should we look for our daughter?*

"I bet you'd never guess that," said Tulip. "Because of my voice. I sound like a baby, don't I?" Her words were slurred. She was pretty loaded. "The owner here told my girlfriend, 'Tulip's butt's too big, but I had to hire her because she sounds like a child and I love to fuck children.'" Tulip giggled. "You get along however you can."

George threw his Coke against the wall. He didn't know he was going to do it, later wondered how he'd decided to aim for the wall instead of the fat, stinking barker, who proved also to be the bouncer. The man was at the table, grabbing George under the armpits, muscling him out before the shards of the glass had hit the floor.

"My money!" cried Tulip, her too-red lips twisted in despair.

"I'm leaving, goddammit! Let me pay her!" The man let go.

George tossed her two twenties and stalked out, Patty trailing.

Blinking in the brightness outside, Patty was pale. "What happened, George? Are you okay?"

"I'm okay." He spoke louder than he needed to, yelled at her, really. They walked in silence to their car. Only when the motor was running did George turn to her. "You read about that stuff, you know? You hear about it."

She nodded, her brows drawn together, as if she were trying to keep her face from falling apart.

"But it doesn't prepare you—I mean, you don't know until you see it. You just don't know."

Patty was shaking. She wasn't crying, she was just shaking, as if she were very cold.

20

Melody took the shuttle back to the Quarter, breathing everyone else's beer fumes and wishing she could have gotten loaded at the JazzFest, could have found someone to buy beer for her. This time, she was really at the end of the line; no turning back. She'd seen someone she knew and been chased. She couldn't sing with the band anymore because people knew what she looked like now; Flip would spread the word. And she couldn't stay with them because it was too sad now that Chris had someone else. They probably wouldn't let her anyway, if she wasn't going to sing.

She could go to the bar on Decatur Street, the one where the runaways and punk rockers hung out, and try to meet someone to stay with, but she was afraid to. She'd had enough of the kindness of strangers for a while. She wanted to see Joel.

He'd be practicing right now with Doug, practicing like crazy because he was going to play when the Boucrees performed to-morrow. She made a decision. It wasn't rational, it was crazy, it was probably even stupid, but her brain wasn't working, only her heart was. Or whatever lonely, longing part of her desperately wanted to be with someone she cared about.

She took the bus to Metairie, walked to the garage, and simply sat down in the yard behind it, where no one ever went at this time of day, and waited till the music stopped; until Doug left. If they had come out together, she'd have had to scrap the plan, but Doug always left first. Joel liked to stick around and work by himself.

"Hey, Joel."

"Huh?" He looked at her in surprise, as if she were a stranger.

Her hand went to her blond and purple hair. "Hey, it's me. Melody."

"Holy shit. That's the ugliest hairdo I've ever seen on a woman who wasn't my mama."

"I know you mean that in the kindest possible way."

He stood up and walked up to her, smiling now. She could tell he was glad to see her. "Hey, Mel, give me a hug."

She hadn't expected that. The only time Joel had ever hugged her was when they won the Battle of the Bands at Valencia. She didn't need to be asked twice. She gave him a lot more of a hug than he probably wanted, and when it wasn't enough, she said, "Hold me tighter, Joel," and proceeded nearly to squeeze the breath out of him.

"Sit down," he said finally.

She did, smiling at him, unable to take her eyes off him; she felt she'd come home.

"Melody, you had us all scared. Real scared."

"Really?" She couldn't believe Joel had actually been worried about her. She didn't know why, she just hadn't thought about it.

"You moron. The whole town's worried about you."

She didn't say anything. She had thought he meant he was.

"I guess you had a good reason for splitting, huh?"

She nodded. "I can't talk about it." Mortified, she realized her voice was going south on her. "Really. I can't. Joel, you're the only one I can trust. I came here because I knew you wouldn't turn me in. I can't go home, Joel. I just can't."

"You can't go home? Melody, listen, what are you saying? Where the hell else are you going to go, girl?"

"Well, I have to figure that out."

"You're sixteen and the whole city's looking for you."

"Yeah, but you didn't recognize me, did you? Listen, I've already had a gig. No kidding, Joel. Tuesday, the day I ran away, I joined a street band. It was easy—I just sang for 'em, and then next thing you knew I was singing with 'em."

"You got a voice and a half, Mel. I always thought that." What she loved about him was his generosity; that and his talent.

"I know it's nothing to you. You've been playing professionally all your life. But it was . . ." She struggled with the enormity of what it had been. "It was a beginning for me. It was the start of my career."

"So is that your plan? To keep singing in the Quarter? Somebody's going to find you, Mel. You'd last three days max."

"There's lots of kids there. I could make friends."

"Yeah, but you couldn't go out in public."

"Well, I could—"

"What? Dance on Bourbon Street? That's still public."

She knew what she had to do. She had to leave town. But she couldn't do it without money. She didn't know how she was going to get the money, she didn't know where to go, and she didn't want to talk about it, even with Joel.

She said, "Oh, Joel, I can't go back. Not yet anyway. I need to be safe for a few days—with no adults around."

"I hear that," he said, and leaned back in his chair, thinking about it. Melody liked that about him too—that he thought about things. "You want me to help you?" he said finally.

"Is there anything you can do?"

"Melody, what happened to you? What's going on with you? Can't you at least tell me that?"

She flared. "I didn't kill my brother."

"You two were real close, weren't you?"

Without the slightest warning, Melody was crying again, shoulders heaving, deep sobs coming up for the eighteenth time. She wondered how long, how many months, how many years, before the crying would stop.

"Oh, Mel, hey." Joel had covered the distance between them and taken her in his arms before she had time to realize that was what he meant to do. No one in her family ever did anything like that. If Melody cried, she was sent to her room to do it in private. "It's okay," he said. "It's okay." He was holding her and stroking her hair. She felt like a big doll, not a person at all, and realized that she had done that herself with her dolls, when they had shed imaginary tears; had held them, stroked them. But she couldn't remember anyone doing it with her. It was almost like having a mother or father. She wondered if Flip would have done it.

Black people are so warm, she thought, and regretted for the millionth time that she wasn't one.

When she was calm again, he held her at arm's length and looked at her, looked in her eyes. She could have melted, but she saw no passion in his eyes, no romance at all, only worry. "You're in bad shape, girl. You need your mama."

She wrenched one of her arms away and swung at him.

"Watch out! What you doing? You crazy?"

"You just don't get it, do you? If I had a mama, I'd be at home. If I had a dad, I'd be home! You've got a mama, you can afford to make statements like that, you don't have any idea what it's like not to have one."

"Whoa, now. Slow down. You telling me you don't get along with your folks?"

"Yes, I'm telling you that!"

"Melody, I think you underestimate them. Betcha if you called 'em right now they'd say they love you."

Why did I think he'd understand? He doesn't know. Nobody from a normal family could know.

The despair was like falling into a bottomless black hole, sinking deeper, deeper, free-floating, no equilibrium, nothing to grab on to, nowhere to put your feet and hands, no night, no day, just falling.

I'm crazy. I'm going crazy because I can't talk to anybody.

But she should try. She should try to explain. There was just a chance, maybe the slightest chance, he would get it. She said, "Joel, what do you think love is?"

"What is this? A philosophical discussion? After I knock off love, want me to tackle reality? Your parents love you, Melody. All parents love their kids."

"Just because they say it doesn't mean they act like it."

"They send you to Country Day. Your mom brings you to school and picks you up every day."

"Because she has to. She hates it. She hates me."

"Melody, at a time like this, they've gotta be hurtin'. You've got to think about them."

Deeper and deeper into the black hole. And now she was spinning, spinning out of control.

"Melody. Melody!" He was rubbing her wrists, pulling at her T-shirt. She was lying on the floor.

"Did I faint again?"

"Yeah. Yeah, I guess that's what you did."

"Good." She closed her eyes for a second, happy, proud of herself. *It's the only sane response. I wish I could do it on command.*

"You doin' drugs?" said Joel.

"No!"

"Well, don't get so mad. Come on, now. Sit up." She obeyed. "Okay, that was *impressive.*"

"It's not fun, though." She would have lain back down, but he caught her around the waist and held her in a sitting position.

"I've got a place you can stay."

"You do?" She suddenly felt better.

It was another garage, much like the one they practiced in, except that it was professionally fitted out. It was the Boucrees' studio. Because people sometimes worked there all night, there was a small bedroom in the back, hardly bigger than a closet, with a single bed in it, and there was what her mother called a "half-bath"—toilet and lavatory, no shower.

"I'll bring you some food," he said. "I can't exactly take you home for red beans and rice."

"Why not?"

"Why do you think? You're too white for this neighborhood."

That made her angry. "You mean your parents are racist?"

He looked at her, uncomprehending. "You're crazy, you know that? Don't be such a baby."

She shut up. If there was anything she hated, it was being thought naive.

"You hungry?"

She checked in with her stomach. "Getting there,"

"I'll be right back. Stay put, okay. This is a black neighborhood. That's B-L-A-C-K, got it? You'd look weird here."

She grumped at him. "O-kay." But she'd have gone exploring if he hadn't said it.

He was gone about an hour, during which there was nothing to do but lie on the narrow bed and think, not her favorite activity of the moment. So she worked on the song awhile, the song about Ham. She was excited about it, knew it was going to be the best thing she'd ever done.

She was ravenous when Joel returned. He came back with corn bread (which he apologized for—it was left over from breakfast) and some of the best gumbo Melody had ever had. Curiously, the food made her sad, made her remember what she didn't have.

What must it be like, she wondered, to have a mother who cooked for you? Who actually got up and made corn bread for breakfast? It wasn't the most feminist idea in the world, she knew that—knew she didn't want to do it for some kid herself. But a mother who did that must surely be a mother who cared.

"They're going to practice here tonight," said Joel. "We have to go out."

She stopped in mid-munch. "Oh. Okay." Going out with Joel was her idea of heaven. The sadness left her. She might have no family, but maybe things worked out somehow. Ham used to quote Mick Jagger, so Melody knew that a pedagogic universe was more likely to bludgeon you into what you needed than treat you to what you wanted. But this seemed the opposite of the song— she needed her brother, a regular family like other kids had, a home—and instead her dreams were coming true. She'd already had a singing career, now she was spending time with Joel. She didn't know what to make of it. But she knew enough to enjoy it while she could.

I might not live that much longer.

The thought didn't exactly shock her, didn't float in out of nowhere. She'd always thought she would die young—that was

why she believed you had to get it while you can. She just hadn't
thought about how young.

"Where shall we go?" she said.

"Now that's a question. Nobody knows you in this neighborhood, but by tomorrow everybody would if we stayed here."

"Not the Quarter. I've had it with the Quarter."

They went to the Burger King on Morrison Road, and Melody
was thrilled that Joel took her to a place in his neighborhood. He
smiled at her. "I'll buy you some dessert."

They sat there for two hours and then, restless, drove out by
the lake and walked there. Finally they ended up in their own
practice garage, not daring to play music, barely whispering; instead of lights, using a candle Melody had brought one day after
a power failure.

Melody had nearly finished the song for Ham, "Blues for a
Brother," and she sang it for Joel. He went crazy. He said it was
the best thing she'd written, but she knew that and he knew she
did. What she wondered was where it stood in the general scheme
of things. Joel, seeming to know that, said it was as good a song
as any the Spin-Offs played, a song that would move people, that
people would remember.

She was embarrassed. "Oh, Joel, don't."

"Why don't?"

"You're such a much better musician than me."

"No, I'm not—Melody, I'm barely adequate. I couldn't get
into NOCCA—didn't you know that?"

He meant New Orleans Center for the Creative Arts. "You
couldn't get in?"

He shifted his weight uncomfortably. "Well, I didn't want to
go anyway. I want to be a doctor—did I ever happen to mention
that?" He sounded defensive.

"But Joel—your music!"

"Yeah, that's what the Boucrees say, some of 'em. 'Specially
my granddaddy's generation." He shrugged. "Music isn't my life,
that's all. It's great and I love it and everything, but I've got other
things I want to do with my life."

"But how could you—I don't understand. If I were as good as you—"

"You're better than me, Melody—don't you get it? You've got the soul; you've got the passion—I just don't."

She was struggling with that, trying to figure out if he was making fun of her, when he said, "I'm too damn well-adjusted."

She had known there had to be a catch. "Only screwballs are musicians, is that it?"

"Art comes out of pain, babe—don't you believe that? Why do you think that song you just wrote is so good?"

"You really think it's good?" She didn't believe him.

"They don't call it blues for nothin'—you of all people ought to know that."

"But you—all the Boucrees. Music's in your blood. It's your heritage."

"Bullshit! Bullshit, bullshit, bullshit!"

"Joel!" He had sounded almost violent.

"My ancestors learned to play the banjo back on the old plantation 'cause that was all they had except a back-breaking life and a bullet to look forward to if they tried to split. A public whipping at the very least. Can you imagine that, Mel? To be tied up and whipped? Don't look at me like that. Your people did it to mine."

"Well, I didn't."

He ignored her. "Why do you think black people converted to Christianity so easily? 'Cause that's where the music was—the only thing that eased the pain. You ever notice how many gospel songs talk about being saved? Why do you think that is? We Boucrees came out of poverty—the ones that weren't musicians were laborers; the women cleaned white ladies' houses."

He said "white ladies" with utter contempt—they were the enemy to him, she saw now, and she wanted to tell him that she wasn't, she'd do anything for him, she worshiped him.

"It's only this generation we've joined the middle class, Mel. You know how weird it is for me to be going to Country Day? Nobody in my whole neighborhood can get over it. But I want to be a doctor—I'll be the first one in my family to get a graduate degree—and my mama didn't want me going to public school and she used to work for a lady who went to Newman and she couldn't stand her. And after she saw the campus, it was Country Day or nothing—but my daddy wanted me to go to NOCCA, just in case; only I didn't make it. My grandparents' generation, they're still poor, at least they think they are.

"My daddy and my uncles made it on their music—made it a lot bigger than the family ever did before. One or two of them had a couple of years of college, but that's all. They smoke a lot of marijuana, do other drugs, I bet, some of them. It hasn't sunk in with them that they've made it, you know that? But me and my brothers and sisters and cousins, we have choices. We're the first Boucrees who ever did, and some of us just aren't as talented as the older generation. I don't know, the talent gets thin or something when you aren't as desperate."

"But what about me?" She was terrified his theory excluded her. "I don't come from a family like that."

"I don't know about you, Melody. You're a real pretty girl from a real nice family. But you're not happy. You couldn't sing and play like you do if you were."

The Boucree garage was deserted when they returned, and Melody fell asleep almost instantly, shimmering thoughts of Joel flitting through her consciousness. It was funny, she hadn't wanted booze or pot all evening. She was falling in love with him. He was enough for her.

Sometime in the night she awoke to someone, she never knew who, playing the piano and singing, unaware she was on the other side of the wall.

My own private concert, she thought, and was as happy as she'd ever been. It wasn't till the music was over, till the place was dark again, that she noticed something was wrong. It had been wrong for hours, had started mid-evening perhaps, but she hadn't wanted to pay it any attention. Now, alone in the dark, a little bit scared, she found it hard to ignore. It was a strange itch between her legs.

21

It was Friday night in the Big Easy, but Skip and Steve were munching a hasty po' boy on her coffee table, having decided there wasn't even time to go out for a bite. Both had to work that night and early the next day.

Skip was wearing a tank top and shorts, fresh from the shower but already sweating again. The ceiling fan was on, but it got hot in the tiny apartment when there were two people in it. And Skip had gotten so she very much liked having Steve in it with her, tight squeeze or no. She was realizing that more and more as the days wore on, the case wore on, and she saw him less and less. She was missing him even though she was living with him.

All of the disadvantages and none of the advantages, she thought. She sighed. It had to be. It was the nature of her work. And his.

"What's wrong?" he said.

"Nothing. I'm just . . . I don't know. I wish we could spend more time hanging out."

"Hey, listen, you're the perfect hostess. Don't give it a thought." He took a long swig of his beer, a huge bite of sandwich.

He was eating as if he hadn't had a meal in a week. "I'm having the time of my life, I'm not kidding."

She sighed again. "I wish I could say that."

"Case got you down?"

"It's still Melody."

"Instant replay of last night."

"Worse. I've talked to a few cops who know something about runaways—kids can hide here forever, you know that? One woman looked solidly for her kid every day for six months and never did find her. The kid called home—turned out she'd been dancing at Bayou Babies. Now how could you overlook that?"

"The mom went there at different times from when the kid was dancing. Or the first time she went, she stupidly identified herself, and every time she came in afterward, someone warned the kid and she split."

"That's it. You stick out when you're looking—and they protect each other. Plus, they sleep all day and only come out at night."

"Besides which, there are just a lot of places they could be at any given time. And they change their appearance, I bet."

"Yeah. Melody did, but her boyfriend spotted her, so now she'll probably do it again." Skip set down her sandwich, feeling even more depressed. "Isn't it weird? You can't walk outside in this town without seeing ten people you know."

"But they're not trying to hide." He made a noise as if clearing his throat.

"You know what they say at Covenant House? They say homeless teenagers have a pretty lousy chance of growing up."

"Makes sense." He seemed distracted.

"Yeah, but guess what the percentage is."

"I give up."

"A big three."

He whistled. "Three percent! What kills them? AIDS and drugs?"

"Not that much. More like murder and suicide. Accidents caused by what they call 'self-destructive behavior'—I guess that could be drugs."

"And that's if you aren't the key to a murder case."

"Yeah. I've got to find her, Steve." She was getting the butter-flies that had taken to coming when she thought about Melody.

But Steve, who normally loved to go on and on about her cases, apparently had something else on his mind. "Listen, Skip, I've got to tell you something. I think I owe you an apology."

Her stomach tightened. There was something about the words "I've got to tell you something" that set off every internal alarm in her body. "An apology?" she said.

"For Mardi Gras. For the way I was then."

She relaxed. But she didn't have a clue what he meant. That was over a year ago.

"I really blew it, trying to get in on your life—get you to let me in on your case and everything. I just should have stuck to doing my own work. That film never did come together, you know that? All that color, all that drama, everything in the world going on, and I really didn't end up with anything at all."

"But you did." She had seen it. It wasn't bad either—it was partly about Mardi Gras, partly about her case, and pretty damned intriguing, she thought.

"Oh, yeah, I got something, enough to satisfy AFI, but it wasn't what I wanted. I just never could settle on a focus—I guess somehow I expected you to give it to me."

He had been pushy. He had been in her face about things she couldn't do for him—like magically turn him into a cop working on the case himself. He had been a pain in the ass, and she deserved an apology. Still, she hadn't expected one at this late date. She was taken aback.

It was what she wanted, if she really thought about it, but she didn't know what it meant. Maybe it meant she'd been a learning experience for him and he was ready to move on. She planned to walk the streets later that night, looking for Melody, and she'd asked him to join her, but he'd declined. He had his own work to do. And she'd been disappointed. Much as she thought it annoyed her, she had to admit to herself that there was something appealing about having him panting like a puppy in her wake.

"You know," she said, "I kind of liked having you under-foot."

"I thought you hated it."

"So did I. Now I'm wishing I had you back."

He laughed. "Never satisfied."

But she didn't laugh with him. It was too close to the truth.

■

Before getting down to the Melody hunt, she had another errand. She'd phoned Johnny Murphy and gotten a grumpy, half-loaded response. She didn't identify herself, just went to find him. He lived in the Faubourg Marigny, in an apartment hardly bigger than hers, and he was about as welcoming as if she'd been from the IRS.

"You mad about what I did with Ti-Belle this afternoon?"

"Hell, no. Bitch deserved it."

"Then talk to me."

"I'm sleepy, okay?" She certainly seemed to have woken him up.

"And hungry, I'll bet. You look like a dog's breakfast. Go shave and I'll buy you dinner."

His hand went to his chin, feeling his beard. Being a musician, and a handsome one—at least formerly—he'd probably had women chasing him for most of his life.

"Oh, okay. For Christ's sake." She figured she'd hit a nerve, complaining about his looks.

While he devoured a plate of gorgeous, crisp-fried catfish, she sipped an iced tea.

"I'm still mad at her," he said. "Mad enough to eat with a cop. What do you think of that?"

"We're talking serious vendetta here."

He looked at her, searching for a twitch, but she stayed dead-pan. "Hey, I'm sorry."

She gave him the smile he wanted. "I'm kidding. I know you're really mad at her. I figure she must have dumped you."

"Two years ago, you b'lieve that? I mean, that I'm still mad? But she did me in good, I'm tellin' you. Took one look at Mr. Hamson Brocato, and said, 'Here's my ticket to the big-time—so long, sucker.' " He stuffed a hunk of catfish down the hatch.

"I found her singin' on the street in Memphis six years ago—little Lacey Longtree, a half-cute gal with a great voice and not a clue in this world. Couldn't even read music. About twenty pounds overweight when I found her—said she'd lost ten pounds since she left home without even trying. Weight kept fallin' off till she got like she is now. I thought she was sick, but she said it wasn't that, this was the way she was s'posed to be." He shoveled in a huge bite, tapped Skip with an angry index finger. "Sounds like sour grapes, but I'm tellin' the gospel truth when I say I taught her everything she knows. And I mean *everything*—I made Ti-Belle Thiebaud out of the pathetic ol' raw material called Lacey Longtree. I figured out there really wasn't a white female singer doing New Orleans rhythm and blues—well, there's Marcia Ball, but she's from Texas and she doesn't have a Cajun name. Find a need and fill it, you know what I mean? And Cajun was where the hole was. Not that she was ever gonna do Cajun music—except just a little to make her look authentic. But what do the folks in Kansas know about that anyway? You got a French-soundin' name, you must be a Cajun singer. Positioning was the whole ball game—she was just gon' have an exotic name and be different from every other singer in the whole country. My idea. All of it. Every bit." He chewed catfish.

"Mine."

"Are you saying Ti-Belle Thiebaud isn't her real name? And she's not a Cajun?"

"I thought you were s'posed to be a detective. I just told you that, lady."

"Well, if she's not a Cajun, where's she from?"

"Funny thing is, she never would say, even when she was a dumb little country girl singin' on the street for quarters." He finished off his beer and ordered another one. "Think I know, though. I saw a letter to her mom once, addressed to Doradale, Alabama."

"So you were with her four years."

"Four years and plannin' on the rest of my life. I thought we were a couple. Like it was understood." His mouth set in a hard, disappointed line when he spoke of it. An angry line that said it was a very poor plan to cross Johnny Murphy.

"What was she like to live with? Have you ever known her to be violent?"

"Violent! Ti-Belle Thiebaud? We are talkin' a very primitive creature here, with just a thin civilized patina spread over some true savagery." He stared off into space and laughed, clearly off in the past. "We had to replace all our plates regularly—she loved to throw everything in the kitchen at me. Fought in bars too. Only woman I've ever seen who does that. Did, I guess. She quit when she started gettin' famous, but even then I had to beg her. She loved it, I think—I really think she did."

He stared out into astroland again, and came back. "Mind if I smoke?" He lit up before she had a chance to answer. "You know that movie, *Thelma & Louise?* That's Ti-Belle all over. Mad! *Real* mad right below the surface. Some guy'd say casually, 'Hey, hon, lookin' good tonight,' and she'd say, 'Shut up, asshole,' 'cause it was always some ol' redneck looked like he was eight months pregnant, and it just outraged her that a guy like that had the nerve to get smart with her. So she'd call him asshole and he was always bound to say, 'Who you callin asshole?' or somethin' just about as dumb, and she'd slug him. Just haul off and sink her fist in his oversized breadbasket. Sometimes he'd try and hit her back, and then somebody'd help her out—usually me, I couldn't help it. And she'd just love it when she got the whole bar to brawlin'. She'd be in there mixin' it up like a man. I told her, 'Ti-Belle, you watch out or you're gon' lose some of those pretty teeth and it's gon' cost us.' But she was always lucky. You ever know a woman who hit people?"

She smiled at him. There was something about him that charmed her. "I've been tempted myself."

"But you never did, I bet."

"Well, hardly ever." Police work wasn't always conducive to keeping your temper, but she tried to stay civilized.

"Oh, come on now."

"Okay, never. But I pushed somebody once."

"Pushed somebody. Ti-Belle pushed *me* every time she got

in a bad mood. But, hell, that was nothin'—what she really liked was yanking this." He pulled his ponytail over his shoulder. "I think she wanted to drag me around by it. Did too. I just didn't know it."

"Johnny." She gave him a level stare. "She sounds like a thoroughgoing bitch."

"Hell, I like a spirited woman."

"We're talking a little more than spirited. Or are you exaggerating just the tiniest bit?"

He leaned back and guffawed, full of catfish, working on his second beer, and smoking a cigarette. A happy man. "You're pretty smart, after all, Detective. Let me buy you a beer, okay?"

"Another iced tea." She'd have dearly loved a beer, but maybe she'd find Melody later. She'd need all the good sense she could muster.

He signaled the waitress. "Well, I'm Irish. You gotta take that into account."

"Tell me about it."

"But listen, there's a grain of truth in all that. More'n a grain. She did throw all the dishes once and she did yank my hair a couple of times. Got in fights twice—whoooo, that woman has a temper. That's the bottom line—we're talkin' temper. You'd think she was the Irish one." He upended his third beer. "What you're askin' is, is she violent? Does she have those kinds of tendencies? Am I right?"

Skip nodded.

"Well, she is and she does."

Why does a woman scorned get all the bad press? Watch out for scorned men. She said, "Remind me not to ever make you mad."

"Hey, listen, you gotta understand. Ti-Belle wasn't just my girlfriend. I *made* her. I devoted four years of my life to midwifing this country's most famous female Cajun R and B singer. She was an investment."

"I guess that's how she saw Ham."

"Yeah. The name's provocative, ain't it?" He stared off into space, came back as an old philosopher. "In this business, maybe we're all just pieces of meat to each other."

"But, Johnny, what about art?"

He guffawed again, enjoying Skip, she could tell. "Heck, let's keep it around in spite of everything. Life's gotta imitate somethin'."

Skip left thinking she'd found buried treasure. That put her in a good mood, and being with Johnny Murphy had been fun—an unusual occurrence when pumping someone about his ex. She was feeling sociable and wished again for Steve to prowl around with. However, Jimmy Dee would be just as good company, and he needed attention—probably either had more to say about his sister or needed light banter to take his mind off her; most likely both. She phoned him. "Want to take a walk on the wild side?"

"You kidding, officer? You need a brute for that."

"I was thinking of going to bars where teenagers hang."

"Hang? Well, in that case. *Something* should be done about the creatures."

"The Blacksmith Shop in five?"

"Done." It was their neighborhood bar. He was waiting when she got there, dapper in jeans and polo shirt, salt-and-pepper hair curling slightly over the collar. He was a hunk, if rather a smaller one than was suitable for Skip. In his law firm, most people didn't know he was gay, and women were forever fixing him up with their single friends. The swish act he affected with Skip was for her personal amusement.

They headed for Decatur Street, Jimmy Dee keeping up a running commentary on the passing carnival. "Don't you just love the fashion statements?" He pointed out a kid in spiderweb panty hose.

"I can't conceive of having fashion sense at sixteen."

"No offense, my sweet, but I can't conceive of your ever having any."

"I don't know, Dee-Dee, under your tutelage—"

"Green, purple, *and* orange hair—look sharp now."

"The vampire he's with—do you love the black nails?"

"But the 666 tattoo is *too* beastly."

The vampire's face had been whited out with something like Kabuki makeup. She had black around her eyes and her lipstick was bruise-colored. Her outfit had to have taken days to think up and weeks to put together. Skip thought she was a bit too short to be Melody, maybe too heavy, but she couldn't be sure. If she wasn't Melody, she was still somebody's kid, and if she was a runaway, her next door neighbor wouldn't recognize her. How did you find one kid in this mob? The bar they liked, the most nondescript on the whole street, except that it had a few video games, was starting to fill up. They didn't seem to be interested in drinking, just milling. And quite a few of them were already unsteady on their feet—though not from alcohol, was Skip's guess. Quaaludes maybe.

She and Jimmy Dee walked up and down the street, around Jackson Square, over to Bourbon, back again. The night was eerie; the air was heavy as always, but this time with millions of bodies, flying termites swarming the lights. They walked side by side, incapable of making eye contact if they didn't want to be mowed down by the crowds. Skip realized later the side-by-side setup had been a rare opportunity for Jimmy Dee, giving him the distance he needed.

He said, "You know what I told you last night?" and she felt a tightness in her belly, knowing what this was costing him.

"About your sister?" She glanced at him briefly, but he looked away.

"Yes. You know how I said there was more?"

"Uh-huh."

"Well, this is it, Skippy. She's going to die—my only relative except for two. I'm going to have to go back and help her through it."

She longed to give him the gift of her eyes, to show him how he'd gotten to her, but she didn't dare. He'd hate it. She said, "I kind of thought it was something like that." She didn't even say she was sorry. She didn't touch him.

"And that's not even the heavy part."

Now she did turn to him, so surprised she forgot discretion. But he said, "Look—a street band. White punks on dope."

Young white punks, playing illegally late. They were hardly older than Melody—two guys and a girl, but the girl wasn't

Melody for sure; way too heavy. They were fairly mediocre, really; nothing different about them.

Jimmy Dee said, "Y'all need a singer."

The drummer rolled his eyes. "Oh, no, not again. You want to audition?"

The girl said, "He's a lot more my type than the last one."

"What last one?"

She shrugged. "One-day wonder. Fantastic voice—we made more money with her in one night than we do in a week by ourselves." She gestured at the guitarist, a blond, good-looking guy. "But Mr. Stud back there scared her off. So—what do you want to sing?"

Skip said, "Skinny girl? Purple and blond hair?"

The girl, the bass player, opened her mouth, but the lead guitarist did something, pinched her maybe. Skip was about to pull out her badge, but Jimmy Dee's instincts were better. He toyed with a twenty-dollar bill. The girl looked at the bill and then at the blond. "She's gone, Chris, okay? She's not coming back." She turned to Jimmy Dee. "Her name's Janis," she said triumphantly. "Is that who you're looking for?"

He smiled as if she'd given the right answer. "No. Not even close."

"Oh." She was downcast. "Well, maybe it wasn't her real name. I know—I'll tell you what she looked like before we did her over." She never took her eyes off the bill.

Jimmy Dee tore the bill and gave her a half.

"Real skinny, blue eyes. Lots of curly black hair."

Skip brought out the picture. "Is this her?"

"I'm not sure. It doesn't look that much like her."

But the drummer said, as if just realizing it, "She's the girl who was in the paper—whose brother was murdered."

"Who is? The picture or the singer?"

"Janis. Why the hell didn't we put that together?" He turned to Chris. "You knew, didn't you? You had to have known."

The blond just shrugged, didn't open his mouth. Skip thought he'd be death to teenage girls with raging hormones. She took out her badge. "Let's talk about it."

He didn't miss a beat. "She fainted when she read about the guy who died. Said she was sick." He shrugged again. "That was it—she didn't talk much. Just sang with us and split."

"What made her leave?"

The girl said, "She caught him with another girl."

The drummer stared at the blond: "Asshole."

It went on like that until Skip was pretty sure they'd given up every crumb of information they had, plus names and addresses. She gave them her card: "If you see her again, call me. And I mean it—it could be a matter of life and death."

"Hers?"

"Yours if you don't cooperate. By the way, it's after eight—haven't you noticed?"

They didn't answer.

Jimmy Dee said, "Should I give them the other half?"

"Up to you."

He handed it over ceremoniously, kissing the girl's hand. "Stay as sweet as you are," he told her.

And Skip said, "When you think about making that call, remember I've got a rich friend. He might just get generous again."

To Jimmy Dee she said, "Come on, I'll buy you a drink. I owe you about half a dozen."

"I've got to finish telling you," he said urgently.

"Okay."

"You know those other two living relatives? Besides my sister? They're her kids."

"Young?"

"Eleven and thirteen. A boy and a girl. The dad deserted the family a long time ago. His parents are alive, but the grandfather's an alcoholic, and they're really, really poor. They just have a tiny apartment."

Skip finally understood what he was telling her. She stared right at him, simply couldn't play the game any longer. "Jimmy Dee? You're going to be a dad?"

He was sweating. "Jesus. I don't know what else to do." She'd never seen him look so worried. And scared. Downright scared.

255

22

The sounds of breakfast penetrated even to the zendo, where Nick had gone for a few minutes quiet. It was a good zendo, a twelve-mat room, but he must remember to have it soundproofed. He had come here thinking to sit zazen, or at least that was the excuse he'd given, but once in here, surrounded by white walls, breathing the heady scent of incense, he was so happy simply to be alone that he started thinking about that. His life was seeming too complicated all of a sudden.

He'd invited Proctor to come for the JazzFest and stay as long as he wanted—Nick thought it was important to support him while he recovered from his divorce—but now he wanted to take it all back. This thing Proctor had for Ti-Belle was really getting uncomfortable. In fact, that was why he'd left the breakfast table. They weren't saying anything, there was just an atmosphere. Something thick and ugly in the air. He couldn't name it, thought it was more than simple dislike, but they didn't have any history together. He couldn't figure out where it was coming from. Proctor had seen him through twenty-five years of relationships and never acted like this. All Ti-Belle would say was that Proctor didn't like her, she could feel it. She never said a word about not liking him. But even Nick didn't like him much at the moment.

Oh, hell. He's not himself. No one is when they're going through a divorce —I should know.

Should he be more patient? He wasn't even sure he had time for Proctor in his life. He wanted to pursue his spiritual life, spend more time with his kids, and there was another thing—he was starting to feel a weird urge to teach. He thought that was partly behind his wholehearted support of Second Line Square. The part that most excited him was the plan to expand the Heritage School of Music; he wanted to be in on that. It was a weird thing and he didn't have a clue where it was coming from. But Caroline said you had to listen to stuff like that, and Nick saw no reason to doubt her. He could afford to follow any impulse he had, and this looked like a constructive one to him.

Sort of. There was a piece of it he didn't trust—somehow it seemed more appealing to teach music to other people's kids than to figure out how the hell he was supposed to be a dad to his own.

But maybe he could do both.

Then there was the matter of Ti-Belle and the new career she had planned for him. In a strange way, that appealed to him too. But weren't things getting too crowded here? How to sort them all out? He decided to quit trying so hard. Instead he closed his eyes and began to follow his breathing.

But after a while he heard hurried footsteps coming toward him, followed by a knock.

"Nick! I've got to talk to you."

Proctor stomped in without waiting for an answer, holding a just-opened Federal Express box and the heavy book that must have come in it. "I know who she is. I had this really weird reaction to her—I mean like I remembered something really unpleasant and couldn't place it. It's been bugging me like crazy. And yesterday I figured it out. Lacey Longtree from my hometown—she was kind of a Doradale celebrity. My mom taught her tenth-grade English, so I called her and got her to send me this."

The volume he was holding was a yearbook from a high school in Doradale, Alabama. Proctor opened it to the page he'd marked and pointed excitedly to a picture of a girl. She had dark hair, not blond, and she was chubby, not thin, but she did look like Ti-Belle in some kind of way. Something about the eyes, the expression. Still, it was anything but conclusive.

"What's this about, Proctor? You're saying Ti-Belle isn't who she says she is?"

"You bet your sweet ass she's not. Just ask her."

"What's the big deal? Look, a lot of people change their names. Why do you care so much? I don't get this one-man war you're waging."

"Look, she knows what I'm on to. She saw me get the package and she tried to see what it was. She's terrified I'm going to blow her out of the water."

"What are you talking about?"

"She's ripe, man. She'll break. Just show her the picture, okay? That's all I ask."

"Okay," said Nick, and put on his shoes. It had to be done. The Proctor—Ti-Belle thing was blowing apart without any interference from him.

He was actually excited. He wanted to get the thing settled and out of the way. He thought later, blaming himself, that perhaps he should have curbed that feeling, that some of it must have showed when he thrust the open yearbook under Ti-Belle's nose. It had to have been his energy she picked up on, because there wasn't anything else. He didn't say a word, hadn't even thought about what to say.

He expected it to go much slower.

The minute she saw what the book was—surely she didn't have time to spot the picture—she sprang at Proctor, an infuriated feline.

"You *fucker!*"

She got him by the shirtfront, but he ripped himself away, and she started throwing things—a half full bowl of granola, a glass of half-drunk orange juice, a fork, a napkin, a glass of milk one of the kids was drinking. That was as far as she got before Nick caught her. But she was a moving target, slippery and fast. As Proctor dodged, Ti-Belle rushed him, grabbing things as she went around the table, all the while shouting anything that came to mind: "Sonofabitch bastard asshole pussy prick motherfucker." And finally: "Stupido!"

A hoot of laughter escaped one of the kids before she turned her white-hot eyes on him and he turned red and ducked. Nick understood the impulse. The whole pathetic scene would have been funny if it hadn't been terrifying in its suddenness, its intensity. Its irrationality. And worst of all, Ti-Belle's killer eyes. Nick had never seen murder in someone's eyes before, but now he understood the phrase.

He caught her from behind, both arms around her waist, pinning her arms, but she kicked him in the shin with her heel, and the sound she made was like a hiss. He held but she twisted wildly, and they both went down. The kids and guests started to run for cover. Proctor seemed frozen in place. Ti-Belle wriggled away from Nick and rolled under the table, all the way to the other side, where Proctor had run for refuge. It happened fast—Proctor obviously didn't see it coming.

She grabbed his ankle, pulled him off balance, got him down and straddled him, going for his throat. "Ham knew about this, goddammit! Ham knew, damn you! What the fuck did you think you were doing?"

She was choking him, Proctor's hands struggling to loosen hers, his face turning red, his body twisting. Nick hesitated, trying to decide whether to go over, under, or around the table, but a voice, strong and authoritative—chilling, probably, to Ti-Belle—said, "Miss Thiebaud! Police!"

Turning from the tableau on the floor, Nick saw Langdon, the oversized cop, bearing down; not running, just walking very fast, very purposefully. The servants had obviously let her in.

"Let him go," she said. If she'd had a megaphone, she couldn't have sounded more official, more threatening.

Nick couldn't take his eyes off her. But Ti-Belle shouted, "Fuck!" and he saw that she too was staring at Langdon, hands still around Proctor's throat.

"Goddamn you!" Ti-Belle yelled. "God damn you, Proctor Gaither!" She went back to choking him, more methodically if anything. Nick didn't understand why Proctor couldn't fight her off.

The cop grabbed her arms: "Let go!"

Ti-Belle didn't. Her face just got redder and more intense. Nick wondered if he should do something, but it was only a moment before the big cop wrenched Ti-Belle's hands off Proctor, whose hands instantly went to his own throat, as if to reassure himself it was his again. Nick was about to jump over the table and help Proctor up, but before he could budge, Ti-Belle, wriggling away from Langdon, stepped in Proctor's face.

Then she turned on the cop, raking at her with open hands. Claws, Nick thought later. Langdon feinted, saving her face from certain laceration. She said, "Calm down, Ti-Belle." No more Miss Thiebaud. "Calm down or I'm going to have to hit you."

Ti-Belle went for her again, a noise coming out of her throat that could have been a growl. She not only sounded like a cat, she behaved like one; moved gracefully, surefootedly. She was beautiful even now, even doing what she was doing. Nick felt a surge of love for her, and pity. He wondered later where the fear had been; it should have been there.

Perhaps the threat threw her off her stride; Nick wasn't sure. Either she lost steam or the cop moved faster than he'd thought she could. She didn't hit Ti-Belle after all, instead managed to catch her, turn her, and cuff her, so fast Nick found that later on he couldn't reconstruct it in his mind.

"You have the right to an attorney," she said. "You have the right to remain silent . . ."

Somehow that was more shocking to him than Ti-Belle's attack, the sound of her being arrested.

▪

Doradale, Alabama, according to Skip's two-year-old almanac, had a population of 10,919. She'd had to track down the county sheriff, a job she knew wouldn't be easy on a Saturday. But she had to try anyway, had woken up early with Johnny Murphy's tale of Lacey Longtree burning in her brain. Seven o'clock was too early. She waited till eight, figured out what the county seat was, and tried the sheriff's department there. The watch commander said he'd try to get the sheriff but he just didn't see much chance, it being a weekend and all. "Can I tell him what it's about?" he asked, almost as an afterthought.

Skip hated telling one person and then the next, running the risk of getting everything garbled; she usually didn't do it. But without planning it, she answered this time. "It's about somebody who used to live in Doradale—woman named Lacey Longtree."

"Lacey Longtree! Oh shit, do you have her?"

And Skip had known the sheriff would be calling back soon.

Now she had Ti-Belle Thiebaud in an interview room, looking raw and gaunt, her makeup having dissolved in floods of tears that started as soon as they walked out the door of Nick Anglime's house. Floods and floods and floods of tears, maybe some of them for Ham, Skip thought.

Even if you'd killed somebody, you'd miss him. You'd be sorry he was dead and sorry you'd done it at least some of the time.

When the sheriff called, he didn't stand on ceremony, just asked the same question the other cop had: "You got Lacey Long-tree?"

"Not in custody. Why—should I? Who is she?"

"Well, she's Doradale's answer to Lizzie Borden, is Ms. Lacey. I knew she'd turn up sooner or later."

"Are you saying she killed her parents?"

"No, I'm not sayin' that. She ain't really Lizzie. Just close to it."

Skip waited.

"Just like those big-city murderers that get all the ink too. Lacey was the last one you'd think done it. Done anything, for that matter. Mousy little fat thing. Kind of reminded you of the Dormouse. Then one day she came home from school and gave her daddy forty whacks."

"Surely not with an ax."

He laughed as if it were the funniest thing ever happened in Pine County. "Not forty either. Just stabbed him once, to tell you the truth. But hard. Rammed that sucker right up to the hilt—she was fat but she wasn't necessarily strong. But you know what they say—crazy people got superhuman strength."

"What was the weapon?"

"Kitchen knife. Plain ordinary kitchen knife. Homely little crime, nothin' fancy about it, but shore did shake this town up."

"Her daddy was a prominent citizen?"

"Naah. He was a carpenter, I b'lieve. Maybe 'lectrician. Something like that. Lacey was closer to being a local celebrity. Straight-A student, good citizen award, worked on the yearbook. Nobody could believe it."

"Were there witnesses?"

"Well, now. That depends on who you believe. Officially, no, there weren't any witnesses. What happened was, her mom left to pick up her little brother from basketball practice and came back to find daddy dead and Lacey gone. That's what Mom and Bubba say. Coach says there wasn't any practice that day."

"How do you know Mom didn't kill Dad and Lacey both, but somehow got rid of Lacey's body?"

"Detective, you have any idea how small Doradale is? Lacey was seen, of course; at the Greyhound bus station. Bought a ticket to Jackson. But she fooled us—got off at the first or second stop, who knows what happened after that? Trail's been cold for almost fifteen years, but don't think we've forgotten. Spectacular murder by our standards. Been looking for that young woman off and on ever since."

"She was fat, was she?"

"Uh-huh, but kind of tall. Worst possible combination. Big and clumsy."

Well, thanks.

"Much worse than short and fat, I always thought."

Skip said, "Blond?"

"Nope. Dark. Real ordinary-looking kid."

"Sheriff, have you ever heard of someone named Ti-Belle Thiebaud?"

"The singer? Sure. She's one of my favorites. I'm crazy about her."

"Have you seen her on television or anything?"

"Heck, yeah. Been to one of her concerts—why do you ask?"

"Because her drummer says she's Lacey Longtree."

"No!"

"I'm just telling you what he says."

"Oh, fuck. You mean I gave up an hour's sleep for this? I thought you had something."

"She absolutely couldn't be Lacey Longtree?"

"No way in hell."

She hadn't known about Proctor at the time, or she would have asked about him.

▪

Ti-Belle was saying, "I just don't know what happened." She stared at her hands as if they were foreign objects. "I've never done anything like that in my life."

"The sheriff of Pine County, Alabama, says you have."

"Oh, fuck."

Her attorney, Barnes Naismith, hastily called by Anglime, was trying to shush her, had been trying for half an hour, but Ti-Belle apparently had things in her that wanted out. Tears for sure and maybe words, if Skip got lucky.

Ti-Belle got a quizzical look. "You've talked to the sheriff already?"

"He says you killed your dad, Ti-Belle. With one blow; with a kitchen knife; in the kitchen. Just like you killed Ham."

"You bitch." She was half out of her chair before Naismith could stop her.

He got her back down but couldn't shut her up. "I didn't kill Ham. I swear to God I didn't kill him. I didn't love him, I wish I had, but I didn't kill him. I didn't have any reason to kill him. Why in hell would I kill Ham?"

Skip kept her voice low, almost sleepy. "He wanted you to stop seeing Anglime. You fought, he said the wrong thing, it made you furious. What was it he said, Ti-Belle?" She was doing the questioning alone because it was Saturday, and because Cappello wasn't there. She would have loved to work with Cappello on this one. She needed someone to play the good cop.

263

"It wasn't me. Can't you leave me alone, goddammit?"

Naismith turned to Skip as if she were beating babies up. "Can't you?"

She ignored him.

Ti-Belle maundered, a woman in a dream: "I didn't hurt Ham. I could never hurt Ham. His problem was he was too nice. How could you hurt a guy like that?"

"Sleep with another guy?"

That brought on more tears. "I did wrong, I know I did wrong. But I didn't kill him. Don't you see the difference?"

"Tell me about your dad."

She bent her head, laced her fingers behind her neck and stayed that way for a long while. When she straightened up, she said, "My dad was a drunk and a sadist. He started drinking the minute he came home from work, and the minute he started drinking was the minute he started picking on people."

"What people? How?"

"Oh, my mother. My little brother. Me. He did it all the usual ways. Physically. Verbally."

"Sexually?"

Ti-Belle looked surprised. "I don't really know. I don't remember it." She shrugged. "But hell, he did everything else."

Naismith said, "Miss Thiebaud, I really must advise you—"

"Would you just shut up?"

Skip thought: *Maybe it's a good thing there's only me today. Maybe it's less threatening this way.*

"What did he do?" she said.

"He tried to kill my baby brother."

"I thought your brother was thirteen."

"Prentiss was small for his age. Anyway, I was seventeen—I practically raised him." She smiled, and Skip wondered what she remembered. Rocking him to sleep, maybe, the smell of baby powder, soft and reassuring. "He used to call me Sissy," she said.

"My mother was sick; always, always sick. She couldn't take care of us, really. Couldn't even take care of herself." She started to cry again. "It wasn't so bad when he beat me. I always felt every time he did it, it saved them getting hit. He never hit me with the bat.''

''The bat?''

''Prentiss's baseball bat.''

Involuntarily, Skip found herself making a face to ward off the evil. ''He hit you with a baseball bat?''

''No! He hit my mother with a baseball bat. He hit my little brother with it. But just once.'' Her eyes turned lynxlike. ''He only did it once.''

Naismith said, ''Miss Thiebaud, I beg you!''

She turned on him: ''Oh, what difference does it make? Somebody had to recognize me eventually. Better now than when I really have something to give up.'' But her face was sad. Obviously she felt she was giving up a lot.

''Listen to me carefully, Miss Thiebaud. They mean it when they say 'what you say can and will be used against you.' If you say any more, you're going to hear it again in court.''

''I want to talk to Skip. Could you leave us alone for a minute?''

''I don't think that would be a very good idea.''

What Ti-Belle was doing was wildly self-destructive, and yet Skip had seen it a hundred times—there was something in the human animal that wanted to confess.

Ti-Belle said, ''Skip, I can trust you, can't I?''

They hadn't been on a first-name basis before. For a moment Skip had thought she'd gotten to her. But it wasn't that. She thought Skip could be manipulated.

''Trust me to do what?'' she said.

''I don't know.'' Ti-Belle spread her arms, looking helpless, as if she really didn't know. ''I just want to tell you something.''

''Tell me what?''

''I yelled at him to stop; stop hitting Prentiss. And he said, 'Who's gonna stop me?' I had the knife already—I was making dinner. So I just held it up, like I was going to stab him. And I said 'Me.' He laughed like it was the funniest thing he ever heard, and then he tried to hit me with the bat. He was coming at me.'' She

265

stopped and gathered her resources. "I lost my temper. I just lost my temper."

"You stabbed him?"

"I didn't say that."

"Well, if you didn't, who did?"

"Not my mama; you can just forget that idea. And not my little brother."

"Who else was there?"

"I think I should shut up now."

"Ti-Belle, you're in a lot of trouble. You lost your temper then, you did it again with Ham, and you did it today at Nick's."

"I didn't kill Ham! I swear to God I didn't."

"You've got a real bad temper, Ti-Belle."

"I'm famous for my fucking temper!" She was getting mad. "I used to yell at Ham all the time. And today I got madder at Proctor than I've ever been at anybody in my life, except one person. He tried to destroy everything I've worked for. You'd be mad too, wouldn't you?"

"I don't know if I would have tried to kill him."

"I didn't try to kill him."

"Did you try to kill your dad?"

"Of course not! I just . . . I don't even remember anymore."

"Look, it sounds to me as if it was self-defense. Why did you leave town?"

Her eyes filled with despair. Her mouth turned down and twisted. Her face fell in on itself. Through her tears, she said, "Mama made me."

23

Melody had hardly slept at all after the music stopped and so couldn't have been more surprised when she found herself awakened by yelling. Two things about it were surprising: first, she didn't know she'd been to sleep, couldn't believe she'd actually dropped off, considering the circumstances; and second, she wasn't at home. Brocatos yelled, not Boucrees; surely not Boucrees.

Yet it was the Boucrees's studio and yelling was occurring right now, before breakfast.

"Goddammit, Tyrone, what's wrong with you? Couldn't you even make it to the bed we put in here?"

"I got tired. I curled up on the rug. You got a problem with that?"

Oh, no. If he's been here all night, he'll come in to use the bathroom in about two minutes. Silently, she got up and made the bed; rolled under it, holding her crotch, scratching it. She'd gotten up in the night to investigate the funny little itch she'd felt. There were red spots there. The itching wasn't so bad, was hardly any worse, but the fear was making her sweat.

"Motherfucker, you got a problem. Alicia's been up all night

267

worryin' about you, not knowing if you were dead or in some woman's bed. Why you do her like this?'' It was a third voice. The sleeper was being ganged up on.

"Hey, I got an idea. Know that transition we been havin' so much trouble with? I think I got it figured out.''

"Oh, man, you're out of your mind. Your wife and four kids want to know where the fuck you are, that's all you can talk about? Why you think we're here, man? Alicia's been callin' all over everywhere.''

"She call Mama?''

"Hell, yes, she called Mama. Mama's 'bout to have a stroke, thinks you're prob'ly lyin' in a ditch. It wouldn't occur to Mama you're just a lazy, inconsiderate fucker, can't even let his own wife know where he is.''

"Hey, there's a phone here. Is there a phone here?'' The sleeper was getting mad. "You see that phone over there? Alicia might have called all of y'all, but she didn't call me.''

Melody heard someone stomp across the room. "Phone's unplugged,'' a fourth voice said. *How many of them were out there?*

"Well, I didn't unplug it!'' the sleeper hollered. "Why don't you assholes get out of my face. What the fuck's going on here?''

"Tyrone, you're messin' up everything. You're the only one that ever fucks up, you ever notice that?''

"Hey, I been up all night trying to save y'all's sorry asses. We're gonna look like a bunch of jerks up there tomorrow if *y'all* don't get it together.''

"Sucker!'' The word had a lifetime of venom behind it. Melody heard a crack, and a noise like someone stumbling, crashing into the piano. The speaker had hit Tyrone.

Someone else said, "Mark, goddammit, what you want to hit him for? You always been that way—hit, hit, hit! You think that's the way to solve everything.''

She hated the way they were attacking each other, accusing each other, humiliating each other, more than she hated the hitting. Her father did that to her mother. The Brocatos did it to her father. Her mother even did it to her sometimes, mildly: "Melody, you never clean your room. You always leave your clothes on the floor.''

Did her father do it to her? It was so familiar. Oh, yes: ''You're making your mother sick. Why can't you do what she says and quit giving her trouble?''

Without even asking her version. He didn't know anything; he was never around.

She lay under the bed, holding her contaminated crotch, feeling sorry for herself. Feeling hope drain away. Just when something good happened, three bad things happened next.

It's the physical thing. I'm sick, that's what it is. Shit, I wonder what I've got? AIDS doesn't start this way, does it? It could be herpes. Maybe it's herpes. Syphilis! That starts with a bump. Or the clap. Can you still get that?

She had read accounts of people having gonorrhea, and it seemed to her burning had been one of the symptoms. When they urinated, was that it? She broke out in a fresh sweat. Was it going to hurt to go to the bathroom? She had to go now.

''Joel, my man, what you doing here?'' There was a break in the din outside. Melody had let her mind wander for a while, partly out of depression, partly fear. She could be dying. Almost certainly she had a sexually transmitted disease—nothing could have been clearer to her. And yet—there was something funny; Chris had used a condom. Wasn't that supposed to protect you? She felt betrayed by one more thing.

''Hey, how y'all?'' said Joel. ''Hey, Daddy. Mama's waitin' on you.''

''Mornin', Joel,'' said the one named Tyrone. ''Your uncles act like it's the end of the world I fell asleep over here.''

''Well, Mama's a little bent out of shape.''

''Ah, hell, how's that different from usual?''

Melody couldn't believe the sleeper was Joel's father. Joel Boucree had a father as imperfect as hers. She just couldn't believe it.

''I better get back to the old lady,'' he said. ''Joel, you coming?''

''Naah. I think I might practice awhile.''

"All by yourself?" said Mark.

"Where y'all goin'?"

"Back home awhile. We were over by Mama's, heard about Tyrone, came over to see was he here."

"Hell, you knew I would be," Tyrone grumbled, and then Melody heard a lot of exit sounds. She came out from under the bed and sat on top, wishing she could fix her hair, but she was afraid to move around any more than necessary.

Joel knocked. "Hey, Mel?"

"Come in."

"You okay?"

Great, except for the clap. She nodded, unable to speak.

"You don't look so good."

"I was kind of upset about hearing that fight."

He laughed. "Hell, don't let that bother you. They're always like that."

"I thought they'd be nice."

"They're just a family, that's all. You think they'd give Daddy such a hard time if they didn't care about him?"

She didn't answer. It seemed to her a weird way to express affection.

"See, he likes to get out of the house when Mama's drinking and yelling. So he goes, and then she falls asleep and wakes up sober enough so she doesn't slur her words and forgets where he's gone and starts calling people. They don't catch on she's drunk and Daddy won't tell 'em. They just think he's out screwin' around or something."

"Why don't you tell them?"

"Oh, man, I stay out of that shit. Here." He thrust a greasy paper package at her—napkins wrapped around a couple of pieces of toast. "Sorry—this was all I could get away with. I'll get something better later. Listen, will you be okay for a while?"

She nodded, feeling somewhat deserted, but also relieved— she needed to be alone, to figure out what to do.

When he was gone, she went to the bathroom, and was hugely relieved to find it didn't hurt at all. She ate the toast and felt her energy coming back. She sat and sifted things in her mind. Was there a way to avoid seeing a doctor? She closed her eyes and squeezed, trying to figure a way. But her crotch itched and burned like poison ivy.

She had to get to a doctor, and she had to do it now, before the Boucrees came back and trapped her. There was a tiny triumphant thought at the back of her brain—possibly, just possibly, there was a doctor she could trust. It wasn't likely, but it was worth a try. And face it, there was no other choice.

Madeleine Richard, her therapist, was a psychiatrist, which meant she could treat medical problems. Richard might very well turn her in. But it was take the chance or die of crotch rot. Would that be better?

In a way she thought it would, but voices hammered away in her skull: *You have no choice. This is the end of the line. You have no choice. You have no choice. You have no choice.*

Her brain wouldn't get off it. She hoped it wasn't a death wish finally getting the upper hand.

Getting out of Joel's neighborhood was much easier than he'd indicated it would be. No one cursed at her, or even stared very much. She said "Mornin' " to everyone she saw, so maybe they'd think she was comfortable there, and they answered courteously.

She was careful to note the address, to watch which streets she walked down. She asked someone for directions and eventually got a bus.

She didn't know what reaction she'd expected, but it wasn't the one she got. Richard took one look at her, did a double-take when she figured out the disguise, flashed a smile of utter delight, and folded the girl to her chest. Melody had never been held like that, had no idea what a bosom felt like; how warm and soft; how comforting. "Come in. Come in, baby. You look terrible."

She couldn't believe Dr. Richard had called her "baby." She thought only black people did that. Had little nicknames, little pet names for people. When Richard did it, Melody felt a funny warmth in her solar plexus, a new sensation, as if . . . she didn't quite know. If you were loved, was it something like this? Did your mom hug you . . . hold you? She didn't dare dwell on the subject.

"You hungry?"

"I'm sick."

Richard let her in, stroking her hair, patting her, something she'd never done before. They hadn't touched at all—why would they? Richard was just somebody her mother had hired because she thought she ought to. It wasn't like she was a relative or anything.

"What's wrong?"

All of a sudden Melody was shy. "I've got this itching. And red spots."

"Where?"

"Uh—well, I guess I better tell you. I slept with someone."

"You slept with someone?" Richard looked utterly astounded. "Someone other than Flip?"

"Flip and I broke up. It was—" She hesitated, ashamed to admit it was a stranger. "It was someone I never told you about."

"How long ago was this?"

"It was Thursday."

"Mmm. Today's Saturday. Does it hurt to urinate?"

Melody shook her head.

"Any discharge?"

"I don't know. I didn't really look. But anyway, it doesn't feel like it's inside. I mean, it's all around."

"How closely have you examined the area?"

Melody was surprised. "Well, I haven't, I guess. I mean I saw the spots and that was so gross—"

"Okay, go in the bathroom and take a look. See if there's any discharge. And use a mirror. I want to know what it looks like down there."

Melody was grateful Richard didn't ask to look. She went in the bathroom and followed orders. And was so horrified at what she saw that she screamed.

"What is it?" yelled Richard. "Are you all right?"

"Oh my God! Things! Little black things! All over the place."

"That's pubic lice, honey. Come on out and we'll see what we can do about it."

"Lice! Omigod. I've never even heard of anyone having lice."

"Melody, just one thing—get one on your finger and let me have a look at it."

Gross! "I can't do that!"

"Okay, I'll come in and look."

"No!" Melody got one and looked at it. It was so repulsive, she slung it off and reached for the soap. "Oh, God! It looks like a crab."

"Well, that's pretty conclusive. Never mind. You don't have to bring it out."

When she'd pulled up her pants and returned to Richard's living room, where she'd never sat before, her shrink explained to her about crab lice. She could hardly bear to sit, so strong was the feeling of being unclean, unworthy; filthy. "They live in pubic hair. So you can get them even if you use a condom. Or you can get them from the bedding."

"Oh, no!"

"What?"

The Boucrees. Now she'd contaminated their bed. She felt like a roach—a big nasty thing that carried disease. Ignoring the question, she said, "What's the prognosis?"

Richard smiled. "You'll live. There's a drugstore remedy for it. All you have to do is wash your clothes and all your bedding, apply the shampoo, and the little suckers drop dead."

"How much is the cure?"

"How much have you got?"

"About five dollars." Five dollars, no home, no plan. Now her shelter was problematical. If she didn't wash her bedding, the crabs would take up permanent residence. How could she wash it?

"Where are you staying?"

"I'm not sure."

"Melody, we have to talk. Come on, I'll fix you something to eat." She looked at her watch. "I have a client in half an hour."

"On Saturday?"

Richard shrugged. "Not everybody's on nine-to-five."

"What happens when she comes?" Melody tried to keep the fear out of her voice. If Richard went into her office, to a place where Melody couldn't go, she could phone the police, Melody's parents, the FBI if she felt like it.

"Look, I've got the money. I can get the stuff if you tell me what it's called, but I don't have access to a shower right now."

"Melody, are you living on the street? Or what?"

"I'm not ready to talk about it." This was a phrase she'd learned in therapy, that Richard herself had taught her.

"You can stay with me, you know. I won't turn you in."

Melody didn't believe her. She didn't trust Richard—her parents had hired her—and besides, there might be laws. Therapists had to report child abuse; maybe they weren't allowed to harbor runaways. She knew perfectly well adults were capable of lying if they thought it was for your own good—they even lied to each other. How many television dramas had she seen in which a police negotiator talks down a potential roof-leaper with promises that can't be kept?

She followed Dr. Richard into her crammed and messy kitchen. "Bagel and cream cheese?"

Melody nodded. "Sure."

Richard kept talking as she cleared a place on the kitchen table, found a bagel, cut it, and popped it in the microwave. "You must have been through a lot the last few days."

A funny wall had come up that made it okay to talk to Richard right now. It was a numbness; Melody wasn't feeling things at the moment. "It's been an education," she said, and even as the words came out, realized they sounded bratty, far too la-di-da to be sincere.

Richard turned and caught her eyes. "Look, I'm really sorry about Ham."

Melody nodded, turned away.

"Something truly awful must have happened to keep you away from home at a time like this."

"Lots of things."

"It's funny—I haven't heard from your parents."

Melody's heart leaped; that was good. "You haven't?"

"I guess they don't realize how close we are."

Close! We aren't close. You're my parents' hired gun.

"But of course they're right not to ask if I've heard from you. I wouldn't tell them if you didn't want me to."

Sure you wouldn't.

Richard put the bagel on the table. Melody fell upon it. She hadn't realized how hungry she was.

Richard kept talking. "You can take a shower while I'm seeing my client. We can put your clothes through the washer. I'll go get your medicine while you wait."

"And then I can go?"

"I hope you won't. Your parents are beside themselves."

"I thought you hadn't talked to them."

"Melody, they've been on TV and in the paper, begging you to come home—haven't you noticed?"

For some reason, that gave her a lump in her throat. Maybe she should just go home. Maybe none of this was worth it. And then she remembered that her life had been irrevocably changed—she had lost more than one kind of innocence. She couldn't go home.

"Flip dumped me for Blair," she blurted.

"Why, the little creep."

Melody laughed. She liked that about Richard, that way she had of being on her side. But it would extend only so far, and she had to remember that.

"Well, I fixed him. I went out and caught the crabs from the first boy I met."

"So was he cute?"

"He was a doll. And you know what? I sang with the band— he has this band—I sang and people stood around and listened, just like it was a real performance. I'm a pro now, Dr. Richard."

"Congratulations."

"And I had this love affair, but it's over now, and I think I'm falling in love again."

"With someone else?"

"Uh-huh." Richard had poured her orange juice, which she now picked up and drained.

"You've only been gone since Tuesday."

"Well, I've been busy."

Richard let her smile fade. "But you were so close to Ham. You can't make his death go away, Melody. No matter how much you cram into your life, how late you stay up, how much pot and alcohol you do, how many guys you sleep with—Ham's still going to be dead."

There it was. The shrinkage. She knew Richard couldn't have a conversation like a normal person—she was what she was—but it still made Melody mad. "Ham's the reason I ran away in the first place!"

She blurted it, and now she felt hot tears on her cheeks. Damn! She didn't need this.

"Ham? But what did he do to you?"

"He didn't feel me up, if that's what you mean. That's all anybody over twenty ever thinks about. No, my brother did not molest me. There's other things that happen. Things so weird nobody'd believe them."

"I'd believe them, Melody."

She sounded so sanctimonious, Melody could have punched her. "Look, I just want to get out of here."

"You need to be home with your family."

Watch it, Melody, watch it. She'll betray you in a minute. Everyone else has. She said, "I like being on my own."

"What happens when you run out of money? You haven't even got enough for the crab stuff."

"I have friends. People on the street look out for each other."

"Won't you at least talk to your mother? I'll call her."

"No!"

"Okay, okay. Look. My client's coming in a minute. Why not go take a shower? And then I'll take you to get the medicine."

No way. But she didn't say it. She didn't know what to say. Really, all there was to do was run. The minute Richard was out of her sight, she was dead. The whole damn thing had been an exercise in futility.

Richard said, "Melody, are you afraid I'll betray you?"

Still she didn't say anything.

Richard left the room and came back with an unplugged phone and a prescription. She fished in her purse for her car keys. "Look, take my car and the phone." She pulled out two twenties. "And this. Go get your medicine, then come back and take your shower.

I'll give you a change of clothes so you don't have to wait for yours to get washed. While you're gone, I'll be incommunicado. If my house burns down, I can't even call the fire department."

"Why would you do that?"

"Because you've been through something really bad and I want to help you."

"You don't even know what it is. You haven't popped the question."

"What's that?"

"Whether or not I killed my brother."

"That's because I don't care. If you killed him, I'm sure you had a good reason. And you've still been through something really bad."

The doorbell rang. "It's my client. Quick, go out the back. Don't forget the phone."

Once in the car, Melody had a wonderful sense of exhilaration, of having put something over on the enemy. She wondered if she should steal the car. She could drive to Memphis, maybe. Ti-Belle had gone there. She could even go to California. No, she couldn't get that far on forty dollars. Houston, maybe. But what would she do when she got there?

I can't do it. I'm scared.

She hated herself for being chickenshit. If she didn't get out of New Orleans, she was going to get caught.

Did she want to get caught? Dr. Richard had taught her to ask questions like that.

But it wasn't that, she thought. Weighing all the options, for a few days it was probably safer in New Orleans. Kids like her stayed in the Quarter for months and never got caught. She'd have to leave Joel's, though. She'd have to figure out a way to make some money and go back to the Quarter. To the runaway underground.

She found a K&B and got the stuff. It was probably gross beyond belief, but nothing could be worse than feeling like Typhoid Mary. She wondered if she were getting little bugs and nits on Richard's front seat.

Driving back, the exhilaration started to give way. It was being replaced by gratitude. And a weird feeling of tenderness for Dr. Richard. Richard didn't have to help her. Why was she doing it? Melody didn't know, couldn't even begin to figure it out, but she almost loved her for it. "Almost" because she didn't dare go for it.

Still, she was so grateful. So very grateful. She couldn't ever remember anybody but Joel being this nice to her.

Joel.

She wondered if he'd like to go to Houston or somewhere.

But that was preposterous. Joel went to Country Day. He wasn't a liberated minor like Melody, a former and about-to-be professional singer making her own way in the world.

Hang on to that thought, Melody. Just hang on.

That's what would get her through. Keeping her eye on the goal. Focusing.

As she drove up to Richard's house, she saw another car parking, kind of a scruffy one, not very well taken care of. A third car was there too, a nondescript dark one. She barely noticed it until she was in front of it—and then only because she caught a sudden movement. She hadn't realized there was anyone in the car.

A young woman got out of the scruffy car, the one that had just arrived, and turned into Richard's driveway. She was a big woman, a woman who looked as if she could take care of herself.

Richard hadn't said she had two clients. She'd said come back after the one and they'd straighten things out. What was this woman doing here?

Melody put it together with the two cars. Cops. What else could it be? One was watching the house, the other going inside to wait for her.

Her scalp prickled, literally itched with fear.

Bitch! I should have known! Everybody has at least two phones—why did I believe her?

Carefully, so as not to attract attention, she drove to the end of the block and turned the corner. Then she floored it.

Asshole! She meant herself.

24

Skip had a fleeting impression of short blond hair in the handsome little Accord that drove by as she was parking; drove by and hesitated. As she turned into Richard's driveway, she glanced back for a second look and the car took off. Not only took off, but she had the definite feeling the driver had been looking at her, checking her out.

Grateful she hadn't yet tossed her keys in her purse, she hopped back in the car and followed. Another car pulled out ahead of her and momentarily slowed her progress. But to her amazement, it speeded up instantly, took the corner as if it was the one chasing the Honda. And once around the corner, applied pedal unceremoniously to metal. If Melody was the one in the Accord, she had more than one pursuer. Skip's heart started beating fast.

The car had been parked on Richard's street when Skip drove up. She hadn't noticed anyone in it, but then she hadn't looked. And if it were someone tracking Melody, they would have hunched down anyway.

The Honda went through a yellow light, which promptly

turned red, and the dark car ran it. Skip would have followed, but traffic was heavy. There was no way.

She peeled out on green, and had gone five blocks before she realized there wasn't a prayer. Neither car was in sight and there were too many places they could have turned off—she hadn't been able to get a plate number on either one, and had only the most cursory of descriptions. She radioed the detective bureau and asked the desk officer to phone Madeleine Richard, ask her if she had a little silver Accord.

Three more blocks, four more, drivers honking and cursing. Nothing.

The desk officer radioed back—Richard's phone didn't answer.

Damn! Damn, damn, damn! She kept driving, kept looking fruitlessly, depressed and panicky, mentally urging Melody on.

Drive, baby, drive. Outrun that son of a bitch. You can do it. She kept saying it over and over: *You can do it.* Her whole being went into it, backing Melody up, until it seemed as if she was putting more energy into that than into actually trying to find her.

After half an hour she stopped, near tears, knowing it was hopeless. Her adrenaline should have been flowing, she shouldn't have been so worried, so emotionally involved, but all she could think of was how close the second car had been to the Honda, how close the murderer to Melody.

Here's wishing you a green light, baby.

She went back to Richard's. It was a wonderful old Victorian camelback, near Audubon Park. With no Accord parked in front.

Richard wore khaki shorts, T-shirt, and a very worried look. She was pretty, with longish dark hair that was slightly wilted in the heat. She had a lot of color in her face and very white teeth.

The worried look gave way to disappointment when she saw Skip.

"Dr. Richard? Skip Langdon." She showed her badge.

Richard looked suddenly very frightened.

"Do you own a silver Accord?"

"Yes. I lent it to someone. Has there been an accident?" Her voice was urgent.

"No. Not that I know of. But I need to talk to you about it."

Richard relaxed a little. "Come in. Would you like some iced tea?"

The living room had a light, airy, lace-curtain look. It was done up in chintz and antiques, and had a window seat, which gave it a welcoming warmth.

"What a nice room," Skip blurted. Richard smiled, seemed to relax.

"You don't sound like a detective."

"Don't I?" Skip smiled back. "I'd love some tea."

When she came back, Skip said, "Could you tell me where your car is right now?"

"I thought maybe you could tell me."

"Are you saying it's been stolen?"

"I told you. I lent it to someone."

"Melody Brocato's your client, isn't she?"

"I'm afraid that information's confidential."

"Dr. Richard, let me tell you something. The person driving that car was last seen being pursued by someone in another car—a dark-colored American job, fairly old. Does that ring a bell?"

She looked alarmed. "No. Not at all."

"Do you mind telling me who you lent your car to?"

"Yes!" She answered immediately. Then stood up and walked to the window, stared out. "Let me think a minute."

Skip kept quiet.

"I think I have to tell you," she said finally. "It's Melody. She came here with a problem. I lent her my car to—"

"Dr. Richard, every second you stall could endanger Melody's life. What problem?"

She shook her head slightly, waved a hand. "A nothing problem. A minor medical thing—but she didn't know it was minor. I tried to get her to talk, and honestly I think I'd have succeeded if I could have had a little more time, but I had a client I couldn't cancel. I lent her my car to go get the medicine, thinking that would show I trusted her, hoping maybe she'd—"

Skip was losing patience. "What on earth made you think she'd bring the car back?"

"She wanted to take a shower."

"A shower. We're talking life and death here."

Richard's smile turned very cold. "Well, I expect it felt like that to Melody. Detective Langdon, have you ever had crab lice?"

"I beg your pardon?"

"That was Melody's medical problem. Would you agree that's none of your business?"

"So she did tell you she had no place to take a shower."

"Yes, but that's about all. Except that she was in love. It's her second guy since her boyfriend dumped her the day she ran away."

"Why'd she run away?"

"That's what she wouldn't say."

"But she's got a guy with no shower."

"And she sang with a band once or twice. She didn't say much about that either."

"What's the time frame?"

Richard shrugged. "She was only here about half an hour. My client came, Melody left, she didn't come back, and you showed up. That's about it."

"Do you have any idea who's chasing her?"

"I'm afraid I think the same thing you do." The worried look came back.

"If she gets in touch again, get her to come back; or at least find out where she is; get as much information as you can and call me."

"I'll do everything I can," Richard said in a peeved tone, and Skip knew she had a right to it.

"Look, I'm sorry—I know you will, and none of what I asked is going to be easy. But I can't stress how important this is."

She liked Richard. *Watch out*, she told herself. And went back to headquarters to check her record. Richard had no Louisiana criminal past and she did own the Honda, which was her only car, according to the DMV. Still, she could have borrowed the dark car. Could she have chased Melody herself?

Skip called the dispatcher to see if anything had come of her bulletin. Nothing had.

As she hung up the phone, Frank O'Rourke strode in. "Frank. I thought you'd be at the JazzFest."

"Some of us have to work, Langdon. Listen, what do you have on the ex-wife?"

"Ham never got around to making a new will. She does inherit."

"Goddammit! She could have the kid, Langdon. She could be holding her. Have you checked out her house?"

"She doesn't have the kid. I saw Melody myself this morning."

"You what?"

"She seems to have stolen a car." Unhappily, she told him the story, knowing it didn't make her look great.

True to form, he didn't miss an opportunity. "You lost them? You didn't get a license number? What the hell are you telling me?"

"Listen, I could eat my gun about it. I'm worried as hell about that kid."

"I swear to God I don't know why we keep you around, Langdon."

She turned back to the computer and began calling up some imaginary record, anything so she wouldn't have to look at him anymore, so he'd get the idea of shutting his obnoxious trap and going away.

But he said, "Find out if the ex-wife needs money." She nodded very slightly, grudgingly, still staring at the screen. "And do it now."

She stared at him. How dare he?

"Report to me in an hour," he said, knowing it was Saturday and she had very little chance of finding out any such thing.

Cappello, goddamn you! I could kill you for getting hurt.

She sighed. *Well, hell, consider it a challenge. Show the bastard.*

She called her favorite twenty-four-hour, full-service information spewer—Alison Gaillard.

"Skippy, I'm so worried about that poor little girl."

"Me too, Alison. Just about beside myself. Listen, she's

changed her hair—she's a blond with a purple streak if you hear anything."

"Want me to call around?"

"I've got something a little more pressing, if you don't mind. But listen, this is very, very confidential—it's about Mason."

"Mason! Omigod. You don't think she did it, do you?"

"Well, look. I need to know if she needs money, and I'm afraid I kind of need it right away."

Alison laughed, a smug laugh, Skip thought, and that delighted her. "Have you come to the right place. I had lunch with Temple Becknell yesterday, who's Kitsy Coignard's Realtor, and she said Kitsy just heard Mason's putting her house on the market."

"Maybe she's buying a bigger one."

"Uh-uh. Mason made some real bad investments. She went into business with a guy she was living with who was just a wee bit younger and kind of needed a boost to get started—well, it was like this: he had a house, which he sold to get the money to buy this photography studio, and then he moved in with Mason."

"Excuse me—did you say photography studio?"

"In New Orleans, Louisiana—not exactly the home of big-time advertising and hotshot slick companies."

"So what was he taking pictures of?"

"I think he thought he was a photojournalist—I don't know. But at first, business didn't come and she lent him money and then some did and he bought more equipment and he was always on the verge of getting some great job with some company that needed an annual report, and she lent him more and more money."

"How could she be that dumb?"

"Well, she wasn't that dumb. The business would almost catch on and then wouldn't quite—you know how that can be? And he'd pay her back a little when it was doing well. What finally did her in was his sick mom."

"Cancer?"

"Oh, no. Mom wasn't really sick. That was just the boyfriend's story. It turned out Mom owned the house the b.f. claimed to have owned, and he owed her the money he'd invested in his studio. So

Mason took out a third mortgage to lend him money for his mother's illness, having already taken out a second to keep the business going, which she had bought into and therefore had a vested interest in.

"But then, without telling her, the boyfriend decided it was never going to work and declared bankruptcy; and since Mason was his partner—and still solvent—the creditors came after her."

"What a lowdown centipede."

"Well, we still haven't hit the punch line. Have you heard about the Formosan termites that are eating the Quarter?"

"No, but I think I saw some the other night, swarming the lightposts. Is that where she lives—the Quarter?"

"Yes. And she's got termite damage to beat the band. Which she can't afford to fix. So she's selling her house for a song—Kitsy hopes—and finding an apartment."

Skip was reeling. "What about the boyfriend?"

"Oh, she dumped him a month ago."

"What's his name?"

"Chas Gegenheimer. Not very romantic, is it?"

"Omigod, he took my brother's wedding pictures. Gorgeous galoot."

"Well, I hope he's hot in the sack too."

"Alison. How many phone calls away is the answer to that one?"

"Well, if you could see me, you'd know I'm blushing. I know already, of course."

Skip was silent for a moment. Alison had a daughter about two years old and a good marriage, she'd thought.

"Don't be a dork, Skippy. How could I spend all day on the phone if I had time for silly stuff?"

"I didn't say a word."

"Your silence was eloquent. I do not know firsthand, but believe me, I know. However, I really must protect my sources."

Skip hung up laughing. She had seriously underestimated Alison during their college days. The woman was her idol now—the world's greatest detective, and she never even had to step outdoors.

She called her brother, Conrad.

"My sister, the cop," he said, "calling her favorite source." With Conrad, this passed for nice—he usually grumped at her. She figured his new wife, Camille, was the source of the new personality.

"How's the ticket situation?"

"I'm hurtin'. Glad you called." They had a deal. He gave her information, in return for which she fixed his parking tickets—or so she told him. She paid them herself.

Lately, they were costing more, though. Knowing she'd be calling eventually, he tended to ignore them, letting the penalties get out of hand.

"One big one or two littles?"

"I thought you were a big wheel down there."

"Conrad, there's such a thing as discretion. If I do it too much, they're going to make me stop."

"How big and how little?"

"Under fifty dollars is little."

"Six littles or two bigs."

"Jesus, don't you ever park legally?"

"I'm storing up nuts for the winter."

"Okay, four littles, but still only one big."

"No way."

"Okay two bigs, dammit. How well do you know Chas Gegenheimer?"

"Who?"

"The photographer at your wedding."

"Oh. Not at all. He's a friend of a friend."

"Who's the friend?"

"Your victim's ex-wife, as a matter of fact—Mason Brocato. Well, she's not really my friend. She's Camille's."

"I love this town."

"What?"

"Oh, never mind." Growing up, she'd hated the city, hated the web of connections no one could avoid there, hated the way everyone knew everyone else's business. Now she was getting used to it, at times like this even liked it. "Well, look, this is kind of delicate, I guess—it'll be obvious why I'm asking what I'm asking.

Can we talk without this getting back to Camille?"

"Sure. If Mason did it, fuck her."

"Mr. Compassion."

"Hey, I've mellowed. Everybody says so."

"Can you find out what Mason's financial situation is?"

"I already know. She was over here two days ago complaining to Camille that she's putting her house on the market. Claims she's tapped out and it's all Chas's fault."

"Has she actually put it on the market?"

"How would I know? But she did mention her agent—that'd be about real estate, wouldn't it? Jimmy Hollingsworth, who I went to Newman with. Wanted to know if he was married."

"Do you have his phone number?"

"He's too young for you. And he is married." He hadn't mellowed that much.

One phone call to Hollingsworth identifying herself as Conrad's sister, and she had what she needed. In fact, more. Not only did he verify the pending house sale—he said, in that confiding Southern way Skip had come to love, "You know Mason's been going through some hard times lately."

A simple "Oh?" and he poured out the whole story. Nothing you could take to court, but the same story three times—plenty good enough for O'Rourke.

25

■ ■

"So how can we be talking if I have your only phone?"

"Melody, is that you? Thank God you're all right."

"Like you really care. Thanks for turning me in."

"I didn't turn you in. You left, and the next thing I knew a cop turned up saying you were involved in a chase."

"Oh, sure. Like you gave me your only phone."

"I forgot about this phone. I'm not kidding—it's an old one I had in the basement. I only remembered it when you didn't come back." There was a rattling at Richard's end. "Hear that? It's me shaking the phone. I dropped it three times and sometimes it works, sometimes it doesn't. That's why I got a new one."

"You just happened to conveniently forget about it."

"I didn't call the cops. I swear it."

"Well, if you didn't call them, why the hell were they chasing me?"

"Did you see the person in the other car?"

"Not very well—it was just some cop wearing shades and a baseball cap. Really great disguise; fooled the hell out of me."

"Melody, listen, I don't think it was a cop. You've got to go

home—or come here at the very least. You have to get to someplace safe.''

"No thanks. I know how safe I was before.''

"Then why'd you call?''

"You might have turned me in, but I'm still not a car thief. I
parked your goddamn car near the auditorium. I hope it gets
stripped. I already gave your phone to a kid in the neighborhood.''
The Municipal Auditorium was in Tremé, a neighborhood that
terrified most white people.

Melody hung up, furious.

How dumb does she think I am?

She was at a pay phone at a hotel she'd heard about where lots
of kids stayed. More like a flophouse, really—just a few bucks a
night. On the way over, she'd shoplifted a pair of panties from
Maison Blanche and picked up some shorts at the flea market. She'd
showered, applied the Kwell, and was now experiencing blessed
relief. She had just about enough money for lunch and bus fare
back to Joel's.

Hoping the bed harbored no bugs (though it looked like it
did), she sat down and thought about what to do next.

Betrayed by Richard. I still don't believe it.

*Or did I know all the time—unconsciously, as she would say? Did I know
I couldn't trust her or anybody else on this miserable planet?*

How about if I just go walk in front of a bus or something?

She had to lie down. She felt too awful to sit up. She didn't
even want to curl up, to feel her body against itself, comforting
itself. She just lay rigid on her back, arms at her sides, as if she were
dead.

She wished she were. Really, really wished it.

The idea about the bus had struck her fancy.

Got Janis's Ol' Kozmic Blues again.

Janis had been like her. Hadn't fit into her hometown, had
been too different to make it there. And talented. And she'd died
young.

Like me. I could do it.

I wonder how?

The bus plan was a thought. Or maybe she could jump off

something. Take an elevator to the top floor of some building, somehow get to the roof, and just walk into space. She kind of liked that one. She might just get paralyzed from the bus, but she'd never survive a crash from twenty stories up. Even ten.

If she had a hair dryer, she could take it in the bathtub with her. Or any small appliance—but how could she get one? She could shoplift a curling iron maybe—something small. But if she got caught doing it, it was back to her old life. Unless the irony killed her, which struck her as a real possibility.

There was a bittersweet pleasure in thinking these thoughts. It was kind of creative in a macabre way.

But I better think about what it's like to be dead.

It was hard at first. She tried out words.

Cold.

Still.

Motionless.

Quiet.

Like I am right now.

The thought was oddly appealing. But there was something about Janis that was nagging at her, something that wasn't quite right.

It came to her—Janis had a career. She didn't die before she sang, before she became *Janis.*

Melody thought about that for a while. And honestly found she wasn't all that damned interested in a career right now. Lying here, maybe forever, seemed more appealing.

She closed her eyes.

She didn't know how long she'd slept, didn't have a watch, but she was afraid it was too long. She felt hot and panicky. She had to replace the Boucrees's infested sheets before anyone turned up to practice.

She would stay at the Boucrees's one more night, catch their set on Sunday, and then decide what to do. If she was going to die, it couldn't be at their studio. That would be the ultimate betrayal of hospitality.

She took the hotel sheets with her. She'd now stolen three times in one day. What was next—hooking? She stared out the window of the bus, tears tracing hot paths down her face. Her eyes hurt.

If I were dead, I couldn't get the crabs and my eyes wouldn't burn every time I cry.

But I wouldn't cry because I wouldn't feel a damn thing.

Her "dead" words changed subtly. Maybe cool and restful was more like it. As if summoned, the smell of loam came to her, of rotting vegetation in the summertime. She had always loved that smell.

But I'd have no nose if I were dead.

She couldn't convince herself. She thought that if you were in the ground, the cool and peaceful ground, where it was quiet and nothing hurt, you could smell that smell; you had to be able to. You would lie in the ground and you would smell the ground and then you would become part of the ground, part of the smell, a component of the loam; you would be the Earth herself, a goddess, some said. You would have achieved immortality.

I'd be contributing to the ecosystem.

She liked the idea. At the same time, it horrified her to realize it would have made her giggle if she'd been in her right mind. It wasn't funny at all now. She genuinely thought it might be the best contribution she could make.

She got off the bus and made her way to the Boucrees's garage. No one was there, and she was grateful. Sluggishly, feeling nothing except a vague sense of duty, she ripped off the contaminated sheets, replaced them with the stolen ones.

Then there was nothing to do but lie down again. But she didn't. Like a sleepwalker, she went to the piano and sat. She hadn't yet been able to work on Ham's song with her instrument, and that was what she found herself doing. It was funny how it happened. She didn't decide to, it happened. Perhaps alcoholics found themselves drinking with no recollection of having gone to the store for a bottle of bourbon. She knew that compulsive eating was like this, had heard friends talk about suddenly realizing they were holding an empty Oreo package. She thought it odd, what she was doing, but she didn't stop to ponder. She was running on automatic and it was like lying in the ground; nothing hurt.

For the first time, she played the song, and was shocked at how good it sounded. But it needed work. So much, such a ton of work! She'd never get it done.

> *He gave me ice cream on sunny days*
> *and alligator lessons;*
> *He gave me Janis, he gave me Etta, he gave me Irma—*
> *He gave me the blues*
> *and it made me so happy*
>
> *He gave me music.*
> *He gave me music,*
> *He gave me music!*
>
> *When I sang before,*
> *it was just the baby blues—*
> *Now I got the cobalts;*
> *I got the royal-blues;*
> *I got the midnight-blues*
> *for my brother . . . the one*
> *Who gave me music—*

It was working. It was good. *Good.* It was wonderful. She was loving it, she was loving singing it. Before, it had been only a tune in her head, or hummed softly to herself so no one could hear. Now she was pouring it out from her soles, from the floor, from the ground under the building, from the middle of the Earth; and it felt soooo good.

"Holy shit," someone said. "Who is this babe?"

It was a whisper, but it was a shade too loud. Melody screamed into the microphone. Her hands flew up from the keyboard and she whirled.

Two of the Boucrees were there—she didn't know their names, but she thought one was Joel's father, Tyrone. She'd been so engrossed, she hadn't even heard them come in.

"You scared me," she said, embarrassed, and now even more so, for saying such a dumb thing.

"Take it easy now; take it easy. We didn't mean to scare you."
The man sounded as if he were talking to a dog: *Take it easy, girl;
you'll be okay.* She straightened up, got the squeak out of her voice.

"I'm a friend of Joel's. Mel—uh, Janis, Frank." After Anne
Frank; someone else who died young, who had an artist's soul.
Melody was pleased with herself for thinking of her.

"Well, I'm Joel's dad, Tyrone—and this here's my brother,
Chick."

"Baby, you sho' can sing," said Chick. He was a fairly young
guy, probably not more than thirty, with hair cropped short and
round, wire-rimmed glasses; very severe. He reminded Melody of
Delfeayo Marsalis, and she thought that was probably not acciden-
tal. The way he talked, kind of affectedly funky, didn't even begin
to go with the look. He reached out his hand, as if to give her high
five, but then thought better of it and slapped his own leg.
"Mmmmph! You sho' can!"

She felt herself go red as a cardinal. "No! I can't—I just—
really, I can't, I was just kind of . . ." And then she recovered
enough to say, "Well, thank you," in case this wasn't some sort
of cruel joke, which of course it had to be. He must be making fun
of her. The idea took hold like oxalis. Her lips tightened.

She knew with certainty that it was that. Here she was, a white
girl out of her depth, out of her neighborhood, and this was their
territory in more ways than one. She was fair game. And the guy
was probably having an identity crisis, the way he looked like an
intellectual and talked like a street kid—he was probably deeply
disturbed. That made her feel superior, but not much. She looked
down at her lap, trying to think what to do next.

The other one, Tyrone, said, "Young lady, you got talent." He
said it in that upbeat way that parents and teachers have when
they're trying to be encouraging. She'd heard that tone too often.
She knew it was real. She stared up at him, and was glad he
cultivated a more relaxed style than his little brother—slightly
longer hair, a nice moustache, sort of the Allen Toussaint look,
everybody's pal. She liked him a lot, found him very . . . well,
dadlike. In a way that her dad wasn't. Even though he fell asleep
on the floor and didn't go home the way he should.

She gave Chick a second look, with the thought that maybe he hadn't been kidding. He was grinning. Friendly, she thought, not hostile after all. She found she liked him too.

Could this be? Here were two members of the illustrious Boucree family praising her music. For a moment she was glad she wasn't dead. Or maybe she was dead. Maybe in heaven you got to have all your dreams come true and that's where she was. But she didn't believe in heaven or hell or life after death or God. She wasn't about to start now.

And yet, that stuff was about as likely as what was happening now.

"Well, listen," said Tyrone. "Don't let us interrupt you. Go ahead. That's a real pretty song—almost made me cry. Let's hear the end of it."

"Well, actually, that's almost all of it so far. I'm still working on it."

Chick said, "You mean you wrote that song?"

Not sure how to take that, Melody said, "Uh . . . yeah."

He let out his breath, not saying anything, just puffing against his lips. Whether it was meant to be positive or negative, she didn't know.

Tyrone said, "Well, let's hear something. What else can you play?"

"Oh, I don't know. Anything, I guess." No Janis, no Marcia Ball. Something sort of black. Perhaps because she had just heard Ti-Belle sing it, she thought of "St. James Infirmary," and without speaking, turned around and started to play.

She didn't know what happened to her. It was the same thing that had happened before, when she was working on Ham's song, but more powerful. It was like a great force came into her through her feet and swelled up to her diaphragm and then came out like a tornado, singing the song for her. It was singing it, not Melody; and yet a piece of her *was* singing it, was fully conscious even as she channeled, if that's what she was doing. She didn't know what to call it, she just knew she'd no idea she could sing that well. She might have sung herself right into that heaven she didn't believe in if she hadn't heard a disgusted, "Oh, shit."

Joel.

But she didn't stop singing. She wasn't going to anyway, but still it was gratifying when someone said, "Shhhh," and there were slight sounds of a scuffle, as if Chick had cuffed Joel for being so rude.

When she was done, Chick said, "All right!" and applauded. They all did, even Joel. There were five of them now.

"You are one talented lady," said Tyrone, and she was almost as pleased at the adult appellation as at the compliment.

One of them stepped forward and stuck out a big black paw. "I'm Terence. Don't know who you are, but I sure want to shake your hand." Melody grabbed his hand as if she thought he could pull her to safety.

"I'm Janis," she said, looking Joel straight in the eye. "I'm a friend of Joel's. He showed me this place once and I sneaked in to work on this song I'm writing. Listen, it's not his fault, he didn't even know—"

The fourth man interrupted her, speaking not so much to her or his brothers as to the ether. "She's the answer to everything, you know that? She could be, like, our Aaron."

"Raymond, what you on about?"

"Know why we've never made it big? 'Cause we've never had a star, that's why. We play good, but we sing shitty. All of us. What we need's a vocalist, and we always have. Like Aaron Neville, you know what I mean? Like, what would the Neville Brothers be without Aaron? Look here, this white girl sings as good as Aaron does, any day of the week. Well, maybe not quite as good, but the chick's hot." He paused. "And she can play too."

Melody felt as if she should jump up in protest, it was such a travesty using Aaron's name in vain that way. As far as she was concerned, he was the best male singer since Elvis, and what this man was speaking was purest blasphemy. One did not compare a deity with simple Melody Brocato. She was frozen in amazement.

Joel was smiling. He nodded and gave her a thumbs-up sign, as if to say, "I told you so."

Chick said, "You mean, like, ask her to play with us? Like that chick in The Fabulous Baker Boys?"

295

Raymond shrugged. "Well, we all talked about it at the time. Everybody said it was what we needed." He folded his arms smugly.

Melody had seen *The Fabulous Baker Boys*, had cried all the way through it and for days afterward. She had cried for the Jeff Bridges character, the sensitive artist, the true musician unrecognized by an uncaring world. But she had identified with the Michele Pfeiffer character. She wanted her own band to save.

Now she imagined the Boucrees seeing the movie—renting it, probably, after some acquaintance had recommended it—and having the same fantasy.

They needed her, she needed them, just like in the movie.

She smiled, couldn't help smiling, and then dug her nails into her wrist to get back to reality.

Hold it, Melody. They're just talking. This doesn't mean anything.

Terence said, "You know who said they'd catch our set, don't you? Those two A&R men—from Atlantic and Warner."

"Tomorrow?" said Tyrone. "You mean tomorrow? We change our whole act for this girl here?"

Suddenly Melody got angry. One minute it had been all gratuitous compliments and now it was gratuitous put-downs.

She said, "Excuse me, I'm not available," got up and started out the door, cheeks hot, thinking that if she wanted to be discussed in the third person, she could always go home.

"Young lady, you just hold up there a minute." The speaker was Tyrone again, and his tone was decidedly paternal.

She turned around and spoke in what she hoped was a dignified manner. "Thank you for the loan of the piano. I did not come here to apply for a job."

The dignity ran out when the tears came into her voice, and this frustrated her so much, she turned around and started to run again. She wondered if that stuff ever stopped, if she'd ever be able to say what she meant, what she wanted, without crying like a kid.

Joel touched her arm as she went by. "Hey, Mel, come on— nobody meant to hurt your feelings."

She looked at him, and his eyes were so pretty, so moist and brown, so sincere and pleading, that she couldn't leave him. "Janis," she whispered. But she stopped.

Tyrone said, "I'm mighty sorry, young lady—I think I'm the one was out of line. You're a fine, fine singer, and even though you didn't ask for a job, we were just thinking out loud about how we could get you. 'Cause we want you, you know? That goes without sayin'. I didn't mean nothin' by what I said—I was just wonderin' if we could do it—if it could physically be done by tomorrow." He stepped forward and gave her his hand and a big smile. "Could you find it in your heart to accept my apology?"

Melody shook with him and nodded. She couldn't think of anything to say.

Raymond said, "Janis, what you think about singin' with a broken-down old band like us?"

Before she could say a word, Tyrone said, "Now wait just a minute, you're rushin' things."

Terence said, "Well, I think we all agree."

To her amazement, Joel, her buddy and comrade-in-arms, her only friend, blurted, "She's white! What the hell we gon' do about that?"

Raymond gave him a swat. "What's the matter with you, boy, you a racist? You just shut up now."

Joel staggered. Raymond had hit him a good one. It was funny —Melody had imagined he was a boy who'd never been hit, a kid from a family so loving he wouldn't even know what violence was. The strange thing was, the Boucrees did seem loving and warm when they weren't arguing. She wondered if the Brocatos did.

Chick said, "Harry Connick's a white boy. Played the JazzFest with James Booker when he was a baby, almost. And that was so long ago, nobody hardly remembers. We gon' discriminate here in the nineties?"

Tyrone said, "Okay, hush everybody, just hush now. Joel, I don't know why you talk like that."

Melody thought that if Joel had been white, he would have turned scarlet. "I didn't mean anything—I just thought it might look funny." He paused. "I mean, she's a girl, and Harry Connick wasn't. How's it gonna look, a sixteen-year-old white girl up there singing with eight or ten black dudes? Gonna look funny, I can't help it."

The image nearly drove Melody mad with delight. But Tyrone tugged his moustache—apparently something he did when he was thinking. "You got a point, son. I apologize to you."

She couldn't imagine her own father apologizing.

To Melody, Tyrone said, "We got more trouble than that, though, don't we?"

She stared at him, hoping he didn't mean what she thought he did.

"I know who you are, girl. I heard what Joel called you." He said to the others. "Y'all leave us alone for a minute. Joel and I need to talk to this lady."

But Melody couldn't see a reason for that. She felt an irresistible tug toward these people, wanted them, warts and all, to be her family, to adopt her and take them in. She said, "It's okay. They can know. But y'all can't turn me in. You've got to promise me that." She looked at the others, pleading with her eyes, wanting them to know how desperate she was.

Chick snapped his fingers. "Oh, no. Oh, shit. I know who you are too. You gotta be the little sister."

"Huh?" The other two were bewildered.

"Ham Brocato's little sister. The one that's gone missing and every cop in the city's looking for."

"Oh, man!"

"Oh, shit!"

"Look, I have a right to my own life. Things weren't working out for me at home, that's all. I haven't committed any crime."

Terence said, "You didn't kill your brother?"

Joel said, "Shut up, motherfucker!" It pleased her that he was defending her.

"It's okay, Joel," she said. She turned to the others. "No. I didn't kill my brother, do you hear that? No!"

Raymond flinched. "Girl, you sure got a voice on you."

"You might not have committed any crime," said Tyrone, "but I bet we have if we take care of you."

298

Take care of her? What did he mean by that? The phrase made her knees go wobbly.

Chick said, "Listen, y'all. This girl sings like a motherfucker. That's the long and short of it."

"Yeah, but she's sixteen. I bet we got to have her parents' permission or something."

Melody said, "Haven't you ever heard of a liberated minor?" She didn't know exactly what it was, but maybe they didn't either.

"I think they got to be older," Tyrone said gently.

"Look, nobody has to know—I'll just turn black. I can get a wig and skin-tanner."

To her horror, everyone in the room laughed, even Joel—and not polite little titters either; great, heartfelt guffaws. She didn't even begin to get the joke, but knew she was the butt of it. Dying had been a really good idea, and she didn't know why she hadn't gone through with it. Anything was better than this shit. Her eyes went out of control again.

"Hey, what you cryin' about?"

"I wish I were dead!"

"Hey, Mel, take it easy." Joel moved closer, put an arm around her.

Terence took a tentative step forward as well. "We didn't mean nothin', little sister. It was just funny, that's all."

"What was so funny about it?"

Chick started to laugh again, but caught himself.

Terence said, "Somethin' 'bout the way you look, I guess. Those blue eyes, maybe."

"You are so unfair! Chick has blue eyes!"

"Eyes aren't the point," said Tyrone. "The point is we got a sixteen-year-old young lady ought to be home with her parents."

"I can't go home."

"Why not?"

"I just can't, that's all. That part of my life is over."

"Ohhhh, shit. Ohhhh fuck." Chick was moaning like he'd been shot. "You didn't kill your brother, but you know who did. That's it, ain't it?"

299

Melody looked him straight in the eye and told the truth.
"That's not it."

"No, that ain't the whole thing. 'Cause it's worse than that.
Whoever it is knows you know. That's why you can't go back.
'Cause they'd know where to come get you."

Raymond said, "You been watchin' too much television."
Melody twisted her mouth into a kind of ironic half smile. She
shook her head slowly from side to side, as if to say, "Poor Chick.
Pitiful. A candidate for the loony bin."

At least she hoped that's how it would play, but she had a
feeling the distressed look on Tyrone's face reflected her own.

"It's not that! I swear it's not that! Listen, I'll prove it to you.
Let me sing with you tomorrow and I'll go back home and
straighten it all out. I swear it!"

*Just let me have this one chance and life will have been worth living. I'll die
happily if I can just do that. I'll climb up to the roof of that building and take a
short walk to the ground. Just let me sing Ham his song and go.*

Tyrone gave her a hard stare. "You mean that, little sister?"

"I swear it on a stack of bibles." That was easy, she wasn't a
Christian.

"My wife and I are gon' take you there and walk you up to the
door. You okay with that?"

No!

But she'd worry about it later. She could slip away after the gig.
By the time they noticed, she'd be dead.

"Just let me do the gig."

He nodded slightly. "You want it, you got it."

The room exploded.

"All riiiight!" Raymond and Chick slapped each other high
fives. Terence came over and shook Melody's hand.

Joel hollered, "Yes!"

Melody thought she must be missing something. All this fuss
couldn't be about her.

When it had subsided, Tyrone said, "You got a place to stay?"

"Well, I had a hotel room, but—"

"Where?"

"The Oriole."

"Oh, shit! Kid your age at the Oriole? Oh, shit."

"It's full of kids my age. That's mostly who's there."

"Well, you ain't goin' back." He pulled out a wad of bills. "Joel'll take you to a Holiday Inn, someplace like that. You really think you can turn black?"

Melody smiled. "With a little help from my friends."

He turned to Joel. "You know that place ya mama gets her hair fixed? Take her to Louise, see what she can do. Maybe she'll lend you a wig or somethin'. Then go 'round to Billy DuPree's, get her a caftan or somethin' African-looking. If she's wearin' something like that, her skin's dark enough, maybe nobody'll look at her too close. Maybe she'll pass."

To Melody, he said, "A hundred dollars of that money's your costume allowance. The other hundred's an advance on the gig."

She heard someone gasp, maybe Raymond, and knew that meant he was overpaying her, giving her a handout. "I can't—"

But he put up a hand. "Dawlin', aren't you forgettin' something? You're gon' make us rich."

She tried to speak, but couldn't get anything out.

"Now y'all get out of here. Be back at three o'clock. Terence, you call the others. We gon' have one hell of a rehearsal. Melody, what's your best song?"

Joel said, "They're all her best song, Daddy."

Melody thought that maybe she wouldn't die, maybe just go to California or something.

26

Ti-Belle had been running from this all her life. This cell, this stink, this depressing half-light, and the ugly faces, ugly voices of the other prisoners.

Now that she was here, she couldn't believe it hadn't happened years earlier. She'd sung everywhere there was to sing, including on national television, and after the first few years didn't even break out in a sweat at the thought of someone recognizing her. She'd genuinely convinced herself no one ever would. She looked different; she had a different name; she'd grown up.

She had a notion why she'd gotten away with it. Because the only place she ever sang in Doradale was the choir. Nobody had especially noticed her voice, and anyway, the songs she did now were so different.

Yet Proctor had figured her out. Why hadn't anyone else? Probably because they hadn't been with her much and he had. He hadn't gotten it at first—it had taken a while. She'd been so arrogant, she hadn't had the sense to stay away while he was at Nick's.

But she couldn't have stayed away. She might have lost him. She'd had to press her advantage.

Now she had lost him. As well as her career and her liberty.

Today she was going to "bond out," as her lawyer called it— she was only in a holding cell—but she was going to jail if she lived long enough. She'd left prints on the knife and she knew it. She'd thought of that a thousand million times since leaving Doradale.

Should she have fought harder? Denied she was Lacey Long-tree? Yes. Almost certainly. But she couldn't go kicking herself about it now—because she knew she could no more help what she'd said, the way all that came out of her, than she could help attacking Proctor. That was the part she wished she could take back —everything else was irrelevant. Because if they printed her, she was dead, and once they'd booked her for battery, they were going to print her.

Only one thing could keep her out of prison. Her uncle Garnet was twice as mean as her daddy ever thought about being. If he was still alive, she had a good chance of dying instead.

"Come on, Ti-Belle." She hated the way they called you by your first name.

But she might have a few days. There wasn't even a crime lab in Doradale. Who knew where they'd have to send the prints? She could go somewhere—Mexico, Europe. But what was the point? With no Nick and no career, what was the point of anything?

But Nick was waiting for her when they let her go, looking like he was going to cry.

"Nick Anglime, what are you doing here?"

"I thought you might need a ride."

"You came to get me?"

For answer he opened his arms.

"I thought you hated me." But then she remembered that he didn't yet know she'd killed her father.

"Why would I hate you, honey pie?"

But he must know; Proctor must have told him.

"I guess I lost my temper back at your house."

"I like a woman with spirit." And she knew she had him forever. Knew, in fact, that he'd help her with the problem she hadn't mentioned yet. This was a man with more heart than brains. She liked that.

■

Skip watched as they left, fuming. Ti-Belle had spent about an hour in a cell. If the sheriff of Pine County, Alabama, hadn't been so damned arrogant, they might still have her. Just because Ti-Belle said she was Lacey Longtree didn't mean she was—Skip still didn't think she had probable cause on the murder charge. But what to do about the old crime wasn't her decision. She'd called the sheriff and said Ti-Belle had admitted she was Lacey Longtree, but hadn't exactly confessed to the murder. Told him the singer was going to bond out and Skip didn't know if she'd be able to find her later. Was there any way to identify her—a scar or something—as the real Longtree?

The sheriff had guffawed in her face. "Detective, you got somethin' against that little Cajun gal? There ain't one hair of her gorgeous head that looks like Lacey Longtree. I'd love to catch up with Ms. L., I sure would, but I'm just afraid you're barkin' up the wrong tree. You know how these singers are—the beauteous Ti-Belle's probably so full o' drugs she doesn't know her name,"

"Well, look, I'll send you a copy of her prints by Federal Express."

"Hey, I thought New Orleans was supposed to be the Big Easy. Go to the JazzFest, have some popcorn s'rimp. I can wait till Monday, no problem."

He was so dismissive he reminded her of her least favorite sergeant and she was a little thin-skinned about O'Rourke right now. He was the one she was really mad at. She was furious that he'd had the gall to tell her what to do. He'd said not to let Ti-Belle out of her sight—that she'd lead them to Melody.

But if Ti-Belle knew where Melody was, she'd have already found her. She might have killed her daddy and she might have killed Ham, but she no more knew where to find Melody than Skip did. It was a waste of time.

They went to Nick's, of course. About an hour later they came out again.

They drove across the bridge to the West Bank, a place many New Orleanians had never even been. It was like never having had a hurricane at Pat O'Brien's—a matter of pride. When they ended up in Marrero, Skip began to develop a new respect for O'Rourke.

Marrero didn't even look as if it belonged in Louisiana—it could have been a seedy part of California, maybe. Everything was new here, meaning built in the last couple of decades. Every ceiling was low. The whole town looked made for dwarves. On Fourth Street there were mingy little nightclubs that looked more like hamburger stands.

Not far from there, blacks lived in a housing project, cheek-by-jowl with blue-collar whites in mobile homes. On weekends they could run into each other at some of the bars on Fourth Street and bang each other upside the head with pool cues if things got dull.

To Skip, even the project wasn't as depressing as the nasty little lanes lined with cheap bungalows, many of them prefab, a lot of them neat, some falling down, and every single one with heavy-duty bars on every single window. People owned these places, called them home. One of the streets was named Silver Lily. It made you want to cry.

Nick and Ti-Belle drove to a gun store. Skip parked and looked in the window while they bought a gun. A handgun. Ti-Belle was the one doing the talking, testing the thing for heft—and eventually the one paying. Skip couldn't for the life of her think of any plausible, legitimate reason why Ti-Belle Thiebaud would need a handgun. Uptown ladies carried them, fearful of getting mugged in their front yards, if you thought that was legitimate. But Ti-Belle didn't live Uptown. Nick did, but since Audubon Place had a gate at the entrance, it was hardly a paradise for muggers.

They made no more trips, just drove home and went to bed about nine-thirty—or at least the lights went off then. Skip went home depressed. She hadn't seen Steve all day, hadn't talked to him, and didn't think he'd be there.

But he's on a big project, Skip. It's nothing to do with you.

Maybe it is.

305

She couldn't still that second nagging little voice.

Her apartment was stuffy and unwelcoming. She opened the windows and turned on the ceiling fan. The soft light from the lamp spilling on a new purchase, an antique English table, was pretty on her new sofa, her melon walls. But she couldn't get comfortable. She wanted a joint.

Hell, I want Steve.

Failing Steve, she wanted a joint.

But Jimmy Dee wouldn't be too bad either.

She picked up the phone. "Dee-Dee, I need you."

"This is getting to be a habit. What is it, angel? Bear bite?"

"The bear's out. I need conversation." She paused. "And drugs."

"Uh-oh."

"Uh-oh what?"

"You've been Little Miss Nancy Reagan lately. Something must be wrong."

"Get over here, Dee-Dee, and bring a big fat joint."

He came in holding it out to her. "What's the prob?"

They sat together on the couch, companionably passing the joint. "Probs plural. I'm beat. I hate this case. I'm worried silly about the kid. Cappello's on sick leave and O'Rourke's my sergeant."

"Oh, my poor tiny thing. Not the dread O'Rourke!"

"I could kill him."

"And the bear? What about him?"

"The bear." Skip sighed. "Nothing new. I guess I'm still upset that he stayed at Cookie's the other night."

"Jesus. This is why I don't date women, you know that?"

"It is not. You just don't think we're cute."

"I don't think most of you are cute. But you, Margaret Langdon, are tiny and adorable. I would say marry me, but you're too damned insecure."

"I am, aren't I?" She felt horribly sad. "What the hell's wrong with me, Jimmy Dee?"

"You're too dainty and helpless. Such a tiny thing against the world—who *could* cope?"

"Waaah!" She was pretending, but she really was close to tears and she didn't know why.

"Tell Papa."

"He says he loves me. . . ."

"Bleeagh."

"He even acts like he loves me."

"Well, he better. The brute."

"But . . ." She bit her lip, trying not to make too big an ass of herself.

"But what, babycakes?"

"I don't see how he could!" The words burst out of her like air out of a suddenly released balloon, a rubber sphere propelled by its own insides, bouncing off walls, falling finally flat and shrunken.

Dee-Dee's kind eyes reminded her of those of a maid her family had once had, a big, comfortable woman who'd called Skip "dawlin" and held her against a mammoth bosom. "Oh, my precious darling. Give Dee-Dee a hug."

His chest was bonier than Louvina's had been, but it did the trick. "I can't believe I'm acting like such a dork."

"Babykins, I remember sex. I mean, I have to reach pretty far back, but I can just barely barely recollect a tiny bit."

"And what do you remember?"

"Turns strong men to jellyfish. By that I mean myself, of course."

"Oh, Dee-Dee, come off it. You don't have an insecure bone in your body."

"Oh, my dainty darling, hush yo' mouf. You've never seen me in love, do you realize that?"

"Not a pretty sight?"

"Omigod, the pacing. The tearing of hair and gnashing of teeth. The agony! You wouldn't have a moment's peace. I'd keep you on the phone till three A.M. I wouldn't eat, you'd have to feed me intravenously. But of course it would be worth it. I have much better taste in men than you do."

Skip burst out laughing, thinking that a world with Dee-Dee in it couldn't be all bad. "Oh, you idiot, what would I do without you?"

"Well, you won't have to. Unless you move to California with all the fruits and nuts."

"Don't be such a bigot."

"Bigot hell, I'm jealous. We're talking my people." He paused, seemed to reflect, to know that he'd lapsed into the inanity people fall into when they're trying to avoid something—sometimes a good-bye, sometimes another subject; a painful one. He took a deep toke, held it a long time, looked anxious, as if he had something unpleasant to say; something scary. "Listen, I want to talk to you."

Not again. She wanted to be a good friend, but she'd called him because she needed cheering up, not because she felt like offering a shoulder to cry on. In fact, what she felt was bone-tired. Just too tired to cope. A day of her favorite pop Cajun R&B singer had done her in.

She yawned, not bothering to hide it.

"Tired?" said Dee-Dee.

"Getting there." She blinked at him sleepily. She slapped her own face.

"What is it?"

"Nothing. I just realized I'm stoned out of my gourd." She smiled. "I'm out of practice."

"I better go." He started to get up.

"No." She patted the sofa. Suddenly it was important to her to function, to do something for Dee-Dee. She was tired, but suddenly overcome by guilt, accompanied by a tidal wave of sloppy sentimentality. She hoped she wouldn't throw her arms around his neck and tell him she loved him.

"Talk," she said.

"Okay." But he was silent. "This is hard."

"For Christ's sake, you're acting like a straight guy. Only two things make them this nervous. So I'm wondering—are you proposing, or are we breaking up?"

The minute she said it, she got a cold feeling in her stomach. Maybe they were breaking up, in a sense. Maybe he was moving to Minneapolis to take care of his niece and nephew. Dee-Dee gave her a smile as sloppily sentimental as she felt. Then he did the unspeakable—threw his arms around her neck and said he loved her.

"Ick, Dee-Dee! Bleeagh. I love you too, but yuck. If we start carrying on like this, what'll be left when we're eighty?"

He was laughing as only the mightily stoned can do, his whole body shaking, tears pouring. "God, you're a bitch. No wonder that man-mountain's stopped coming around."

"Oh, boy. Who's the bitch?"

"Sorry, I didn't mean it. I mean, I'm sure it's nothing—bimbo attack, probably."

"Oh, can it, Dee-Dee, I thought you wanted to tell me something." She hated herself for breaking the mood. Women always said men wouldn't talk about feelings, but she was the guilty one here. She'd sidetracked sentiment as handily as any clod who'd ever pledged Deke.

"Well, like I was saying, I love ya, baby."

"Likewise, I'm sure."

"I have to make changes in my life—for the kids."

"You're really going to be a dad?"

"What else do you suggest?"

She shrugged. "I don't know. Boarding school, I guess."

He shook his head vigorously. "Uh-uh and no way. I got sent and no kid of mine—"

"Listen to you! One minute you're camping it up and next you're talking no-kid-of-mine."

"Well, dammit, I want to do this. I really want to take care of those kids." He stopped and looked away from her, made sure she couldn't see his face, and said, "Love them."

He said it so low she wasn't sure she'd heard right, but she was starting to come down and she had the sense not to ask.

He turned to her and grimaced. "It's not like I had a sex life or anything. I might as well get a hobby."

"Dee-Dee, you're the worst."

"Well, I mean, guys in feather boas and leather aren't exactly a wholesome influence. Do you think?"

"Depends on the guys." He said it with her, and they split their sides for a while, still deliciously loaded.

"What I want to say first—here's the bottom line—is you're family. Do you understand that? No matter what happens."

"Dee-Dee, what are you saying?"

"Well, I kind of need your apartment."

So that was it. The cold feeling in her stomach came back. "You want me to move?"

"Well, yes and no."

"Dee-Dee, you do or you don't."

"I want you to move and stay here too. What I want to do is take back your apartment and the other two, redo the building as a single-family home, and move the kids in. Plus a nanny or au pair or something—whatever you're supposed to get."

She shrugged. "Beats me." She didn't know what she'd do if it were she, suddenly a mom without a clue.

"It'll be gorgeous, don't you think? Can you see the possibilities?"

"It'll be great." *I wish I could live in it.*

"And I want you to take the slave quarters."

"What?" He lived there himself, and it was a showplace. "Dee-Dee that's sweet of you, but I don't think—"

"At the same rent, my dainty darling. A teensy-weensy little rent for a teensy-weensy girl."

"No."

"Yes. *Mais certainement.*"

"I can't."

"But you must. I can't go through this alone." It was a joke, he said it like a joke, but she caught an involuntary twitch in his neck, knew that it was true, that he was tense right now, afraid she'd turn him down.

She said, "You just want a built-in babysitter."

"Wrong. I need a cop in the house. 'Cause you know what kids do? They make you watch Freddy Krueger movies and then you have nightmares and wake up scared. I need you to protect me."

Skip was jerked upright by the sweet domestic image—Uncle Jimmy and his niece and nephew watching scary movies in their newly redone French Quarter home. Munching microwave pop-corn. No lights on. The kids on the floor, Skip too. Everybody giggling at funny old Freddy and his fake fingernails.

It seemed doable. Alien, but doable. She was excited by it in a funny way, somewhere deep in her belly felt fuzzy little stirrings.

I want this. She was surprised.

She turned to Jimmy Dee and raised an eyebrow. "You're getting weird, Dee-Dee."

"I'll go make up the lease—okay?"

"They have to call me Auntie. That's non-negotiable."

27

They were hugging when Steve came in. A curious domesticity had come over them, a weird blissful peace, as if they'd found something they were looking for.

"You two getting married?"

"No. We're going to be single parents."

"Am I missing something?"

"That's my cue," said Jimmy Dee. " 'Bye now." He floated out with a campy flick of the wrist.

Steve stared after him. "Like I said. Am I missing something?"

Skip got up and gave him a hug, but she felt resistance and was hurt. "What's the matter?"

"You and Dee-Dee. You looked like you were in love."

"Well, we are, sort of. It's like *Tootsie*—if he'd cut out the drag act, maybe we could get something going."

He stepped away from her. "You're stoned."

It was like a slap, sudden, sharp, painful, and utterly sobering. "Well, I was. I think I'm coming down. I'm sorry about the scene with Dee-Dee. I have a hard time remembering you get jealous of him."

"I'm not jealous!"

"Would you like to sit down, by any chance? Could I get you a beer maybe?"

He relaxed, dug into his eyes with the heels of his hands. "Good God, yes."

She got him the beer and made some instant iced tea for herself, thinking about what she wanted to say. "Listen, I'm sorry I got stoned."

He reached for her in that easy way he had. He was affectionate and she liked that in a man. He didn't seem even slightly threatened by being close to her. "It's okay. You've got a right to get stoned. I was just noticing, that's all.

"You know, I hardly ever do it anymore. Tonight I was feeling insecure."

"Your case?"

"No, you."

"Me!" He couldn't have looked more bewildered if she'd set him on fire.

"I guess I was upset that you went to Cookie's the other night."

"But why?" Now he seemed hurt too—as if she'd said she wanted to break up.

"I guess I thought you didn't want to be with me."

"I didn't want to be with you?" He leaned back to look at her. "Listen, Skip, you don't have to worry about that. You can believe what I say. If I say I want to give you some space, you don't have to think I got a better offer or something. Tell me you aren't feeling crowded in here."

She shrugged, starting to feel embarrassed. "Sometimes. But it's getting better, don't you think?"

"I thought it might be getting worse. The three-day guest theory, you know?"

"I feel silly."

"Don't feel silly, feel secure. I want you to feel secure."

"Okay." It was all she could think of to say. On the one hand, he'd made her feel ridiculous for being so absurdly neurotic; on the other, she was conscious of a funny resentment she couldn't identify.

What am I mad at? He's perfect.

It's easy to be perfect when you only have to do it a week or two at a time.

So that's what it was. She wanted a bigger piece of him. Well, that was her problem and she'd have to get it under control.

He said, "Remember that first time I was here? At Mardi Gras a year ago? How I didn't know anything and you had to keep giving me New Orleans lessons?"

"And you more or less thought you'd landed on Mars?"

"I can barely remember that now. This place is starting to seem like home to me. I bet you never notice the air here."

He got up and took his beer to the open window. It was a window that opened from the floor and reached almost to the ceiling. The legs of his shorts blew slightly in the breeze. "It's like velvet," he said. "Soft and deep, like you could fall into it and sink; you can hardly stand it on your skin it's so soft. But it can be smothery too. Like wool sweaters in July."

"I do notice it; I notice it all the time. I think I might be addicted to it."

He nodded. "Yes. Maybe that's what gets you about the place. I miss this air."

"I'd think in L.A. you'd miss any air."

"You know, you've still never come to visit me there."

"Well, I want to; it just hasn't worked out yet."

He sat beside her again. "This place is its own little world."

"Well, we like it."

"Hey, don't get defensive. You're the ones who call it a Third World country."

"It's not exactly an apple pie kind of place. The last bastion of hedonism."

"That's not all. Remember when you had that case that had us all going to twelve-step programs?"

"You only went once or twice, I thought."

"Shows how much you know. I went to three or four. And, actually, I'd been to one or two in California."

"Why, Steve Steinman, you never said so."

He looked embarrassed. "Well, I went with a friend. And in California, they're extremely polite. No 'cross talk'—you can't answer back—"

"I thought there was always no cross talk."

"There's never supposed to be. And there's a certain language for these things. Everybody's real sincere; kind of reverent, like it's church or something."

"They're like that here too."

"Ha! The first one I went to, the speaker calls on this guy and he says, 'I've really been giving it some thought lately and I've decided Al-Anon is for neurotic wimps with no brains and no balls.' " He paused. "What do you think the speaker did?"

"Said 'thank you' and called on the next person—that's the protocol."

"Fat chance. He started arguing with the guy."

"What do you mean? Those people don't do that."

"Well, they did. So, then the next person who gets called on puts in her two cents worth, and the speaker answers her back. Then the original 'neurotic wimps' guy answers him. Next thing you know, everybody's mixing it up."

Skip was laughing now, able to see the scene all too clearly, to recognize the rugged individualists of her home state in a true-life vignette. "The Louisiana legislature's exactly the same way."

"That's what Ham said when I told him about it."

Ham. The word had a sobering effect on Skip. She drew in her breath, but Steve didn't seem to notice.

"You know what I thought when I saw that? I thought, I've got to find some way to move here—people this crazy are my kind of people. A whole state like the Rum Tum Tugger."

"Like what?" She was only listening with half an ear.

"One of the cats in Cats: 'He do do what he will do and there's no doing anything about it.' "

She gave him a vague smile.

"So what do you think?"

"About what?"

"About my moving here. Did you hear a word I said?"

"What—you're moving here? Sorry. I was thinking about Melody."

He turned away. "Well, I thought I might."

It started to sink in. *"You're moving here?"*

"We need to talk about it. I'm in deep, you know."

"Uh—well, I— What does that mean exactly?"

"With you, Skip. In deep with you." He touched her arm lightly, but that was all. He was behaving shyly, which wasn't like him. "I wasn't trying to get away from you last night. I'm falling more and more in love with you."

"You are?" She wanted to look around and see if there was anyone else in the room.

"Look at me!" Her eyes must have followed her impulse. "You know, it doesn't make me feel really great to have you looking around for a way out."

"That's not it. Believe me, it's not it. Would you really move here?"

"Well, half-time maybe. Something like that. If I could get work. Maybe I could get a more or less regular gig with the foundation. Or something else—all I need is one semiregular kind of thing."

"You mean it? You really mean it?"

"Yeah, I mean it. And you know what else I mean? You are the most beautiful, curly-headed, green-eyed amazon I ever saw in my life."

"Amazon?"

"Goddess. I misspoke. Would you make love to a mortal?" He was tugging on her arm.

"I'm all sweaty."

"Well, okay, let's get in the shower."

If the air felt like velvet, the water felt like liquid silk. It washed the case away, washed away her worry about Melody, even temporarily banished what she was beginning to see as her towering insecurity.

She could swear she saw rainbows, but there wasn't enough light.

316

"Turn around."

She turned away from him, in a haze of love and passion, her mind mud, mud so wet it shook like jelly. Her focus slipped to the center of her body and her legs shook, like the mud of her mind. Steve ran his hands once over her butt and let them settle on her hips, lightly, so very lightly, and then her eyelids exploded in gold and silver stars, rivers of them, bursting out of a sun somewhere in her head.

"Skip, don't fall. Hold on, help me or you're going to fall."

His voice brought her back; she had almost fainted from the pleasure of him. She was desperate to put her arms around him, but she couldn't or they would disconnect. A little scream of love and delight and frustration came out of her, and then she slipped away again.

Next he was holding her tight against the shower wall, literally keeping her up with his body, and finally her legs stopped shaking.

Later, lying squeaky clean on her folded-out sofa, she said, "Do you see things when we make love?"

"I saw purple irises this time."

They did it again, and she saw a Japanese landscape, perfect in the moonlight, orderly and ideal, unlike the rest of the flotsam that cluttered her mind. Steve saw the ocean—and a mermaid, he said, but she thought he embellished.

▪

When the Boucrees were together and they played, it was some of the finest music Melody ever hoped to hear. When they weren't playing, it was a wall of sound. For some reason, she'd associated the old phrase *gumbo ya-ya*—everybody talks at once—with women. It was clear to her now that men had invented it. They were like a bunch of black Brocatos, she thought sometimes, always arguing over business matters, digging at each other, hurting, going for the weak spots. They could be nasty, and that upset her. She'd run away for the same old thing?

But they were warm too. They'd solve the problem and then they'd make up and play the piece they were arguing about and the music would be all the sweeter for it. All the more soulful, Melody

thought, and wondered if that was racist. But she thought it wasn't
—soul meant feeling to her. The Boucrees wore not merely their
hearts on their sleeves, but their spleens and guts and balls as well.
They might not be perfect, might have their differences, but they
made it work for them.

Raymond said, "Fuck it, Tyrone, you're screwing up again."

"Fuck you, Raymond. What the fuck do you know?"

"I know what I know. Hey, Daddy, tell Tyrone to knock that
shit off, will you?"

"Knock what shit off, baby brother?"

"That cornball crap, that white paddy bullshit you were just
playin'."

"Why you talk that way in front of our guest?"

Raymond remembered his manners and apologized. But Melody, mind made up so firmly on the Boucree side, convinced they
were turning their troubles into art, couldn't help wondering how
long she could stand them. Maybe being a Boucree was as much
a pain in the ass as being what she was.

She was watching Joel to see how he took it. When they got
into it, he dragged his drumsticks on the floor and kind of hunched
over till it passed. He even looked a little as if he were taking a nap.
She wondered if this was why he didn't want to be a musician. A
doctor worked alone.

She particularly wondered about his relationship with Tyrone.
As far as she could see, the man was pretty close to a saint. She
loved the way he'd been with her—firm and strong, but at the
same time gentle and warm. Perfect qualities for a dad—hers had
none of them except strength, and he used it only to erect a wall
between the two of them.

He never speaks to me as if he actually likes me, she thought with
surprise. No wonder it hurt so much to be around him.

Joel seemed genuinely fond of Tyrone, had always spoken
fondly of him, and seeing them together was good: they were nice
to each other. Yet this model father had had his whole family
yelling at him this morning, purportedly for abandoning his wife.
As Joel seemed to take his side about that, Melody did too. But still
she wondered.

Is anything simple?

Not lately, anyway.

There were eleven of the Boucree Brothers, but one was usually drunk or out of town or otherwise unavailable, and tonight was no exception. The one named Mark was said to be "indisposed." But ten male Boucrees of three generations, instruments and all, were crowded into that garage, every one of them focused on Melody.

At first they argued about her too—the four who "discovered" her had to sell her to the others, and the negotiations weren't pleasant. What it came down to was that Melody had to audition for them, something she hadn't counted on, and that made her so nervous she nearly blew it. But Tyrone had said, "Take your time now. Start over. That's it. Just sing it like you sang it this morning. Take your time now." His voice had been so gentle, so encouraging, she'd felt she could do anything, but he nearly clutched till he sat down with her and started playing "Brickyard Blues."

"Play something sweet, play something mellow . . ."

She chimed in on the next part:

"Play something I can sink my teeth in like Jell-O."

She finished it with him and by then was so warmed up, she swung into a completely new song, abandoning "St. James Infirmary" for Janis's "Ball and Chain," which the other brothers— who didn't know her—liked so much they wanted to close the set with it.

But Melody wanted to close with "Blues for a Brother," having finished it after her shopping trip, flying so high on adrenaline it only took about half an hour. Tyrone said that was a much better idea, that "Ball and Chain" wasn't really a nineties kind of song, and anyway, they'd never learn it by tomorrow.

The real question was what to begin with. Melody wanted to do another of Janis's songs—"Turtle Blues." To which Tyrone and Terence and Joel, of all people, objected violently, the band having settled yesterday on "Iko Iko." But at least three other Boucrees said that was the most overdone song since "Jambalaya," and that was good for twenty minutes. In the end they agreed on the tried-and-true "Something's Got a Hold on Me," with "Turtle Blues" to follow.

After a couple of hours they took her home for dinner, and she thought she'd died and gone to heaven. It was so different from her house—so many people, so little furniture, the television on with everybody talking. There was a picture of Martin Luther King—she'd never seen that in anyone's house—and lots of family pictures. And there was a strange altar with colored bottles on it. Joel said his family were members of the Spiritual Church, but when Melody asked what that was, he got vague. His mama had made greens and fried chicken, and fried okra and rice. Patty would have fainted at the fat content.

They went back and worked five hours, and Melody wasn't even tired when it was over. It was the most exciting time of her life. They wanted her. They loved her. They changed their whole act for her and loved doing it. Despite the constant arguing, the jabs and digs, the rivalry and meanness (none of which was directed at her), they were taking care of business like a team of Clydesdales. Heavy lifting was getting done.

She hadn't worked with pros before, except for Joel, and she couldn't believe how exhilarating it was. She wished—almost wished—she was going to live to do it again.

Joel drove her to the Holiday Inn near the Rivergate, only to find it filled. Melody was glad, in a way. There was something too comfortable about a hotel like that—it would remind her of things she'd put behind her.

"It's okay," she said. "I never checked out of the Oriole. My room's still there, and anyway, I think I forgot something."

"What were you doing there anyway? I thought you were staying with us?"

"Well, I wanted a shower. Look, could we walk by the river awhile? I've got to come down."

Joel nodded. "Me too. The Boucrees'll do it to you. High maintainance, huh?"

"High voltage."

320

Melody was so far gone on adrenaline she knew she wouldn't sleep for hours. She wanted a beer, but didn't dare—wanted to be perfectly tuned for her biggest and last public performance, the pinnacle of her short life, and her second-to-last act. (The last would be finding the right building to take the walk from.)

"I'm sorry I said that thing about your being white."

She was surprised. "That's okay. You explained it."

"Yeah, but that's only what I thought. I mean, I guess I thought that. It seemed logical. But it wasn't what I was feeling. I felt mean when I said it, *mean*, Mel, like I knew deep down I wasn't doin' right."

She couldn't think of anything to say.

"I guess I really had to face how jealous I am of you."

"Jealous? But you've always been so supportive."

He smiled. "Well, I guess it was just a cover-up. When it comes right down to it . . ."

She waited, but he didn't seem inclined to finish. "Yes? When it comes right down to it . . . ?"

"I guess I'd kill to have your talent. I mean, I never thought so before, I thought I'd be happy being a doctor, and I guess I will, but maybe . . ."

"What?" He was driving her crazy, stopping in the middle.

"Maybe what we all want is to be a star. I mean at least a star in your own family. When I saw everybody fussin' over you, arranging everything just for you, making you the big cheese, I thought 'I wish that was me. I wish my daddy thought as much of me as he does of Melody.' "

She was embarrassed. "I'm no star."

"Mel, listen to me—something's wrong with you. You've got no confidence, and I don't know why. You *are* a star. A star's exactly what you are. You're not going to want to sing with the Boucrees very long. You're going to cast us aside like a snake shedding its skin, and you're going on to the big-time. You're gonna leave Ti-Belle Thiebaud in the dust, did you know that?" He didn't give her time to answer. "No, you didn't. 'Cause you got no confidence. You gotta wake up, girl!"

She loved him so much she could barely take in what he said.

321

All that stuff about being a star. But it was true about the craving to be a star in your own family, in your own neighborhood, even, your own hometown. Nobody at home, or school or anywhere, had particularly thought she could sing. Except Ti-Belle, and Ti-Belle had never indicated she was *that* good, as good as she herself, and Melody knew she would have if she thought so. Ti-Belle just thought she was a talented kid.

There was Ham, of course. Ham had always told her she was the greatest, but that was just Ham.

Maybe Joel could take Ham's place. If he could love her, maybe it was a reason to live. Maybe somehow she could find a way. He could help her; all the Boucrees could. Maybe she and Joel could just get married and barricade themselves against the world. It was worth a try. It could keep her alive.

They were standing side by side, looking at the river, the wind blowing a little. When they talked, they looked at the West Bank, not at each other. His skin looked so smooth, his cheek, in profile, so round; so perfect. There was a magnetic field between them; surely he could feel it. Something this strong had to be mutual.

She whispered his name, and the sound was so different, he did look at her. She touched his face, leaned forward to kiss him, and automatically he put an arm around her. But he didn't kiss back.

"Hey, hey, Mel. What you doing?"

What the hell. Why not say it? It was life or death. "I think I'm falling in love with you."

He turned full face toward her, took both her wrists and held them, as if to ward off an attack. "No, you aren't."

"How do you know what I feel?"

"Melody, we're friends. You're a real good friend to me. And you're a great musician. But I don't see us being anything else."

She wriggled out of his grasp, so embarrassed she thought she'd die on the spot. And angry.

Furious. "Well, why not?"

"Are you crazy? You're a Capulet and I'm a Montague. Haven't you got enough trouble without that crap?"

"You're such a racist!"

"I am not. I just know this city. I know what would happen. Who needs it?"

"Well, what would happen?"

He shrugged. "People wouldn't speak to us, in both our families, probably. Lots of your friends'd get pissed off. Some of mine too probably, at Country Day. And here in the real world, all of 'em would. I got friends you haven't even met, and won't. They don't like white folks."

"I can't believe black people are such racists."

"Minority people can't be racists. It doesn't apply."

"The hell it doesn't."

He lowered his voice. It was obviously an effort. "Mel. Let me take you back, okay? We're both tired."

She slept in her clothes that night, on a bare mattress, having stolen the sheets earlier. The meanness of it, the deprivation of it, suited her.

28

Infuriated, hot, impatient beyond endurance, Skip sat in her car on Audubon Place, waiting for Ti-Belle to surface. Today was a prime day to look for Melody—Skip was sure she'd go to the JazzFest, was positive she'd try to see the Boucree Brothers, and O'Rourke had saddled her with Ti-Belle. Skip was sending her silent psychic messages to get out to the fairgrounds, to have a yen for Boucrees. They were on at one. At twelve Ti-Belle came out, picked some flowers, and went back in.

But a few minutes later she came out again with Nick, both in the official JazzFest uniform—shorts, T-shirt, running shoes (it was too dusty for sandals, and anyway, people stepped on your feet), straw hat, sunglasses, and belly pack containing cash and sunscreen. In an hour they'd be as sweaty as everyone else, and probably sticky from having strawberry sno balls spilled on them. Ti-Belle's hair, pinned up against the heat, would be starting to escape in the same limp tendrils as the hair of the masses. JazzFest was a great leveler.

Still, Skip wondered. Did you really just go out and mingle if you were a celeb? Of course they'd have backstage passes, but that didn't seem like enough. There was still going to be the dealing-with-the-crowds problem, the spilled sno balls, the stepped-on feet, the prodigious lines for food, the pushing and shoving. It was the last day of the festival—the fans would be nearly eighty thousand strong, and it was eighty-five in the shade. Or would have been if there'd been any shade. Somehow, she couldn't see these two braving the roiling sea of humanity for such a busman's holiday.

She hated to give O'Rourke any credit, but did Ti-Belle have the same idea Skip did? To track Melody down at the Boucrees' performance? If ever Skip knew anyone had a gun, she knew Ti-Belle did. Maybe it was in her belly pack. In crowds like they'd be in, she could get within inches of Melody, shoot her, and melt away, just another straw hat and pair of khaki shorts. But what about Nick? He'd gone with her to buy the gun, but she could have given him some half-baked reason for needing it. Maybe she'd said her father had a brother who'd come gunning for her.

Sure enough, Ti-Belle dropped Nick off at a friend's. He opened the trunk, unloaded golf clubs, and kissed her good-bye. She drove straight to the fairgrounds.

Skip's heart was pounding. It wasn't going to be easy, keeping anyone in sight in these crowds. Where were the Boucrees scheduled to play? She'd left her program in the car and couldn't stop to get another or she'd lose her quarry. At first Ti-Belle moseyed like she didn't have a thing on her mind, even standing in line for a rosemint tea. Then she started walking fast, cutting across to Congo Square and then toward the WVUE/WNOE stage, the one at the opposite end from the Ray-Ban stage, the biggest and most important—the one, now that she thought of it, where the Boucrees were most likely to play. It wasn't what she'd expected. If Ti-Belle was going after Melody, surely she'd expect her to be at the Boucrees's set.

"Skip!" She looked around. She was being videotaped by a playful Steve.

"Goddammit!" It was all she could do to keep from making childish obscene gestures. Later she thought perhaps it was only the thought of being taped that had kept her from it. "I haven't got time for this," she hollered, and looked around for Ti-Belle.

She'd lost her.

Seventy thousand people at the fairgrounds, and no Ti-Belle in sight. What were the odds of finding her again? She probably had a better chance of winning the lottery.

"Shit! Fuck! Kill!" People were staring at her. She decided to keep going in the same direction.

"Skip! Wait up!"

"Shut up, goddammit!" What was he trying to do, get her to strangle him in front of half the world?

He caught up. "What's going on?"

She didn't stop, kept barreling through the crowd. "My assignment, in case you've forgotten, is keeping Ti-Belle in sight. I saw her buy a gun yesterday, have good reason to think she's going to try to kill Melody, and thanks to you I've lost her."

"Oh, shit."

"I quite agree."

"Hey, wait. Is that her?"

"Are you kidding? Is what her?"

"Up there. In the hat."

She tried to keep the sarcasm out of her voice. "Which of the thirty thousand hats in view would that be?'

"Pink band. Matches her T-shirt."

"Yes! Where?"

"Come on." He threaded through the crowd, close enough that Skip spotted her. Ti-Belle was still headed toward the stage at the far end of the fairgrounds.

"Who's at that stage?" she asked Steve.

"Dixie Cups? No, their set's over. I can't remember; I've got to tape the Boucrees."

"At the Ray-Ban stage?"

"Yeah."

"Damn! Why can't I be two people?" She should have called in another officer, and there was no time now. She couldn't risk losing Ti-Belle again.

"Can I help?"

"If anybody gets killed, just get it on tape." There was no point telling him to look for Melody. He couldn't do that and do his job too.

The band onstage was a hot pop group, judging from the huge crowd, but Skip didn't know them. And didn't like them particularly, couldn't understand why a singer like Ti-Belle wanted to brave the crowds to hear them.

Ti-Belle skirted the edges of the crowd, undoubtedly looking for the backstage entrance. Skip wasn't quite sure what to do. She could follow by using her badge, but the backstage area, the marked-off spot for VIP fans, was so small she'd be spotted. Or rather, there were so few people in there, she couldn't hide in the crowd. The actual area was huge. You entered from the back, walked across a long green space, then ended up in front of the stage and slightly to the right, separated only from the hoi polloi by metal barricades. The barricades were close to the stage at the front, but extended about fifty feet on the three other sides. It would take forever to walk around them, to push through the crowds, to observe Ti-Belle from the front of the stage. And if she decided to leave before Skip got there, Skip would lose her.

That meant she had to follow her in. She sighed. Getting spotted might even be a deterrent. Ti-Belle wasn't going to shoot anybody with Skip watching.

Skip kept her distance, standing well behind the backstage crowd, behind Ti-Belle, and felt frustrated.

It isn't O'Rourke's fault. He did me a favor—I'd never have known about the gun if he hadn't given me that stupid order.

Ti-Belle was boogying to the music, acting like anyone, the bass player's girlfriend or something, anyone at all but a famous singer. She seemed blissed out, the last person in the world who'd shoot anyone.

Should I leave?

But in her heart she knew the chances of finding Melody at the Ray-Ban stage—even if she hadn't changed her appearance again —were next to none.

Yes, but at least I'd know I tried.

■

327

Melody woke up, teeth chattering, at six A.M. She pulled the bed-spread over her, and the blanket, which she had disdained the night before because it was rough and because she thought it might be harboring worse vermin than the ones she'd brought there herself. Bundled up, she realized she wasn't cold. She was nervous.

She tried deep breathing, then tensing and relaxing her muscles, but her tricks ran out with that one. Insomnia was new to her.

Finally she just lay there, waiting for it to be late enough to get up. And realized she had the flu. She got up and threw up.

But it wasn't the flu. It was nerves.

What the hell, she thought. *I'm going to die today. No wonder I'm nervous.*

She was surprised when she heard bustling and traffic. She must have dropped off after all, like the other night when she had the crabs.

That was last night.

It seemed years away. She got up and went to the restaurant downstairs, knowing she had to eat to get through the performance. But she could get nothing down except some coffee, which left her wired and more nauseous still.

She lay down for a little while, trying to recover, but her stomach felt like an entire Social and Pleasure club was marching in it.

Finally she got up and applied the makeup that turned her black, wishing some magic could make it really happen. She thought about being reborn as a black person. How would that be? She couldn't imagine it at all.

Next the wig. Shopping with Joel, she'd considered a turban, but that emphasized her features too much, drew too much attention. Louise had wanted to sell them a wig with tumbling curls that she could shake around to hide her face, but it looked too much like her usual hair. She'd opted for a sleek, straight, shoulder-length one with long bangs that hung in her eyes; maybe they'd hide the blue. Billy DuPree had had plenty of sarong-type things in African fabrics, but too much skin would be exposed. She might get hot and the makeup might run. So she'd gotten a fabulous huge caftan with flowing long sleeves, which meant she had only her face, neck, hands, forearms, and feet, which would be in sandals, to worry about.

Already she was sweating. The day was hot, the wig was hot, and the caftan was a furnace. Yet she had to dress here, because otherwise someone might see her white skin.

She went back down to the air-conditioned restaurant and got a biscuit, which she crammed down, really felt she must. It was like a mud pie, baked dry in the sun.

"Well, if it ain't the African queen." It was Terence, come up behind her. "Mama, you look fine."

His eyes were so obviously admiring, she actually believed him. He hadn't looked at her like that when she was white, and that told her something; something painful. Joel would like her better this way too and she couldn't produce it for him. She had convinced herself before she slept last night that Joel had rejected her for her own protection. Because he knew how hard it would be, being part of an interracial couple, and he wanted to spare her the pain. He loved her and he couldn't bear to see her go through what black people had to go through as a matter of course.

In the cold light of day, with Terence admiring her African magnificence, she saw this as pathetic grasping for straws. And she knew Joel hadn't come for her because he was too embarrassed; or too frightened she'd pounce on him again.

"I don't feel so good," she said, and ran for the door. She threw up at the curb.

"You got the worst case of stage fright I ever saw in my life."

"I've got to go back up and brush my teeth."

She blocked everything out of her mind.

Just get through it!

But why? Why not just die now?

Because I don't want to! I want to sing before I die. I want to perform just once. Just this once.

But she wasn't sure she really did. She felt tired now, tired and wired at the same time. She wanted to lie down on the bed and stay there till she could gather enough strength to find a tall building.

She went downstairs. She wasn't going to ask where Joel was, she had too much pride for that, but Terence said, "Joel's sorry he couldn't come. His daddy made him pack up all the equipment."

"It's okay."

But she thought he understood how sad she was, wondered if Joel had told him why he didn't want to come. He said, "You look just like Rwanda Zaire, you know that?"

It was the name they'd decided to give her. Raymond had said, "Janis Frank! It sounds like a poor man's Janis Joplin."

"We need a show biz kind of name," said Martin, the patriarch, the one three or four of them called Daddy. "Something that sounds made-up and African. Kind of modern and political."

"Yeah," Joel said. "Something to explain the weird outfit."

Rwanda Zaire was what they'd come up with. Melody liked it. It was stage magic, sleight of hand—if she kept saying she was black in a thousand different ways—her outfit, her skin, her name—it wasn't going to occur to people that she wasn't. She'd heard it said that magicians worked by telling the audience to look at their left hand while they did the trick with their right. She was an octopus with seven arms to distract them; it had to work.

Terence said, "You know what, Rwanda? You're lucky you got me instead of Joel. 'Cause I got somethin' that straight-arrow'd never have in a million years. Cure that stage fright so fast you forget its name."

"What?"

"Hash. I got some hash you're not gonna believe."

He packed a pipe—it couldn't have been easy while driving, but he'd obviously had plenty of practice. "You light it."

She did, to be a good sport, but she was afraid to really inhale, not at all sure what it would do to her performance. "I'll be okay," she said. "I don't really need it."

Sweat was running down her neck, and her teeth were chattering. Her heart was a jackhammer. Just as they pulled up to the fairgrounds, she said, "Terence? Could I change my mind?"

He handed her the pipe. "Listen. We can't close with 'Blues for a Brother.' "

She sucked on the pipe, knowing she'd made the right decision, hoping the hash would knock out the pain of the blow, her last and greatest disappointment. The great gesture she wanted to leave the planet with, and Terence was telling her she wasn't going to get to do it. Her last fucking act on Earth!

She said, "I sing that song or I don't go onstage."

"What you so excited about? We're gon' do the song. Why you think we wouldn't do the song? It's a great song, we're gon' do it. It just can't be last, that's all."

"What are we going to close with?"

" 'Tell It Like It Is.' "

She'd argued against doing that one at all. It belonged to Aaron Neville and she couldn't see the point. But they said that was the point—the audience knew it and loved it. It was a favorite.

She didn't care. The hash was working. She was going to sing Ham's song and nothing else mattered.

A couple of tokes was all it took. But Terence looked at her like a doctor: "That ain't gon' last long. Here." He gave her a little bit to eat.

She was a new person, a floaty, African kind of person, someone who glided rather than walked, and who couldn't remember how she got onstage. All she knew was that Tyrone had said, "Miss Rwanda Zaire!" and she, Melody Brocato, was on the Ray-Ban stage at the New Orleans Jazz and Heritage Festival. Singing to thousands and thousands of people. Singing her heart out. Belting "Something's Got a Hold on Me"; belting like Janis; maybe better. She wasn't aware of anyone or anything except the music, how damn good it felt to be there, to be doing it, singing it, feeling it, feeling the thing whatever it was, that came up through her feet and worked her body and her voice. Melody had melted. Even Rwanda had melted. There was nothing but the music.

She could have sworn the Boucrees were playing at the top of their form, even better than usual, and she was with them. They were a unit, each note blending with each other note, her instrument blending with theirs, she blending with them, with each of them, and it was as close to a religious experience as she'd ever had or was ever likely to have. This was what music was. This was art, this was life!

This was happiness.

She was giddy with the happiness of it. The crowd liked her, she could tell that right away, but after "Turtle Blues," they went crazy. Jumped up and down and hollered. It had been taking a chance to do that song, she knew that, but it showcased her—it was perfect for her. Tyrone was so excited he came forward and introduced her again. "Miss Rwanda Zaire, ladies and gentlemen. Miss Rwanda Zaire!" Melody took her bow like a pro, and they swung into "Tipitina." Then two more upbeat songs and after that "Blues for a Brother."

■

Steve grabbed Skip from behind, for once having the sense not to shout her name and alert Ti-Belle. But she jumped as if stuck with a pin.

"I've found Melody. Come on."

She followed without another word until they were out of the backstage area.

"Where is she?"

"She's singing with the Boucrees."

"Onstage? You mean just standing there in front of the whole world?"

"Come on." He pressed urgently through the crowd. "She's now Rwanda Zaire, black blues singer. Her mirror wouldn't know her. And let me tell you something—she's fantastic. One of the best singers I ever heard."

"You've got to be kidding."

"She's a phenomenon."

"Better than Ti-Belle?"

"Much."

"But nobody told me. I mean, her parents or anybody."

"Interesting, isn't it? Oops, sorry." He had knocked a plate of jambalaya out of a kid's hand. The kid started to cry, but they couldn't stop to comfort him. On the other hand, going wasn't a lot different from stopping. The crowd was not only thick, but lazy; no one was moving fast.

"Steve, how did you recognize her?"

"I didn't at first. Who could? She looks as black as anyone I ever saw. But she sang this song—this amazing, haunting song about a guy who taught her about music. It was sad, Skip—when you know who wrote it. It's all about how she had nothing in her life, how hopeless she felt, and this dude gave her a new life."

"I still don't get it."

"Well, the folks went crazy, and so the Boucrees announced the name of the song and said it was her own composition. 'Blues for a Brother.' How does that grab you?" It was hard to hear because she was ahead of him—had to be to use her badge to push through the crowd.

She was pondering, thinking it was still a big leap, when he said, "Then I remembered 'Turtle Blues.' Who was the last person you heard sing that?"

She was puzzled. "I don't even know it."

"Janis Joplin used to sing it. Remember, Melody's a Joplin fan? See, there's a line about Janis in the brother song, so I put it together. And then of course there were these amazing blue eyes."

Skip looked at her watch. Time for the set to be over. They were close, but she didn't hear music. Had the Boucrees already finished? She held her badge over her head and yelled, "Police! Coming through!"

It helped some, for a while, but as they got closer to the Ray-Ban stage, it became apparent the Boucrees were still playing —they were doing "Tell It Like It Is," and they sounded great. The audience was entranced, so much so that even loud cries of "Police!" didn't do much to break the trance.

They finished the song and thanked the audience. Rwanda Zaire, who looked so much like a black woman Skip thought Steve might have been wrong, took a bow, and the crowd shouted for more. She disappeared. The crowd kept stomping and yelling. Skip and Steve were nearly there.

The Boucrees started their encore—without Rwanda. Good. She'd be joining them in a minute.

Skip leaped over the barricade, ran to the side of the stage, just behind the musicians. People tried to stop her, but only till they saw the badge. "Where's Rwanda?"

The man in charge, a good-looking white man with gray hair, older than she'd have thought, looked confused. He shrugged, opened his arms. Skip didn't have time for conversation. "Did she leave the stage?"

He scanned the area. "She must have. Tyrone was looking for her." He pointed. "She could have gone to the trailer."

But she wasn't there and there was no evidence she had been. She could simply have slipped away, via the backstage barricade opening, and then left the fairgrounds. It would have been easy from here.

And then she could have gotten a taxi or one of the shuttles that ran between the fairgrounds and other places.

But where would she head? Skip had to wait till the end of the damn song to ask the Boucrees.

29

Melody took a bus to the Jax Brewery, one of the shuttles, and then walked to the hotel, cursing herself for forgetting a change of clothes. She was dying in the caftan. And she was so high from the performance and the hash that she could barely remember why she'd left the stage. That the end of the road had come. Suddenly she didn't feel even slightly suicidal.

She felt hot, restless; eager to get the makeup off and get into some shorts. In seven minutes flat she was dressed, white, but still black-haired. She'd put the wig in a ponytail. She planned to sneak out without paying the bill, and after that she wasn't sure what to do—just get away to think, that was the extent of her plan.

Was there, finally, a way she could work this out? That she could go back home to her mom and dad and be safe? She didn't think so. She thought she'd probably end up in jail. If she got lucky.

But she had to think. Maybe she'd overlooked something. She'd never experienced anything like the rush she got on that stage, and it just killed her that she'd had to bug out. Life seemed suddenly worth living.

She bounded down the stairs, still riding the crest of the high, and heard a familiar voice. She stopped dead. The person she least wanted to see was talking to the desk clerk, undoubtedly asking for her.

Melody cursed herself. It would have been so easy. Someone could have watched her leave, seen her board the bus, and then it would have been a simple matter of going to the Jax Brewery to wait for it. Or if the bus got there first, as it obviously had, to prowl the streets looking for the only woman for miles in an African caftan. The only reason Melody had got this far had to be that her tracker had guessed wrong, thought she'd turn downtown, and had searched there first. After that, all you'd have to do was try the other way, asking bums, anybody who looked like they'd been there awhile, if they'd seen the spectacle Melody had made of herself.

Oh, dumb, dumb, dumb! I could just kill myself!

She eased up the steps and out of sight. She'd registered as Janis Frank, which would mean nothing to anyone else, and anyway, the hotel probably wouldn't give out her room number. Still, she was a minor . . . there might be ways to pressure them. Or bribes.

She looked for a back way. There were only stairs that led to a basement, a filthy sweltering hellhole with lots of nasty scraping noises; rat sounds.

She hid in a barrel of heavy cardboard, and as she huddled in the hot, filthy dark, the hash turned on her. Each scrape of a rat's toe seemed like doom, her killer come to drag her off to her fate. The heat was so oppressive she couldn't breathe. She'd be dead soon.

But she hadn't meant to go this way. Her body would be found stuffed in a stupid barrel in a fetid basement, and it wasn't fair, she could *sing!* She'd proved that today.

It could have been the start of a great career. Should have been. But she was going to die here; of suffocation, if the killer didn't get her first.

A sob escaped and a new wave of panic swept over her. She couldn't stay where she was. She'd been crazy to think she could hide here. She was overcome with a desperate need to get out of the barrel, to breathe some air. She was like an animal caught in a trap. But getting in the barrel had been a lot easier than getting out was going to be. She'd pulled a wooden box up to it and stepped on it. To get out she had to raise a leg practically over her head and then step down, hoping to reach the box. She was sweating gallons.

She missed the box. And came crashing to the floor, barrel and all, hitting her head on the box. The pain was excruciating. Yet not nearly so bad, she thought, as the noise, which reverberated like an explosion.

She tried to sit up, heart threatening to rip her ribs out, and the last thing she remembered was the sensation of slipping, her mind slipping, her soul, not her body: the ghastly feeling that meant the end of consciousness.

It was quiet when she woke up, groaning, still sweating, head aching, but nothing more threatening than rats were approaching. She lay there with her eyes closed, listening to the quiet, grateful for it. She'd been out only a moment, she thought. She had to get away, someone could have heard the crash, could be on their way.

She couldn't move. She didn't know whether it was from the fear or the fall, but her body was giving the orders and it was saying stay put. Her teeth were chattering again, her legs were weak and twitchy, her heart pounding, sweat pouring, stomach heaving.

It's the hash. I shouldn't have had the hash.

That helped—remembering there was a physical reason for her body turning on her. She felt calmer. Gradually the twitching stopped, the sweating stopped, even some of the fear left.

Not fear—I'm going to die anyway. Paranoia.

Still no one came. The danger must be over. Cautiously she sat up. The sick feeling was gone, her energy had come back; her body surged with it.

She left the basement and found a back exit, slipped out. She heard the clang of a streetcar, a friendly, beckoning sound. On a streetcar she'd be safe. She could hide there, and think. She got on but didn't think, kept her mind blank, just holding herself together, shivering once again in fear.

She got off at Audubon Park and went to the zoo, hoping for

grounding, some communion with the animals that would connect her with something; with the Earth perhaps.

Ti-Belle had told her something once she said she'd never told anyone. Two things. That she was running from something, someone was after her, Melody didn't know who—an ex-boyfriend maybe—but Ti-Belle couldn't go back; could never go back home. And that she'd turned tricks. Melody wasn't sure why she told her this; she'd probably been stoned. Or maybe she'd had a kind of premonition—seen something of herself in Melody.

Melody knew she couldn't live like this, like she was living now. Always afraid, not knowing what to do next. Having no home, no parents.

Could she turn tricks? She thought about it. Picked out a stranger, a fairly young, slightly puffy white man wearing a baseball cap. Could she have sex with him? She thought about it.

Maybe. But he'd probably smell bad.

She picked out another one. An old guy, his face destroyed by gravity. She'd hate to see his chest, his shoulders. Could she do it with him? She imagined his hands on her, his mouth . . . and felt her gorge rising. She swallowed hard, repeatedly, till the sensation went away.

She didn't think she could do it. Not if she was going to throw up in his face. And shoplifting was too dangerous. If she got caught, she'd get sent home.

Okay. Think about it again. What about home?

Suddenly she could remember being at the zoo, this zoo, with her mom and dad. She was on her dad's shoulders and there was a gibbon there, its throat swelling with its odd, wonderful, mischievous cries. Melody could remember pointing at it, unable to keep her eyes off, and her mother laughing.

I want my mommy and daddy.

She did. She'd been trying to keep the feeling at bay for the past few days, but that was what she wanted. She wanted a career and all that, of course, or her mind and her heart did, but she, Melody, in her soul wanted her family back.

Could she have it?

Suddenly she saw that she might have if she hadn't run away, that running away was the worst possible thing she could have done. Now it was too late . . . the police would come, her parents couldn't protect her, there wasn't a way out.

Who am I kidding? I don't have parents.

The more she tried to think of a way out, the more depressed she got. She told herself it was the hash, but she couldn't shake it and after a while she quit trying. The time had come. She would die.

She sat for a long time watching the alligators, wondering if she dared jump in with them.

Go out with a splash.

They didn't bite you in two; she'd heard they dragged you down and drowned you.

It could be quiet.

It could even be peaceful. She might experience the rapture of the deep.

But when she thought of them chasing their prey, fast, threatening on those short powerful legs, like speeded-up film, the next image was always the same—teeth and blood; red and white; splashing, flailing. No screaming, just the sound of the alligators, a sort of snorting as she imagined it, maybe something to do with dragon stories.

It wasn't the way to go.

But going out with a splash had merit. She could turn her death into art. It couldn't be beautiful, that would require a white robe and flowers, something along those lines, far too elaborate at this point.

What then? Poetic? Ironic?

Yes. Yes to both.

I know! I'll die singing.

I'll fry singing.

It was so perfect it made her laugh.

The tricky part was getting back to the garage, but she did it the same way she'd gotten out—took a bus out Airline Highway and got off by Schwegmann's. She went in and got some twine and a paring knife; her last purchases.

Then she followed the railroad tracks as far as she could and took surface streets to the garage.

She felt light, exhilarated. The paranoia had left and a feeling of certainty, of solidity, had taken its place. She knew this was the right thing. Her only regret was that there would be no flowers in the vase she would use.

What should she wear? Her wig, certainly. Rwanda Zaire was a part of her now. Anyhow, it looked better than what was underneath.

Anything else? It was either shorts and T-shirt, bra and panties, or nothing. Nothing would be far the most dramatic, but somehow she couldn't stand the thought of poor Joel or Doug finding her naked. There was something pathetic about it.

I'd be so obviously dead meat.

The thought of her own dead body didn't frighten or repel her; seemed right somehow. But she hoped finding it wouldn't be too hard on the person who did. She especially hoped the wig didn't slip when she fell, making it look like she had two heads. Would she fall? She hoped she'd slump gracefully over the piano, but didn't think it likely. Electrocution made you jerk around. She'd seen it in a movie once.

Her most prized possession, her little electric piano, was going to be her instrument of death.

As it had been her instrument of life, had kept her going when the depression wouldn't let up. It had poetry and it had irony.

She would leave her clothes on.

She pulled the piano to a space underneath a shelf; there was already a vase there, from the time her parents had sent her flowers when the Spin-Offs won the Battle of the Bands. She filled the vase with water and tied the string to it. Pulled it.

Perfect. The water spilled on the piano wire. And now she had a nice puddle to put her feet in, just to make double sure.

With the paring knife, she cut a piece of insulation off the wire. A pretty big section so the water couldn't miss.

All that remained was to pick the song. This was important, the most important part of all, even though no one would ever know.

Something elegiac? At jazz funerals they did gospel songs at the

wake service the night before, and dirges on the way to the cemetery. On the way back they did celebratory songs: "The Saints" and
"Didn't He Ramble."

She'd heard two versions of the tradition. One held that at the
wake, to the tune of "Down by the Riverside" and the like, the idea
was to reminisce about the "good life" of the dead person, and the
joyous songs celebrated his "bad life." But she hated that. That was
what she despised most about religion as she'd been taught it: joy
must be bad.

Forget it. I'm not a Christian.

Another version said the dirges were for the mourners, to say
good-bye, to express their sadness, and the send-off songs celebrated the release of the dead person's soul. That worked better for
her. Release: that was the idea.

"Breakaway."

The words were perfect. Perfectly metaphorical. And the thing
had symmetry—it was almost the first song she'd ever sung professionally.

Did she dare do it twice? No. Once was dicey enough. Someone might hear and come to investigate.

She'd do it once and pull the vase on the last line.

Maybe before if I feel like it.

She refilled the vase, plugged in the piano and took off her
shoes. She was careful not to let the wire drag in the puddle, not
to wet her feet quite yet. She felt an odd tingling in her lower torso,
whether belly or lower still she wasn't sure, but it was vaguely
sexual. Some kind of prickly excitement.

And why not? This is the greatest adventure of all.

She started to sing:

> "*I've made my reservations,*
> *I'm leaving town tomorrow*
> *I'll find somebody new and*
> *There'll be no more sorrow.*"

God, this is fun.

"That's what I say each time,
But I can't follow through
I can't break away from . . . you make me cry
I can't break away, can't say good-bye
No! No! No no no no! No! No!
No! No! No no no no! No! No!
I'll never ever break away from you!"

I wish I could do it twice!

"I made a vow to myself
You and I are through
Nothing can change my mind
'Sorry' just won't do."

For the first time since she'd had the great idea, she was sad. If I die, I can't ever do this again.

"That's what I say each time,
But I can't follow through
I can't break away from . . . you make me cry
I can't break away, can't say good-bye
No! No! No no no no! No! No!
No! No! No no no no! No! No!
I'll never ever break away from you!"

I have to do it. There's no choice.

"Even though you treat me bad
Little words are so fine
You have got a spell on me
That just can't be broken."

But I don't want to.

"I'll snatch your picture down
And throw it away

> There'll be no waiting 'round
> For you to call each day."

Yes, I do. I really, really do.

The end was near, and it was so perfect, the part where it said, "I'll never ever break away from you." That was the problem, she couldn't break away, she just couldn't; she'd tried and it didn't work. So now she was pulling a different kind of breakaway, guaranteed to work and keep working.

She would sing like she never had before. She'd put the full force of her young body into the last two lines, go out with a bang as well as a splash.

> "That's what I say each time,
> but I can't follow through . . ."

I can. I'm going to.

Her fingers were starting to itch. Irma did the last line repeatedly, dragging it out and out and out before the final "you," and Melody would too. She'd pull the string on the "you." She could feel her muscles gathering. The music would carry her—she could feel the momentum—

> "I'll never ever break away from—
> Never ever break away from—"

Irma did it five times, to be exact, but who was counting?

> "Never ever—"

"Melody!"

She came back from the tunnel she'd been in, the odd gray space between death and life. Or perhaps she merely awoke from the deep trance of the music. She never knew, knew only that her mother's voice brought her back to consciousness. She screamed.

Patty said, "What on earth are you doing?"

Surely her mother didn't know, couldn't tell from such a

343

cursory glance, but nonetheless Patty strode instantly to the other
side of the garage and unplugged the piano.

"Young lady, *what* have you done to your hair?"

It wasn't the tearful reunion a daughter might have hoped for,
but Melody reminded herself that Patty knew she hadn't been
kidnapped and murdered; knew she'd run away and knew why.
Patty had reason to kill her, not save her. Yet she had saved her, had
disabled her weapon, seemingly without even thinking about it.
Still, this hurt. Somewhere deep in Melody's gut was a yearning
that gnawed and burned; the way a bullet wound would feel, she
thought—deep, hot pain.

"Hello, Mother. Did you hear me sing?"

Patty nodded. "I didn't know it was you at first."

"I saw you at the Oriole."

"I've been frantic, Melody. I've been trying to find you for
days, just to talk to you. Look, the cops may have had the same
thought I did. For all I know, they've been watching the garage. I
have, when I could manage. So let's be fast." She opened her purse.
"This is for you."

She held out a packet of money, went back for another, held
it out as well. "It's fifty thousand dollars. That's the best we can do.
Your father and I understand why you did what you did; we agree
you have to leave, it's the only real answer right now." She looked
at her watch. "Come on. I'll drive you to the airport."

"I suppose you already have a ticket for me?"

"I'll buy you one. To wherever you want to go."

"My father doesn't know about this."

"What?"

"You're lying. You killed my brother, didn't you? And now
you think you can get rid of me just as easily. You never wanted
me in the first place. I was just a convenience for you."

"I didn't kill Ham and you know it."

"The hell I know it! Nobody else could have." Melody didn't
shout the words, didn't hurl them as she wanted to. She could
speak only in a hoarse whisper. Her throat was nearly closed
against the rage inside, boiling rage, a force all its own, gathering
itself into a maelstrom, a live thing sucking desperately downward,

roiling and circling endlessly upon itself, gathering black, ugly energy as it circled.

Her mother spoke calmly. "You're a child. You don't know anything about the world."

"I'm a child! I'm a child and I don't know anything about the world! And you're fucking kicking me out." She was trying to grasp it, that her mother could do this. She was conscious of an odd ringing in her ears, as if she were falling through space so fast the pressure kept changing.

"Watch your mouth, Melody." Her mother's own mouth curled in annoyance, and that was the only emotion Melody could see on her face. There was something else there, but it was not a feeling, not anger or self-pity or love for her child, nothing so human as any of these. It was a terrifying determination, a steeliness, an adamancy so unyielding it made Melody think of pictures she had seen of New York, of the Chrysler Building, the Empire State Building. This thing, this obduracy, this force, seemed as solid, as impossible to move, as one of those.

It frightened Melody, but it fueled the rage.

It's not right. This isn't a mother!

She knew that. She might be a child with a child's knowledge of the world, but she knew she had been cheated, she deserved better.

"Watch my mouth? Watch my fucking mouth! You kill my brother and try to buy me off and all you can say is don't say fuck? Well, fuck, Mother!" She was screaming now, the whirlpool had worked its way past the block of fear and grief in her throat. "Fuck fuck fuck fuck fuck! Fuck you, Mother!"

"I swear to God I don't know why I don't just leave you here to kill yourself. That's what you were trying to do, wasn't it? Why don't you do it, Melody?" She plugged the piano in again. "We'd all be better off."

"You want me dead." She said the words slowly. It took a moment to sink in. And then she flew off the piano stool, knocking off the carefully placed vase of water as she did it, but she had moved too fast, she wasn't touching the piano now. She was pummeling her mother, tearing her hair out, kicking her. Yelling,

"Die, you bitch! Die!" Even when Patty fell over and hit her head on the concrete floor of the garage, Melody didn't stop. Simply jumped on top and beat her all the more. Even when she heard a command that brooked no argument: "Stop! Melody, stop!"

She didn't. But then she felt strong arms grab hers, pull her off, and by then it was too late to face the intruder, to turn around. It was all over anyway. Her energy was spent, the maelstrom dissolved. She felt hot and ashamed, couldn't believe what she'd done. The sight of her mother crumpled on the floor made her want to cry. But it didn't stop her from fighting.

30

The girl writhed and twisted in Skip's arms like some species of giant worm. Skip heard herself saying over and over: "It's okay. It's okay, Melody," as if the girl were listening, or cared. She might as well have been in a coma for all she probably heard. And meanwhile she was dragging Skip around the garage like a teddy bear.

Finally she changed her tactic and shouted, "Melody, be still!" and the girl came out of it. Quit fighting, twisted, and looked up at her. "Who the hell are you?"

"Detective Skip Langdon, NOPD."

Melody went limp. "Oh. It's over."

"No, it isn't." It was Patty. Skip had nearly forgotten about her. She whirled, still holding Melody.

Patty was holding a gun in both hands. Skip's heart leapt to her throat. How had Patty gotten her gun?

But it wasn't hers. It was probably one she'd pulled from her purse, one of the little gifts from a doting husband that Uptown ladies wouldn't be caught dead without. In New Orleans, people didn't just complain about crime, they all thought they were Dirty Harry.

347

"Patty, it's okay. Put the gun down."

"Let her go."

"Drop the gun first and we'll talk."

"Let her go or I'll shoot." Her voice had risen.

Gingerly, Skip let Melody loose, but the girl didn't move.

Patty said, "Melody, step to Skip's right."

She obeyed, rubbing her elbows as if she were cold.

"Patty, everything's under control now. Give me the gun."

"Shut up!"

"She's going to kill us," said Melody. "There's nothing else she can do now. She tried to buy me off, but I didn't go for it. So she has to kill me."

"Shut up!"

Skip said, "Patty. Think about what you're doing."

"Ham was my father! My own mother slept with her stepson and lied to everybody for the next seventeen years. Did you really think I'd go away quietly, Mother? I'd just take your money and go? Just because I had no father and no mother either?" She spat out the last sentence as if it were poison she'd somehow ingested.

Skip was terrified. This was guaranteed to push Patty over the edge. She spoke in the calmest voice she could muster. "Melody, we can talk about all that later. For right now, let's just—"

But Patty interrupted as if mother and daughter were alone. "I had to, goddammit! You think I wanted to? I had a sick mother and a family to support, and a husband who was too drunk to get it up. What the hell was I supposed to do?" Skip made a quick calculation: Ham had been thirty-four when he died, and Melody was now sixteen. Allowing for pregnancy, that meant Ham must have been about seventeen at the time—and rather a geeky kid, according to Alison. Patty had been twenty-three and must have looked like a Christmas package to a boy like that. If she'd wanted him, she could certainly have had him. But the question was, why would she want him? By all accounts she was devoted to George and always had been.

"I loved your father very very much, Melody."

"Which father, Mother?"

"You selfish little bitch—you wouldn't know what it's like to love anybody but your own bony little self. I had a whole family to take care of. And you know what? Your father hated me. We know now it was the booze, but he swore at me, he called me names—I'm going to tell you something you should know, young lady—he even raised his hand to me."

"My father wouldn't hit anybody."

"He threatened me. He threatened to divorce me."

"Oh." The look on Melody's face said she finally understood why her whole world had been destroyed. It was so wise and so sad, tears sprung to Skip's eyes, the last thing she needed now.

"But he wouldn't," said the girl, "if you had a baby. George just wouldn't do that. You were going to lose your meal ticket."

If she had a baby, legally George would have to support the child. But there was probably more to it than that. Patty had probably calculated—quite correctly—that he would want the baby even if he didn't want her; and so he'd stay married to her.

"You don't understand a lot of things, little girl, and this is one of them. I loved your dad more than anything. I sometimes think I used my mother and family as an excuse because I wanted to keep him so bad."

A wised-up woman a moment ago, Melody was now the jeering teenager. "Oh, sure you did! Oh, sure! And my dad saw right through your game. He wasn't nasty to you 'cause he was a drunk, Mo-ther. He was trying to get rid of you because he saw through you. He saw what a money-grubbing, gold-digging bitch you were!"

Skip said, "Melody, why don't we—"

But it was too late. Patty had fired and Melody was lying on the floor; Skip couldn't tell if she'd been hit or had dropped down for protection. Patty took a step back.

Skip held out her hand. "Patty, it's okay. We'll get some help right away. Just give me the gun and it'll all be okay."

She fired again. Knocked off her pins, either by the impact or the shock, Skip hit the floor as well, aware of searing, burning pain. And blood. Lots of it, pouring out of her, pouring onto the floor.

Melody screamed, "Oh, my God! Oh, my God!" and sat up. She seemed fine, hadn't been hit.

Skip stared up at her executioner, wondering if she'd keep firing, one shot after another, to make sure she was dead.

But Patty pointed the gun at Melody. Her eyes looked red, as if she'd been crying, and her hands were shaking. She kept staring at the girl, losing her grip a little more and a little more, her hands getting shakier and shakier. Skip didn't say a word. This was a woman capable of shooting her own daughter, at least at that moment. She was having trouble with it, but that didn't mean she wouldn't do it. Hoping Melody would have the sense to keep her mouth shut, Skip held her breath. She saw Patty bunch her muscles, gathering her strength, and braced herself for the report. But Patty didn't move. A tear fell from her left eye.

And then she turned and bolted, dropping the gun.

Skip scrambled up, ignoring the pain, and ran after her, chased her down the street, tackled her, hit her in the face she was so mad. Blood dripped onto her, onto Patty's nose, and she screamed. The blood had come from Skip's head. How long could she stay conscious?

Melody said, "Don't move."

She was pointing Patty's gun at the two of them. Damn! Why hadn't Skip thought of that scenario?

"Uh . . . do you need your cuffs?"

"That's okay. I think you should put the gun down, though." She put a knee in Patty's back, pulled her cuffs from her belly pack, but saw that simple cuffing wasn't going to be good enough. She was going to pass out any second, and Melody still had the gun; if Patty tried to run, she might shoot her.

"Come on," she said, but Patty didn't budge.

How much strength did she have left? Mustering all of it, she dragged Patty off the sidewalk and cuffed her to the rail of an iron fence.

Then she put out her hand for the gun. Its comforting heft in her palm, she gasped, "Call 911." And sat down gratefully, waiting for oblivion. Melody pulled off her T-shirt, applied it to Skip's head, and disappeared.

But as her breathing slowed, Skip realized she didn't even feel faint. And yet she must have lost a lot of blood, not to mention having a bullet in her skull. She pulled herself up and caught her reflection in a car window.

The bullet wasn't in her after all. She was fine. But what she saw made her feel a lot fainter than the wound—the thing had taken out a path of hair as it traveled along the right side of her head.

Well, no way was she going to the hospital. *No way!* These two were hers and she was doing the questioning.

O'Rourke was surprisingly docile about it.

Maybe he thinks I'll bleed to death.

She got some first aid from colleagues while she waited for George Brocato and two lawyers to arrive—one for Patty and one for Melody. After Melody conferred with her father and lawyer, Skip joined her in Juvenile. She seemed in good spirits, glad to see Skip. "Hi. You look good. Do you feel okay? You were really white for a while."

She'd been wearing Rwanda's wig at the garage. Now her hair was a lifeless white, with the purple streak Flip had described.

She managed a smile, and it was pretty. There was something about her face—an alertness, an eagerness, a willingness to meet the world—that reminded Skip of the look in the eyes of a six-week-old kitten. A look of optimism a cat would outgrow the first time it met a German shepherd. A baby-animal look so vulnerable, so hopeful, it made you want to rush right out and repair the hole in the ozone. Skip had done nothing but worry about this child for a week, and now Melody was worried about her.

"I'm fine, thanks, but my hairdresser had a stroke."

"You should get a CAT scan."

"I will. How about you? You okay?"

Melody nodded.

"I've been worried about you."

"They told me you were looking for me. Thanks, I guess."

"I almost caught up with you once. At Madeleine Richard's. But someone else got there first."

"My mom, I guess. I think she borrowed my Aunt Des's car. Is she all right?"

"I haven't seen her yet."

"I'm sorry I beat her up."

"I guess you were mad."

"That's an understatement."

George cleared his throat.

Skip took the hint. "Do you feel up to talking?"

George said, "Does it have to be now?"

"It's okay, Daddy. I'd rather."

"Only if I sit in," said George. He was wearing a Ralph Lauren polo shirt, dressed for a Sunday. Tension showed in every inch of him.

Melody said, "Ummm. I don't know."

"What?"

"Could it be just Anthony?" Her lawyer.

"There are things you don't want me to hear?"

"Not yet. I'll tell you, but not yet, okay?"

Skip got Melody some coffee, and when they were settled, she said, "Melody, I have to ask you something important. Did you actually see her kill Ham?"

Melody opened her mouth to answer, closed it again, stared out the window for a while. Finally she said, "I guess I heard it. I didn't want to think that's really what it was, but"—she looked down at her lap—"I guess it was."

"What happened, Melody? You overheard them fighting?"

"Well, I had a bad day that day—"

"I know all about Flip and Blair."

A slight tinge of pink appeared on Melody's cheeks. Even with the blond and purple hair, her young skin managed to look healthy. "I guess you do. I went to Ham's all upset and just let myself in, as usual. But he and Patty were yelling so loud they didn't hear me." *Patty, not Mother.*

"I heard my name, so I tiptoed down the hall and listened. He was trying to get her to do something, I guess—it must have been about selling the business. They had this offer that they were all fighting over. Patty had a vote, but she always took my father's side. He didn't want to sell, but I guess Ham did. I know he'd put a lot of his money into Second Line Square and he'd lent a lot to Ti-Belle. I guess he needed the sale because he needed money." She shrugged. "I mean, I've had several days to try to piece it together, and that's what it must have been. I guess she refused and he threatened her—and that's about where I came in. He said he'd tell Dad and he'd tell me. About—you know. But then, I didn't know. That's why I listened.

"I couldn't believe what he said. I couldn't forget it, though: 'What would Melody think if she knew I was her father?' " She closed her eyes and shook her head.

"I still don't believe it. Do you know how it is when you've thought one thing all your life—the most basic thing, the simplest thing—and that thing isn't true? Your world's upside down—nothing is right. You just can't figure anything out. And then there was Blair and Flip and all—I just didn't have a life anymore. I had to leave. I don't believe what a baby I was. How innocent."

"Why do you say that?"

"Because when I left, I thought that was the worst thing that could happen to me."

She must have awakened the next day to the news that her brother was dead and known then that her mother was the murderer—and that she was the only witness.

"You poor kid."

Melody looked away, embarrassed.

"What happened when you heard all that? Did you say anything?"

"I jumped her. Just like I did this morning." She shook her head again—this was something else that wouldn't sink in. "I tried to kill my own mother. Twice."

Her lawyer started. "Melody!"

"Why did you stop?"

"Ham pulled me off and I ran out of the house. Didn't think, just ran. I had to get the hell out."

"Did you hear anything else?"

"No. Well, maybe. It might have been my imagination."

"What?"

"I thought I heard a scream."

"Patty screamed?"

"No. Ham, I thought."

"Did he say anything?"

"No. Just yelled, like . . ."

"Like what?"

"Well, I guess . . . I mean I thought later . . . I guess that's when she did it."

Skip tried to keep her face impassive. She couldn't say "poor kid" again. "And that was all?"

"I just kept running."

"Okay, let's stop for now. Your dad can take you home."

"I can go?"

She sighed. She'd gotten through the interview fine. For the first time she looked frightened. "What am I going back to?"

It was the moan of a motherless child.

▪

Skip went to get Patty. "Is George still here?" she asked.

"He took Melody home. But your lawyer's waiting for us." Gray Renegar was one of the best criminal lawyers in the state. George was nothing if not a good provider.

Patty sighed. "George'll be unhappy. He doesn't like Gray's advice."

Skip wondered what she meant. As they made their way to the interview room where they'd meet Renegar, Patty said, "I'm sorry I shot you. I guess I went a little crazy."

A more accomplished Southerner than she, Skip thought, would come up with a polite reply. She couldn't.

When they reached their destination and everyone was seated, Skip said, "Do you understand your rights?"

Patty nodded. "I want to waive them."

"What?" She stared at Renegar, who spoke automatically to Patty.

"I have to advise you against that."

"George wants me to."

"Patty, has it occurred to you that you and George might have a conflict in this thing? I'm your lawyer and I'm telling you to keep your mouth shut."

Patty looked surprised, apparently unused to such talk. She said, "He's right, Gray. I want to plead guilty. If I stand trial, Melody will have to testify. Neither of us wants that."

What do you know—a shred of maternal feeling. Or is she just mouthing George's words?

The latter, Skip thought. Definitely the latter. She felt oddly let down. She'd expected more of a fight. But she could hear Melody's words of a few minutes before, now metaphorically fraught: *Patty had a vote, but she always took my father's side.*

"He doesn't know what happened," Patty said. "He just knows I killed Ham. I told him that."

Her hair was the hair of a woman used to having others groom her; it was sticking out all over, stiff with spray and sweat. Crying had eroded her makeup. She looked haggard and beaten.

Renegar said, "Patty, I have to advise you—"

"Shut up!"

His eyes were the color of his name, and hard. "Could we just get it on the record, please?"

She kept quiet while he told her again to keep her trap shut. And then she said, voice dripping with sarcasm: "May I start now?" A lot of anger was about to come out.

"He turned my own child against me—and now my husband. My own husband would rather see me in jail than . . . oh, never mind.

"He threatened me—he threatened to tell George and Melody if I didn't vote to sell the business. They only needed one vote, you see. But I couldn't do that, it wasn't what George wanted, so of course I wasn't about to."

"And what did he threaten you with?"

"Oh, about being Melody's father." She seemed distracted, wanting to get on with it—she'd already told this story.

Renegar looked as if he were going to have a cow.

"I thought he'd forgotten," she said.

"Forgotten!" Skip blurted it, unable to keep quiet.

"Well, it only happened two or three times. I mean, I just—waited until George was out getting drunk and Ham was asleep.

355

Then I'd take off my clothes and get in bed with him. He didn't say a word. He was seventeen—would any seventeen-year-old boy in the world say no?"

Still a child.

Skip wondered if she'd let him down easy or even mentioned the fun was over. Probably not, she thought. And of course she'd have been sure to seduce George around that time—or tell him she had if he was the kind of drunk who wouldn't remember.

"We never said a word about it."

"You and Ham?"

She shook her head. "We never did until the other day. I really thought he—I don't know—didn't even know, maybe. Thought he was dreaming or something."

Oh, sure.

"Anyway, she was really George's baby. Ham's genes were his genes."

Renegar cleared his throat. "Can we get on with it, please?"

Skip said, "So Ham threatened to tell George and Melody he was Melody's father."

"He called and asked me to come over—I knew it was going to be bad, I knew it. He'd asked me before about the vote. He'd been begging me. The bastard, it was none of his business. And then he sounded so serious on the phone. He said, 'Look, it's to your advantage to show up.' So I had some wine before I left, and then I had some with him. I was drunk. I didn't know what I was doing."

"What did you do when he threatened you?"

"Nothing. Melody just came out of nowhere and started beating me. He pulled her off, but I realized what had happened—he'd turned my own child against me. The lowlife, scum-sucking bastard! I work all these years to raise this beautiful little family, and along comes Ham and poof—my own child tries to kill me. I could just—"

"And you did, didn't you?"

"Yes, goddammit! I did. I didn't even think. I was in a white-hot rage—I can get in it again just thinking about it—and I picked up the knife before I thought. I don't remember stabbing him, but

I must have because—'' She stopped, sobered for the moment, color draining.

"Because what?"

"He made a horrible noise."

"Like a scream?"

"Like a snuffle. And the knife was in him."

He'd probably been dead before Melody hit the sidewalk.

■

Later, telling Steve about it, Skip said, "So Renegar asked, 'How'd you feel then, Patty? Sorry?' And do you think she took the hint? Oh, no. Poor man. It didn't even occur to her to pretend she knew she'd committed a tiny little sin against society."

"What did she say?"

"She said she was scared so she left. Just drove aimlessly for a while, but did the horror of what she'd done take hold? Hell, no. She remembered she was supposed to pick up Melody, and then she caught on she could be in big trouble. So she coolly goes back —goes *back*, can you believe it?—to wash the glasses and wipe the knife. Then she drives over to Blair's, saying she's late because she stopped at the store to get something for dinner. And then she actually does go shopping so the story will check out. Arrives home with a pound and a half of shrimp."

Steve whistled. "Boy, do I feel sorry for that kid."

It was raining, but the front windows were up because the roof of the balcony protected it. Skip got up and walked over. She didn't know why, just knew the thought of Melody made her want to feel the wet warmth, smell the ozone.

She had been born a pawn in a game, born to a mother forever locked in a dance of wills with her father—one desperate to be loved, the other determined to withhold love. Skip didn't know why, and wondered. Patty had been so desperate she'd forgotten Melody, forgotten she had a daughter to love, or perhaps she was simply so self-involved she couldn't have been much of a mother anyway.

That was bad enough, but it happened to lots of kids. What Melody had suffered seemed unbearable. Skip wondered how she

357

would get through. Whether she could recover.

Steve came up behind her, held her against his chest. "What are you thinking?"

"It's funny, I've only seen Melody once, but I feel close to her. I wish I could—you know . . ."

"Be friends with her?"

"I guess."

"That's the down side of the job."

"A million stories in the naked city."

"Ships that pass in the night."

"Another day, another case." They were trying to be brave, to cheer each other up, but it wasn't going to work. Tonight they'd feel sad. And make love and wake up feeling better.

She was glad to have Steve with her.

31

On the way to the cemetery, the band playing "Just a Closer Walk
With Thee," George was grappling once again with the alien idea
that he had lost a son.

Sometimes I wonder if I ever knew I had one.

Now he felt the loss in his chest, in his gut, in his temples. And
the feeling was almost too much, as if his body was stretched to
the limit, a balloon inflated past capacity. It started to come out his
eyes, then his throat. He was crying. He, George Brocato, was
crying in public.

But it wasn't in public. It was in a limousine with his daughter.
Still, he was the father, he wasn't supposed to cry. He turned his
face to the window, hoping no one could see in. But he was
making noise; he couldn't stop that. He was almost as panicked at
the thought Melody would know as he was sad. And then he felt
her hand take his and intertwine her fingers. She didn't say a word.

When he had regained control, he looked at her, wondering
how she was. There were only three options: terrible, worse, and
on the verge of collapse. Yet she looked all right. Her jaw worked,
and she had on sunglasses so he couldn't see her eyes, but other-

wise she seemed almost stony. She was holding it in.

How terrible, he thought, to be sixteen and go through this and not even be able to cry. He said, "Darlin', you can cry if you want. Daddy's here." He never referred to himself in the third person; everything was different today.

She shook her head. "It's okay, Daddy. It doesn't feel real. It's like a dream."

It was shock. He'd been through it too, days ago, when Ham died. He felt like a different person now. Certainly he belonged to a different family, and in a way it was better. He had lost his son, he had lost his wife, it was hard to imagine anything worse— except, he thought, the way he'd been living most of his life: as if those people didn't matter, as if Melody didn't, George himself didn't.

He felt as if he'd found some lost part of himself that could be with Melody now in a way he'd never been able to before. The saddest, most pathetic part of it all was that he had been responsible for everything. For being a drunk, for letting Patty down when they were first married, for treating her like a piece of property, creating an atmosphere in which she had to do something to protect herself; and the thing she'd done was have a child with his son. It was monstrous, and yet he knew, it was so clear to him now, that this was his monster. The enormity of it made him feel shriveled and impotent, a spider in a flame.

But worse, so much worse, was Patty's killing Ham—also his doing, to George's way of thinking, this new, strange, weight-of-the-world way that had him looking back practically to childhood at the ways he'd botched his life. His doing because he hadn't loved Patty, because her whole life had been devoted to winning him: her husband of seventeen years.

He had tried to tell Melody. He wanted her to know what he had become. Her reply shocked him: "Dad, you can't feel guilty, it'll eat you up. You just have to take responsibility for what's yours and let Mother take what's hers. I mean, it isn't *all* yours."

She was right, he saw that, and couldn't imagine how she could have known such a thing, and then he remembered that Patty had insisted on sending her to a psychiatrist, that Dr. Richard. He hadn't seen the point, but he supposed this was the sort of thing that came out if it, and it wasn't bad. At her age she knew more than he did.

When he got the news, when the call came, he somehow wasn't surprised at what Patty had done. He had lived with this woman for seventeen years, and much as he'd tried to keep his distance from her, to hold back, to live a separate life, he had an inkling of who she was. And what their life was. He knew, he knew when Melody told him, he knew with a thud like an anvil landing that there had been something between Patty and Ham, that Melody was not his child in the same way she was Patty's.

He didn't know how he knew this, or that he'd known it all her life, he just knew that he had. Perhaps it was something about the timing of the birth, or something in Ham's manner toward Patty; perhaps Melody was like Ham in some way that suggested paternity. He couldn't put his finger on it, couldn't remember much at all from the drunken period. But he knew now that this was why he'd held back from Melody, that there had been something in him like revulsion regarding her. He thought now that she —or his feelings about her—set thoughts in motion, memories, emotions; stirred things up that he didn't want disturbed.

Now that he knew all this, he understood that odd feeling he'd had when Ham died—of relief, almost, instead of grief. All those years, in some way he couldn't yet get to the bottom of, he must have been jealous of his own son.

He wondered briefly if the old, unacknowledged wound was what kept him from Patty as well, but felt a tug in his gut that told him it wasn't that, or wasn't just that, that there was a lot more. He thought about the rest of it, the other things. These were things he'd always known as well. It amazed him to see them now, fanned out like a poker hand, and know that they'd always been there, held closely.

Now I know this. I could change. Maybe it's not too late for Patty and me. But it was. She'd killed his son.

▪

The sad music was soothing, Melody found. Made her feel better instead of worse, gave her a little distance, a chance to think.

She was trying to get used to this unaccustomed, unwieldy feeling in her chest. It hurt, it felt like a lump of cement. She thought it was love. Well, she knew it was. But she had thought love felt good, felt happy and joyous, and this thing felt distant and unattainable. It was taking the form of longing; she knew because this was a feeling as familiar to her as her own blue eyes, only usually it seemed to come from somewhere outside.

The love was for her dad. It was just so new to her she didn't know what to do with it, and that was what the longing was about.

He'd gone to sleep yesterday after picking her up at the police station—had simply left her and gone to sleep! She'd been so desperate, she'd ended up taking his car—without permission—over to Ti-Belle's. And miraculously, Ti-Belle had been there. She was having a glass of iced tea with a strange man. (Though she was quick to explain that he was a drummer, someone whose set she'd just caught at the JazzFest because she was getting rid of Johnny Murphy.) Melody didn't care about that—she just wanted Ti-Belle alone, to herself, wanted to bury her face in her chest and cry. Later, she realized she could have gone to Richard—that Richard hadn't turned on her after all, but she hadn't thought of that. Ti-Belle was the closest thing she had to a sister—to any kind of real relative, her mother being in jail and her father the sort of person who could fall asleep an hour after learning his wife had been arrested for the murder of his son.

But later it turned out he hadn't been asleep. He'd been thinking—maybe crying, Melody didn't know. What she did know was the person who came out of that room wasn't the father she remembered. It was a beaten, vulnerable, much softer man. Or was she different—had he always been like that? But he said it himself: Ham's death had changed him.

It wasn't the first thing he said. If he wanted to win her over, he'd certainly begun on the right foot: "Melody, I want to do everything I can to help with your music. I know I haven't been very supportive, and I regret that."

It was stiff and his delivery was a little pompous, almost seemed to contain a note of belligerence, but she put that down to embarrassment. She heard what he was saying—he was saying he was taking her seriously in a way he never had before.

He hadn't ever had the least interest in her music, hadn't even gone to her piano recitals, and later, when she'd started singing, his disinterest had been more like disdain. He'd stopped a hair short of ridicule.

"I want to be a different person from now on."

She couldn't believe what she was hearing.

"When you disappeared, I knew how much—" He couldn't finish. Was he going to say that he loved her? He didn't know how. And yet her chest fluttered in a way that said something important was going on. If he'd just glibly said "how much I love you," in a meaningless monotone, without affect, it wouldn't have been nearly so moving, she thought.

"I know, Dad."

He looked relieved. "Will you sit down?" He led her into the living room, where they'd probably never sat together in their lives.

He sat on a sofa, legs crossed formally, she on a chair, feeling awkward in her shorts. "Ham died; you ran away. I saw what I'd been missing and I knew that I was the cause of it. I saw that I really wasn't a good father, either to you or to Ham, and I wasn't a good husband. Patty is the way she is because of me."

"No, she isn't, Dad. She picked you because she couldn't really . . . couldn't do it either." She noticed that she too had shied from the L word. "Dr. Richard told me that."

"You discuss us in there?"

In spite of everything, Melody had laughed. "Daaaad! What do you think therapy's all about?"

"I guess I thought she'd just tell you not to be such a brat and that'd be that."

Could this be her father? Making a joke?

"Look, Melody, remember when you were a little girl? We were close then, weren't we?"

"I think so. I can't remember that well."

"I do better with little kids than big kids. And a lot better than I do with adults."

"Sure. You can control them. People with minds of their own are too threatening."

Now, in the limousine, the memory of it made her laugh. You could have knocked him over with a feather. He had no idea she'd know things like that.

That was fun. It was the first good thing she'd gotten out of knowing what she knew. Just because you knew it didn't mean you could change it. Richard said she could only change herself, and she'd tried; she'd wanted to be a person who didn't have to live with these people. And now she didn't; her mother was going to jail and her father was metamorphosing right before her eyes. Richard didn't know every damn thing.

Her dad had said, "So that makes me a control freak, huh?"

She'd said, "Just a wimp, Daddy." And they'd laughed together like they were used to it.

After the cemetery service, suffering the hugs and murmurings of dozens of powdered, sweaty, perfumed adults she didn't care about, she thought she'd faint; only the memory of how unpleasant that was kept her upright.

She wanted to be alone, she told herself, but at the same time she was thrilled that these people were here for Ham—the mayor, everyone from Uptown, every music figure in town, and that meant plenty of nationwide importance. And lots and lots of people she didn't know, and that Ham probably hadn't known. People who appreciated his work, probably. She was proud of her brother.

People were there for her too—Joel; Dr. Richard; Flip and Blair; even that nice cop, that Skip. She knew the cop was there for her, she sensed it, and she felt loved, protected by her presence, though they didn't really know each other and probably never would.

The band for the funeral had probably been assembled from lots of bands—that was her guess anyway. The Olympia Brass Band, the Magnificent Seven Brass Band, Dejan's, Pin Stripe, the

Young Tuxedos; some of the Boucrees were marching in it, and she knew they were there for her too.

As they left the cemetery, the band played "The Saints," and when they got warmed up, they swung into "Didn't He Ramble," and for the first time that day Melody cried. She thought it ironic that she'd gotten through the dirges fine, but the happy songs made her sad. It was because they reminded her of Ham, because they celebrated his "bad life," his earthly life, brought back the Ham she'd loved. He wouldn't hear these songs again; he wouldn't ramble and he wouldn't march. That was what hurt.

But it was a sweet hurt, for the songs also celebrated the release of his soul.

And mine. The sad part of my life is over. With these songs it's over.

She said it like an incantation and was tempted to add, "Begone!" as if she were banishing a demon.

She knew how pathetic she looked to the world; she had seen the look on Richard's face. Her brother was in the ground, her mother in jail, Ti-Belle in trouble.

She missed Ham already, like she'd miss a hand or a foot. In spite of everything, she was going to miss her mother.

But she wouldn't miss her childhood, and she was saying good-bye to that. Today she was like a saint: marching in.

ABOUT THE AUTHOR

Julie Smith's *New Orleans Mourning* won the 1991 Edgar Allan Poe Award given by the Mystery Writers of America for best novel, making Smith the first woman to win the Edgar in that category since 1956. Officer Skip Langdon, introduced in *New Orleans Mourning*, returned in *The Axeman's Jazz*, Smith's second New Orleans mystery.

A former reporter for the *New Orleans Times-Picayune* and the *San Francisco Chronicle*, Julie Smith is also the creator of two San Francisco sleuths: lawyer-detective Rebecca Schwartz, who appears in *Death Turns a Trick*, *The Sourdough Wars*, *Tourist Trap*, and *Dead in the Water*, and ex-reporter-turned-mystery-writer Paul MacDonald, who appears in *True-Life Adventure* and *Huckleberry Fiend*.

Julie Smith lives in Oakland, California.